On its 25th birthday, Penguin Books I... ether
25 of its b...

Ruskin Bond	
Vikram Chandra	
William Dalrymple	
Gurcharan Das	*... the*
Shobhaa Dé	*...arry Nights*
Anita Desai	*The Village by the Sea*
Kiran Desai	*The Inheritance of Loss*
M.K. Gandhi	*My Experiments with Truth*
Amitav Ghosh	*In an Antique Land*
A.P.J. Abdul Kalam	*Ignited Minds: Unleashing the Power within India*
Sunil Khilnani	*The Idea of India*
Dalai Lama	*The Path to Tranquillity: Daily Meditations*
Yann Martel	*Life of Pi*
Suketu Mehta	*Maximum City: Bombay Lost and Found*
R.K. Narayan	*The Guide*
Jawaharlal Nehru	*The Discovery of India*
Nandan Nilekani	*Imagining India: Ideas for the New Century*
Arundhati Roy	*The God of Small Things*
Salman Rushdie	*Haroun and the Sea of Stories*
P. Sainath	*Everybody Loves a Good Drought: Stories from India's Poorest Districts*
Sankar	*Chowringhee*
Arshia Sattar	*The Ramayana*
Amartya Sen	*The Argumentative Indian: Writings on Indian Culture, History and Identity*
Khushwant Singh	*Train to Pakistan*
Rabindranath Tagore	*Gitanjali*

www.popularpenguins.co.in

PENGUIN BOOKS

THE GOD OF SMALL THINGS

ARUNDHATI ROY won the Booker Prize for *The God of Small Things* in 1997. She is the author of five volumes of non-fiction writing: *The Algebra of Infinite Justice* (2001), *An Ordinary Person's Guide to Empire* (2005), *Listening to Grasshoppers* (2009), *Broken Republic* (2011) and *Walking with the Comrades* (2011). *The Shape of the Beast*, a collection of her interviews, was published in 2008.

THE GOD OF SMALL THINGS

ARUNDHATI ROY

PENGUIN BOOKS

PENGUIN BOOKS
Published by the Penguin Group
Penguin Books India Pvt. Ltd, 11 Community Centre, Panchsheel Park,
New Delhi 110 017, India
Penguin Group (USA) Inc., 375 Hudson Street, New York, New York 10014, USA
Penguin Group (Canada), 90 Eglinton Avenue East, Suite 700, Toronto,
Ontario, M4P 2Y3, Canada (a division of Pearson Penguin Canada Inc.)
Penguin Books Ltd, 80 Strand, London WC2R 0RL, England
Penguin Ireland, 25 St Stephen's Green, Dublin 2, Ireland
(a division of Penguin Books Ltd)
Penguin Group (Australia), 250 Camberwell Road, Camberwell, Victoria
3124, Australia (a division of Pearson Australia Group Pty Ltd)
Penguin Group (NZ), 67 Apollo Drive, Rosedale, Auckland 0632, New Zealand
(a division of Pearson New Zealand Ltd)
Penguin Group (South Africa) (Pty) Ltd, 24 Sturdee Avenue, Rosebank,
Johannesburg 2196, South Africa

Penguin Books Ltd, Registered Offices: 80 Strand, London WC2R 0RL, England

First published in India by IndiaInk 1997
Published by Penguin Books India 2002
This edition published 2012

10 9 8 7 6 5 4 3 2 1

This is a work of fiction. Names, characters, places and incidents are either the product of the author's imagination or are used fictitiously and any resemblance to any actual person, living or dead, events or locales is entirely coincidental.

ISBN 9780143417880

For sale in the Indian Subcontinent only

Printed at Thomson Press India Ltd, New Delhi

ACKNOWLEDGEMENTS

Pradip Krishen, my most exacting critic, my closest friend, my love. Without you this book wouldn't have been *this* book.

Pia and Mithva for being mine.

Aradhana, Arjun, Bete, Chandu, Carlo, Golak, Indu, Joanna, Naheed, Philip, Sanju, Veena and Viveka, for seeing me through the years it took me to write this book.

Pankaj Mishra for flagging it off on its journey into the world.

Alok Rai and Shomit Mitter, for being the kind of readers that writers dream about.

David Godwin, flying agent, guide and friend. For taking that impulsive trip to India. For making the waters part.

Neelu, Sushma & Krishnan for keeping my spirits up and my hamstrings in working order.

And finally but immensely, Dadi and Dada. For their love and support.

Thank you.

For Mary Roy who grew me up.
Who taught me to say 'excuse me' before interrupting her in Public.
Who loved me enough to let me go.

For LKC, who, like me, survived.

Never again will a single story be told as
though it's the only one.

JOHN BERGER

CONTENTS

I

Paradise Pickles & Preserves

May in Ayemenem is a hot, brooding month. The days are long and humid. The river shrinks and black crows gorge on bright mangoes in still, dustgreen trees. Red bananas ripen. Jackfruits burst. Dissolute bluebottles hum vacuously in the fruity air. Then they stun themselves against clear windowpanes and die, fatly baffled in the sun.

The nights are clear but suffused with sloth and sullen expectation.

But by early June the south-west monsoon breaks and there are three months of wind and water with short spells of sharp, glittering sunshine that thrilled children snatch to play with. The countryside turns an immodest green. Boundaries blur as tapioca fences take root and bloom. Brick walls turn mossgreen. Pepper vines snake up electric poles. Wild creepers burst through laterite banks and spill across the flooded roads. Boats ply in the bazaars. And small fish appear in the puddles that fill the PWD potholes on the highways.

It was raining when Rahel came back to Ayemenem. Slanting silver ropes slammed into loose earth, ploughing it up like gunfire. The old house on the hill wore its steep, gabled roof pulled over its ears like a low hat. The walls, streaked with moss, had grown soft, and bulged a little with dampness that seeped up from the ground. The wild, overgrown garden was full of the whisper and scurry of small lives. In the undergrowth a rat snake rubbed itself against a glistening stone. Hopeful yellow bullfrogs cruised the scummy pond for mates. A drenched mongoose flashed across the leaf-strewn driveway.

The house itself looked empty. The doors and windows were locked. The front verandah bare. Unfurnished. But the skyblue Plymouth with chrome tailfins was still parked outside, and inside, Baby Kochamma was still alive.

She was Rahel's baby grand aunt, her grandfather's younger sister. Her name was really Navomi, Navomi Ipe, but everybody called her Baby. She became Baby Kochamma when she was old enough to be an aunt. Rahel hadn't come to see her, though. Neither niece nor baby grand aunt laboured under any illusions on that account. Rahel had come to see her brother, Estha. They were two-egg twins. 'Dizygotic' doctors called them. Born from separate but simultaneously fertilized eggs. Estha Esthappen – was the older by eighteen minutes.

They never did look much like each other, Estha and Rahel, and even when they were thin-armed children, flat-chested, worm-ridden and Elvis Presley-puffed, there was none of the usual 'Who is who?' and 'Which is which?' from oversmiling relatives or the Syrian Orthodox Bishops who frequently visited the Ayemenem house for donations.

The confusion lay in a deeper, more secret place.

In those early amorphous years when memory had only just begun, when life was full of Beginnings and no Ends, and Everything was For Ever, Esthappen and Rahel thought of themselves together as Me, and separately, individually, as We or Us. As though they were a rare breed of Siamese twins, physically separate, but with joint identities.

Now, these years later, Rahel has a memory of waking up one night giggling at Estha's funny dream.

She has other memories too that she has no right to have.

She remembers, for instance (though she hadn't been there), what the Orangedrink Lemondrink Man did to Estha in

Abhilash Talkies. She remembers the taste of the tomato sandwiches – *Estha's* sandwiches, that *Estha* ate – on the Madras Mail to Madras.

And these are only the small things.

Anyway, now she thinks of Estha and Rahel as *Them*, because separately, the two of them are no longer what *They* were or ever thought *They'd* be.

Ever.

Their lives have a size and a shape now. Estha has his and Rahel hers.

Edges, Borders, Boundaries, Brinks and Limits have appeared like a team of trolls on their separate horizons. Short creatures with long shadows, patrolling the Blurry End. Gentle half-moons have gathered under their eyes and they are as old as Ammu was when she died. Thirty-one.

Not old.

Not young.

But a viable die-able age.

They were nearly born on a bus, Estha and Rahel. The car in which Baba, their father, was taking Ammu, their mother, to hospital in Shillong to have them, broke down on the winding tea estate road in Assam. They abandoned the car and flagged down a crowded State Transport bus. With the queer compassion of the very poor for the comparatively well off, or perhaps only because they saw how hugely pregnant Ammu was, seated passengers made room for the couple and for the rest of the journey Estha and Rahel's father had to hold their mother's stomach (with them in it) to prevent it from wobbling. That was before they were divorced and Ammu came back to live in Kerala.

According to Estha, if they'd been born on the bus, they'd have got free bus rides for the rest of their lives. It wasn't clear where he'd got this information from, or how he knew these things, but for years the twins harboured a faint resentment against their parents for having diddled them out of a lifetime of free bus rides.

They also believed that if they were killed on a zebra crossing, the Government would pay for their funerals. They had the definite impression that that was what zebra crossings were meant for. Free funerals. Of course there were no zebra crossings to get killed on in Ayemenem, or, for that matter, even in Kottayam, which was the nearest town, but they'd seen some from the car window when they went to Cochin, which was a two hour drive away.

The Government never paid for Sophie Mol's funeral because she wasn't killed on a zebra crossing. She had hers in Ayemenem in the old church with the new paint. She was Estha and Rahel's cousin, their uncle Chacko's daughter. She was visiting from England. Estha and Rahel were seven years old when she died. Sophie Mol was almost nine. She had a special child-sized coffin.

Satin-lined.

Brass handle shined.

She lay in it in her yellow Crimplene bellbottoms with her hair in a ribbon and her Made-in-England go-go bag that she loved. Her face was pale and as wrinkled as a dhobi's thumb from being in water for too long. The congregation gathered around the coffin, and the yellow church swelled like a throat with the sound of sad singing. The priests with curly beards swung pots of frankincense on chains and never smiled at babies the way they did on usual Sundays.

The long candles on the altar were bent. The short ones weren't.

An old lady masquerading as a distant relative (whom nobody recognized), but who often surfaced next to bodies at funerals (a funeral junkie? a latent necrophiliac?) put cologne on a wad of cotton wool and with a devout and gently challenging air, dabbed it on Sophie Mol's forehead. Sophie Mol smelled of cologne and coffinwood.

Margaret Kochamma, Sophie Mol's English mother, wouldn't let Chacko, Sophie Mol's biological father, put his arm around her to comfort her.

The family stood huddled together. Margaret Kochamma, Chacko, Baby Kochamma, and next to her, her sister-in-law, Mammachi – Estha and Rahel's (and Sophie Mol's) grandmother. Mammachi was almost blind and always wore dark glasses when she went out of the house. Her tears trickled down from behind them and trembled along her jaw like raindrops on the edge of a roof. She looked small and ill in her crisp off-white sari. Chacko was Mammachi's only son. Her own grief grieved her. His devastated her.

Though Ammu, Estha and Rahel were allowed to attend the funeral, they were made to stand separately, not with the rest of the family. Nobody would look at them.

It was hot in the church, and the white edges of the arum lilies crisped and curled. A bee died in a coffin flower. Ammu's hands shook and her hymnbook with it. Her skin was cold. Estha stood close to her, barely awake, his aching eyes glittering like glass, his burning cheek against the bare skin of Ammu's trembling, hymnbook-holding arm.

Rahel, on the other hand, was wide awake, fiercely vigilant and brittle with exhaustion from her battle against Real Life.

She noticed that Sophie Mol was awake for her funeral. She showed Rahel Two Things.

Thing One was the newly painted high dome of the yellow church that Rahel hadn't ever looked at from the inside. It was painted blue like the sky, with drifting clouds and tiny whizzing jet planes with white trails that crisscrossed in the clouds. It's true (and must be said) that it would have been easier to notice these things lying in a coffin looking up than standing in the pews, hemmed in by sad hips and hymnbooks.

Rahel thought of the someone who had taken the trouble to go up there with cans of paint, white for the clouds, blue for the sky, silver for the jets, and brushes, and thinner. She imagined him up there, someone like Velutha, bare bodied and shining, sitting on a plank, swinging from the scaffolding in the high dome of the church, painting silver jets in a blue church sky.

She thought of what would happen if the rope snapped. She imagined him dropping like a dark star out of the sky that he had made. Lying broken on the hot church floor, dark blood spilling from his skull like a secret.

By then Esthappen and Rahel had learned that the world had other ways of breaking men. They were already familiar with the smell. Sicksweet. Like old roses on a breeze.

Thing Two that Sophie Mol showed Rahel was the bat baby.

During the funeral service, Rahel watched a small black bat climb up Baby Kochamma's expensive funeral sari with gently clinging curled claws. When it reached the place between her sari and her blouse, her roll of sadness, her bare midriff, Baby Kochamma screamed and hit the air with her hymnbook. The singing stopped for a 'Whatisit? Whathappened?' and for a furrywhirring and a sariflapping.

The sad priests dusted out their curly beards with goldringed fingers as though hidden spiders had spun sudden cobwebs in them.

The baby bat flew up into the sky and turned into a jet plane without a crisscrossed trail.

Only Rahel noticed Sophie Mol's secret cartwheel in her coffin.

The sad singing started again and they sang the same sad verse twice. And once more the yellow church swelled like a throat with voices.

When they lowered Sophie Mol's coffin into the ground in the little cemetery behind the church, Rahel knew that she still wasn't dead. She heard (on Sophie Mol's behalf), the softsounds of the red mud and the hardsounds of the orange laterite that spoiled the shining coffin polish. She heard the dullthudding through the polished coffin wood, through the satin coffin lining. The sad priests' voices muffled by mud and wood.

We entrust into thy hands, most merciful Father,
The soul of this our child departed,
And we commit her body to the ground,
Earth to earth, ashes to ashes, dust to dust.

Inside the earth Sophie Mol screamed, and shredded satin with her teeth. But you can't hear screams through earth and stone.

Sophie Mol died because she couldn't breathe.

Her funeral killed her. *Dus to dus to dus to dus to dus.* On her tombstone it said *A Sunbeam Lent To Us Too Briefly.*

Ammu explained later that Too Briefly meant For Too Short a While.

After the funeral Ammu took the twins back to the Kottayam police station. They were familiar with the place. They had spent a good part of the previous day there. Anticipating the sharp, smoky stink of old urine that permeated the walls and furniture, they clamped their nostrils shut well before the smell began.

Ammu asked for the Station House Officer and when she was shown into his office, she told him that there had been a terrible mistake and that she wanted to make a statement. She asked to see Velutha.

Inspector Thomas Mathew's moustaches bustled like the friendly Air India Maharajah's, but his eyes were sly and greedy.

'It's a little too late for all this, don't you think?' he said. He spoke the coarse Kottayam dialect of Malayalam. He stared at Ammu's breasts as he spoke. He said the police knew all they needed to know and that the Kottayam Police didn't take statements from *veshyas* or their illegitimate children. Ammu said she'd see about that. Inspector Thomas Mathew came around his desk and approached Ammu with his baton.

'If I were you,' he said, 'I'd go home quietly.' Then he tapped her breasts with his baton. Gently. *Tap, tap.* As though he was choosing mangoes from a basket. Pointing out the ones that he wanted packed and delivered. Inspector Thomas Mathew seemed to know whom he could pick on and whom he couldn't. Policemen have that instinct.

Behind him a red and blue board said:

P oliteness
O bedience
L oyalty
I ntelligence
C ourtesy
E fficiency

When they left the police station Ammu was crying, so Estha and Rahel didn't ask her what *veshya* meant. Or for that matter, *illegitimate.* It was the first time they'd seen their mother cry. She wasn't sobbing. Her face was set like stone, but the tears welled up in her eyes and ran down her rigid cheeks. It made the twins sick with fear. Ammu's tears made everything that had so far seemed unreal, real. They went back to Ayemenem by bus. The conductor, a narrow man in khaki, slid towards them on the bus rails. He balanced his bony hips against the back of a seat and clicked his ticket-puncher at Ammu. *Where to?* the click was meant to mean. Rahel could smell the sheaf of bus tickets and the sourness of the steel bus-rails on the conductor's hands.

'He's dead,' Ammu whispered to him. 'I've killed him.'

'Ayemenem,' Estha said quickly, before the conductor lost his temper.

He took the money out of Ammu's purse. The conductor gave him the tickets. Estha folded them carefully and put them in his pocket. Then he put his little arms around his rigid, weeping mother.

Two weeks later, Estha was Returned. Ammu was made to send him back to their father, who had by then resigned his lonely tea estate job in Assam and moved to Calcutta to work for a company that made carbon black. He had remarried, stopped drinking (more or less), and suffered only occasional relapses.

Estha and Rahel hadn't seen each other since.

And now, twenty-three years later, their father had re-Returned Estha. He had sent him back to Ayemenem with a suitcase and a letter. The suitcase was full of smart new clothes. Baby Kochamma showed Rahel the letter. It was written in a slanting, feminine, convent school hand, but the signature underneath was their father's. Or at least the name was. Rahel wouldn't have recognized the signature. The letter said that he, their father, had retired from his carbon black job and was emigrating to Australia where he had got a job as Chief of Security at a ceramics factory, and that he couldn't take Estha with him. He wished everybody in Ayemenem the very best and said that he would look in on Estha if he ever came back to India, which, he went on to say, was a bit unlikely.

Baby Kochamma told Rahel that she could keep the letter if she wanted to. Rahel put it back into its envelope. The paper had grown soft, and folded like cloth.

She had forgotten just how damp the monsoon air in Ayemenem could be. Swollen cupboards creaked. Locked windows burst open. Books got soft and wavy between their covers. Strange insects appeared like ideas in the evenings and burned themselves on Baby Kochamma's dim 40-watt bulbs. In the daytime their crisp, incinerated corpses littered the floor and windowsills, and until Kochu Maria swept them away in her plastic dustpan, the air smelled of Something Burning.

It hadn't changed, the June Rain.

Heaven opened and the water hammered down, reviving the reluctant old well, greenmossing the pigless pigsty, carpet bombing still, tea-coloured puddles the way memory bombs still, tea-coloured minds. The grass looked wetgreen and pleased. Happy earthworms frolicked purple in the slush. Green nettles nodded. Trees bent.

Further away, in the wind and rain, on the banks of the river, in the sudden thunderdarkness of the day, Estha was walking. He was wearing a crushed-strawberry-pink T-shirt, drenched darker now, and he knew that Rahel had come.

Estha had always been a quiet child, so no one could pinpoint with any degree of accuracy exactly when (the year, if not the month or day) he had stopped talking. Stopped talking altogether, that is. The fact is that there wasn't an 'exactly when'. It had been a gradual winding down and closing shop. A barely noticeable quietening. As though he had simply run out of conversation and had nothing left to say. Yet Estha's silence was never awkward. Never intrusive. Never noisy. It wasn't an accusing, protesting silence as much as a sort of aestivation, a dormancy, the psychological equivalent of what lungfish do to get themselves through the dry season, except that in Estha's case the dry season looked as though it would last for ever.

Over time he had acquired the ability to blend into the background of wherever he was – into bookshelves, gardens, curtains, doorways, streets – to appear inanimate, almost invisible to the untrained eye. It usually took strangers a while to notice him even when they were in the same room with him.

It took them even longer to notice that he never spoke. Some never noticed at all.

Estha occupied very little space in the world.

After Sophie Mol's funeral, when Estha was Returned, their father sent him to a boys' school in Calcutta. He was not an exceptional student, but neither was he backward, nor particularly bad at anything. *An average student*, or *Satisfactory work* were the usual comments that his teachers wrote in his Annual Progress Reports. *Does not participate in Group Activities* was another recurring complaint. Though what exactly they meant by 'Group Activities' they never said.

Estha finished school with mediocre results, but refused to go to college. Instead, much to the initial embarrassment of his father and stepmother, he began to do the housework. As though in his own way he was trying to earn his keep. He did the sweeping, swabbing and all the laundry. He learned to cook and shop for vegetables. Vendors in the bazaar, sitting behind pyramids of oiled, shining vegetables, grew to recognize him and would attend to him amidst the clamouring of their other customers. They gave him rusted film cans in which to put the vegetables he picked. He never bargained. They never cheated him. When the vegetables had been weighed and paid for, they would transfer them to his red plastic shopping basket (onions at the bottom, brinjal and tomatoes on the top) and always a sprig of coriander and a fistful of green chillies for free. Estha carried them home in the crowded tram. A quiet bubble floating on a sea of noise.

At meal times when he wanted something, he got up and helped himself.

Once the quietness arrived, it stayed and spread in Estha. It reached out of his head and enfolded him in its swampy arms. It rocked him to the rhythm of an ancient, foetal heartbeat. It sent its stealthy, suckered tentacles inching along the insides of his skull, hoovering the knolls and dells of his memory, dislodging old sentences, whisking them off the tip of his tongue. It stripped his thoughts of the words that described them and left them pared and naked. Unspeakable. Numb. And to an observer therefore, perhaps barely there. Slowly, over the years, Estha withdrew from the world. He grew accustomed to the uneasy octopus that lived inside him and squirted its inky tranquillizer on his past. Gradually the reason for his silence was hidden away, entombed somewhere deep in the soothing folds of the fact of it.

When Khubchand, his beloved, blind, bald, incontinent seventeen-year-old mongrel, decided to stage a miserable, long-drawn-out death, Estha nursed him through his final ordeal as though his own life somehow depended on it. In the last months of his life, Khubchand, who had the best of intentions but the most unreliable of bladders, would drag himself to the top-hinged dog-flap built into the bottom of the door that led out into the back garden, push his head through it and urinate unsteadily, bright yellowly, *inside.* Then with bladder empty and conscience clear he would look up at Estha with opaque green eyes that stood in his grizzled skull like scummy pools and weave his way back to his damp cushion, leaving wet footprints on the floor. As Khubchand lay dying on his cushion, Estha could see the bedroom window reflected in his smooth, purple balls. And the sky beyond. And once a bird that flew across. To Estha – steeped in the smell of old roses, blooded on memories of a broken man – the fact that something so fragile, so unbearably tender had survived, had been *allowed* to exist, was a miracle. A bird in flight reflected in an old dog's balls. It made him smile out loud.

After Khubchand died Estha started his walking. He walked for hours on end. Initially he patrolled only the neighbourhood, but gradually went further and further afield.

People got used to seeing him on the road. A well-dressed

man with a quiet walk. His face grew dark and outdoorsy. Rugged. Wrinkled by the sun. He began to look wiser than he really was. Like a fisherman in a city. With sea-secrets in him.

Now that he'd been re-Returned, Estha walked all over Ayemenem.

Some days he walked along the banks of the river that smelled of shit, and pesticides bought with World Bank loans. Most of the fish had died. The ones that survived suffered from fin-rot and had broken out in boils.

Other days he walked down the road. Past the new, freshly baked, iced, Gulf-money houses built by nurses, masons, wire-benders and bank clerks who worked hard and unhappily in faraway places. Past the resentful older houses tinged green with envy, cowering in their private driveways among their private rubber trees. Each a tottering fiefdom with an epic of its own.

He walked past the village school that his great-grandfather built for Untouchable children.

Past Sophie Mol's yellow church. Past the Ayemenem Youth Kung Fu Club. Past the Tender Buds Nursery School (for Touchables), past the ration shop that sold rice, sugar, and bananas that hung in yellow bunches from the roof. Cheap soft-porn magazines about fictitious South Indian sex fiends were clipped with clothes pegs to ropes that hung from the ceiling. They spun lazily in the warm breeze, tempting honest ration buyers with glimpses of ripe, naked women lying in pools of fake blood.

Sometimes Estha walked past Lucky Press – old Comrade K. N. M. Pillai's printing press, once the Ayemenem office of the Communist Party, where midnight study meetings were held, and pamphlets with rousing lyrics of Marxist Party songs were printed and distributed. The flag that fluttered on the roof had grown limp and old. The red had bled away.

Comrade Pillai himself came out in the mornings in a greying

Aertex vest, his balls silhouetted against his soft white mundu. He oiled himself with warm, peppered coconut oil, kneading his old, loose flesh that stretched willingly off his bones, like chewing gum. He lived alone now. His wife, Kalyani, had died of ovarian cancer. His son, Lenin, had moved to Delhi, where he worked as a services contractor for foreign embassies.

If Comrade Pillai was outside his house oiling himself when Estha walked past, he made it a point to greet him.

'Estha Mon!' he would call out, in his high, piping voice, frayed and fibrous now, like sugarcane stripped of its bark. 'Good morning! Your daily constitutional?'

Estha would walk past, not rude, not polite. Just quiet.

Comrade Pillai would slap himself all over to get his circulation going. He couldn't tell whether Estha recognized him after all those years or not. Not that he particularly cared. Though his part in the whole thing had by no means been a small one, Comrade Pillai didn't hold himself in any way personally responsible for what had happened. He dismissed the whole business as the Inevitable Consequence of Necessary Politics. The old omelette and eggs thing. But then, Comrade K. N. M. Pillai was essentially a political man. A professional omeletteer. He walked through the world like a chameleon. Never revealing himself, never appearing not to. Emerging through chaos unscathed.

He was the first person in Ayemenem to hear of Rahel's return. The news didn't perturb him as much as excite his curiosity. Estha was almost a complete stranger to Comrade Pillai. His expulsion from Ayemenem had been so sudden and unceremonious, and so very long ago. But Rahel Comrade Pillai knew well. He had watched her grow up. He wondered what had brought her back. After all these years.

It had been quiet in Estha's head until Rahel came. But with her she had brought the sound of passing trains, and the light and shade that falls on you if you have a window seat. The world, locked out for years, suddenly flooded in, and now Estha couldn't hear himself for the noise. Trains. Traffic. Music. The Stock Market. A dam had burst and savage waters swept everything up in a swirling. Comets, violins, parades, loneliness, clouds, beards, bigots, lists, flags, earthquakes, despair were all swept up in a scrambled swirling.

And Estha, walking on the riverbank, couldn't feel the wetness of the rain, or the suddenshudder of the cold puppy that had temporarily adopted him and squelched at his side. He walked past the old mangosteen tree and up to the edge of a laterite spur that jutted out into the river. He squatted on his haunches and rocked himself in the rain. The wet mud under his shoes made rude, sucking sounds. The cold puppy shivered – and watched.

Baby Kochamma and Kochu Maria, the vinegar-hearted, short-tempered, midget cook, were the only people left in the Ayemenem house when Estha was re-Returned. Mammachi, their grandmother, was dead. Chacko lived in Canada now, and ran an unsuccessful antiques business.

As for Rahel.

After Ammu died (after the last time she came back to Ayemenem, swollen with cortisone and a rattle in her chest that sounded like a faraway man shouting), Rahel drifted. From school to school. She spent her holidays in Ayemenem, largely ignored by Chacko and Mammachi (grown soft with sorrow, slumped in their bereavement like a pair of drunks in a toddy bar) and largely ignoring Baby Kochamma. In matters related to the raising of Rahel, Chacko and Mammachi tried, but couldn't. They provided the care (food, clothes, fees), but withdrew the concern.

The Loss of Sophie Mol stepped softly around the Ayemenem House like a quiet thing in socks. It hid in books and food. In

Mammachi's violin case. In the scabs of the sores on Chacko's shins that he constantly worried. In his slack, womanish legs.

It is curious how sometimes the memory of death lives on for so much longer than the memory of the life that it purloined. Over the years, as the memory of Sophie Mol (the seeker of small wisdoms: *Where do old birds go to die? Why don't dead ones fall like stones from the sky?* The harbinger of harsh reality: *You're both whole wogs and I'm a half one.* The guru of gore: *I've seen a man in an accident with his eyeball swinging on the end of a nerve, like a yo-yo*) slowly faded, the Loss of Sophie Mol grew robust and alive. It was always there. Like a fruit in season. Every season. As permanent as a Government job. It ushered Rahel through childhood (from school to school) into womanhood.

Rahel was first blacklisted in Nazareth Convent at the age of eleven, when she was caught outside her Housemistress's garden gate decorating a knob of fresh cowdung with small flowers. At Assembly the next morning she was made to look up *depravity* in the Oxford Dictionary and read aloud its meaning. '*The quality or condition of being depraved or corrupt*,' Rahel read, with a row of stern-mouthed nuns seated behind her and a sea of sniggering schoolgirl faces in front. '*Perverted quality: Moral perversion; The innate corruption of human nature due to original sin; Both the elect and the non-elect come into the world in a state of total d. and alienation from God, and can, of themselves do nothing but sin. J. H. Blunt.*'

Six months later she was expelled after repeated complaints from senior girls. She was accused (quite rightly) of hiding behind doors and deliberately colliding with her seniors. When she was questioned by the Principal about her behaviour (cajoled, caned, starved), she eventually admitted that she had done it to find out whether breasts hurt. In that Christian institution, breasts were not acknowledged. They weren't supposed to exist, and if they didn't could they hurt?

That was the first of three expulsions. The second for

smoking. The third for setting fire to her Housemistress's false hair bun which, under duress, Rahel confessed to having stolen.

In each of the schools she went to, the teachers noted that she:

(a) Was an extremely polite child.
(b) Had no friends.

It appeared to be a civil, solitary form of corruption. And for this very reason, they all agreed (savouring their teacherly disapproval, touching it with their tongues, sucking it like a sweet) – all the more serious.

It was, they whispered to each other, *as though she didn't know how to be a girl.*

They weren't far off the mark.

Oddly, neglect seemed to have resulted in an accidental release of the spirit.

Rahel grew up without a brief. Without anybody to arrange a marriage for her. Without anybody who would pay her a dowry and therefore without an obligatory husband looming on her horizon.

So as long as she wasn't noisy about it, she remained free to make her own enquiries: into breasts and how much they hurt. Into false hair buns and how well they burned. Into life and how it ought to be lived.

When she finished school, she won admission into a mediocre college of Architecture in Delhi. It wasn't the outcome of any serious interest in Architecture. Nor even, in fact, of a superficial one. She just happened to take the entrance exam, and happened to get through. The staff were impressed by the size (enormous), rather than the skill, of her charcoal still-life sketches. The careless, reckless lines were mistaken for artistic confidence, though in truth, their creator was no artist.

She spent eight years in college without finishing the five-year undergraduate course and taking her degree. The fees were low and it wasn't hard to scratch out a living, staying in the hostel, eating in the subsidized student mess, rarely going to class, working instead as a draughtsman in gloomy architectural firms that exploited cheap student labour to render their presentation drawings and to blame when things went wrong. The other students, particularly the boys, were intimidated by Rahel's waywardness and almost fierce lack of ambition. They left her alone. She was never invited to their nice homes or noisy parties. Even her professors were a little wary of her – her bizarre, impractical building plans, presented on cheap brown paper, her indifference to their passionate critiques.

She occasionally wrote to Chacko and Mammachi, but never returned to Ayemenem. Not when Mammachi died. Not when Chacko emigrated to Canada.

It was while she was at the School of Architecture that she met Larry McCaslin who was in Delhi collecting material for his doctoral thesis on *Energy Efficiency in Vernacular Architecture.* He first noticed Rahel in the School library and then again, a few days later, in Khan Market. She was in jeans and a white T-shirt. Part of an old patchwork bedspread was buttoned around her neck and trailed behind her like a cape. Her wild hair was tied back to look straight though it wasn't. A tiny diamond gleamed in one nostril. She had absurdly beautiful collarbones and a nice athletic run.

There goes a jazz tune, Larry McCaslin thought to himself, and followed her into a bookshop where neither of them looked at books.

Rahel drifted into marriage like a passenger drifts towards an unoccupied chair in an airport lounge. With a Sitting Down sense. She returned with him to Boston.

When Larry held his wife in his arms, her cheek against his heart, he was tall enough to see the top of her head, the dark tumble of her hair. When he put his finger near the corner of her mouth he could feel a tiny pulse. He loved its location. And that faint, uncertain jumping, just under her skin. He would touch it, listening with his eyes, like an expectant father feeling his unborn baby kick inside its mother's womb.

He held her as though she was a gift. Given to him in love. Something still and small. Unbearably precious.

But when they made love he was offended by her eyes. They behaved as though they belonged to someone else. Someone watching. Looking out of the window at the sea. At a boat in the river. Or a passer-by in the mist in a hat.

He was exasperated because he didn't know what that look *meant*. He put it somewhere between indifference and despair. He didn't know that in some places, like the country that Rahel came from, various kinds of despair competed for primacy. And that *personal* despair could never be desperate enough. That something happened when personal turmoil dropped by at the wayside shrine of the vast, violent, circling, driving, ridiculous, insane, unfeasible, public turmoil of a nation. That Big God howled like a hot wind, and demanded obeisance. Then Small God (cosy and contained, private and limited) came away cauterized, laughing numbly at his own temerity. Inured by the confirmation of his own inconsequence, he became resilient and truly indifferent. Nothing mattered much. Nothing much mattered. And the less it mattered, the less it mattered. It was never important enough. Because Worse Things had happened. In the country that she came from, poised forever between the terror of war and the horror of peace, Worse Things kept happening.

So Small God laughed a hollow laugh, and skipped away cheerfully. Like a rich boy in shorts. He whistled, kicked stones. The source of his brittle elation was the relative smallness of his misfortune. He climbed into people's eyes and became an exasperating expression.

What Larry McCaslin saw in Rahel's eyes was not despair at all, but a sort of enforced optimism. And a hollow where

Estha's words had been. He couldn't be expected to understand that. That the emptiness in one twin was only a version of the quietness in the other. That the two things fitted together. Like stacked spoons. Like familiar lovers' bodies.

After they were divorced, Rahel worked for a few months as a waitress in an Indian restaurant in New York. And then for several years as a night clerk in a bullet-proof cabin at a gas station outside Washington, where drunks occasionally vomited into the money tray, and pimps propositioned her with more lucrative job offers. Twice she saw men being shot through their car windows. And once a man who had been stabbed, ejected from a moving car with a knife in his back.

Then Baby Kochamma wrote to say that Estha had been re-Returned. Rahel gave up her job at the gas station and left America gladly. To return to Ayemenem. To Estha in the rain.

In the old house on the hill, Baby Kochamma sat at the dining table rubbing the thick, frothy bitterness out of an elderly cucumber. She was wearing a limp, checked, seersucker nightgown with puffed sleeves and yellow turmeric stains. Under the table she swung her tiny, manicured feet, like a small child on a high chair. They were puffy with oedema, like little foot-shaped air cushions. In the old days whenever anybody visited Ayemenem, Baby Kochamma made it a point to call attention to their large feet. She would ask to try on their slippers and say, 'Look how big for me they are!' Then she would walk around the house in them, lifting her sari a little so that everybody could marvel at her tiny feet.

She worked on the cucumber with an air of barely concealed triumph. She was delighted that Estha had not spoken to Rahel. That he had looked at her and walked straight past. Into the rain. As he did with everyone else.

She was eighty-three. Her eyes spread like butter behind her thick glasses.

'I told you, didn't I?' she said to Rahel. 'What did you expect? Special treatment? He's lost his mind, I'm telling you! He doesn't *recognize* people any more! What did you think?'

Rahel said nothing.

She could feel the rhythm of Estha's rocking, and the wetness of rain on his skin. She could hear the raucous, scrambled world inside his head.

Baby Kochamma looked up at Rahel uneasily. Already she regretted having written to her about Estha's return. But then, what else could she have done? Had him on her hands for the rest of her life? Why *should* she? He wasn't her responsibility.

Or was he?

The silence sat between grand-niece and baby grand aunt like a third person. A stranger. Swollen. Noxious. Baby Kochamma reminded herself to lock her bedroom door at night. She tried to think of something to say.

'How d'you like my bob?'

With her cucumber hand she touched her new haircut. She left a riveting bitter blob of cucumber froth behind.

Rahel could think of nothing to say. She watched Baby Kochamma peel her cucumber. Yellow slivers of cucumber skin flecked her bosom. Her hair, dyed jetblack, was arranged across her scalp like unspooled thread. The dye had stained the skin of her forehead a pale grey, giving her a shadowy second hairline. Rahel noticed that she had started wearing make-up. Lipstick. Kohl. A sly touch of rouge. And because the house was locked and dark, and because she only believed in 40-watt bulbs, her lipstick mouth had shifted slightly off her real mouth.

She had lost weight on her face and shoulders, which had turned her from being a round person into a conical person. But sitting at the dining table with her enormous hips concealed, she managed to look almost fragile. The dim, dining-room light had rubbed the wrinkles off her face leaving it looking – in a strange, sunken way – younger. She was wearing a lot of jewellery. Rahel's dead grandmother's jewellery. All of it. Winking rings. Diamond earrings. Gold bangles and a beautifully crafted flat gold chain that she touched from time to time reassuring herself that it was there and that it was hers. Like a young bride who couldn't believe her good fortune.

She's living her life backwards, Rahel thought.

It was a curiously apt observation. Baby Kochamma *had* lived her life backwards. As a young woman she had renounced the material world, and now, as an old one, she seemed to embrace it. She hugged it and it hugged her back.

When she was eighteen, Baby Kochamma fell in love with a handsome young Irish monk, Father Mulligan, who was in Kerala for a year on deputation from his seminary in Madras. He was studying Hindu scriptures, in order to be able to denounce them intelligently.

Every Thursday morning Father Mulligan came to Ayemenem to visit Baby Kochamma's father, Reverend E. John Ipe, who was a priest of the Mar Thoma church. Reverend Ipe was well known in the Christian community as the man who had been blessed personally by the Patriarch of Antioch, the sovereign head of the Syrian Christian Church – an episode which had become part of Ayemenem's folklore.

In 1876, when Baby Kochamma's father was seven years old, his father had taken him to see the Patriarch who was visiting the Syrian Christians of Kerala. They found themselves right in front of a group of people whom the Patriarch was addressing in the westernmost verandah of the Kalleny house, in Cochin. Seizing his opportunity, his father whispered in his young son's ear and propelled the little fellow forward. The future Reverend, skidding on his heels, rigid with fear, applied his terrified lips to the ring on the Patriarch's middle finger, leaving it wet with spit. The patriarch wiped his ring on his sleeve, and blessed the little boy. Long after he grew up and became a priest, Reverend

Ipe continued to be known as *Punnyan Kunju* – Little Blessed One – and people came down the river in boats all the way from Alleppey and Ernakulam, with children to be blessed by him.

Though there was a considerable age difference between Father Mulligan and Reverend Ipe, and though they belonged to different denominations of the Church (whose only common sentiment was their mutual disaffection), both men enjoyed each other's company, and more often than not, Father Mulligan would be invited to stay for lunch. Of the two men, only one recognized the sexual excitement that rose like a tide in the slender girl who hovered around the table long after lunch had been cleared away.

At first Baby Kochamma tried to seduce Father Mulligan with weekly exhibitions of staged charity. Every Thursday morning, just when Father Mulligan was due to arrive, Baby Kochamma force-bathed a poor village child at the well with hard red soap that hurt its protruding ribs.

'Morning, Father!' Baby Kochamma would call out when she saw him, with a smile on her lips that completely belied the vice-like grip that she had on the thin child's soapslippery arm.

'Morning to you, Baby!' Father Mulligan would say, stopping and folding his umbrella.

'There's something I wanted to ask you, Father,' Baby Kochamma would say. 'In First Corinthians, chapter ten, verse twenty-three, it says . . . "All things are lawful for me, but all things are not expedient". Father, how can *all* things be lawful unto Him? I mean I can understand if *some* things are lawful for Him, but –'

Father Mulligan was more than merely flattered by the emotion he aroused in the attractive young girl who stood before him with a trembling, kissable mouth and blazing, coal-black eyes. For he was young too, and perhaps not wholly unaware that the solemn explanations with which he dispelled her bogus biblical doubts were completely at odds with the thrilling promise he held out in his effulgent emerald eyes.

Every Thursday, undaunted by the merciless midday sun, they would stand there by the well. The young girl and the intrepid Jesuit, both quaking with unchristian passion. Using the Bible as a ruse to be with each other.

Invariably, in the middle of their conversation, the unfortunate soapy child that was being force-bathed would manage to slip away, and Father Mulligan would snap back to his senses and say, 'Oops! We'd better catch him before a cold does.'

Then he would reopen his umbrella and walk away in chocolate robes and comfortable sandals, like a high-stepping camel with an appointment to keep. He had young Baby Kochamma's aching heart on a leash, bumping behind him, lurching over leaves and small stones. Bruised and almost broken.

A whole year of Thursdays went by. Eventually the time came for Father Mulligan to return to Madras. Since charity had not produced any tangible results, the distraught young Baby Kochamma invested all her hope in faith.

Displaying a stubborn single-mindedness (which in a young girl in those days was considered as bad as a physical deformity – a harelip perhaps, or a club foot), Baby Kochamma defied her father's wishes and became a Roman Catholic. With special dispensation from the Vatican, she took her vows and entered a convent in Madras as a trainee novice. She hoped somehow that this would provide her with legitimate occasion to be with Father Mulligan. She pictured them together, in dark sepulchral rooms with heavy velvet drapes, discussing Theology. That was all she wanted. All she ever dared to hope for. Just to be near him. Close enough to smell his beard. To see the coarse weave of his cassock. To love him just by looking at him.

Very quickly she realized the futility of this endeavour. She found that the Senior Sisters monopolized the priests and bishops with biblical doubts more sophisticated than hers would ever be, and that it might be years before she got anywhere near Father Mulligan. She grew restless and unhappy in the convent. She developed a stubborn allergic rash on her scalp from the constant chafing of her wimple. She felt she spoke much better English than everybody else. This made her lonelier than ever.

Within a year of her joining the convent, her father began to receive puzzling letters from her in the mail. *My dearest Papa, I am well and happy in the service of Our Lady. But Koh-i-noor appears to be unhappy and homesick. My dearest Papa, Today Koh-i–noor vomited after lunch and is running a temperature. My dearest Papa, Convent food does not seem to suit Koh-i-noor, though I like it well enough. My dearest Papa, Koh-i-noor is upset because her family seems to neither understand nor care about her wellbeing . . .*

Other than the fact that it was (at the time) the name of the world's biggest diamond, Reverend E. John Ipe knew of no other Koh-i-noor. He wondered how a girl with a Muslim name had ended up in a Catholic Convent.

It was Baby Kochamma's mother who eventually realized that Koh-i-noor was none other than Baby Kochamma herself. She remembered that long ago she had shown Baby Kochamma a copy of her father's (Baby Kochamma's grandfather's) will in which, describing his grandchildren he had written: *I have seven jewels one of which is my Koh-i-noor.* He went on to bequeath little bits of money and jewellery to each of them, never clarifying which one he considered his Koh-i-noor. Baby Kochamma's mother realized that Baby Kochamma, for no reason that she could think of, had assumed that he had meant *her* – and all those years later at the convent, knowing that all her letters were read by the Mother Superior before they were posted, had resurrected Koh-i-noor to communicate her troubles to her family.

Reverend Ipe went to Madras and withdrew his daughter from the convent. She was glad to leave, but insisted that she would not reconvert, and for the rest of her days remained a Roman Catholic. Reverend Ipe realized that his daughter had by now developed a 'reputation' and was unlikely to find a husband. He decided that since she couldn't have a husband there was no harm in her having an education. So he made arrangements for her to attend a course of study at the University of Rochester in America.

Two years later, Baby Kochamma returned from Rochester with a diploma in Ornamental Gardening, but more in love with Father Mulligan than ever. There was no trace of the slim, attractive girl that she had been. In her years at Rochester, Baby Kochamma had grown extremely large. In fact, let it be said, obese. Even timid little Chellappen Tailor at Chungam Bridge insisted on charging bush-shirt rates for her sari blouses.

To keep her from brooding, her father gave Baby Kochamma charge of the front garden of the Ayemenem House, where she raised a fierce, bitter garden that people came all the way from Kottayam to see.

It was a circular, sloping patch of ground, with a steep gravel driveway looping around it. Baby Kochamma turned it into a lush maze of dwarf hedges, rocks and gargoyles. The flower she loved the most was the anthurium. Anthurium *andraeanum.* She had a collection of them, the 'Rubrum', the 'Honeymoon' and a host of Japanese varieties. Their single succulent spathes ranged from shades of mottled black to blood red and glistening orange. Their prominent, stippled spadices always yellow. In the centre of Baby Kochamma's garden, surrounded by beds of canna and phlox, a marble cherub peed an endless silver arc into a shallow pool in which a single blue lotus bloomed. At each corner of the pool lolled a pink plaster-of-Paris gnome with rosy cheeks and a peaked red cap.

Baby Kochamma spent her afternoons in her garden. In sari and gumboots. She wielded an enormous pair of hedge shears in her bright orange gardening gloves. Like a lion-tamer she tamed twisting vines and nurtured bristling cacti. She limited bonsai plants and pampered rare orchids. She waged war on the weather. She tried to grow edelweiss and chinese guava.

Every night she creamed her feet with real cream and pushed back the cuticles on her toe-nails.

Recently, after enduring more than half a century of relentless, pernickety attention, the ornamental garden had been abandoned. Left to its own devices, it had grown knotted and wild, like a circus whose animals had forgotten their tricks. The weed that people call communist patcha (because it flourished in Kerala like communism) smothered the more exotic plants. Only the vines kept growing, like toe-nails on a corpse. They reached through the nostrils of the pink plaster gnomes and blossomed in their hollow heads, giving them an expression half surprised, half sneeze-coming.

The reason for this sudden, unceremonious dumping was a new love. Baby Kochamma had installed a dish antenna on the roof of the Ayemenem house. She presided over the World in her drawing room on satellite TV. The impossible excitement that this engendered in Baby Kochamma wasn't hard to understand. It wasn't something that happened gradually. It happened overnight. Blondes, wars, famines, football, sex, music, coups d'état – they all arrived on the same train. They unpacked together. They stayed at the same hotel. And in Ayemenem, where once the loudest sound had been a musical bus horn, now whole wars, famines, picturesque massacres and Bill Clinton could be summoned up like servants. And so, while her ornamental garden wilted and died, Baby Kochamma followed American NBA league games, one-day cricket and all the Grand Slam tennis tournaments. On weekdays she watched *The Bold and The Beautiful* and *Santa Barbara*, where brittle blondes with lipstick and hairstyles rigid with spray seduced androids and defended their sexual empires. Baby Kochamma loved their shiny clothes and the smart, bitchy repartee. During the day disconnected snatches of it came back to her and made her chuckle.

Kochu Maria, the cook, still wore the thick gold earrings that had disfigured her earlobes for ever. She enjoyed the WWF *Wrestling Mania* shows, where Hulk Hogan and Mr Perfect, whose necks were wider than their heads, wore spangled Lycra leggings and beat each other up brutally. Kochu Maria's laugh had that slightly cruel ring to it that young children's sometimes have.

All day they sat in the drawing room, Baby Kochamma on the long-armed planter's chair or the chaise longue (depending on the condition of her feet), Kochu Maria next to her on the floor (channel surfing when she could), locked together in a noisy Television silence. One's hair snow white, the other's dyed coal black. They entered all the contests, availed themselves of all the discounts that were advertised and had, on two occasions, won a T-shirt and a Thermos flask that Baby Kochamma kept locked away in her cupboard.

Baby Kochamma loved the Ayemenem house and cherished the furniture that she had inherited by outliving everybody else. Mammachi's violin and violin stand, the Ooty cupboards, the plastic basket chairs, the Delhi beds, the dressing table from Vienna with cracked ivory knobs. The rosewood dining table that Velutha made.

She was frightened by the BBC famines and Television wars that she encountered while she channel surfed. Her old fears of the Revolution and the Marxist-Leninist menace had been rekindled by new television worries about the growing numbers of desperate and dispossessed people. She viewed ethnic cleansing, famine and genocide as direct threats to her furniture.

She kept her doors and windows locked, unless she was using them. She used her windows for specific purposes. For a Breath of Fresh Air. To Pay for the Milk. To Let Out a Trapped Wasp (which Kochu Maria was made to chase around the house with a towel).

She even locked her sad, paint-flaking fridge where she kept her week's supply of cream buns that Kochu Maria brought her from Bestbakery in Kottayam. And the two bottles of rice-water that she drank instead of ordinary water. In the shelf below the baffle tray, she kept what was left of Mammachi's willow-pattern dinner service.

She put the dozen or so bottles of insulin that Rahel brought her in the cheese and butter compartment. She suspected that these days, even the innocent and the round-eyed could be crockery crooks, or cream-bun cravers, or thieving diabetics cruising Ayemenem for imported insulin.

She didn't even trust the twins. She deemed them Capable of Anything. Anything at all. *They might even steal their present back*, she thought, and realized with a pang how quickly she had reverted to thinking of them as though they were a single unit once again. After all those years. Determined not to let the past creep up on her she altered her thought at once. *She. She might steal her present back.*

She looked at Rahel standing at the dining table and noticed the same eerie stealth, the ability to keep very still and very quiet that Estha seemed to have mastered. Baby Kochamma was a little intimidated by Rahel's quietness.

'So!' she said. Her voice shrill, faltering. 'What are your plans? How long will you be staying? Have you decided?'

Rahel tried to say something. It came out jagged. Like a piece of tin. She walked to the window and opened it. For a Breath of Fresh Air.

'Shut it when you've finished with it,' Baby Kochamma said, and closed her face like a cupboard.

You couldn't see the river from the window any more.

You could, until Mammachi had had the back verandah closed in with Ayemenem's first sliding-folding door. The oil portraits of Reverend E. John Ipe and Aleyooty Ammachi (Estha and Rahel's great-grandparents), were taken down from the back verandah and put up in the front one.

They hung there now, the Little Blessed One and his wife, on either side of the stuffed, mounted bison head.

Reverend Ipe smiled his confident-ancestor smile out across the road instead of the river.

Aleyooty Ammachi looked more hesitant. As though she would have liked to turn around but couldn't. Perhaps it wasn't as easy for her to abandon the river. With her eyes she looked in the direction that her husband looked. With her heart she looked away. Her heavy, dull gold kunukku earrings (tokens of the Little Blessed One's Goodness) had stretched her earlobes and hung all the way down to her shoulders. Through the holes in her ears you could see the hot river and the dark trees that bent into it. And the fishermen in their boats. And the fish.

Though you couldn't see the river from the house any more, like a seashell always has a sea-sense, the Ayemenem house still had a river-sense.

A rushing, rolling, fishswimming sense.

From the dining-room window where she stood, with the wind in her hair, Rahel could see the rain drum down on the rusted tin roof of what used to be their grandmother's pickle factory.

Paradise Pickles & Preserves.

It lay between the house and the river.

They used to make pickles, squashes, jams, curry powders and canned pineapples. And banana jam (illegally) after the FPO (Food Products Organization) banned it because according to their specifications it was neither jam nor jelly. Too thin for jelly and too thick for jam. An ambiguous, unclassifiable consistency, they said.

As per their books.

Looking back now, to Rahel it seemed as though this difficulty that their family had with classification ran much deeper than the jam-jelly question.

Perhaps, Ammu, Estha and she were the worst transgressors. But it wasn't just them. It was the others too. They all broke the rules. They all crossed into forbidden territory. They all tampered with the laws that lay down who should be loved and how. And how much. The laws that make grandmothers grandmothers, uncles uncles, mothers mothers, cousins cousins, jam jam, and jelly jelly.

It was a time when uncles became fathers, mothers lovers, and cousins died and had funerals.

It was a time when the unthinkable became thinkable and the impossible really happened.

Even before Sophie Mol's funeral, the police found Velutha.

His arms had goosebumps where the handcuffs touched his skin. Cold handcuffs with a sourmetal smell. Like steel bus rails and the smell of the bus conductor's hands from holding them.

After it was all over, Baby Kochamma said, 'As ye sow, so shall ye reap.' As though *she* had had nothing to do with the Sowing and the Reaping. She returned on her small feet to her cross-stitch embroidery. Her little toes never touched the floor. It was her idea that Estha be Returned.

Margaret Kochamma's grief and bitterness at her daughter's death coiled inside her like an angry spring. She said nothing, but slapped Estha whenever she could in the days she was there before she returned to England.

Rahel watched Ammu pack Estha's little trunk.

'Maybe they're right,' Ammu's whisper said. 'Maybe a boy does need a Baba.'

Rahel saw that her eyes were a redly dead.

They consulted a Twin Expert in Hyderabad. She wrote back to say that it was not advisable to separate monozygotic twins, but that two-egg twins were no different from ordinary siblings and that while they would certainly suffer the natural distress that children from broken homes underwent, it would be nothing more than that. Nothing out of the ordinary.

And so Estha was Returned in a train with his tin trunk and his beige and pointy shoes rolled into his khaki holdall. First class, overnight on the Madras Mail to Madras and then with a friend of their father's from Madras to Calcutta.

He had a tiffin carrier with tomato sandwiches. And an Eagle flask with an eagle. He had terrible pictures in his head.

Rain. Rushing, inky water. And a smell. Sicksweet. Like old roses on a breeze.

But worst of all, he carried inside him the memory of a young man with an old man's mouth. The memory of a swollen face and a smashed, upside-down smile. Of a spreading pool of clear liquid with a bare bulb reflected in it. Of a bloodshot eye that had opened, wandered and then fixed its gaze on him. Estha. And what had Estha done? He had looked into that beloved face and said: Yes.

Yes, it was him.

The word Estha's octopus couldn't get at: *Yes.* Hoovering didn't seem to help. It was lodged there, deep inside some fold or furrow, like a mango hair between molars. That couldn't be worried loose.

In a purely practical sense it would probably be correct to say that it all began when Sophie Mol came to Ayemenem. Perhaps it's true that things can change in a day. That a few dozen hours can affect the outcome of whole lifetimes. And that when they do, those few dozen hours, like the salvaged remains of a burned house – the charred clock, the singed photograph, the scorched furniture – must be resurrected from the ruins and examined. Preserved. Accounted for.

Little events, ordinary things, smashed and reconstituted.

Imbued with new meaning. Suddenly they become the bleached bones of a story.

Still, to say that it all began when Sophie Mol came to Ayemenem is only one way of looking at it.

Equally, it could be argued that it actually began thousands of years ago. Long before the Marxists came. Before the British took Malabar, before the Dutch Ascendency, before Vasco da Gama arrived, before the Zamorin's conquest of Calicut. Before three purple-robed Syrian Bishops murdered by the Portuguese were found floating in the sea, with coiled sea serpents riding on their chests and oysters knotted in their tangled beards. It could be argued that it began long before Christianity arrived in a boat and seeped into Kerala like tea from a teabag.

That it really began in the days when the Love Laws were made. The laws that lay down who should be loved, and how.

And how much.

HOWEVER, for practical purposes, in a hopelessly practical world . . .

2

Pappachi's Moth

. . . it was a skyblue day in December sixty-nine (the nineteen silent). It was the kind of time in the life of a family when something happens to nudge its hidden morality from its resting place and make it bubble to the surface and float for a while. In clear view. For everyone to see.

A skyblue Plymouth, with the sun in its tailfins, sped past young rice-fields and old rubber trees, on its way to Cochin. Further east, in a small country with similar landscape (jungles, rivers, rice-fields, communists), enough bombs were being dropped to cover all of it in six inches of steel. Here, however, it was peacetime and the family in the Plymouth travelled without fear or foreboding.

The Plymouth used to belong to Pappachi, Rahel and Estha's grandfather. Now that he was dead, it belonged to Mammachi, their grandmother, and Rahel and Estha were on their way to Cochin to see *The Sound of Music* for the third time. They knew all the songs.

After that they were all going to stay at Hotel Sea Queen with the oldfood smell. Bookings had been made. Early next morning they would go to Cochin Airport to pick up Chacko's ex-wife – their English aunt, Margaret Kochamma – and their cousin, Sophie Mol, who were coming from London to spend Christmas at Ayemenem. Earlier that year, Margaret Kochamma's second husband, Joe, had been killed in a car accident.

When Chacko heard about the accident he invited them to Ayemenem. He said that he couldn't bear to think of them spending a lonely, desolate Christmas in England. In a house full of memories.

Ammu said that Chacko had never stopped loving Margaret Kochamma. Mammachi disagreed. She liked to believe that he had never loved her in the first place.

Rahel and Estha had never met Sophie Mol. They'd heard a lot about her, though, that last week. From Baby Kochamma, from Kochu Maria, and even Mammachi. None of them had met her either, but they all behaved as though they already knew her. It had been the *What Will Sophie Mol Think?* week.

That whole week Baby Kochamma eavesdropped relentlessly on the twins' private conversations, and whenever she caught them speaking in Malayalam, she levied a small fine which was deducted at source. From their pocket money. She made them write lines – 'impositions' she called them – *I will always speak in English, I will always speak in English.* A hundred times each. When they were done, she scored them out with her red pen to make sure that old lines were not recycled for new punishments.

She had made them practise an English car song for the way back. They had to form the words properly, and be particularly careful about their pronunciation. Prer *NUN* sea ayshun.

Rej-Oice in the Lo-Ord Or-Orlways
And again I say rej-Oice,
RejOice,
RejOice,
And again I say rej-Oice.

Estha's full name was Esthappen Yako. Rahel's was Rahel. For the Time Being they had no surname because Ammu was considering reverting to her maiden name, though she said that choosing between her husband's name and her father's name didn't give a woman much of a choice.

Estha was wearing his beige and pointy shoes and his Elvis puff. His Special Outing Puff. His favourite Elvis song was 'Party'. '*Some people like to rock, some people like to roll,*' he would croon, when nobody was watching, strumming a badminton racquet, curling his lip like Elvis. '*But moonin' an' a-groonin' gonna satisfy mah soul, less have a pardy . . .* '

Estha had slanting, sleepy eyes and his new front teeth were still uneven on the ends. Rahel's new teeth were waiting inside her gums, like words in a pen. It puzzled everybody that an eighteen-minute age difference could cause such a discrepancy in front-tooth timing.

Most of Rahel's hair sat on top of her head like a fountain. It was held together by a Love-in-Tokyo – two beads on a rubber band, nothing to do with Love or Tokyo. In Kerala Love-in-Tokyos have withstood the test of time, and even today if you were to ask for one at any respectable A-1 Ladies' Store, that's what you'd get. Two beads on a rubber band.

Rahel's toy wristwatch had the time painted on it. Ten to two. One of her ambitions was to own a watch on which she could change the time whenever she wanted to (which according to her was what Time was meant for in the first place). Her yellow-rimmed red plastic sunglasses made the world look red. Ammu said that they were bad for her eyes and had advised her to wear them as seldom as possible.

Her Airport Frock was in Ammu's suitcase. It had special matching knickers.

Chacko was driving. He was four years older than Ammu. Rahel and Estha couldn't call him Chachen because when they did, he called them Chetan and Cheduthi. If they called him Ammaven he called them Appoi and Ammai. If they called him Uncle he called them Aunty, which was embarrassing in Public. So they called him Chacko.

Chacko's room was stacked from floor to ceiling with books. He had read them all and quoted long passages from them for no apparent reason. Or at least none that anyone else could fathom. For instance, that morning, as they drove out through the gate, shouting their goodbyes to Mammachi in the verandah, Chacko suddenly said: '*Gatsby turned out all right at the end; it is what preyed on Gatsby, what foul dust floated in the wake of his dreams that temporarily closed out my interest in the abortive sorrows and short-winded elations of men.*'

Everyone was so used to it that they didn't bother to nudge each other or exchange glances. Chacko had been a Rhodes Scholar at Oxford and was permitted excesses and eccentricities nobody else was.

He claimed to be writing a Family Biography that the Family would have to pay him not to publish. Ammu said that there was only one person in the family who was a fit candidate for biographical blackmail and that was Chacko himself.

Of course that was then. Before the Terror.

In the Plymouth, Ammu was sitting in front, next to Chacko. She was twenty-seven that year, and in the pit of her stomach she carried the cold knowledge that for her, life had been lived. She had had one chance. She made a mistake. She married the wrong man.

Ammu finished her schooling the same year that her father retired from his job in Delhi and moved to Ayemenem. Pappachi insisted that a college education was an unnecessary expense for a girl, so Ammu had no choice but to leave Delhi and move with them. There was very little for a young girl to do in Ayemenem other than to wait for marriage proposals while she helped her mother with the housework. Since her father did not have enough money to raise a suitable dowry, no proposals came Ammu's way. Two years went by. Her eighteenth birthday came and went. Unnoticed, or at least unremarked upon by her parents. Ammu grew desperate. All day she dreamed of escaping from Ayemenem and the clutches of her ill-tempered father and bitter, long-suffering mother. She hatched several wretched little plans. Eventually, one worked. Pappachi agreed to let her spend the summer with a distant aunt who lived in Calcutta.

There, at someone else's wedding reception, Ammu met her future husband.

He was on vacation from his job in Assam where he worked as an assistant manager of a tea estate. His family were once-wealthy zamindars who had migrated to Calcutta from East Bengal after Partition.

He was a small man, but well-built. Pleasant-looking. He wore old-fashioned spectacles that made him look earnest and completely belied his easy-going charm and juvenile but totally disarming sense of humour. He was twenty-five and had already been working on the tea estates for six years. He hadn't been to college, which accounted for his schoolboy humour. He proposed to Ammu five days after they first met. Ammu didn't pretend to be in love with him. She just weighed the odds and accepted. She thought that *anything*, anyone at all, would be better than returning to Ayemenem. She wrote to her parents informing them of her decision. They didn't reply.

Ammu had an elaborate Calcutta wedding. Later, looking back on the day, Ammu realized that the slightly feverish glitter in her bridegroom's eyes had not been love, or even excitement at the prospect of carnal bliss, but approximately eight large pegs of whisky. Straight. Neat.

Ammu's father-in-law was Chairman of the Railway Board and had a Boxing Blue from Cambridge. He was the Secretary of the BABA – the Bengal Amateur Boxing Association. He gave the young couple a custom-painted, powder-pink Fiat as a present which after the wedding he drove off in himself, with all the jewellery and most of the other presents that they had been given. He died before the twins were born – on the operating table while his gall bladder was being removed. His cremation was attended by all the boxers in Bengal. A congregation of mourners with lantern jaws and broken noses.

When Ammu and her husband moved to Assam, Ammu, beautiful, young and cheeky, became the toast of the Planters' Club. She wore backless blouses with her saris and carried a silver lamé purse on a chain. She smoked long cigarettes in a silver cigarette holder and learned to blow perfect smoke rings. Her husband turned out to be not just a heavy drinker but a full-blown alcoholic with all of an alcoholic's deviousness and tragic charm. There were things about him that Ammu never understood. Long after she left him, she never stopped wondering why he lied so outrageously when he didn't need to. *Particularly* when he didn't need to. In a conversation with friends he would talk about how much he loved smoked salmon when Ammu knew he hated it. Or he would come home from the club and tell Ammu that he saw *Meet Me in St Louis* when they'd actually screened *The Bronze Buckaroo*. When she confronted him about these things, he never explained or apologized. He just giggled, exasperating Ammu to a degree she never thought herself capable of.

Ammu was eight months pregnant when war broke out with China. It was October of 1962. Planters' wives and children were evacuated from Assam. Ammu, too pregnant to travel, remained on the estate. In November, after a hair-raising, bumpy bus ride to Shillong, amidst rumours of Chinese occupation and India's impending defeat, Estha and Rahel were born. By candlelight. In a hospital with the windows blacked out. They emerged without much fuss, within eighteen minutes of each other. Two little ones, instead of one big one. Twin seals, slick with their mother's juices. Wrinkled with the effort of being born. Ammu checked them for deformities before she closed her eyes and slept.

She counted four eyes, four ears, two mouths, two noses, twenty fingers and twenty perfect toe-nails.

She didn't notice the single Siamese soul. She was glad to have them. Their father, stretched out on a hard bench in the hospital corridor, was drunk.

By the time the twins were two years old their father's drinking, aggravated by the loneliness of tea estate life, had driven him into an alcoholic stupor. Whole days went by during which he just lay in bed and didn't go to work. Eventually, his English manager, Mr Hollick, summoned him to his bungalow for a 'serious chat'.

Ammu sat in the verandah of her home waiting anxiously for her husband to return. She was sure the only reason that Hollick wanted to see him was to sack him. She was surprised when he returned looking despondent but not devastated. Mr Hollick had proposed something, he told Ammu, that he needed to discuss with her. He began a little diffidently, avoiding her gaze, but he gathered courage as he went along. Viewed practically, in the long run it was a proposition that would benefit both of them, he said. In fact *all* of them, if they considered the children's education.

Mr Hollick had been frank with his young assistant. He informed him of the complaints he had received from the labour as well as from the other assistant managers.

'I'm afraid I have no option,' he said, 'but to ask for your resignation.'

He allowed the silence to take its toll. He allowed the pitiful man sitting across the table to begin to shake. To weep. Then Hollick spoke again.

'Well, actually there *may* be an option . . . perhaps we could work something out. Think positive, is what I always say. Count your blessings.' Hollick paused to order a pot of black coffee. 'You're a very lucky man, you know, wonderful family, beautiful children, such an attractive wife . . .' He lit a cigarette and allowed the match to burn until he couldn't hold it any more. 'An *extremely* attractive wife . . .'

The weeping stopped. Puzzled brown eyes looked into lurid, red-veined, green ones. Over coffee, Mr Hollick proposed that Baba go away for a while. For a holiday. To a clinic perhaps, for treatment. For as long as it took him to get better. And for the period of time that he was away, Mr Hollick suggested that Ammu be sent to his bungalow to be 'looked after'.

Already there were a number of ragged, lightskinned children on the estate that Hollick had bequeathed on tea-pickers whom he fancied. This was his first incursion into management circles.

Ammu watched her husband's mouth move as it formed words. She said nothing. He grew uncomfortable and then infuriated by her silence. Suddenly he lunged at her, grabbed her hair, punched her and then passed out from the effort. Ammu took down the heaviest book she could find in the bookshelf – *The Reader's Digest World Atlas* – and hit him with it as hard as she could. On his head. His legs. His back and shoulders. When he regained consciousness, he was puzzled by his bruises. He apologized abjectly for the violence, but immediately began to badger her about helping with his transfer. This fell into a pattern. Drunken violence followed by post-drunken badgering. Ammu was repelled by the medicinal smell of stale alcohol that seeped through his skin, and the dry, caked vomit that encrusted his mouth like a pie every morning. When his bouts of violence began to include the children, and the war with Pakistan began, Ammu left her husband and returned, unwelcomed, to her parents in Ayemenem. To everything that she had fled from only a few years ago. Except that now she had two young children. And no more dreams.

Pappachi would not believe her story – not because he thought well of her husband, but simply because he didn't believe that an Englishman, *any* Englishman, would covet another man's wife.

Ammu loved her children (of course), but their wide-eyed vulnerability, and their willingness to love people who didn't really love them, exasperated her and sometimes made her want to hurt them – just as an education, a protection.

It was as though the window through which their father disappeared had been kept open for anyone to walk in and be welcomed.

To Ammu her twins seemed like a pair of small bewildered frogs engrossed in each other's company, lolloping arm in arm down a highway full of hurtling traffic. Entirely oblivious of what trucks can do to frogs. Ammu watched over them fiercely. Her watchfulness stretched her, made her taut and tense. She was quick to reprimand her children, but even quicker to take offence on their behalf.

For herself she knew that there would be no more chances. There was only Ayemenem now. A front verandah and a back verandah. A hot river and a pickle factory.

And in the background, the constant, high, whining mewl of local disapproval.

Within the first few months of her return to her parents' home, Ammu quickly learned to recognize and despise the ugly face of sympathy. Old female relations with incipient beards and several wobbling chins made overnight trips to Ayemenem to commiserate with her about her divorce. They squeezed her knee and gloated. She fought off the urge to slap them. Or twiddle their nipples. With a spanner. Like Chaplin in *Modern Times*.

When she looked at herself in her wedding photographs, Ammu felt the woman that looked back at her was someone else. A foolish jewelled bride. Her silk sunset-coloured sari shot with gold. Rings on every finger. White dots of sandalwood paste over her arched eyebrows. Looking at herself like this, Ammu's soft mouth would twist into a small, bitter smile at the memory – not of the wedding itself so much as the fact that she had permitted herself to be so painstakingly decorated before being led to the gallows. It seemed so absurd. So futile.

Like polishing firewood.

She went to the village goldsmith and had her heavy wedding ring melted down and made into a thin bangle with snakeheads that she put away for Rahel.

Ammu knew that weddings were not something that could be avoided altogether. At least not practically speaking. But for the rest of her life she advocated *small* weddings in *ordinary* clothes. It made them less ghoulish, she thought.

Occasionally, when Ammu listened to songs that she loved on the radio, something stirred inside her. A liquid ache spread under her skin, and she walked out of the world like a witch, to a better, happier place. On days like this, there was something restless and untamed about her. As though she had temporarily set aside the morality of motherhood and divorceehood. Even her walk changed from a safe mother-walk to another wilder sort of walk. She wore flowers in her hair and carried magic secrets in her eyes. She spoke to no one. She spent hours on the riverbank with her little plastic transistor shaped like a tangerine. She smoked cigarettes and had midnight swims.

What was it that gave Ammu this Unsafe Edge? This air of unpredictability? It was what she had battling inside her. An unmixable mix. The infinite tenderness of motherhood and the reckless rage of a suicide bomber. It was this that grew inside her, and eventually led her to love by night the man her children loved by day. To use by night the boat that her children used by day. The boat that Estha sat on, and Rahel found.

On the days that the radio played Ammu's songs, everyone was a little wary of her. They sensed somehow that she lived in the penumbral shadows between two worlds, just beyond the grasp of their power. That a woman that they had already damned, now had little left to lose, and could therefore be dangerous. So on the days that the radio played Ammu's songs, people avoided her, made little loops around her, because everybody agreed that it was best to just Let Her Be.

On other days she had deep dimples when she smiled.

She had a delicate, chiselled face, black eyebrows angled like a soaring seagull's wings, a small straight nose and luminous nutbrown skin. On that skyblue December day, her wild, curly hair had escaped in wisps in the car wind. Her shoulders in her sleeveless sari blouse shone as though they had been polished with a high-wax shoulder polish. Sometimes she was the most beautiful woman that Estha and Rahel had ever seen. And sometimes she wasn't.

On the back seat of the Plymouth, between Estha and Rahel, sat Baby Kochamma. Ex-nun, and incumbent baby grand aunt. In the way that the unfortunate sometimes dislike the co-unfortunate, Baby Kochamma disliked the twins, for she considered them doomed, fatherless waifs. Worse still, they were Half-Hindu Hybrids whom no self-respecting Syrian Christian would ever marry. She was keen for them to realize that they (like herself) lived on sufferance in the Ayemenem House, their maternal grandmother's house, where they really had no right to be. Baby Kochamma resented Ammu, because she saw her quarrelling with a fate that she, Baby Kochamma herself, felt she had graciously accepted. The fate of the wretched Man-less woman. The sad, Father Mulligan-less Baby Kochamma. She had managed to persuade herself over the years that her unconsummated love for Father Mulligan had been entirely due to *her* restraint and *her* determination to do the right thing.

She subscribed wholeheartedly to the commonly held view that a married daughter had no position in her parents' home. As for a *divorced* daughter – according to Baby Kochamma, she had no position anywhere at all. And as for a *divorced* daughter from a *love* marriage, well, words could not describe Baby Kochamma's outrage. As for a *divorced* daughter from a *intercommunity love* marriage – Baby Kochamma chose to remain quiveringly silent on the subject.

The twins were too young to understand all this, so Baby Kochamma grudged them their moments of high happiness when a dragonfly they'd caught lifted a small stone off their palms with its legs, or when they had permission to bathe the pigs, or they found an egg – hot from a hen. But most of all, she grudged them the comfort they drew from each other. She expected from them some token unhappiness. At the very least.

On the way back from the airport, Margaret Kochamma would sit in front with Chacko because she used to be his wife. Sophie Mol would sit between them. Ammu would move to the back.

There would be two flasks of water. Boiled water for Margaret Kochamma and Sophie Mol, tap water for everybody else.

The luggage would be in the boot.

Rahel thought that *boot* was a lovely word. A much better word, at any rate, than *sturdy*. *Sturdy* was a terrible word. Like a dwarf's name. *Sturdy Koshy Oommen* – a pleasant, middle-class, God-fearing dwarf with low knees and a side parting.

On the Plymouth roof rack there was a four-sided tin-lined, plywood billboard that said, on all four sides, in elaborate writing, *Paradise Pickles & Preserves.* Below the writing there were painted bottles of mixed-fruit jam and hot-lime pickle in edible oil, with labels that said, in elaborate writing, *Paradise Pickles & Preserves.* Next to the bottles there was a list of all the Paradise products and a kathakali dancer with his face green and skirts swirling. Along the bottom of the S-shaped swirl of his billowing skirt, it said, in an S-shaped swirl, *Emperors of the Realm of Taste* – which was Comrade K. N. M. Pillai's unsolicited contribution. It was a literal translation of *Ruchi lokathinde Rajavu*, which sounded a little less ludicrous than *Emperors of the Realm of Taste.* But since Comrade Pillai had already printed them, no one had the heart to ask him to re-do the whole print order. So, unhappily, *Emperors of the Realm of Taste* became a permanent feature on the Paradise Pickle labels.

Ammu said that the kathakali dancer was a Red Herring and had nothing to do with anything. Chacko said that it gave the products a Regional Flavour and would stand them in good stead when they entered the Overseas Market.

Ammu said that the billboard made them look ridiculous. Like a travelling circus. With tailfins.

Mammachi had started making pickles commercially soon after Pappachi retired from Government service in Delhi and came to live in Ayemenem. The Kottayam Bible Society was having a fair and asked Mammachi to make some of her famous banana jam and tender mango pickle. It sold quickly, and Mammachi found that she had more orders than she could cope with. Thrilled with her success, she decided to persist with the pickles and jam, and soon found herself busy all year round. Pappachi, for his part, was having trouble coping with the ignominy of retirement. He was seventeen years older than Mammachi, and realized with a shock that he was an old man when his wife was still in her prime.

Though Mammachi had conical corneas and was already practically blind, Pappachi would not help her with the pickle-making, because he did not consider pickle-making a suitable job for a high-ranking ex-Government official. He had always been a jealous man, so he greatly resented the attention his wife was suddenly getting. He slouched around the compound in his immaculately tailored suits, weaving sullen circles around mounds of red chillies and freshly powdered yellow turmeric, watching Mammachi supervise the buying, the weighing, the salting and drying, of limes and tender mangoes. Every night he beat her with a brass flower vase. The beatings weren't new. What was new was only the frequency with which they took place. One night Pappachi broke the bow of Mammachi's violin and threw it in the river.

Then Chacko came home for a summer vacation from Oxford. He had grown to be a big man, and was, in those days, strong from rowing for Balliol. A week after he arrived he found Pappachi beating Mammachi in the study. Chacko strode into the room, caught Pappachi's vase-hand and twisted it around his back.

'I never want this to happen again,' he told his father. 'Ever.'

For the rest of that day Pappachi sat in the verandah and stared stonily out at the ornamental garden, ignoring the plates of food that Kochu Maria brought him. Late at night he went into his study and brought out his favourite mahogany rocking chair. He put it down in the middle of the driveway and smashed it into little bits with a plumber's monkey wrench. He left it there in the moonlight, a heap of varnished wicker and splintered wood. He never touched Mammachi again. But he never spoke to her either as long as he lived. When he needed anything he used Kochu Maria or Baby Kochamma as intermediaries.

In the evenings, when he knew visitors were expected, he would sit on the verandah and sew buttons that weren't missing onto his shirts, to create the impression that Mammachi neglected him. To some small degree he did succeed in further corroding Ayemenem's view of working wives.

He bought the skyblue Plymouth from an old Englishman in Munnar. He became a familiar sight in Ayemenem, coasting importantly down the narrow road in his wide car, looking outwardly elegant but sweating freely inside his woollen suits. He wouldn't allow Mammachi or anyone else in the family to use it, or even to sit in it. The Plymouth was Pappachi's revenge.

Pappachi had been an Imperial Entomologist at the Pusa Institute. After Independence, when the British left, his designation was changed from Imperial Entomologist to Joint

Director, Entomology. The year he retired, he had risen to a rank equivalent to Director.

His life's greatest setback was not having had the moth that *he* had discovered named after him.

It fell into his drink one evening while he was sitting in the verandah of a rest house after a long day in the field. As he picked it out he noticed its unusually dense dorsal tufts. He took a closer look. With growing excitement he mounted it, measured it and the next morning placed it in the sun for a few hours for the alcohol to evaporate. Then he caught the first train back to Delhi. To taxonomic attention and, he hoped, fame. After six unbearable months of anxiety, to Pappachi's intense disappointment he was told that his moth had finally been identified as a slightly unusual race of a well-known species that belonged to the tropical family Lymantriidae.

The real blow came twelve years later, when, as a consequence of a radical taxonomic reshuffle, lepidopterists decided that Pappachi's moth *was* in fact a separate species and genus hitherto unknown to science. By then, of course, Pappachi had retired and moved to Ayemenem. It was too late for him to assert his claim to the discovery. His moth was named after the Acting Director of the Department of Entomology, a junior officer whom Pappachi had always disliked.

In the years to come, even though he had been ill-humoured long before he discovered the moth, Pappachi's Moth was held responsible for his black moods and sudden bouts of temper. Its pernicious ghost – grey, furry and with unusually dense dorsal tufts – haunted every house that he ever lived in. It tormented him and his children and his children's children.

Until the day he died, even in the stifling Ayemenem heat, every single day, Pappachi wore a well-pressed three-piece suit and his gold pocket watch. On his dressing table, next to his cologne and silver hairbrush, he kept a picture of himself as a young man, with his hair slicked down, taken in a photographer's studio in Vienna where he had done the six-month diploma course that had qualified him to apply for the post of Imperial Entomologist. It was during those few months they spent in Vienna that Mammachi took her first lessons on the violin. The lessons were abruptly discontinued when Mammachi's teacher, Launsky-Tieffenthal, made the mistake of telling Pappachi that his wife was exceptionally talented and, in his opinion, potentially concert class.

Mammachi pasted, in the family photograph album, the clipping from the *Indian Express* that reported Pappachi's death. It said:

> Noted entomologist, Shri Benaan John Ipe, son of late Rev. E. John Ipe of Ayemenem (popularly known as *Punnyan Kunju*), suffered a massive heart attack and passed away at the Kottayam General Hospital last night. He developed chest pains around 1.05 a.m. and was rushed to hospital. The end came at 2.45 a.m. Shri Ipe had been keeping indifferent health since last six months. He is survived by his wife Soshamma and two children.

At Pappachi's funeral, Mammachi cried and her contact lenses slid around in her eyes. Ammu told the twins that Mammachi was crying more because she was used to him than because she loved him. She was used to having him slouching around the pickle factory, and was used to being beaten from time to time. Ammu said that human beings were creatures of habit, and it was amazing the kind of things they could get used to. You only had to look around you, Ammu said, to see that beatings with brass vases were the least of them.

After the funeral Mammachi asked Rahel to help her to locate and remove her contact lenses with the little orange pipette that came in its own case. Rahel asked Mammachi whether, after Mammachi died, she could inherit the pipette. Ammu took her out of the room and smacked her.

'I never want to hear you discussing people's deaths with them again,' she said.

Estha said Rahel deserved it for being so insensitive.

The photograph of Pappachi in Vienna, with his hair slicked down, was reframed and put up in the drawing room.

He was a photogenic man, dapper and carefully groomed, with a little man's largeish head. He had an incipient second chin that would have been emphasized had he looked down or nodded. In the photograph he had taken care to hold his head high enough to hide his double chin, yet not so high as to appear haughty. His light brown eyes were polite, yet maleficent, as though he was making an effort to be civil to the photographer while plotting to murder his wife. He had a little fleshy knob on the centre of his upper lip that dropped down over his lower lip in a sort of effeminate pout – the kind that children who suck their thumbs develop. He had an elongated dimple on his chin which only served to underline the threat of a lurking manic violence. A sort of contained cruelty. He wore khaki jodhpurs though he had never ridden a horse in his life. His riding boots reflected the photographer's studio lights. An ivory-handled riding crop lay neatly across his lap.

There was a watchful stillness to the photograph that lent an underlying chill to the warm room in which it hung.

When he died, Pappachi left trunks full of expensive suits and a chocolate tin full of cuff-links that Chacko distributed among the taxi drivers in Kottayam. They were separated and made into rings and pendants for unmarried daughters' dowries.

When the twins asked what cuff-links were for – 'To link cuffs together,' Ammu told them – they were thrilled by this morsel of logic in what had so far seemed an illogical language. *Cuff+link = Cuff-link.* This, to them, rivalled the precision and logic of mathematics. *Cuff-links* gave them an inordinate (if exaggerated) satisfaction, and a real affection for the English language.

Ammu said that Pappachi was an incurable British CCP, which was short for *chhi-chhi poach* and in Hindi meant shit-wiper.

Chacko said that the correct word for people like Pappachi was *Anglophile.* He made Rahel and Estha look up *Anglophile* in the *Reader's Digest Great Encyclopaedic Dictionary*. It said *Person well disposed to the English.* Then Estha and Rahel had to look up *disposed.*

It said:

(1) *Place suitably in particular order.*
(2) *Bring mind into certain state.*
(3) *Do what one will with, get off one's hands, stow away, demolish, finish, settle, consume (food), kill, sell.*

Chacko said that in Pappachi's case it meant (2) *Bring mind into certain state.* Which, Chacko said, meant that Pappachi's mind had been *brought into a state* which made him like the English.

Chacko told the twins that though he hated to admit it, they were all Anglophiles. They were a *family* of Anglophiles. Pointed in the wrong direction, trapped outside their own history, and unable to retrace their steps because their footprints had been swept away. He explained to them that history was like an old house at night. With all the lamps lit. And ancestors whispering inside.

'To understand history,' Chacko said, 'we have to go inside and listen to what they're saying. And look at the books and the pictures on the wall. And smell the smells.'

Estha and Rahel had no doubt that the house Chacko meant was the house on the other side of the river, in the middle of the abandoned rubber estate where they had never been. Kari Saipu's house. The Black Sahib. The Englishman who had 'gone native'. Who spoke Malayalam and wore mundus. Ayemenem's own Kurtz. Ayemenem his private Heart of Darkness. He had shot himself through the head ten years ago when his young lover's parents had taken the boy away from him and sent him to school. After the suicide, the property had become the subject of extensive litigation between Kari Saipu's cook and his secretary. The house had lain empty for years. Very few people had seen it. But the twins could picture it.

The History House.

With cool stone floors and dim walls and billowing ship-shaped shadows. Plump, translucent lizards lived behind old pictures, and waxy, crumbling ancestors with tough toe-nails and breath that smelled of yellow maps gossiped in sibilant, papery whispers.

'But we can't go in,' Chacko explained, 'because we've been locked out. And when we look in through the windows, all we see are shadows. And when we try and listen, all we hear is a whispering. And we cannot understand the whispering, because our minds have been invaded by a war. A war that we have won and lost. The very worst sort of war. A war that captures dreams and re-dreams them. A war that has made us adore our conquerors and despise ourselves.'

'*Marry* our conquerors, is more like it,' Ammu said drily, referring to Margaret Kochamma. Chacko ignored her. He made the twins look up *Despise*. It said: *To look down upon; to view with contempt; to scorn or disdain.*

Chacko said that in the context of the war he was talking about – the War of Dreams – *Despise* meant all those things.

'We're Prisoners of War,' Chacko said. 'Our dreams have been doctored. We belong nowhere. We sail unanchored on troubled seas. We may never be allowed ashore. Our sorrows will never be sad enough. Our joys never happy enough. Our dreams never big enough. Our lives never important enough. To matter.'

Then, to give Estha and Rahel a sense of historical perspective (though perspective was something which, in the weeks to follow, Chacko himself would sorely lack), he told them about the Earth Woman. He made them imagine that the earth – four thousand six hundred million years old – was a forty-six-year-old woman

– as old, say, as Aleyamma Teacher, who gave them Malayalam lessons. It had taken the whole of the Earth Woman's life for the earth to become what it was. For the oceans to part. For the mountains to rise. The Earth Woman was eleven years old, Chacko said, when the first single-celled organisms appeared. The first animals, creatures like worms and jellyfish, appeared only when she was forty. She was over forty-five – just eight months ago – when dinosaurs roamed the earth.

'The whole of human civilization as we know it,' Chacko told the twins, 'began only *two hours* ago in the Earth Woman's life. As long as it takes us to drive from Ayemenem to Cochin.'

It was an awe-inspiring and humbling thought, Chacko said (*Humbling* was a nice word, Rahel thought. *Humbling along without a care in the world*), that the whole of contemporary history, the World Wars, the War of Dreams, the Man on the Moon, science, literature, philosophy, the pursuit of knowledge – was no more than a blink of the Earth Woman's eye.

'And we, my dears, everything we are and ever will be – are just a twinkle in her eye,' Chacko said grandly, lying on his bed, staring at the ceiling.

When he was in this sort of mood, Chacko used his Reading Aloud voice. His room had a church-feeling. He didn't care whether anyone was listening to him or not. And if they were, he didn't care whether or not they had understood what he was saying. Ammu called them his Oxford Moods.

Later, in the light of all that happened, *twinkle* seemed completely the wrong word to describe the expression in the Earth Woman's eye. Twinkle was a word with crinkled, happy edges.

Though the Earth Woman made a lasting impression on the twins, it was the History House – so much closer at hand – that really fascinated them. They thought about it often. The house on the other side of the river.

Looming in the Heart of Darkness.

A house they couldn't enter, full of whispers they couldn't understand.

They didn't know then, that soon they *would* go in. That they would cross the river and be where they weren't supposed to be, with a man they weren't supposed to love. That they would watch with dinner-plate eyes as history revealed itself to them in the back verandah.

While other children of their age learned other things, Estha and Rahel learned how history negotiates its terms and collects its dues from those who break its laws. They heard its sickening thud. They smelled its smell and never forgot it.

History's smell.

Like old roses on a breeze.

It would lurk for ever in ordinary things. In coat-hangers. Tomatoes. In the tar on the roads. In certain colours. In the plates at a restaurant. In the absence of words. And the emptiness in eyes.

They would grow up grappling with ways of living with what happened. They would try to tell themselves that in terms of geological time it was an insignificant event. Just a blink of the Earth Woman's eye. That Worse Things had happened. That Worse Things kept happening. But they would find no comfort in the thought.

Chacko said that going to see *The Sound of Music* was an extended exercise in Anglophilia.

Ammu said, 'Oh come on, the whole world goes to see *The Sound of Music*. It's a World Hit.'

'Nevertheless, my dear,' Chacko said in his Reading Aloud voice. 'Never. The. Less.'

Mammachi often said that Chacko was easily one of the cleverest men in India. 'According to whom?' Ammu would say. 'On *what* basis?' Mammachi loved to tell the story (Chacko's story) of how one of the dons at Oxford had said that in his opinion, Chacko was brilliant, and made of prime ministerial material.

To this, Ammu always said, 'Ha! Ha! Ha!' like people in the comics.

She said:

(a) Going to Oxford didn't necessarily make a person clever.

(b) Cleverness didn't necessarily make a good prime minister.

(c) If a person couldn't even run a pickle factory profitably, how was that person going to run a whole country?

And, most important of all:

(d) All Indian mothers are obsessed with their sons and are therefore poor judges of their abilities.

Chacko said:

(a) You don't *go* to Oxford. You *read* at Oxford.

And

(b) After *reading* at Oxford you *come down.*

'Down to earth, d'you mean?' Ammu would ask. '*That* you definitely do. Like your famous airplanes.'

Ammu said that the sad but entirely predictable fate of Chacko's airplanes was an impartial measure of his abilities.

Once a month (except during the monsoons), a parcel would arrive for Chacko by VPP. It always contained a balsa aeromodelling kit. It usually took Chacko between eight and ten days to assemble the aircraft with its tiny fuel tank and motorized propellor. When it was ready, he would take Estha and Rahel to the rice-fields in Nattakom to help him fly it. It never flew for more than a minute. Month after month, Chako's carefully constructed planes crashed in the slushgreen paddy fields into which Estha and Rahel would spurt, like trained retrievers, to salvage the remains.

A tail, a tank, a wing.

A wounded machine.

Chacko's room was cluttered with broken wooden planes.

And every month, another kit would arrive. Chacko never blamed the crashes on the kit.

It was only after Pappachi died that Chacko resigned his job as lecturer at the Madras Christian College, and came to Ayemenem with his Balliol Oar and his Pickle Baron dreams. He commuted his pension and provident fund to buy a Bharat bottle-sealing machine. His oar (with his team mates' names inscribed in gold) hung from iron hoops on the factory wall.

Up to the time Chacko arrived, the factory had been a small but profitable enterprise. Mammachi just ran it like a large kitchen. Chacko had it registered as a partnership and informed Mammachi that she was the sleeping partner. He invested in equipment (canning machines, cauldrons, cookers) and expanded the labour force. Almost immediately, the financial slide began, but was artificially buoyed by extravagant bank loans that Chacko raised by mortgaging the family's rice-fields around the Ayemenem House. Though Ammu did as much work in the factory as Chacko, whenever he was dealing with food inspectors or sanitary engineers, he always referred to it as *my* factory, *my* pineapples, *my* pickles. Legally, this was the case because Ammu, as a daughter, had no claim to the property.

Chacko told Rahel and Estha that Ammu had no Locusts Stand I.

'Thanks to our wonderful male chauvinist society,' Ammu said.

Chacko said, 'What's yours is mine and what's mine is also mine.'

He had a surprisingly high laugh for a man of his size and fatness. And when he laughed, he shook all over without appearing to move.

Until Chacko arrived in Ayemenem, Mammachi's factory had no name. Everybody just referred to her pickles and jams as Sosha's Tender Mango, or Sosha's Banana Jam. Sosha was Mammachi's first name. Soshamma.

It was Chacko who christened the factory Paradise Pickles & Preserves and had labels designed and printed at Comrade K. N. M. Pillai's press. At first he had wanted to call it Zeus Pickles & Preserves, but that idea was vetoed because everybody said that Zeus was too obscure and had no local relevance, whereas Paradise did. (Comrade Pillai's suggestion – Parashuram Pickles – was vetoed for the opposite reason: too *much* local relevance.)

It was Chacko's idea to have a billboard painted and installed on the Plymouth's roof rack.

On the way to Cochin now, it rattled and made fallingoff noises.

Near Vaikom they had to stop to buy some rope to secure it more firmly. That delayed them by another twenty minutes. Rahel began to worry about being late for *The Sound of Music.*

Then, as they approached the outskirts of Cochin, the red and white arm of the railway level-crossing gate went down. Rahel knew that this had happened because she had been hoping that it wouldn't.

She hadn't learned to control her Hopes yet. Estha said that that was a Bad Sign.

So now they were going to miss the beginning of the picture. When Julie Andrews starts off as a speck on the hill and gets bigger and bigger till she bursts on to the screen with her voice like cold water and her breath like peppermint.

The red sign on the red and white arm said STOP in white.

'POTS,' Rahel said.

A yellow hoarding said BE INDIAN, BUY INDIAN in red.

'NAIDNI YUB, NAIDNI EB,' Estha said.

The twins were precocious with their reading. They had raced through *Old Dog Tom, Janet and John* and their *Ronald Ridout*

Workbooks. At night Ammu read to them from Kipling's *Jungle Book.*

Now Chil the Kite brings home the night
That Mang the Bat sets free –

The down on their arms would stand on end, golden in the light of the bedside lamp. As she read, Ammu could make her voice gravelly, like Shere Khan's. Or whining, like Tabaqui's.

'Ye choose and ye do not choose! What talk is this of choosing? By the bull that I killed, am I to stand nosing into your dog's den for my fair dues? It is I Shere Khan, who speak!

'And it is I, Raksha [The Demon], who answer,' the twins would shout in high voices. Not together, but almost.

'*The man's cub is* mine *Lungri* – mine *to* me*! He shall not be killed. He shall live to run with the Pack and to hunt with the Pack; and in the end, look you, hunter of little naked cubs – frog eater – fish killer – he shall hunt* thee!'

Baby Kochamma, who had been put in charge of their formal education, had read them a version of *The Tempest* abridged by Charles and Mary Lamb.

'*Where the bee sucks, there suck I,*' Estha and Rahel would go about saying. *'In a cowslip's bell I lie.'*

So when Baby Kochamma's Australian missionary friend, Miss Mitten, gave Estha and Rahel a baby book – *The Adventures of Susie Squirrel* – as a present when she visited Ayemenem, they were deeply offended. First they read it forwards. Miss Mitten, who belonged to a sect of born-again Christians, said that she was a Little Disappointed in them when they read it aloud to her, backwards.

'ehT serutnevdA fo eisuS lerriuqS. enO gnirps gninrom eisuS lerriuqS ekow pu.'

They showed Miss Mitten how it was possible to read both *Malayalam* and *Madam I'm Adam* backwards as well as forwards. She wasn't amused and it turned out that she didn't even know what Malayalam was. They told her it was the language everyone spoke in Kerala. She said she had been under the impression that it was called Keralese. Estha, who had by then taken an active dislike to Miss Mitten, told her that as far as he was concerned it was a Highly Stupid Impression.

Miss Mitten complained to Baby Kochamma about Estha's rudeness, and about their reading backwards. She told Baby Kochamma that she had seen Satan in their eyes. *nataS in their seye.*

They were made to write *In future we will not read backwards. In future we will not read backwards.* A hundred times. Forwards.

A few months later Miss Mitten was killed by a milk van in Hobart, across the road from a cricket oval. To the twins there was hidden justice in the fact that the milk van had been *reversing.*

More buses and cars had stopped on either side of the level crossing. An ambulance that said *Sacred Heart Hospital* was full of a party of people on their way to a wedding. The bride was staring out of the back window, her face partially obscured by the flaking paint of the huge red cross.

The buses all had girls' names. Lucykutty, Mollykutty, Beena Mol. In Malayalam, Mol is Little Girl and Mon is Little Boy. Beena Mol was full of pilgrims who'd had their heads shaved at Tirupati. Rahel could see a row of bald heads at the bus window, above evenly spaced vomit streaks. She was more than a little curious about vomiting. She had never vomited. Not once. Estha had, and when he did, his skin grew hot and shiny, and his eyes helpless and beautiful, and Ammu loved him more than usual. Chacko said that Estha and Rahel were indecently healthy. And so was Sophie Mol. He said it was because they didn't suffer from Inbreeding like most Syrian Christians. And Parsees.

Mammachi said that what her grandchildren suffered from was far worse than Inbreeding. She meant having parents who were divorced. As though these were the only choices available to people: Inbreeding or Divorce.

Rahel wasn't sure what she suffered from, but occasionally she practised sad faces, and sighing in the mirror.

'*It is a far, far better thing that I do, than I have ever done,*' she would say to herself sadly. That was Rahel being Sydney Carton being Charles Darnay, as he stood on the steps, waiting to be guillotined, in the Classics Illustrated comic's version of *A Tale of Two Cities.*

She wondered what had caused the bald pilgrims to vomit so uniformly, and whether they had vomited together in a single, well-orchestrated heave (to music perhaps, to the rhythm of a bus bhajan), or separately, one at a time.

Initially, when the level crossing had just closed, the Air was full of the impatient sound of idling engines. But when the man that manned the crossing came out of his booth, on his backward bending legs and signalled with his limp, flapping walk to the tea stall that they were in for a long wait, drivers switched off their engines and milled about, stretching their legs.

With a desultory nod of his bored and sleepy head, the Level Crossing Divinity conjured up beggars with bandages, men with trays selling pieces of fresh coconut, parippu vadas on banana leaves. And cold drinks. Coca-Cola, Fanta, Rosemilk.

A leper with soiled bandages begged at the car window.

'That looks like Mercurochrome to me,' Ammu said, of his inordinately bright blood.

'Congratulations,' Chacko said. 'Spoken like a true bourgeoise.'

Ammu smiled and they shook hands, as though she really was being awarded a Certificate of Merit for being an honest-to-goodness Genuine Bourgeoise. Moments like these, the twins treasured and threaded like precious beads on a (somewhat scanty) necklace.

Rahel and Estha squashed their noses against the Plymouth's quarter-windows. Yearning marshmallows with cloudy children behind them. Ammu said, 'No,' firmly, and with conviction.

Chacko lit a Charminar. He inhaled deeply and then removed a little flake of tobacco that had stayed behind on his tongue.

Inside the Plymouth, it wasn't easy for Rahel to see Estha, because Baby Kochamma rose between them like a hill. Ammu had insisted that they sit separately to prevent them from fighting. When they fought, Estha called Rahel a Refugee Stick Insect. Rahel called him Elvis the Pelvis and did a twisty, funny kind of dance that infuriated Estha. When they had serious physical fights, they were so evenly matched that the fights went on for ever, and things that came in their way – table lamps, ashtrays and water jugs – were smashed or irreparably damaged.

Baby Kochamma was holding on to the back of the front seat with her arms. When the car moved, her armfat swung like heavy washing in the wind. Now it hung down like a fleshy curtain, blocking Estha from Rahel.

On Estha's side of the road was the tea shack that sold tea and stale glucose biscuits in dim glass cases with flies. There was lemon soda in thick bottles with blue marble stoppers to keep the fizz in. And a red ice-box that said rather sadly *Things go better with Coca-Cola.*

Murlidharan, the level-crossing lunatic, perched cross-legged and perfectly balanced on the milestone. His balls and penis dangled down, pointing towards the sign which said:

COCHIN
23

Murlidharan was naked except for the tall plastic bag that somebody had fitted onto his head like a transparent chef's cap through which the view of the landscape continued – dimmed, chef-shaped, but uninterrupted. He couldn't remove his cap even if had wanted to because he had no arms. They had been blown off in Singapore in '42, within the first week of his running away from home to join the fighting ranks of the Indian National Army. After Independence he had himself registered as a Grade I Freedom Fighter and had been allotted a free first-class railway pass for life. This too he had lost (along with his mind), so he could no longer live on trains or in refreshment rooms in railway stations. Murlidharan had no home, no doors to lock, but he had his old keys tied carefully around his waist. In a shining bunch. His mind was full of cupboards, cluttered with secret pleasures.

An alarm clock. A red car with a musical horn. A red mug for the bathroom. A wife with a diamond. A briefcase with important papers. A coming home from the office. An *I'm sorry, Colonel Sabhapathy, but I'm afraid I've said my say.* And crisp banana chips for the children.

He watched the trains come and go. He counted his keys.

He watched governments rise and fall. He counted his keys.

He watched cloudy children at car windows with yearning marshmallow noses.

The homeless, the helpless, the sick, the small and lost, all filed past his window. Still he counted his keys.

He was never sure which cupboard he might have to open, or when. He sat on the burning milestone with his matted hair and eyes like windows, and was glad to be able to look away sometimes. To have his keys to count and countercheck.

Numbers would do.

Numbness would be fine.

Murlidharan moved his mouth when he counted, and made well-formed words.

Onner.
Runder.
Moonner.

Estha noticed that the hair on his head was curly grey, the hair in his windy, armless armpits was wispy black, and the hair in his crotch was black and springy. One man with three kinds of hair. Estha wondered how that could be. He tried to think of whom to ask.

The Waiting filled Rahel until she was ready to burst. She looked at her watch. It was ten to two. She thought of Julie Andrews and Christopher Plummer kissing each other sideways so that their noses didn't collide. She wondered whether people always kissed each other sideways. She tried to think of whom to ask.

Then, from a distance, a hum approached the held-up traffic and covered it like a cloak. The drivers who'd been stretching their legs got back into their vehicles and slammed doors. The beggars and vendors disappeared. Within minutes there was no one on the road. Except Murlidharan. Perched with his bum on the burning milestone. Unperturbed and only mildly curious.

There was hustle-bustle. And police whistles.

From behind the line of waiting, oncoming traffic, a column of men appeared, with red flags and banners and a hum that grew and grew.

'Put up your windows,' Chacko said. 'And stay calm. They're not going to hurt us.'

'Why not join them, comrade?' Ammu said to Chacko. 'I'll drive.'

Chacko said nothing. A muscle tensed below the wad of fat on his jaw. He tossed away his cigarette and rolled up his window.

Chacko was a self-proclaimed Marxist. He would call pretty women who worked in the factory to his room, and on the pretext of lecturing them on labour rights and trade union law, flirt with them outrageously. He would call them Comrade, and insist that they call him Comrade back (which made them giggle). Much to their embarrassment and Mammachi's dismay, he forced them to sit at table with him and drink tea.

Once he even took a group of them to attend Trade Union classes that were held in Alleppey. They went by bus and returned by boat. They came back happy, with glass bangles and flowers in their hair.

Ammu said it was all hogwash. Just a case of a spoiled princeling playing *Comrade! Comrade!* An Oxford avatar of the old zamindar mentality – a landlord forcing his attentions on women who depended on him for their livelihood.

As the marchers approached, Ammu put up her window. Estha his. Rahel hers. (Effortfully, because the black knob on the handle had fallen off.)

Suddenly the skyblue Plymouth looked absurdly opulent on the narrow, pitted road. Like a wide lady squeezing down a narrow corridor. Like Baby Kochamma in church, on her way to the bread and wine.

'Look down!' Baby Kochamma said, as the front ranks of the procession approached the car. 'Avoid eye contact. That's what really provokes them.'

On the side of her neck, her pulse was pounding.

Within minutes, the road was swamped by thousands of marching people. Automobile islands in a river of people. The air was red with flags, which dipped and lifted as the marchers ducked under the level-crossing gate and swept across the railway tracks in a red wave.

The sound of a thousand voices spread over the frozen traffic like a Noise Umbrella.

'Inquilab Zindabad!
Thozhilali Ekta Zindabad!'

'Long Live the Revolution!' they shouted. 'Workers of the World Unite!'

Even Chacko had no really complete explanation for why the Communist Party was so much more successful in Kerala than it had been almost anywhere else in India, except perhaps in Bengal.

There were several competing theories. One was that it had to do with the large population of Christians in the state. Twenty per cent of Kerala's population were Syrian Christians, who believed that they were descendants of the one hundred Brahmins whom Saint Thomas the Apostle converted to Christianity when he travelled east after the Resurrection. Structurally – this somewhat rudimentary argument went – Marxism was a simple substitute for Christianity. Replace God with Marx, Satan with the bourgeoisie, Heaven with a classless society, the Church with the Party, and the form and purpose of the journey remained similar. An obstacle race, with a prize at the end. Whereas the Hindu mind had to make more complex adjustments.

The trouble with this theory was that in Kerala the Syrian Christians were, by and large, the wealthy, estate-owning (pickle-factory-running) feudal lords, for whom communism represented a fate worse than death. They had always voted for the Congress Party.

A second theory claimed that it had to do with the comparatively high level of literacy in the state. Perhaps. Except that the high literacy level was largely *because* of the communist movement.

The real secret was that communism crept into Kerala insidiously. As a reformist movement that never overtly questioned the traditional values of a caste-ridden, extremely traditional community. The Marxists worked from *within* the communal divides, never challenging them, never appearing not to. They offered a cocktail revolution. A heady mix of Eastern Marxism and orthodox Hinduism, spiked with a shot of democracy.

Though Chacko was not a card-holding member of the Party, he had been converted early and had remained, through all its travails, a committed supporter.

He was an undergraduate at Delhi University during the euphoria of 1957, when the Communists won the State Assembly elections and Nehru invited them to form a government. Chacko's hero, Comrade E. M. S. Namboodiripad, the flamboyant Brahmin high priest of Marxism in Kerala, became Chief Minister of the first ever democratically elected communist government in the world. Suddenly the communists found themselves in the extraordinary – critics said absurd – position of having to govern a people and foment revolution simultaneously. Comrade E. M. S. Namboodiripad evolved his own theory about how he would do this. Chacko studied his treatise on *The Peaceful Transition to Communism* with an adolescent's obsessive diligence and an ardent fan's unquestioning approval. It set out in detail how Comrade E. M. S. Namboodiripad's government intended to enforce land reforms, neutralize the police, subvert the judiciary and 'Restrain the Hand of the Reactionary Anti-People Congress Government at the Centre'.

Unfortunately, before the year was out, the Peaceful part of the Peaceful Transition came to an end.

Every morning at breakfast the Imperial Entomologist derided his argumentative Marxist son by reading out newspaper reports of the riots, strikes and incidents of police brutality that convulsed Kerala.

'So, Karl Marx!' Pappachi would sneer when Chacko came to the table. 'What shall we do with these bloody students now? The stupid goons are agitating against our People's Government. Shall we annihilate them? Surely students aren't People any more?'

Over the next two years the political discord, fuelled by the Congress Party and the Church, slid into anarchy. By the time Chacko finished his BA and left for Oxford to do another one, Kerala was on the brink of civil war. Nehru dismissed the Communist Government and announced fresh elections. The Congress Party returned to power.

It was only in 1967 – almost exactly ten years after they first came to power – that Comrade E. M. S. Namboodiripad's party was re-elected. This time as part of a coalition between what had now become two separate parties – the Communist Party of India, and the Communist Party of India (Marxist). The CPI and the CPI(M).

Pappachi was dead by then. Chacko divorced. Paradise Pickles was seven years old.

Kerala was reeling in the aftermath of famine and a failed monsoon. People were dying. Hunger had to be very high up on any government list of priorities.

During his second term in office, Comrade E. M. S. went about implementing the Peaceful Transition more soberly. This earned him the wrath of the Chinese Communist Party. They denounced him for his 'Parliamentary Cretinism' and accused him of 'providing relief to the people and thereby blunting the People's Consciousness and diverting them from the Revolution'.

Peking switched its patronage to the newest, most militant faction of the CPI(M) – the Naxalites – who had staged an armed insurrection in Naxalbari, a village in Bengal. They organized peasants into fighting cadres, seized land, expelled the owners and established People's Courts to try Class Enemies. The Naxalite movement spread across the country and struck terror in every bourgeois heart.

In Kerala, they breathed a plume of excitement and fear into the already frightened air. Killings had begun in the north. That May there was a blurred photograph in the papers of a landlord in Palghat who had been tied to a lamp post and beheaded.

His head lay on its side, some distance away from his body, in a dark puddle that could have been water, could have been blood. It was hard to tell in black and white. In the grey pre-dawn light.

His surprised eyes were open.

Comrade E. M. S. Namboodiripad (*Running Dog, Soviet Stooge*) expelled the Naxalites from his party and went on with the business of harnessing anger for parliamentary purposes.

The march that surged around the skyblue Plymouth on that skyblue December day was a part of that process. It had been organized by the Travancore-Cochin Marxist Labour Union. Their comrades in Trivandrum would march to the Secretariat and present the Charter of People's Demands to Comrade E. M. S. himself. The orchestra petitioning its conductor. Their demands were that paddy workers, who were made to work in the fields for eleven and a half hours a day – from seven in the morning to six-thirty in the evening – be permitted to take a one-hour lunch break. That women's wages be increased from one rupee twenty-five paisa a day, to three rupees, and men's from two rupees fifty paisa to four rupees fifty paisa a day. They were also demanding that Untouchables no longer be addressed by their caste names. They demanded *not* to be addressed as Achoo *Parayan*, or Kelan *Paravan*, or Kuttan *Pulayan*, but just as Achoo, or Kelan, or Kuttan.

Cardamom Kings, Coffee Counts and Rubber Barons – old boarding school buddies – came down from their lonely, far-flung estates and sipped chilled beer at the Sailing Club. They raised their glasses. '*A rose by any other name . . .*' they said, and sniggered to hide their rising panic.

The marchers that day were party workers, students, and the labourers themselves. Touchables and Untouchables. On their shoulders they carried a keg of ancient anger, lit with a recent fuse. There was an edge to this anger that was Naxalite, and new.

Through the Plymouth window, Rahel could see that the loudest word they said was *Zindabad.* And that the veins stood out in their necks when they said it. And that the arms that held the flags and banners were knotted and hard.

Inside the Plymouth it was still and hot.

Baby Kochamma's fear lay rolled up on the car floor like a damp, clammy cheroot. This was just the beginning of it. The fear that over the years would grow to consume her. That would make her lock her doors and windows. That would give her two hairlines and both her mouths. Hers, too, was an ancient, age-old fear. The fear of being dispossessed.

She tried to count the green beads on her rosary, but couldn't concentrate. An open hand slammed against the car window.

A balled fist banged down on the burning skyblue bonnet. It sprang open. The Plymouth looked like an angular blue animal in a zoo asking to be fed.

A bun.

A banana.

Another balled fist slammed down on it, and the bonnet closed. Chacko rolled down his window and called out to the man who had done it.

'Thanks, *keto*!' he said. '*Valarey* thanks!'

'Don't be so ingratiating, comrade,' Ammu said. 'It was an accident. He didn't really mean to help. How could he *possibly* know that in this old car there beats a truly Marxist heart?'

'Ammu,' Chacko said, his voice steady and deliberately casual, 'is it at all possible for you to prevent your washed-up cynicism from completely colouring everything?'

Silence filled the car like a saturated sponge. *Washed-up* cut like a knife through a soft thing. The sun shone with a shuddering sigh. This was the trouble with families. Like invidious doctors, they knew just where it hurt.

Just then Rahel saw Velutha. Vellya Paapen's son, Velutha. Her most beloved friend Velutha. Velutha marching with a red flag. In a white shirt and mundu with angry veins in his neck. He never usually wore a shirt.

Rahel rolled down her window in a flash.

'Velutha! Velutha!' she called to him.

He froze for a moment, and listened with his flag. What he heard was a familiar voice in a most unfamiliar circumstance. Rahel, standing on the car seat, had grown out of the Plymouth window like the loose, flailing horn of a car-shaped herbivore. With a fountain in a Love-in-Tokyo and yellow-rimmed red plastic sunglasses.

'Velutha! *Ividay!* Velutha!' And she too had veins in her neck.

He stepped sideways and disappeared deftly into the angriness around him.

Inside the car Ammu whirled around, and her eyes were angry. She slapped at Rahel's calves, which were the only part of her left in the car to slap. Calves and brown feet in Bata sandals.

'Behave yourself!' Ammu said.

Baby Kochamma pulled Rahel down, and she landed on the seat with a surprised thump. She thought there'd been a misunderstanding.

'It was Velutha!' she explained with a smile. 'And he had a flag!'

The flag had seemed to her a most impressive piece of equipment. The right thing for a friend to have.

'You're a stupid silly little girl!' Ammu said.

Her sudden, fierce anger pinned Rahel against the car seat. Rahel was puzzled. Why was Ammu so angry? About what?

'But it *was* him!' Rahel said.

'Shut up!' Ammu said.

Rahel saw that Ammu had a film of perspiration on her forehead and upper lip, and that her eyes had become hard, like marbles. Like Pappachi's in the Vienna studio photograph. (How Pappachi's Moth whispered in his children's veins!)

Baby Kochamma rolled up Rahel's window.

Years later, on a crisp fall morning in upstate New York, on a Sunday train from Grand Central to Croton Harmon, it suddenly came back to Rahel. That expression on Ammu's face. Like a rogue piece in a puzzle. Like a question mark that drifted through the pages of a book and never settled at the end of a sentence.

That hard marble look in Ammu's eyes. The glisten of perspiration on her upper lip. And the chill of that sudden, hurt silence.

What had it all meant?

The Sunday train was almost empty. Across the aisle from Rahel a woman with chapped cheeks and a moustache coughed up phlegm and wrapped it in twists of newspaper that she tore off the pile of Sunday papers on her lap. She arranged the little packages in neat rows on the empty seat in front of her as though she was setting up a phlegm stall. As she worked she chatted to herself in a pleasant, soothing voice.

Memory was that woman on the train. Insane in the way she sifted through dark things in a closet and emerged with the most unlikely ones – a fleeting look, a feeling. The smell of smoke. A windscreen wiper. A mother's marble eyes. Quite sane in the way she left huge tracts of darkness veiled. Unremembered.

Her co-passenger's madness comforted Rahel. It drew her closer into New York's deranged womb. Away from the other, more terrible thing that haunted her. *A sourmetal smell, like steel bus-rails, and the smell of the bus conductor's hands from holding them. A young man with an old man's mouth.*

Outside the train, the Hudson shimmered, and the trees were the redbrown colours of fall. It was just a little cold.

'There's a nipple in the air,' Larry McCaslin said to Rahel, and laid his palm gently against the suggestion of protest from a chilly nipple through her cotton T-shirt. He wondered why she didn't smile.

She wondered why it was that when she thought of home, it was always in the colours of the dark, oiled wood of boats, and the empty cores of the tongues of flame that flickered in brass lamps.

It *was* Velutha.

That much Rahel was sure of. She'd seen him. He'd seen her. She'd have known him anywhere, any time. And if he hadn't been wearing a shirt, she would have recognized him from behind. She knew his back. She'd been carried on it. More times than she could count. It had a light brown birthmark, shaped like a pointed dry leaf. He said it was a lucky leaf, that made the monsoons come on time. A brown leaf on a black back. An autumn leaf at night.

A lucky leaf that wasn't lucky enough.

Velutha wasn't supposed to be a carpenter.

He was called Velutha – which means White in Malayalam – because he was so black. His father, Vellya Paapen, was a Paravan. A toddy tapper. He had a glass eye. He had been shaping a block of granite with a hammer when a chip flew into his left eye and sliced right through it.

As a young boy, Velutha would come with Vellya Paapen to the back entrance of the Ayemenem House to deliver the coconuts they had plucked from the trees in the compound. Pappachi would not allow Paravans into the house. Nobody would. They were not allowed to touch anything that Touchables touched. Caste Hindus and Caste Christians. Mammachi told Estha and Rahel that she could remember a time, in her girlhood, when Paravans were expected to crawl backwards with a broom, sweeping away their footprints so that Brahmins or Syrian Christians would not defile themselves by accidentally stepping into a Paravan's footprint. In Mammachi's time, Paravans, like other Untouchables, were not allowed to walk on public roads, not allowed to cover their upper bodies, not allowed to carry umbrellas. They had to put their hands over their mouths when they spoke, to divert their polluted breath away from those whom they addressed.

When the British came to Malabar, a number of Paravans, Pelayas and Pulayas (among them Velutha's grandfather, Kelan) converted to Christianity and joined the Anglican Church to escape the scourge of Untouchability. As added incentive they were given a little food and money. They were known as the Rice-Christians. It didn't take them long to realize that they had jumped from the frying pan into the fire. They were made to have separate churches, with separate services, and separate priests. As a special favour they were even given their own separate Pariah Bishop. After Independence they found they were not entitled to any Government benefits like job reservations or bank loans at low interest rates, because officially, on paper, they were Christians, and therefore casteless. It was a little like having to sweep away your footprints without a broom. Or worse, not being *allowed* to leave footprints at all.

It was Mammachi, on vacation from Delhi and Imperial Entomology, who first noticed little Velutha's remarkable facility with his hands. Velutha was eleven then, about three years younger than Ammu. He was like a little magician. He could make intricate toys – tiny windmills, rattles, minute jewel boxes out of dried palm reeds; he could carve perfect boats out of tapioca stems and figurines on cashew nuts. He would bring them for Ammu, holding them out on his palm (as he had been taught) so she wouldn't have to touch him to take them. Though he was younger than she was, he called her Ammukutty – Little Ammu. Mammachi persuaded Vellya Paapen to send him to the Untouchables' School that her father-in-law, Punnyan Kunju, had founded.

Velutha was fourteen when Johann Klein, a carpenter from a carpenters' guild in Bavaria, came to Kottayam and spent three years with the Christian Mission Society, conducting a workshop with local carpenters. Every afternoon, after school, Velutha caught a bus to Kottayam where he worked with Klein till dusk. By the time he was sixteen, Velutha had finished high school and was an accomplished carpenter. He had his own set of carpentry tools and a distinctly German design sensibility. He built Mammachi a Bauhaus dining table with twelve dining chairs in rosewood and a traditional Bavarian chaise longue in lighter jack. For Baby Kochamma's annual Nativity plays he made her a stack of wire-framed angels' wings that fitted onto children's backs like knapsacks, cardboard clouds for the Angel Gabriel to appear between, and a dismantleable manger for Christ to be born in. When her garden cherub's silver arc dried up inexplicably, it was Dr Velutha who fixed its bladder for her.

Apart from his carpentry skills, Velutha had a way with machines. Mammachi (with impenetrable Touchable logic) often said that if only he hadn't been a Paravan, he might have become an engineer. He mended radios, clocks, water-pumps. He looked after the plumbing and all the electrical gadgets in the house.

When Mammachi decided to enclose the back verandah, it was Velutha who designed and built the sliding-folding door that later became all the rage in Ayemenem.

Velutha knew more about the machines in the factory than anyone else.

When Chacko resigned his job in Madras and returned to Ayemenem with a Bharat bottle-sealing machine, it was Velutha who reassembled it and set it up. It was Velutha who maintained the new canning machine and the automatic pineapple slicer.

Velutha who oiled the water-pump and the small diesel generator. Velutha who built the aluminium sheet-lined, easy-to-clean cutting surfaces, and the ground-level furnaces for boiling fruit.

Velutha's father, Vellya Paapen, however, was an Old World Paravan. He had seen the Crawling Backwards Days and his gratitude to Mammachi and her family for all that they had done for him, was as wide and deep as a river in spate. When he had his accident with the stone chip, Mammachi organized and paid for his glass eye. He hadn't worked off his debt yet, and though he knew he wasn't expected to, that he wouldn't ever be able to – he felt that his eye was not his own. His gratitude widened his smile and bent his back.

Vellya Paapen feared for his younger son. He couldn't say what it was that frightened him. It was nothing that he had said. Or done. It was not *what* he said, but the *way* he said it. Not *what* he did, but the *way* he did it.

Perhaps it was just a lack of hesitation. An unwarranted assurance. In the way he walked. The way he held his head. The quiet way he offered suggestions without being asked. Or the quiet way in which he disregarded suggestions without appearing to rebel.

While these were qualities that were perfectly acceptable, perhaps even desirable in Touchables, Vellya Paapen thought that in a Paravan they could (and would, and indeed, *should*) be construed as insolence.

Vellya Paapen tried to caution Velutha. But since he couldn't put his finger on what it was that bothered him, Velutha misunderstood his muddled concern. To him it appeared as though his father grudged him his brief training and his natural skills. Vellya Paapen's good intentions quickly degenerated into nagging and bickering and a general air of unpleasantness between father and son. Much to his mother's dismay, Velutha began to avoid going home. He worked late. He caught fish in the river and cooked it on an open fire. He slept outdoors, on the banks of the river.

Then one day he disappeared. For four years nobody knew where he was. There was a rumour that he was working on a building site for the Department of Welfare and Housing in Trivandrum. And more recently, the inevitable rumour that he had become a Naxalite. That he had been to prison. Somebody said they had seen him in Quilon.

There was no way of reaching him when his mother, Chella, died of tuberculosis. Then Kuttappen, his older brother, fell off a coconut tree and damaged his spine. He was paralysed and unable to work. Velutha heard of the accident a whole year after it happened.

It had been five months since he returned to Ayemenem. He never talked about where he had been, or what he had done.

Mammachi rehired Velutha as the factory carpenter and put him in charge of general maintenance. It caused a great deal of resentment among the other Touchable factory workers because, according to them, Paravans were not *meant* to be carpenters. And certainly, prodigal Paravans were not meant to be rehired.

To keep the others happy, and since she knew that nobody else would hire him as a carpenter, Mammachi paid Velutha less than she would a Touchable carpenter but more than she would a Paravan. Mammachi didn't encourage him to enter the house (except when she needed something mended or installed). She thought that he ought to be grateful that he was allowed on the factory premises at all, and allowed to touch things that Touchables touched. She said that it was a big step for a Paravan.

When he returned to Ayemenem after his years away from home, Velutha still had about him the same quickness. The sureness. And Vellya Paapen feared for him now more than ever. But this time he held his peace. He said nothing.

At least not until the Terror took hold of him. Not until he saw, night after night, a little boat being rowed across the river. Not until he saw it return at dawn. Not until he saw what his Untouchable son had touched. More than touched.

Entered.

Loved.

When the Terror took hold of him, Vellya Paapen went to Mammachi. He stared straight ahead with his mortgaged eye. He wept with his own one. One cheek glistened with tears. The other stayed dry. He shook his own head from side to side to side till Mammachi ordered him to stop. He trembled his own body like a man with malaria. Mammachi ordered him to stop it but he couldn't, because you can't order fear around. Not even a Paravan's. Vellya Paapen told Mammachi what he had seen. He asked God's forgiveness for having spawned a monster. He offered to kill his son with his own bare hands. To destroy what he had created.

In the next room Baby Kochamma heard the noise and came to find out what it was all about. She saw Grief and Trouble ahead, and secretly, in her heart of hearts, she exulted.

She said (among other things) – '*How could she stand the smell? Haven't you noticed, they have a particular smell, these Paravans?*'

And she shuddered theatrically, like a child being force-fed spinach. She preferred an Irish-Jesuit smell to a particular Paravan smell.

By far. By far.

Velutha, Vellya Paapen and Kuttappen lived in a little laterite hut, downriver from the Ayemenem house. A three-minute run through the coconut trees for Esthappen and Rahel. They had only just arrived at Ayemenem with Ammu and were too young to remember Velutha when he left. But in the months since he had returned, they had grown to be the best of friends. They were forbidden from visiting his house, but they did. They would sit with him for hours, on their haunches – hunched punctuation marks in a pool of wood shavings – and wonder how he always seemed to know what smooth shapes waited inside the wood for him. They loved the way wood, in Velutha's hands, seemed to soften and become as pliable as Plasticine. He was teaching them to use a planer. His house (on a good day) smelled of fresh wood shavings and the sun. Of red fish curry cooked with black tamarind. The best fish curry, according to Estha, in the whole world.

It was Velutha who made Rahel her luckiest ever fishing rod and taught her and Estha to fish.

And on that skyblue December day, it *was* him that she saw through her red sunglasses, marching with a red flag at the level crossing outside Cochin.

Steelshrill police whistles pierced holes in the Noise Umbrella. Through the jagged umbrella holes Rahel could see pieces of red sky. And in the red sky, hot red kites wheeled, looking for rats. In their hooded yellow eyes there was a road and red flags marching. And a white shirt over a black back with a birthmark.

Marching.

Terror, sweat and talcum powder blended into a mauve paste between Baby Kochamma's rings of neckfat. Spit coagulated into little white gobs at the corners of her mouth. She imagined she saw a man in the procession who looked like the photograph in the newspapers of the Naxalite called Rajan, who was rumoured to have moved south from Palghat. She imagined he had looked straight at her.

A man with a red flag and a face like a knot opened Rahel's door because it wasn't locked. The doorway was full of men who'd stopped to stare.

'Feeling hot, baby?' the man like a knot asked Rahel kindly in Malayalam. Then unkindly, 'Ask your daddy to buy you an Air Condition!' and he hooted with delight at his own wit and timing. Rahel smiled back at him, pleased to have Chacko mistaken for her father. Like a normal family.

'Don't answer!' Baby Kochamma whispered hoarsely. 'Look down! Just look down!'

The man with the flag turned his attention to her. She was looking down at the floor of the car. Like a coy, frightened bride who had been married off to a stranger.

'Hello, sister,' the man said carefully in English. 'What is your name please?'

When Baby Kochamma didn't answer, he looked back at his co-hecklers.

'She has no name.'

'What about Modalali Mariakutty?' someone suggested with a giggle. Modalali in Malayalam means landlord.

'A, B, C, D, X, Y, Z,' somebody else said, irrelevantly.

More students crowded around. They all wore handkerchiefs or printed Bombay Dyeing hand towels on their heads to stave off the sun. They looked like extras who had wandered off the sets of the Malayalam version of *Sinbad: The Last Voyage.*

The man like a knot gave Baby Kochamma his red flag as a present. 'Here,' he said. 'Hold it.'

Baby Kochamma held it, still not looking at him.

'Wave it,' he ordered.

She had to wave it. She had no choice. It smelled of new cloth and a shop. Crisp and dusty. She tried to wave it as though she wasn't waving it.

'Now say *Inquilab Zindabad*!'

'*Inquilab Zindabad*,' Baby Kochamma whispered.

'Good girl.'

The crowd roared with laughter. A shrill whistle blew.

'Okay then,' the man said to Baby Kochamma in English, as though they had successfully concluded a business deal. 'Bye-bye!'

He slammed the skyblue door shut. Baby Kochamma wobbled. The crowd around the car unclotted and went on with its march.

Baby Kochamma rolled the red flag up and put it on the ledge behind the back seat. She put her rosary back into her blouse where she kept it with her melons. She busied herself with this and that, trying to salvage some dignity.

After the last few men walked past, Chacko said it was all right now to roll down the windows.

'Are you sure it was him?' Chacko asked Rahel.

'Who?' Rahel said, suddenly cautious.

'Are you sure it was Velutha?'

'Hmmm . . . ?' Rahel said, playing for time, trying to decipher Estha's frantic thought signals.

'I said, are you sure that the man you saw was Velutha?' Chacko said for the third time.

'Mmm . . . nyes . . . nn . . . nnalmost,' Rahel said.

'You're almost sure?' Chacko said.

'No . . . it was almost Velutha,' Rahel said. 'It almost looked like him . . .'

'So you're *not* sure then?'

'Almost not.' Rahel slid a look at Estha for approval.

'It must have been him,' Baby Kochamma said. 'It's Trivandrum that's done this to him. They all go there and come back thinking they're some great politicos.'

Nobody seemed particularly impressed by her insight.

'We should keep an eye on him,' Baby Kochamma said. 'If he starts this union business in the factory . . . I've noticed some signs, some rudeness, some ingratitude . . . The other day I asked him to help me with the rocks for my scree bed and he –'

'I saw Velutha at home before we left,' Estha said brightly. 'So how could it be him?'

'For his own sake,' Baby Kochamma said, darkly, 'I hope it wasn't. And next time, Esthappen, don't interrupt.'

She was annoyed that nobody asked her what a scree bed was.

In the days that followed, Baby Kochamma focused all her fury at her public humiliation on Velutha. She sharpened it like a pencil. In her mind he grew to represent the march. And the man who had forced her to wave the Marxist Party flag. And the man who christened her Modalali Mariakutty. And all the men who had laughed at her.

She began to hate him.

From the way Ammu held her head, Rahel could tell that she was still angry. Rahel looked at her watch. Ten to two. Still no train. She put her chin on the window sill. She could feel the grey gristle of the felt that cushioned the window glass pressing into her chinskin. She took off her sunglasses to get a better look at the dead frog squashed on the road. It was so dead and squashed so flat that it looked more like a frog-shaped stain on the road than a frog. Rahel wondered if Miss Mitten had been squashed into a Miss Mitten-shaped stain by the milk truck that killed her.

With the certitude of a true believer, Vellya Paapen had assured the twins that there was no such thing in the world as a black cat. He said that there were only black cat-shaped holes in the Universe.

There were so many stains on the road.

Squashed Miss Mitten-shaped stains in the Universe.

Squashed frog-shaped stains in the Universe.

Squashed crows that had tried to eat the squashed frog-shaped stains in the Universe.

Squashed dogs that ate the squashed crow-shaped stains in the Universe.

Feathers. Mangoes. Spit.

All the way to Cochin.

The sun shone through the Plymouth window directly down at Rahel. She closed her eyes and shone back at it. Even behind her eyelids the light was bright and hot. The sky was orange, and the coconut trees were sea anemones waving their tentacles, hoping to trap and eat an unsuspecting cloud. A transparent spotted snake with a forked tongue floated across the sky. Then a transparent Roman soldier on a spotted horse. The strange thing about Roman soldiers in the comics, according to Rahel, was the amount of trouble they took over their armour and their helmets, and then, after all that, they left their legs bare. It didn't make any sense at all. Weatherwise or otherwise.

Ammu had told them the story of Julius Caesar and how he was stabbed by Brutus, his best friend, in the Senate. And how he fell to the floor with knives in his back and said, '*Et tu? Brute? – Then fall Caesar.*'

'It just goes to show,' Ammu said, 'that you can't trust anybody. Mother, father, brother, husband, bestfriend. Nobody.'

With children, she said (when they asked), it remained to be seen. She said it was entirely possible, for instance, that Estha could grow up to be a Male Chauvinist Pig.

At night, Estha would stand on his bed with his sheet wrapped around him and say, '"*Et tu? Brute?* – Then fall Caesar!"' and crash into bed without bending his knees, like a stabbed corpse. Kochu Maria, who slept on the floor on a mat, said that she would complain to Mammachi.

'Tell your mother to take you to your father's house,' she said. 'There you can break as many beds as you like. These aren't your beds. This isn't *your* house.'

Estha would rise from the dead, stand on his bed and say, '*Et tu? Kochu Maria?* – Then fall Estha!' and die again.

Kochu Maria was sure that *Et tu* was an obscenity in English and was waiting for a suitable opportunity to complain about Estha to Mammachi.

The woman in the neighbouring car had biscuit crumbs on her mouth. Her husband lit a bent after-biscuit cigarette. He exhaled two tusks of smoke through his nostrils and for a fleeting moment looked like a wild boar. Mrs Boar asked Rahel her name in a Baby Voice.

Rahel ignored her and blew an inadvertent spit-bubble.

Ammu hated them blowing spit-bubbles. She said it reminded her of Baba. Their father. She said that he used to blow spit-bubbles and shiver his leg. According to Ammu, only clerks behaved like that, not aristocrats.

Aristocrats were people who didn't blow spit-bubbles or shiver their legs. Or gobble.

Though Baba wasn't a clerk, Ammu said he often behaved like one.

When they were alone, Estha and Rahel sometimes pretended that they were clerks. They would blow spit-bubbles and shiver their legs and gobble like turkeys. They remembered their father whom they had known between wars. He once gave them puffs from his cigarette and got annoyed because they had sucked it and wet the filter with spit.

'It's not a ruddy sweet!' he said, genuinely angry.

They remembered his anger. And Ammu's. They remembered being pushed around a room once, from Ammu to Baba to Ammu to Baba like billiard balls. Ammu pushing Estha away: 'Here, you keep one of them. I can't look after them both.' Later, when Estha asked Ammu about that, she hugged him and said he mustn't imagine things.

In the only photograph they had seen of him (which Ammu allowed them to look at once), he was wearing a white shirt and glasses. He looked like a handsome, studious cricketer. With one arm he held Estha on his shoulders. Estha was smiling, with his chin resting on his father's head. Rahel was held against his body with his other arm. She looked grumpy and bad-tempered, with her babylegs dangling. Someone had painted rosy blobs on to their cheeks.

Ammu said that he had only carried them for the photograph

and even then had been so drunk that she was scared he'd drop them. Ammu said she'd been standing just outside the photograph, ready to catch them if he did. Still, except for their cheeks, Estha and Rahel thought it was a nice photograph.

'Will you stop that!' Ammu said, so loudly that Murlidharan, who had hopped off the milestone to stare into the Plymouth, backed off, his stumps jerking in alarm.

'What?' Rahel said, but knew immediately what. Her spit-bubble. 'Sorry, Ammu.'

'Sorry doesn't make a dead man alive,' Estha said.

'Oh come on!' Chacko said. 'You can't dictate what she does with her own *spit*!'

'Mind your own business,' Ammu snapped.

'It brings back memories,' Estha, in his wisdom, explained to Chacko.

Rahel put on her sunglasses. The World became angry-coloured.

'Take off those ridiculous glasses!' Ammu said.

Rahel took off her ridiculous glasses.

'It's fascist, the way you deal with them,' Chacko said. 'Even children have some rights, for God's sake!'

'Don't use the name of the Lord in vain,' Baby Kochamma said.

'I'm not,' Chacko said. 'I'm using it for a very good reason.'

'Stop posing as the children's Great Saviour!' Ammu said. 'When it comes down to brass tacks, you don't give a damn about them. Or me.'

'Should I?' Chacko said. 'Are they *my* responsibility?' He said that Ammu and Estha and Rahel were millstones around his neck.

The backs of Rahel's legs went wet and sweaty. Her skin slipped on the foamleather upholstery of the car seat. She and Estha knew about millstones. In *Mutiny on the Bounty*, when people died at sea, they were wrapped in white sheets and thrown overboard with millstones around their necks so that the corpses wouldn't float. Estha wasn't sure how they decided how many millstones to take with them before they set off on their voyage.

Estha put his head in his lap.

His puff was spoiled.

A distant train rumble seeped upwards from the frog-stained road. The yam leaves on either side of the railway track began to nod in mass consent. *Yesyesyesyesyes.*

The bald pilgrims in Beena Mol began another bhajan.

'I tell you, these Hindus,' Baby Kochamma said piously. 'They have no sense of *privacy*.'

'They have horns and scaly skins,' Chacko said sarcastically. 'And I've heard that their babies hatch from eggs.'

Rahel had two bumps on her forehead that Estha said would grow into horns. At least one of them would because she was half-Hindu. She hadn't been quick enough to ask him about *his* horns. Because whatever She was, He was too.

The train slammed past under a column of dense black smoke. There were thirty-two bogies, and the doorways were full of young men with helmety haircuts who were on their way to the Edge of the World to see what happened to the people who fell off. Those of them who craned too far fell off the edge themselves. Into the flailing darkness, their haircuts turned inside out.

The train was gone so quickly that it was hard to imagine that everybody had waited so long for so little. The yam leaves continued to nod long after the train had gone, as though they agreed with it entirely and had no doubts at all.

A gossamer blanket of coaldust floated down like a dirty blessing and gently smothered the traffic.

Chacko started the Plymouth. Baby Kochamma tried to be jolly. She started a song.

'There's a sad sort of clanging
From the clock in the Hall
And the bells in the stee-ple too.
And up in the nursery
An abs-urd
Litt-le Bird
Is popping out to say –'

She looked at Estha and Rahel, waiting for them to say *Cu-ckoo.*

They didn't.

A carbreeze blew. Greentrees and telephone poles flew past the windows. Still birds slid by on moving wires, like unclaimed baggage at the airport.

A pale daymoon hung hugely in the sky and went where they went. As big as the belly of a beer-drinking man.

3

Big Man the Laltain, Small Man the Mombatti

Filth had laid siege to the Ayemenem house like a medieval army advancing on an enemy castle. It clotted every crevice and clung to the windowpanes.

Midges whizzed in teapots. Dead insects lay in empty vases.

The floor was sticky. White walls had turned an uneven grey. Brass hinges and doorhandles were dull and greasy to the touch. Infrequently used plug points were clogged with grime. Lightbulbs had a film of oil on them. The only things that shone were the giant cockroaches that scurried around like varnished gofers on a film set.

Baby Kochamma had stopped noticing these things long ago. Kochu Maria, who noticed everything, had stopped caring.

The chaise longue on which Baby Kochamma reclined had crushed peanut shells stuffed into the crevices of its rotting upholstery.

In an unconscious gesture of television-enforced democracy, mistress and servant both scrabbled unseeingly in the same bowl of nuts. Kochu Maria tossed nuts into her mouth. Baby Kochamma *placed* them decorously in hers.

On the *Best of Donahue* the studio audience watched a clip from a film in which a black busker was singing *Somewhere Over the Rainbow* in a subway station. He sang sincerely, as though he really believed the words of the song. Baby Kochamma sang with him, her thin, quavering voice thickened with peanut paste. She smiled as the lyrics came back to her. Kochu Maria looked at her as though she had gone mad, and grabbed more than her fair share of nuts. The busker threw his head back when he hit the high notes (the *where* of *somewhere*), and the ridged, pink roof of his mouth filled the television screen. He was as ragged as a rock star, but his missing teeth and the unhealthy pallor of his skin spoke eloquently of a life of privation and despair. He had to stop singing each time a train arrived or left, which was often.

Then the lights went up in the studio and Donahue presented the man himself, who, on a prearranged cue, started the song from exactly the point that he had had to stop (for a train) – cleverly achieving a touching victory of Song over Subway.

The next time the busker was interrupted mid-song was only when Phil Donahue put his arm around him and said, 'Thank you. Thank you very much.'

Being interrupted by Phil Donahue was of course entirely different from being interrupted by a subway rumble. It was a pleasure. An honour.

The studio audience clapped and looked compassionate.

The busker glowed with Prime-Time Happiness, and for a few moments, deprivation took a back seat. It had been his dream to sing on the Donahue show, he said, not realizing that he had just been robbed of that too.

There are big dreams and little ones. 'Big Man the Laltain sahib, Small Man the Mombatti,' an old Bihari coolie, who met Estha's school excursion party at the railway station (unfailingly, year after year) used to say of dreams.

Big Man the Lantern. Small man the Tallow-stick.

Huge man the Strobe Lights, he omitted to say. And *Small Man the Subway Station.*

The Masters would haggle with him as he trudged behind them with the boys' luggage, his bowed legs further bowed, cruel schoolboys imitating his gait. Balls-in-Brackets they used to call him.

Smallest Man the Varicose Veins, he clean forgot to mention, as he wobbled off with less than half the money he had asked for and less than a tenth of what he deserved.

Outside, the rain had stopped. The grey sky curdled and the clouds resolved themselves into little lumps, like substandard mattress-stuffing.

Esthappen appeared at the kitchen door, wet (and wiser than he really was). Behind him the long grass sparkled. The puppy stood on the steps beside him. Raindrops slid across the curved bottom of the rusted gutter on the edge of the roof, like shining beads on an abacus.

Baby Kochamma looked up from the television.

'Here he comes,' she announced to Rahel, not bothering to lower her voice. 'Now watch. He won't say anything. He'll walk *straight* to his room. Just watch!'

The puppy seized the opportunity and tried to stage a combined entry. Kochu Maria hit the floor fiercely with her palms and said, 'Hup! Hup! *Poda Patti!*'

So the puppy, wisely, desisted. It appeared to be familiar with this routine.

'Watch!' Baby Kochamma said. She seemed excited. 'He'll walk *straight* to his room and wash his clothes. He's very over-clean . . . he won't say a *word*!'

She had the air of a game warden pointing out an animal in the grass. Taking pride in her ability to predict its movements. Her superior knowledge of its habits and predilections.

Estha's hair was plastered down in clumps, like the inverted petals of a flower. Slivers of white scalp shone through. Rivulets of water ran down his face and neck. He walked to his room.

A gloating halo appeared around Baby Kochamma's head. 'See?' she said.

Kochu Maria used the opportunity to switch channels and watch a bit of *Prime Bodies*.

Rahel followed Estha to his room. Ammu's room. Once.

The room had kept his secrets. It gave nothing away. Not in the disarray of rumpled sheets, nor the untidiness of a kicked off shoe, or a wet towel hung over the back of a chair. Or a half-read book. It was like a room in a hospital after the nurse had just been. The floor was clean, the walls white. The cupboard closed. Shoes arranged. The dustbin empty.

The obsessive cleanliness of the room was the only positive sign of volition from Estha. The only faint suggestion that he had, perhaps, some Design for Life. Just the whisper of an unwillingness to subsist on scraps offered by others. On the wall by the window, an iron stood on an ironing board. A pile of folded, crumpled clothes waited to be ironed.

Silence hung in the air like secret loss.

The terrible ghosts of impossible-to-forget toys clustered on the blades of the ceiling fan. A catapult. A Qantas koala (from Miss Mitten) with loosened button eyes. An inflatable goose (that had been burst with a policeman's cigarette). Two ballpoint pens with silent streetscapes and red London buses that floated up and down in them.

Estha put on the tap and water drummed into a plastic bucket. He undressed in the gleaming bathroom. He stepped out of his sodden jeans. Stiff. Dark blue. Difficult to get out of. He pulled his crushed-strawberry T-shirt over his head, smooth, slim, muscular arms crossed over his body. He didn't hear his sister at the door.

Rahel watched his stomach suck inwards and his ribcage rise as his wet T-shirt peeled away from his skin, leaving it wet and honey-coloured. His face and neck and a V-shaped triangle at the base of his throat were darker than the rest of him. His arms too were double-coloured. Paler where his shirtsleeves ended. A dark brown man in pale honey clothes. Chocolate with a twist of coffee. High cheekbones and hunted eyes. A fisherman in a white-tiled bathroom, with sea-secrets in his eyes.

Had he seen her? Was he really mad? Did he know that she was there?

They had never been shy of each other's bodies, but they had never been old enough (together) to know what shyness was.

Now they were. Old enough.

Old.

A viable die-able age.

What a funny word *old* was on its own, Rahel thought, and said it to herself: *Old.*

Rahel at the bathroom door. Slim-hipped. ('Tell her she'll need a Caesarean!' a drunk gynaecologist had said to her husband while they waited for their change at the gas station.) A lizard on a map on her faded T-shirt. Long wild hair with a glint of deep henna-red, sent unruly fingers down into the small of her back. The diamond in her nostril flashed. Sometimes. And sometimes not. A thin, gold, serpent-headed bangle glowed like a circle of orange light around her wrist. Slim snakes whispering to each other, head to head. Her mother's melted wedding ring. Down softened the sharp lines of her thin, angular arms.

At first glance she appeared to have grown into the skin of her mother. High cheekbones. Deep dimples when she smiled. But she was longer, harder, flatter, more angular than Ammu had been. Less lovely perhaps to those who liked roundness and softness in women. Only her eyes were incontestably more beautiful. Large. Luminous. *Drownable in*, as Larry McCaslin had said and discovered to his cost.

Rahel searched her brother's nakedness for signs of herself. In the shape of his knees. The arch of his instep. The slope of his shoulders. The angle at which the rest of his arm met his elbow. The way his toe-nails tipped upwards at the ends. The sculpted hollows on either side of his taut, beautiful buns. Tight plums. Men's bums never grow up. Like school satchels, they evoke in an instant memories of childhood. Two vaccination marks on his arm gleamed like coins. Hers were on her thigh.

Girls always have them on their thighs, Ammu used to say.

Rahel watched Estha with the curiosity of a mother watching her wet child. A sister a brother. A woman a man. A twin a twin.

She flew these several kites at once.

He was a naked stranger met in a chance encounter. He was the one that she had known before Life began. The one who had once led her (swimming) through their lovely mother's cunt.

Both things unbearable in their polarity. In their irreconcilable far-apartness.

A raindrop glistened on the end of Estha's earlobe. Thick, silver in the light, like a heavy bead of mercury. She reached out. Touched it. Took it away.

Estha didn't look at her. He retreated into further stillness. As though his body had the power to snatch its senses inwards (knotted, egg-shaped), away from the surface of his skin, into some deeper more inaccessible recess.

The silence gathered its skirts and slid, like Spiderwoman, up the slippery bathroom wall.

Estha put his wet clothes in a bucket and began to wash them with crumbling, bright blue soap.

4

Abhilash Talkies

Abhilash Talkies advertised itself as the first cinema hall in Kerala with a 70mm CinemaScope screen. To drive home the point, its façade had been designed as a cement replica of a curved cinemascope screen. On top (cement writing, neon lighting) it said *Abhilash Talkies* in English and Malayalam.

The toilets were called HIS and HERS. HERS for Ammu, Rahel and Baby Kochamma. HIS for Estha alone, because Chacko had gone to see about the bookings at the Hotel Sea Queen.

'Will you be okay?' Ammu said, worried.

Estha nodded.

Through the red Formica door that closed slowly on its own, Rahel followed Ammu and Baby Kochamma into HERS. She turned to wave across the slipperoily marble floor at Estha Alone (with a comb), in his beige and pointy shoes. Estha waited in the dirty marble lobby with the lonely, watching mirrors till the red door took his sister away. Then he turned and padded off to HIS.

In HERS, Ammu suggested that Rahel balance in the air to piss. She said that Public Pots were Dirty. Like Money was. You never knew who'd touched it. Lepers. Butchers. Car Mechanics. (Pus. Blood. Grease.)

Once when Kochu Maria took her to the butcher's shop, Rahel noticed that the green five-rupee note that he gave them had a tiny blob of red meat on it. Kochu Maria wiped the blob away with her thumb. The juice left a red smear. She put the money into her bodice. Meat-smelling blood money.

Rahel was too short to balance in the air above the pot, so Ammu and Baby Kochamma held her up, her legs hooked over their arms. Her feet pigeon-toed in Bata sandals. High in the air with her knickers down. For a moment nothing happened, and Rahel looked up at her mother and baby grand aunt with naughty (now what?) question marks in her eyes.

'Come on,' Ammu said. 'Sssss . . .'

Sssss for the sound of Soo-soo. Mmmmm for the Sound of Myooozick.

Rahel giggled. Ammu giggled. Baby Kochamma giggled. When the trickle started they adjusted her aerial position. Rahel was unembarrassed. She finished and Ammu had the toilet paper.

'Shall you or shall I?' Baby Kochamma said to Ammu.

'Either way,' Ammu said. 'Go ahead. You.'

Rahel held her handbag. Baby Kochamma lifted her rumpled sari. Rahel studied her baby grand aunt's enormous legs. (Years later during a history lesson being read out in school – *The Emperor Babur had a wheatish complexion and pillar-like thighs* – this scene would flash before her. Baby Kochamma balanced like a big bird over a public pot. Blue veins like lumpy knitting running up her translucent shins. Fat knees dimpled. Hair on them. Poor little tiny feet to carry such a load!) Baby Kochamma waited for half of half a moment. Head thrust forward. Silly smile. Bosom swinging low. Melons in a blouse. Bottom up and out. When the gurgling, bubbling sound came, she listened with her eyes. A yellow brook burbled through a mountain pass.

Rahel liked all this. Holding the handbag. Everyone pissing in front of everyone. Like friends. She knew nothing then, of how precious a feeling this was. *Like friends.* They would never be together like this again. Ammu, Baby Kochamma and she.

When Baby Kochamma finished, Rahel looked at her watch. 'So long you took, Baby Kochamma,' she said. 'It's ten to two.'

Rubadub dub (Rahel thought),
Three women in a tub,
Tarry a while said Slow.

She thought of Slow being a person. Slow Kurien. Slow Kutty. Slow Mol. Slow Kochamma.

Slow Kutty. Fast Verghese. And Kuriakose. Three brothers with dandruff.

Ammu did hers in a whisper. Against the side of the pot so you couldn't hear. Her father's hardness had left her eyes and they were Ammu-eyes again. She had deep dimples in her smile and didn't seem angry any more. About Velutha or the spit-bubble.

That was a Good Sign.

Estha Alone in HIS had to piss onto naphthalene balls and cigarette stubs in the urinal. To piss in the pot would be Defeat. To piss in the urinal, he was too short. He needed Height. He searched for Height, and in a corner of HIS, he found it. A dirty broom, a squash bottle half-full of a milky liquid (phenyl) with floaty black things in it. A limp floorswab, and two rusty tin cans of nothing. They could have been Paradise Pickle products. Pineapple chunks in syrup. Or slices. Pineapple slices. His honour redeemed by his grandmother's cans, Estha Alone organized the rusty cans of nothing in front of the urinal. He stood on them, one foot on each, and pissed carefully, with minimal wobble. Like a Man. The cigarette stubs, soggy then, were wet now, and swirly. Hard to light. When he finished, Estha moved the cans to the basin in front of the mirror. He washed his hands and wet his hair. Then, dwarfed by the size of Ammu's comb that was too big for him, he reconstructed his puff carefully. Slicked back, then pushed forward and swivelled sideways at the very end. He returned the comb to his pocket, stepped off the tins and put them back with the bottle and swab and broom. He bowed to them all. The whole shooting match. The bottle, the broom, the cans, the limp floorswab.

'Bow,' he said, and smiled, because when he was younger, he had been under the impression that you had to say 'Bow' when you bowed. That you had to *say* it to do it. 'Bow, Estha,' they'd say. And he'd bow and say, 'Bow,' and they'd look at each other and laugh, and he'd worry.

Estha Alone of the uneven teeth.

Outside, he waited for his mother, his sister and his baby grand aunt. When they came out, Ammu said 'Okay, Esthappen?'

Estha said, 'Okay,' and shook his head carefully to preserve his puff.

Okay? Okay. He put the comb back into her handbag. Ammu felt a sudden clutch of love for her reserved, dignified little son in his beige and pointy shoes, who had just completed his first adult assignment. She ran loving fingers through his hair. She spoiled his puff.

The Man with the steel Eveready Torch said that the picture had started, so to hurry. They had to rush up the red steps with the old red carpet. Red staircase with red spit stains in the red corner. The Man with the Torch scrunched up his mundu and held it tucked under his balls, in his left hand. As he climbed, his calf muscles hardened under his climbing skin like hairy cannonballs. He held the torch in his right hand. He hurried with his mind.

'It started longago,' he said.

So they'd missed the beginning. Missed the rippled velvet curtain going up, with lightbulbs in the clustered yellow tassels. Slowly up, and the music would have been *Baby Elephant Walk* from *Hatari*. Or *Colonel Bogey's March*.

Ammu held Estha's hand. Baby Kochamma, heaving up the steps, held Rahel's. Baby Kochamma, weighed down by her melons, would not admit to herself that she was looking forward to the picture. She preferred to feel that she was only doing it for the children's sake. In her mind she kept an organized, careful account of Things She'd Done For People, and Things People Hadn't Done For Her.

She liked the early nun-bits best, and hoped they hadn't missed them. Ammu explained to Estha and Rahel that people always loved best what they *Identified* most with. Rahel supposed she Identified most with Christopher Plummer who acted as Captain von Trapp. Chacko didn't Identify with him at all and called him Captain von Clapp Trapp.

Rahel was like an excited mosquito on a leash. Flying. Weightless. Up two steps. Down two. Up one. She climbed five flights of red stairs for Baby Kochamma's one.

I'm Popeye the sailor man dum dum
I live in a cara-van dum dum
I op-en the door

And Fall-on the floor

I'm Popeye the sailor man dum dum

Up two. Down two. Up one. Jump, jump.

'Rahel,' Ammu said, 'you haven't learned your Lesson yet. Have you?'

Rahel had: *Excitement Always Leads to Tears.* Dum dum.

They arrived at the Princess Circle lobby. They walked past the Refreshment Counter where the orangedrinks were waiting. And the lemondrinks were waiting. The orange too orange. The lemon too lemon. The chocolates too melty.

The Torch Man opened the heavy Princess Circle door into the fan-whirring, peanut-crunching darkness. It smelled of breathing people and hairoil. And old carpets. A magical, *Sound of Music* smell that Rahel remembered and treasured. Smells, like music, hold memories. She breathed deep, and bottled it up for posterity.

Estha had the tickets. Little Man. He lived in a cara-van. Dum dum.

The Torch Man shone his light on the pink tickets. Row J. Numbers 17, 18, 19, 20. Estha, Ammu, Rahel, Baby Kochamma. They squeezed past irritated people who moved their legs this way and that to make space. The seats of the chairs had to be pulled down. Baby Kochamma held Rahel's seat down while she climbed on. She wasn't heavy enough, so the chair folded her into itself like sandwich stuffing, and she watched from between her knees. Two knees and a fountain. Estha, with more dignity that that, sat on the edge of his chair.

The shadows of the fans were on the sides of the screen where the picture wasn't.

Off with the torch. On with the World Hit.

The camera soared up in the skyblue (car-coloured) Austrian sky with the clear, sad sound of church bells.

Far below, on the ground, in the courtyard of the abbey, the cobblestones were shining. Nuns walked across it. Like slow cigars. Quiet nuns clustered quietly around their Reverend Mother, who never read their letters. They gathered like ants around a crumb of toast. Cigars around a Queen Cigar. No hair on their knees. No melons in their blouses. And their breath like peppermint. They had complaints to make to their Reverend Mother. Sweetsinging complaints. About Julie Andrews, who was still up in the hills, singing *The Hills Are Alive with the Sound of Music* and was, once again, late for mass.

She climbs a tree and scrapes her knee

the nuns sneaked musically.

Her dress has got a tear.
She waltzes on her way to Mass
And whistles on the stair . . .

People in the audience were turning around.

'Shhh!' they said.

Shh! Shh! Shh!

And underneath her wimple
she has curlers in her hair!

There was a voice from outside the picture. It was clear and true, cutting through the fan-whirring, peanut-crunching darkness. There was a nun in the audience. Heads twisted around like bottle caps. Black-haired backs of heads became faces with mouths and moustaches. Hissing mouths with teeth like sharks. Many of them. Like stickers on a card.

'Shhh!' they said together.

It was Estha who was singing. A nun with a puff. An Elvis Pelvis Nun. He couldn't help it.

'Get him out of here!' the Audience said, when they found him.

Shutup or Getout. Getout or Shutup.

The Audience was a Big Man. Estha was a Little Man, with the tickets.

'Estha, for heaven's sake, shut UP!' Ammu's fierce whisper said.

So Estha shut UP. The mouths and moustaches turned away. But then, without warning, the song came back, and Estha couldn't stop it.

'Ammu, can I go and sing it outside?' Estha said (before Ammu smacked him). 'I'll come back after the song.'

'But don't ever expect me to bring you out again,' Ammu said. 'You're embarrassing *all* of us.'

But Estha couldn't help it. He got up to go. Past angry Ammu. Past Rahel concentrating through her knees. Past Baby Kochamma. Past the Audience that had to move its legs again. Thiswayandthat. The red sign over the door said EXIT in a red light. Estha EXITed.

In the lobby, the orangedrinks were waiting. The lemondrinks were waiting. The melty chocolates were waiting. The electric blue foamleather car-sofas were waiting. The *Coming Soon!* posters were waiting.

Estha Alone sat on the electric blue foamleather car-sofa, in the Abhilash Talkies Princess Circle lobby, and sang. In a nun's voice, as clear as clean water.

But how do you make her stay
And listen to all you say?

The man behind the Refreshments Counter, who'd been asleep on a row of stools, waiting for the interval, woke up. He saw, with gummy eyes, Estha Alone in his beige and pointy shoes. And his spoiled puff. The Man wiped his marble counter with a dirtcoloured rag. And he waited. And waiting he wiped. And wiping he waited. And watched Estha sing.

How do you keep a wave upon the sand?
Oh, how do you solve a problem like Maree . . . yah?

'Ay! *Eda cherukka!*' the Orangedrink Lemondrink Man said, in a gravelley voice thick with sleep. 'What the hell d'you think you're doing?'

How do you hold a
moonbeam
in your hand?

Estha sang.

'Ay!' the Orangedrink Lemondrink Man said. 'Look, this is my Resting Time. Soon I'll have to wake up and work. So I can't have you singing English songs here. Stop it.' His gold wristwatch was almost hidden by his curly forearm hair. His gold chain was almost hidden by his chest hair. His white Terylene shirt was unbuttoned to where the swell of his belly began. He looked like an unfriendly jewelled bear. Behind him there were mirrors for people to look at themselves in while they bought cold drinks and refreshments. To reorganize their puffs and settle their buns. The mirrors watched Estha.

'I could file a Written Complaint against you,' the Man said to Estha. 'How would you like that? A Written Complaint?'

Estha stopped singing and got up to go back in.

'Now that I'm up,' the Orangedrink Lemondrink Man said. 'now that you've woken me up from my Resting Time, now that you've *disturbed* me, at least come and have a drink. It's the least you can do.'

He had an unshaven, jowly face. His teeth, like yellow piano keys, watched little Elvis the Pelvis.

'No thank you,' Elvis said politely. 'My family will be expecting me. And I've finished my pocket money.'

'*Porketmunny?*' the Orangedrink Lemondrink Man said with his teeth still watching. 'First English songs, and now *Porketmunny*! Where d'you live? On the moon?'

Estha turned to go.

'Wait a minute!' the Orangedrink Lemondrink Man said sharply. 'Just a minute!' he said again, more gently. 'I thought I asked you a question.'

His yellow teeth were magnets. They saw, they smiled, they sang, they smelled, they moved. They mesmerized.

'I asked you where you lived,' he said, spinning his nasty web.

'Ayemenem,' Estha said. 'I live in Ayemenem. My grandmother owns Paradise Pickles & Preserves. She's the Sleeping Partner.'

'Is she, now?' the Orangedrink Lemondrink Man said. 'And who does she sleep with?' He laughed a nasty laugh that Estha couldn't understand. 'Never mind. You wouldn't understand.'

'Come and have a drink,' he said. 'A Free Cold Drink. Come. Come here and tell me all about your grandmother.'

Estha went. Drawn by yellow teeth.

'Here. Behind the counter,' the Orangedrink Lemondrink Man said. He dropped his voice to a whisper. 'It has to be a secret because drinks are not allowed before the interval. It's a Theatre Offence.'

'Cognizable,' he added after a pause.

Estha went behind the Refreshments Counter for his Free Cold Drink. He saw the three high stools arranged in a row for the Orangedrink Lemondrink Man to sleep on. The wood shiny from his sitting.

'Now if you'll kindly hold this for me,' the Orangedrink Lemondrink Man said, handing Estha his penis through his soft white muslin dhoti, 'I'll get you your drink. Orange? Lemon?'

Estha held it because he had to.

'Orange? Lemon?' the Man said. 'Lemonorange?'

'Lemon, please,' Estha said politely.

He got a cold bottle and a straw. So he held a bottle in one hand and a penis in the other. Hard, hot, veiny. Not a moonbeam.

The Orangedrink Lemondrink Man's hand closed over Estha's. His thumbnail was long like a woman's. He moved Estha's hand up and down. First slowly. Then fastly.

The lemondrink was cold and sweet. The penis hot and hard.

The piano keys were watching.

'So your grandmother runs a factory?' the Orangedrink Lemondrink Man said. 'What kind of factory?'

'Many products,' Estha said, not looking, with the straw in

his mouth. 'Squashes, pickles, jams, curry powders. Pineapple slices.'

'Good,' the Orangedrink Lemondrink Man said. 'Excellent.'

His hand closed tighter over Estha's. Tight and sweaty. And faster still.

Fast faster fest
Never let it rest
Until the fast is faster,
And the faster's fest.

Through the soggy paper straw (almost flattened with spit and fear), the liquid lemon sweetness rose. Blowing through the straw (while his other hand moved), Estha blew bubbles into the bottle. Stickysweet lemon bubbles of the drink he couldn't drink. In his head he listed his grandmother's produce.

PICKLES	SQUASHES	JAMS
Mango	*Orange*	*Banana*
Green pepper	*Grape*	*Mixed fruit*
Bitter gourd	*Pineapple*	*Grapefruit marmalade*
Garlic	*Mango*	
Salted lime		

Then the gristly-bristly face contorted, and Estha's hand was wet and hot and sticky. It had egg white on it. White egg white. Quarter-boiled.

The lemondrink was cold and sweet. The penis was soft and shrivelled like an empty leather change-purse. With his dirtcoloured rag, the man wiped Estha's other hand.

'Now finish your drink,' he said, and affectionately squished a cheek of Estha's bottom. Tight plums in drainpipes. And beige and pointy shoes. 'You mustn't waste it,' he said. 'Think of all the poor people who have nothing to eat or drink. You're a lucky rich boy, with porketmunny and a grandmother's factory to inherit. You should Thank God that you have no worries. Now finish your drink.'

And so, behind the Refreshments Counter, in the Abhilash Talkies Princess Circle lobby, in the hall with Kerala's first 70mm CinemaScope screen, Esthappen Yako finished his free bottle of fizzed, lemon-flavoured fear. His lemontoolemon, too cold. Too sweet. The fizz came up his nose. He would be given another bottle soon (free, fizzed fear). But he didn't know that yet. He held his sticky Other Hand away from his body.

It wasn't supposed to touch anything.

When Estha finished his drink, the Orangedrink Lemondrink Man said, 'Finished? Goodboy.'

He took the empty bottle and the flattened straw, and sent Estha back into *The Sound of Music.*

Back inside the hairoil darkness, Estha held his Other Hand carefully (upwards, as though he was holding an imagined orange). He slid past the Audience (their legs moving thisway-andthat), past Baby Kochamma, past Rahel (still tilted back), past Ammu (still annoyed). Estha sat down, still holding his sticky orange.

And there was Captain von Clapp-Trapp. Christopher Plummer. Arrogant. Hardhearted. With a mouth like a slit. And a steelshrill police whistle. A captain with seven children. Clean children, like a packet of peppermints. He pretended not to love them, but he did. He loved them. He loved her (Julie Andrews), she loved him, they loved the children, the children loved them. They all loved each other. They were clean, white children, and their beds were soft with Ei. Der. Downs.

The house they lived in had a lake and gardens, a wide staircase, white doors and windows, and curtains with flowers.

The clean white children, even the big ones, were scared of the thunder. To comfort them, Julie Andrews put them all in her clean bed, and sang them a clean song about a few of her favourite things. These were a few of her favourite things:

(1) Girls in white dresses with blue satin sashes.
(2) Wild geese that flew with the moon on their wings.
(3) Bright copper kettles.
(4) Doorbells and sleighbells and schnitzel with noodles.
(5) Etc.

And then, in the minds of certain two-egg twin members of the audience in Abhilash Talkies, some questions arose, that needed answers, i.e.:

(a) *Did Captain von Clapp-Trapp shiver his leg?*
He did not.
(b) *Did Captain von Clapp-Trapp blow spit-bubbles? Did he?*
He did most certainly not.
(c) *Did he gobble?*
He did not.

Oh Captain von Trapp, Captain von Trapp, could you love the little fellow with the orange in the smelly auditorium?

He's just held the Orangedrink Lemondrink Man's soo-soo in his hand, but could you love him still?

And his twin sister? Tilting upwards with her fountain in a Love-in-Tokyo? Could you love her too?

Captain von Trapp had some questions of his own.

(a) *Are they clean white children?*
No. (*But Sophie Mol is.*)
(b) *Do they blow spit-bubbles?*
Yes. (*But Sophie Mol doesn't.*)
(c) *Do they shiver their legs? Like clerks?*
Yes. (*But Sophie Mol doesn't.*)
(d) *Have they, either or both, ever held strangers' soo-soos?*
N . . . Nyes. (*But Sophie Mol hasn't.*)

'Then I'm sorry,' Captain von Clapp-Trapp said. 'It's out of the question. I cannot love them. I cannot be their Baba. Oh no.'

Captain von Clapp-Trapp couldn't.

Estha put his head in his lap.

'What's the matter?' Ammu said. 'If you're sulking again, I'm taking you straight home. Sit up please. And watch. That's what you've been brought here for.'

Finish the drink.

Watch the picture.

Think of all the poor people.

Lucky rich boy with porketmunny. No worries.

Estha sat up and watched. His stomach heaved. He had a greenwavy, thick-watery, lumpy, seaweedy, floaty, bottomless-bottomful feeling.

'Ammu?' he said.

'Now WHAT?' The *WHAT* snapped, barked, spat out.

'Feeling vomity,' Estha said.

'Just feeling or d'you want to?' Ammu's voice was worried.

'Don't know.'

'Shall we go and try?' Ammu said. 'It'll make you feel better.'

'Okay,' Estha said.

Okay? Okay.

'Where're you going?' Baby Kochamma wanted to know.

'Estha's going to try and vomit,' Ammu said.

'Where're you going?' Rahel asked.

'Feeling vomity,' Estha said.

'Can I come and watch?'

'No,' Ammu said.

Past the Audience again (legs thiswayandthat). Last time to sing. This time to try and vomit. Exit through the EXIT. Outside in the marble lobby, the Orangedrink Lemondrink man was eating a sweet. His cheek was bulging with a moving sweet. He made soft, sucking sounds like water draining from a basin.

There was a green Parry's wrapper on the counter. Sweets were free for this man. He had a row of free sweets in dim bottles. He wiped the marble counter with his dirt-coloured rag that he held in his hairy watch hand. When he saw the luminous woman with polished shoulders and the little boy, a shadow slipped across his face. Then he smiled his portable piano smile.

'Out again sosoon?' he said.

Estha was already retching. Ammu moonwalked him to the Princess Circle bathroom. HERS.

He was held up, wedged between the notclean basin and Ammu's body. Legs dangling. The basin had steel taps, and rust stains. And a brownwebbed mesh of hairline cracks, like the roadmap of some great, intricate city.

Estha convulsed, but nothing came. Just thoughts. And they floated out and floated back in. Ammu couldn't see them. They hovered like storm clouds over the Basin City. But the basin men and basin women went about their usual basin business. Basin cars, and basin buses, still whizzed around. Basin Life went on.

'No?' Ammu said.

'No,' Estha said.

No? No.

'Then wash your face,' Ammu said. 'Water always helps. Wash your face and let's go and have a fizzy lemondrink.'

Estha washed his face and hands and face and hands. His eyelashes were wet and bunched together.

The Orangedrink Lemondrink Man folded the green sweet wrapper and fixed the fold with his painted thumbnail. He stunned a fly with a rolled magazine. Delicately, he flicked it over the edge of the counter onto the floor. It lay on its back and waved its feeble legs.

'Sweetboy this,' he said to Ammu. 'Sings nicely.'

'He's my son,' Ammu said.

'Really?' the Orangedrink Lemondrink Man said, and looked

at Ammu with his teeth. 'Really? You don't look old enough!'

'He's not feeling well,' Ammu said. 'I thought a cold drink would make him feel better.'

'Of course,' the Man said. 'Ofcourseofcourse. Orangelemon? Lemonorange?'

Dreadful, dreaded question.

'No thank you.' Estha looked at Ammu. Greenwavy, seaweedy, bottomless-bottomful.

'What about you?' the Orangedrink Lemondrink Man asked Ammu.

'Coca-ColaFanta? IcecreamRosemilk?'

'No. Not for me. Thank you,' Ammu said. Deep-dimpled, luminous woman.

'Here,' the Man said, with a fistful of sweets, like a generous air hostess. 'These are for your little Mon.'

'No thank you,' Estha said, looking at Ammu.

'Take them, Estha,' Ammu said. 'Don't be rude.'

Estha took them.

'Say Thank you,' Ammu said.

'Thank you,' Estha said. (For the sweets, for the white egg white.)

'No mention,' the Orangedrink Lemondrink Man said in English.

'So!' he said. 'Mon says you're from Ayemenem?'

'Yes,' Ammu said.

'I come there often,' the Orangedrink Lemondrink Man said. 'My wife's people are Ayemenem people. I know where your factory is. Paradise Pickles, isn't it? He told me. Your Mon.'

He knew where to find Estha. That was what he was trying to say. It was a warning.

Ammu saw her son's bright feverbutton eyes.

'We must go,' she said. 'Mustn't risk a fever. Their cousin is coming tomorrow,' she explained to Uncle. And then, added casually, 'From London.'

'From London?' A new respect gleamed in Uncle's eyes. For a family with London connections.

'Estha, you stay here with Uncle. I'll get Baby Kochamma and Rahel,' Ammu said.

'Come,' Uncle said. 'Come and sit with me on a high stool.'

'No, Ammu! No, Ammu, no! I want to come with you!'

Ammu, surprised at the unusually shrill insistence from her usually quiet son, apologized to the Orangedrink Lemondrink Uncle.

'He's not usually like this. Come on then, Esthappen.'

The back-inside smell. Fan shadows. Backs of heads. Necks. Collars. Hair. Buns. Plaits. Ponytails.

A fountain in a Love-in-Tokyo. A little girl and an ex-nun.

Captain von Trapp's seven peppermint children had had their peppermint baths, and were standing in a peppermint line with their hair slicked down, singing in obedient peppermint voices to the woman the Captain nearly married. The blonde Baroness who shone like a diamond.

The hills are alive
with the sound of music.

'We have to go,' Ammu said to Baby Kochamma and Rahel.

'But, Ammu!' Rahel said. 'The Main Things haven't even happened yet! He hasn't even *kissed* her! He hasn't even torn up the Hitler flag yet! They haven't even been *betrayed* by Rolf the Postman!'

'Estha's sick,' Ammu said. 'Come on!'

'The Nazi soldiers haven't even come!'

'Come on,' Ammu said. 'Get up!'

'They haven't even done "*High on a hill was a lonely goatherd*"!'

'Estha has to be well for Sophie Mol, doesn't he?' Baby Kochamma said.

'He doesn't,' Rahel said, but mostly to herself.

'What did you say?' Baby Kochamma said, getting the general drift, but not what was actually said.

'Nothing,' Rahel said.

'I *heard* you,' Baby Kochamma said.

Outside, Uncle was reorganizing his dim bottles. Wiping with his dirtcoloured rag the ring-shaped water-stains they had left on his marble Refreshments Counter. Preparing for the Interval. He was a Clean Orangedrink Lemondrink Uncle. He had an air hostess's heart trapped in a bear's body.

'Going then?' he said.

'Yes,' Ammu said. 'Where can we get a taxi?'

'Out the gate, up the road, on your left,' he said, looking at Rahel. 'You never told me you had a little Mol too.' And holding out another sweet 'Here, Mol – for you.'

'Take mine!' Estha said quickly, not wanting Rahel to go near the man.

But Rahel had already started towards him. As she approached him, he smiled at her and something about that portable piano smile, something about the steady gaze in which he held her, made her shrink from him. It was the most hideous thing she had ever seen. She spun around to look at Estha.

She backed away from the hairy man.

Estha pressed his Parry's sweets into her hand and she felt his fever hot fingers whose tips were as cold as death.

''Bye, Mon,' Uncle said to Estha. 'I'll see you in Ayemenem sometime.'

So, the redsteps once again. This time Rahel lagging. Slow. No I don't want to go. A ton of bricks on a leash.

'Sweet chap, that Orangedrink Lemondrink fellow,' Ammu said.

'Chhi!' Baby Kochamma said.

'He doesn't look it, but he was surprisingly sweet with Estha,' Ammu said.

'So why don't you marry him then?' Rahel said petulantly.

Time stopped on the red staircase. Estha stopped. Baby Kochamma stopped.

'Rahel,' Ammu said.

Rahel froze. She was desperately sorry for what she had said. She didn't know where those words had come from. She didn't know that she'd had them in her. But they were out now, and wouldn't go back in. They hung about that red staircase like clerks in a Government office. Some stood, some sat and shivered their legs.

'Rahel,' Ammu said. 'Do you realize what you have just done?'

Frightened eyes and a fountain looked back at Ammu.

'It's all right. Don't be scared,' Ammu said. 'Just answer me. Do you?'

'What?' Rahel said in the smallest voice she had.

'Realize what you've just done?' Ammu said.

Frightened eyes and a fountain looked back at Ammu.

'D'you know what happens when you hurt people?' Ammu said. 'When you hurt people, they begin to love you less. That's what careless words do. They make people love you a little less.'

A cold moth with unusually dense dorsal tufts landed lightly on Rahel's heart. Where its icy legs touched her, she got goose bumps. Six goose bumps on her careless heart.

A little less her Ammu loved her.

And so, out the gate, up the road, and to the left. The taxi stand. A hurt mother, an ex-nun, a hot child and a cold one. Six goose bumps and a moth.

The taxi smelled of sleep. Old clothes rolled up. Damp towels. Armpits. It was, after all, the taxi driver's home. He lived in it. It was the only place he had to store his smells. The seats had been killed. Ripped. A swathe of dirty yellow sponge spilled out and shivered on the back seat like an immense jaundiced liver. The driver had the ferrety alertness of a small rodent. He had a hooked Roman nose and a Little Richard moustache. He was so small that he watched the road through the steering wheel. To passing traffic it looked like a taxi with passengers but no driver. He drove fast, pugnaciously, darting into empty spaces, nudging other cars out of their lanes. Accelerating at zebra crossings. Jumping lights.

'Why not use a cushion or a pillow or something?' Baby Kochamma suggested in her friendly voice. 'You'll be able to see better.'

'Why not mind your own business, sister?' the driver suggested in his unfriendly one.

Driving past the inky sea, Estha put his head out of the window. He could taste the hot, salt breeze in his mouth. He could feel it lift his hair. He knew that if Ammu found out about what he had done with the Orangedrink Lemondrink Man, she'd love him less as well. Very much less. He felt the shaming churning heaving turning sickness in his stomach. He longed for the river. Because water always helps.

The sticky neon night rushed past the taxi window. It was hot inside the taxi, and quiet. Baby Kochamma looked flushed and excited. She loved not being the cause of ill feeling. Every time a pye-dog strayed onto the road, the driver made a sincere effort to kill it.

The moth on Rahel's heart spread its velvet wings, and the chill crept into her bones.

In the Hotel Sea Queen car park, the skyblue Plymouth gossiped with other, smaller cars. *Hslip Hslip Hsnooh-snah.* A big lady at a small ladies' party. Tailfins aflutter.

'Room numbers 313 and 327,' the man at the reception said. 'Non-airconditioned. Twin beds. Lift is closed for repair.'

The bellboy who took them up wasn't a boy and hadn't a bell. He had dim eyes and two buttons missing on his frayed maroon coat. His greyed undershirt showed. He had to wear his silly bellhop's cap tilted sideways, its tight plastic strap sunk into his sagging dewlap. It seemed unnecessarily cruel to make an old man wear a cap sideways like that and arbitrarily reorder the way in which age chose to hang from his chin.

There were more red steps to climb. The same red carpet from the cinema hall was following them around. Magic flying carpet.

Chacko was in his room. Caught feasting. Roast chicken, finger chips, sweetcorn and chicken soup, two parathas and vanilla ice cream with chocolate sauce. Sauce in a sauceboat. Chacko often said that his ambition was to die of overeating. Mammachi said it was a sure sign of suppressed unhappiness. Chacko said it was no such thing. He said it was Sheer Greed.

Chacko was puzzled to see everybody back so early, but pretended otherwise. He kept eating.

The original plan had been that Estha would sleep with Chacko, and Rahel with Ammu and Baby Kochamma. But now that Estha wasn't well and Love had been reapportioned (Ammu loved her a little less), Rahel would have to sleep with Chacko, and Estha with Ammu and Baby Kochamma.

Ammu took Rahel's pyjamas and toothbrush out of the suitcase and put them on the bed.

'Here,' Ammu said.

Two clicks to close the suitcase.

Click. And click.

'Ammu,' Rahel said, 'shall I miss dinner as my punishment?'

She was keen to exchange punishments. No dinner, in exchange for Ammu loving her the same as before.

'As you please,' Ammu said. 'But I advise you to eat. If you want to grow, that is. Maybe you could share some of Chacko's chicken.'

'Maybe and maybe not,' Chacko said.

'But what about my punishment?' Rahel said. 'You haven't given me my punishment!'

'Some things come with their own punishments,' Baby Kochamma said. As though she was explaining a sum that Rahel couldn't understand.

Some things come with their own punishments. Like bedrooms with built-in cupboards. They would all learn more about punishments soon. That they came in different sizes. That some were so big they were like cupboards with built-in bedrooms. You could spend your whole life in them, wandering through dark shelving.

Baby Kochamma's goodnight kiss left a little spit on Rahel's cheek. She wiped it off with her shoulder.

'Goodnight Godbless,' Ammu said. But she said it with her back. She was already gone.

'Goodnight,' Estha said, too sick to love his sister.

Rahel Alone watched them walk down the hotel corridor like silent but substantial ghosts. Two big, one small, in beige and pointy shoes. The red carpet took away their feet sounds.

Rahel stood in the hotel room doorway, full of sadness.

She had in her the sadness of Sophie Mol coming. The sadness of Ammu's loving her a little less. And the sadness of whatever the Orangedrink Lemondrink Man had done to Estha in Abhilash Talkies.

A stinging wind blew across her dry, aching eyes.

Chacko put a leg of chicken and some finger chips onto a quarter plate for Rahel.

'No thank you,' Rahel said, hoping that if she could somehow effect her own punishment, Ammu would rescind hers.

'What about some ice cream with chocolate sauce?' Chacko said.

'No thank you,' Rahel said.

'Fine,' Chacko said. 'But you don't know what you're missing.'

He finished all the chicken and then all the ice cream.

Rahel changed into her pyjamas.

'Please don't tell me what it is you're being punished for,' Chacko said. 'I can't bear to hear about it.' He was mopping the last of the chocolate sauce from the sauceboat with a piece of paratha. His disgusting, after-sweet sweet. 'What was it? Scratching your mosquito bites till they bled? Not saying "Thankyou" to the taxi driver?'

'Something much worse than that,' Rahel said, loyal to Ammu.

'Don't tell me,' Chacko said. 'I don't want to know.'

He rang for room service, and a tired bearer came to take away the plates and bones. He tried to catch the dinner smells, but they escaped and climbed into the limp brown hotel curtains.

A dinnerless niece and her dinnerfull uncle brushed their teeth together in the Hotel Sea Queen bathroom. She, a forlorn, stubby convict in striped pyjamas and a Fountain in a Love-in-Tokyo. He, in his cotton vest and underpants. His vest, taut and stretched over his round stomach like a second skin, went slack over the depression of his belly-button.

When Rahel held her frothing toothbrush still and moved her teeth instead, he didn't say she mustn't.

He wasn't a fascist.

They took it in turns to spit. Rahel carefully examined her white Binaca froth as it dribbled down the side of the basin carefully, to see what she could see.

What colours and strange creatures had been ejected from the spaces between her teeth?

None tonight. Nothing unusual. Just Binaca bubbles.

Chacko put off the Big Light.

In bed, Rahel took off her Love-in-Tokyo and put it by her sunglasses. Her fountain slumped a little, but stayed standing.

Chacko lay in bed in the pool of light from his bedside lamp. A fat man on a dark stage. He reached over to his shirt lying crumpled at the foot of his bed. He took his wallet out of the pocket, and looked at the photograph of Sophie Mol that Margaret Kochamma had sent him two years ago.

Rahel watched him and her cold moth spread its wings again. Slow out. Slow in. A predator's lazy blink.

The sheets were coarse, but clean.

Chacko closed his wallet and put out the light. Into the night he lit a Charminar and wondered what his daughter looked like now. Nine years old. Last seen when she was red and wrinkled. Barely human. Three weeks later, Margaret his wife, his only love, had cried and told him about Joe.

Margaret told Chacko that she couldn't live with him any more. She told him that she needed her own space. As though Chacko had been using *her* shelves for *his* clothes. Which, knowing him, he probably had.

She asked him for a divorce.

Those last few tortured nights before he left her, Chacko would slip out of bed with a torch and look at his sleeping child. To learn her. Imprint her on his memory. To ensure that when he thought of her, the child that he invoked would be accurate. He memorized the brown down on her soft skull. The shape of her puckered, constantly moving mouth. The spaces between her toes. The suggestion of a mole. And then, without meaning to, he found himself searching his baby for signs of Joe. The baby clutched his index finger while he conducted his insane, broken, envious, torchlit study. Her belly button protruded from her satiated satin stomach like a domed monument on a hill. Chacko laid his ear against it and listened with wonder at the rumblings from within. Messages being sent from here to there. New organs getting used to each other. A new government setting up its systems. Organizing the division of labour, deciding who would do what.

She smelled of milk and urine. Chacko marvelled at how someone so small and undefined, so vague in her resemblances, could so completely command the attention, the love, the *sanity*, of a grown man.

When he left, he felt that something had been torn out of him. Something big.

But Joe was dead now. Killed in a car crash. Dead as a doorknob. A Joe-shaped hole in the universe.

In Chacko's photograph, Sophie Mol was seven years old. White and blue. Rose-lipped, and Syrian Christian nowhere. Though Mammachi, peering at the photograph, insisted she had Pappachi's nose.

'Chacko?' Rahel said, from her darkened bed. 'Can I ask you a question?'

'Ask me two,' Chacko said.

'Chacko, do you love Sophie Mol Most in the World?'

'She's my daughter,' Chacko said.

Rahel considered this.

'Chacko? Is it *necessary* that people HAVE to love their own children Most in the World?'

'There are no rules,' Chacko said. 'But people usually do.'

'Chacko, for example,' Rahel said. 'Just for *example*, is it possible that Ammu can love Sophie Mol more than me and Estha? Or for you to love me more than Sophie Mol, for *example*?'

'Anything's possible in Human Nature,' Chacko said in his Reading Aloud voice. Talking to the darkness now, suddenly insensitive to his little fountain-haired niece. 'Love. Madness. Hope. Infinite joy.'

Of the four things that were Possible in Human Nature, Rahel thought that *Infinnate Joy* sounded the saddest. Perhaps because of the way Chacko said it.

Infinnate Joy. With a church sound to it. Like a sad fish with fins all over.

A cold moth lifted a cold leg.

The cigarette smoke curled into the night. And the fat man and the little girl lay awake in silence.

A few rooms away, while his baby grand aunt snored, Estha awoke.

Ammu was asleep and looked beautiful in the barred-blue streetlight that came in through the barred-blue window. She smiled a sleepsmile that dreamed of dolphins and a deep barred blue. It was a smile that gave no indication that the person who belonged to it was a bomb waiting to go off.

Estha Alone walked weavily to the bathroom. He vomited a clear, bitter, lemony, sparkling, fizzy liquid. The acrid aftertaste of a Little Man's first encounter with Fear. Dum dum.

He felt a little better. He put on his shoes and walked out of his room, laces trailing, down the corridor, and stood quietly outside Rahel's door.

Rahel stood on a chair and unlatched the door for him.

Chacko didn't bother to wonder how she could possibly have known that Estha was at the door. He was used to their sometimes strangeness.

He lay like a beached whale on the narrow hotel bed and wondered idly if it had indeed been Velutha that Rahel saw. He didn't think it likely. Velutha had too much going for him. He was a Paravan with a future. He wondered whether Velutha had become a card-holding member of the Marxist Party. And whether he had been seeing Comrade K. N. M. Pillai lately.

Earlier in the year, Comrade Pillai's political ambitions had been given an unexpected boost. Two local Party members, Comrade J. Kattukaran and Comrade Guhan Menon had been expelled from the Party as suspected Naxalites. One of them – Comrade Guhan Menon – was tipped to be the Party's candidate for the Kottayam by-elections to the Legislative Assembly due next March. His expulsion from the Party created a vacuum that a number of hopefuls were jockeying to fill. Among them Comrade K. N. M. Pillai.

Comrade Pillai had begun to watch the goings-on at Paradise Pickles with the keenness of a substitute at a soccer match. To bring in a new labour union, however small, in what he hoped would be his future constituency, would be an excellent beginning for a journey to the Legislative Assembly.

Until then, at Paradise Pickles, *Comrade! Comrade!* (as Ammu put it) had been no more than a harmless game played outside working hours. But if the stakes were raised, and the conductor's baton wrested from Chacko's hands, everybody (except Chacko) knew that the factory, already steeped in debt, would be in trouble.

Since things were not going well financially, the labour was paid less than the minimum rates specified by the trade union. Of course it was Chacko himself who pointed this out to them and promised that as soon as things picked up, their wages would be revised. He believed that they trusted him and knew that he had their best interests at heart.

But there was someone who thought otherwise. In the evenings, after the factory shift was over, Comrade K. N. M. Pillai waylaid the workers of Paradise Pickles and shepherded them into his printing press. In his reedy, piping voice he urged them on to revolution. In his speeches he managed a clever mix of pertinent local issues and grand Maoist rhetoric which sounded even grander in Malayalam.

'People of the World,' he would chirrup, 'be courageous, *dare* to fight, *defy* difficulties and advance wave upon wave. Then the whole world will belong to the People. Monsters of all kinds shall be destroyed. You must demand what is rightfully yours. Yearly bonus. Provident fund. Accident insurance.' Since these speeches were in part rehearsal for when, as the local Member of the Legislative Assembly, Comrade Pillai would address thronging millions, there was something odd about their pitch and cadence. His voice was full of green rice-fields and red banners that arced across blue skies instead of a small hot room and the smell of printer's ink.

Comrade K. N. M. Pillai never came out openly against Chacko. Whenever he referred to him in his speeches he was careful to strip him of any human attributes and present him as an abstract functionary in some larger scheme. A theoretical construct. A pawn in the monstrous bourgeois plot to subvert the Revolution. He never referred to him by name, but always as 'the Management'. As though Chacko was many people. Apart from it being tactically the right thing to do, this disjunction between the man and his job helped Comrade Pillai to keep his conscience clear about his own private business dealings with Chacko. His contract for printing the Paradise Pickles labels gave him an income that he badly needed. He told himself that Chacko-the-client and Chacko-the-Management were two different people. Quite separate of course from Chacko-the-Comrade.

The only snag in Comrade K. N. M. Pillai's plans was Velutha. Of all the workers at Paradise Pickles, he was the only card-holding member of the Party, and that gave Comrade Pillai an ally he would rather have done without. He knew that all the other Touchable workers in the factory resented Velutha for ancient reasons of their own. Comrade Pillai stepped carefully around this wrinkle, waiting for a suitable opportunity to iron it out.

He stayed in constant touch with the workers. He made it his business to know exactly what went on at the factory. He ridiculed them for accepting the wages they did, when their *own* government, the People's Government, was in power.

When Punnachen the accountant, who read Mammachi the papers every morning, brought news that there had been talk among the workers of demanding a raise, Mammachi was furious. 'Tell them to read the papers. There's a famine on. There are no jobs. People are starving to death. They should be grateful they have any work *at all.*'

Whenever anything serious happened in the factory, it was always to Mammachi and not Chacko that the news was brought. Perhaps this was because Mammachi fitted properly into the conventional scheme of things. She was the Modalali. She played her part. Her responses, however harsh, were straightforward and predictable. Chacko, on the other hand, though he was the Man of the House, though he said, '*My* pickles, *my* jam, *my* curry powders,' was so busy trying on different costumes that he blurred the battle lines.

Mammachi tried to caution Chacko. He heard her out, but didn't really listen to what she was saying. So despite the early rumblings of discontent on the premises of Paradise Pickles, Chacko, in rehearsal for the Revolution, continued to play *Comrade! Comrade!*

That night, on his narrow hotel bed, he thought sleepily about pre-empting Comrade Pillai by organizing his workers into a sort of private labour union. He would hold elections for them. Make them vote. They could take turns at being elected representatives. He smiled at the idea of holding round-table negotiations with Comrade Sumathi, or, better still, Comrade Lucykutty, who had much the nicer hair.

His thoughts returned to Margaret Kochamma and Sophie Mol. Fierce bands of love tightened around his chest until he could barely breathe. He lay awake and counted the hours for them to leave for the airport.

On the next bed, his niece and nephew slept with their arms around each other. A hot twin and a cold one. He and She. We and Us. Somehow, not wholly unaware of the hint of doom and all that waited in the wings for them.

They dreamed of their river.

Of the coconut trees that bent into it and watched, with

coconut eyes, the boats slide by. Upstream in the mornings. Downstream in the evenings. And the dull, sullen sound of the boatmen's bamboo poles as they thudded against the dark, oiled boatwood.

It was warm, the water. Greygreen. Like rippled silk.

With fish in it.

With the sky and trees in it.

And at night, the broken yellow moon in it.

When they grew tired of waiting, the dinner smells climbed off the curtains and drifted through the Sea Queen windows to dance the night away on the dinner-smelling sea.

The time was ten to two.

5

God's Own Country

Years later, when Rahel returned to the river, it greeted her with a ghastly skull's smile, with holes where teeth had been, and a limp hand raised from a hospital bed.

Both things had happened.

It had shrunk. And she had grown.

Downriver, a saltwater barrage had been built, in exchange for votes from the influential paddy-farmer lobby. The barrage regulated the inflow of saltwater from the backwaters that opened into the Arabian Sea. So now they had two harvests a year instead of one. More rice, for the price of a river.

Despite the fact that it was June, and raining, the river was no more than a swollen drain now. A thin ribbon of thick water that lapped wearily at the mud banks on either side, sequinned with the occasional silver slant of a dead fish. It was choked with a succulent weed, whose furred brown roots waved like thin tentacles under water. Bronze-winged lily-trotters walked across it. Splay-footed, cautious.

Once it had had the power to evoke fear. To change lives. But now its teeth were drawn, its spirit spent. It was just a slow, sludging green ribbon lawn that ferried fetid garbage to the sea. Bright plastic bags blew across its viscous, weedy surface like subtropical flying-flowers.

The stone steps that had once led bathers right down to the water, and Fisher People to the fish, were entirely exposed and led from nowhere to nowhere, like an absurd corbelled monument that commemorated nothing. Ferns pushed through the cracks.

On the other side of the river, the steep mud banks changed abruptly into low mud walls of shanty hutments. Children hung their bottoms over the edge and defecated directly onto the squelchy, sucking mud of the exposed river bed. The smaller ones left their dribbling mustard streaks to find their own way down. Eventually, by evening, the river would rouse itself to accept the day's offerings and sludge off to the sea, leaving wavy lines of thick white scum in its wake. Upstream, clean mothers washed clothes and pots in unadulterated factory effluents. People bathed. Severed torsos soaping themselves, arranged like dark busts on a thin, rocking, ribbon lawn.

On warm days the smell of shit lifted off the river and hovered over Ayemenem like a hat.

Further inland, and still across, a five-star hotel chain had bought the Heart of Darkness.

The History House (where map-breath'd ancestors with tough toe-nails once whispered) could no longer be approached from the river. It had turned its back on Ayemenem. The hotel guests were ferried across the backwaters, straight from Cochin. They arrived by speedboat, opening up a V of foam on the water, leaving behind a rainbow film of gasoline.

The view from the hotel was beautiful, but here too the water was thick and toxic. *No Swimming* signs had been put up in stylish calligraphy. They had built a tall wall to screen off the slum and prevent it from encroaching on Kari Saipu's estate. There wasn't much they could do about the smell.

But they had a swimming pool for swimming. And fresh tandoori pomfret and crêpe suzette on their menu.

The trees were still green, the sky still blue, which counted for something. So they went ahead and plugged their smelly paradise – 'God's Own Country' they called it in their brochures

– because they knew, those clever Hotel People, that smelliness, like other people's poverty, was merely a matter of getting used to. A question of discipline. Of Rigour and Air-conditioning. Nothing more.

Kari Saipu's house had been renovated and painted. It had become the centrepiece of an elaborate complex, crisscrossed with artificial canals and connecting bridges. Small boats bobbed in the water. The old colonial bungalow with its deep verandah and Doric columns, was surrounded by smaller, older, wooden houses – ancestral homes – that the hotel chain had bought from old families and transplanted in the Heart of Darkness. Toy Histories for rich tourists to play in. Like the sheaves of rice in Joseph's dream, like a press of eager natives petitioning an English magistrate, the old houses had been arranged around the History House in attitudes of deference. 'Heritage', the hotel was called.

The Hotel People liked to tell their guests that the oldest of the wooden houses, with its air-tight, panelled storeroom which could hold enough rice to feed an army for a year, had been the ancestral home of Comrade E. M. S. Namboodiripad, 'Kerala's Mao Tse-tung,' they explained to the uninitiated. The furniture and knick-knacks that came with the house were on display. A reed umbrella, a wicker couch. A wooden dowry box. They were labelled with edifying placards which said *Traditional Kerala Umbrella* and *Traditional Bridal Dowry Box*.

So there it was then, History and Literature enlisted by commerce. Kurtz and Karl Marx joining palms to greet rich guests as they stepped off the boat.

Comrade Namboodiripad's house functioned as the hotel's dining room, where semi-suntanned tourists in bathing suits sipped tender coconut water (served in the shell), and old communists, who now worked as fawning bearers in colourful ethnic clothes, stooped slightly behind their trays of drinks.

In the evenings (for that Regional Flavour) the tourists were treated to truncated kathakali performances ('Small attention spans,' the Hotel People explained to the dancers). So ancient stories were collapsed and amputated. Six-hour classics were slashed to twenty-minute cameos.

The performances were staged by the swimming pool. While the drummers drummed and the dancers danced, hotel guests frolicked with their children in the water. While Kunti revealed her secret to Karna on the river bank, courting couples rubbed suntan oil on each other. While fathers played sublimated sexual games with their nubile teenaged daughters, Poothana suckled young Krishna at her poisoned breast. Bhima disembowelled Dushasana and bathed Draupadi's hair in his blood.

The back verandah of the History House (where a posse of Touchable policemen converged, where an inflatable goose was burst) had been enclosed and converted into the airy hotel kitchen. Nothing worse than kebabs and caramel custard happened there now. The Terror was past. Overcome by the smell of food. Silenced by the humming of cooks. The cheerful chop-chop-chopping of ginger and garlic. The disembowelling of lesser mammals – pigs, goats. The dicing of meat. The scaling of fish.

Something lay buried in the ground. Under grass. Under twenty-three years of June rain.

A small forgotten thing.

Nothing that the world would miss.

A child's plastic wristwatch with the time painted on it.

Ten to two it said.

A band of children followed Rahel on her walk.

'Hello, hippie,' they said, twenty-five years too late. 'Whatisyourname?'

Then someone threw a small stone at her, and her childhood fled, flailing its thin arms.

On her way back, looping around the Ayemenem House, Rahel emerged onto the main road. Here too, houses had mushroomed, and it was only the fact that they nestled under trees, and that the narrow paths that branched off the main road and led to them were not motorable, that gave Ayemenem the semblance of rural quietness. In truth, its population had swelled to the size of a little town. Behind the fragile facade of greenery lived a press of people who could gather at a moment's notice. To beat to death a careless bus driver. To smash the windscreen of a car that dared to venture out on the day of an Opposition bandh. To steal Baby Kochamma's imported insulin and her cream buns that came all the way from Bestbakery in Kottayam.

Outside Lucky Press, Comrade K. N. M. Pillai was standing at his boundary wall talking to a man on the other side. Comrade Pillai's arms were crossed over his chest, and he clasped his own armpits possessively, as though someone had asked to borrow them and he had just refused. The man across the wall shuffled through a bunch of photographs in a plastic sachet, with an air of contrived interest. The photographs were mostly pictures of Comrade K. N. M. Pillai's son, Lenin, who lived and worked in Delhi – he took care of the painting, plumbing, and any electrical work – for the Dutch and German embassies. In order to allay any fears his clients might have about his political leanings, he had altered his name slightly. Levin he called himself now. P. Levin.

Rahel tried to walk past unnoticed. It was absurd of her to have imagined that she could.

'*Aiyyo*, Rahel Mol!' Comrade K. N. M. Pillai said, recognizing her instantly. '*Orkunnilley?* Comrade Uncle?'

'*Oower*,' Rahel said.

Did she remember him? She did indeed.

Neither question nor answer was meant as anything more than a polite preamble to conversation. Both she and he knew that there are things that can be forgotten. And things that cannot – that sit on dusty shelves like stuffed birds with baleful, sideways staring eyes.

'So!' Comrade Pillai said. 'I think so you are in Amayrica now?'

'No,' Rahel said. 'I'm here.'

'Yes yes,' he sounded a little impatient, 'but otherwise in Amayrica, I suppose?'

Comrade Pillai uncrossed his arms. His nipples peeped at Rahel over the top of the boundary wall like a sad St Bernard's eyes.

'Recognized?' Comrade Pillai asked the man with the photographs, indicating Rahel with his chin.

The man hadn't.

'The Old Paradise Pickle Kochamma's daughter's daughter,' Comrade Pillai said.

The man looked puzzled. He was clearly a stranger. And not a pickle-eater. Comrade Pillai tried a different tack.

'Punnyan Kunju?' he asked. The Patriarch of Antioch appeared briefly in the sky – and waved his withered hand.

Things began to fall into place for the man with the photographs. He nodded enthusiastically.

'Punnyan Kunju's son? Benaan John Ipe? Who used to be in Delhi?' Comrade Pillai said.

'*Oower, oower, oower*,' the man said.

'His daughter's daughter is this. In Amayrica now.'

The nodder nodded as Rahel's ancestral lineage fell into place for him.

'*Oower, oower, oower.* In Amayrica now, isn't it.' It wasn't a question. It was sheer admiration.

He remembered vaguely a whiff of scandal. He had forgotten the details, but remembered that it had involved sex and death. It had been in the papers. After a brief silence and another series of small nods, the man handed Comrade Pillai the sachet of photographs.

'Okaythen, comrade, I'll be off.'

He had a bus to catch.

'So!' Comrade Pillai's smile broadened as he turned all his attention like a searchlight on Rahel. His gums were startlingly pink, the reward for a lifetime's uncompromising vegetarianism. He was the kind of man whom it was hard to imagine had once been a boy. Or a baby. He looked as though he had been *born* middle-aged. With a receding hairline.

'Mol's husband?' he wanted to know.

'Hasn't come.'

'Any photos?'

'No.'

'Name?'

'Larry. Lawrence.'

'*Oower.* Lawrence.' Comrade Pillai nodded as though he agreed with it. As though given a choice, it was the very one he would have picked.

'Any issues?'

'No,' Rahel said.

'Still in planning stages, I suppose? Or expecting?'

'No.'

'One is must. Boy girl. Anyone,' Comrade Pillai said. 'Two is of course your choice.'

'We're divorced.' Rahel hoped to shock him into silence.

'Die-vorced?' His voice rose to such a high register that it cracked on the question mark. He even pronounced the word as though it were a form of death.

'That is most unfortunate,' he said, when he had recovered. For some reason resorting to uncharacteristic, bookish language. 'Mo-stunfortunate.'

It occurred to Comrade Pillai that this generation was perhaps paying for its forefathers' bourgeois decadence.

One was mad. The other die-vorced. Probably barren.

Perhaps *this* was the real revolution. The Christian bourgeoisie had begun to self-destruct.

Comrade Pillai lowered his voice as though there were people listening, though there was no one about.

'And Mon?' he whispered confidentially. 'How is he?'

'Fine,' Rahel said. 'He's fine.'

Fine. Flat and honey-coloured. He washes his clothes with crumbling soap.

'Aiyyo paavam,' Comrade Pillai whispered, and his nipples drooped in mock dismay. 'Poor fellow.'

Rahel wondered what he gained by que tioning her so closely and then completely disregarding her answers. Clearly he didn't expect the truth from her, but why didn't he at least bother to pretend otherwise?

'Lenin is in Delhi now,' Comrade Pillai came out with it finally, unable to hide his pride. 'Working with foreign embassies. See!'

He handed Rahel the Cellophane sachet. They were mostly photographs of Lenin and his family. His wife, his child, his new Bajaj scooter. There was one of Lenin shaking hands with a very well-dressed, very pink man.

'German First Secretary,' Comrade Pillai said.

They looked cheerful in the photographs, Lenin and his wife. As though they had a new refrigerator in their drawing room, and a down payment on a DDA flat.

Rahel remembered the incident that made Lenin swim into focus as a Real Person for her and Estha, when they stopped regarding him as just another pleat in his mother's sari. She and Estha were five, Lenin perhaps three or four years old. They met in the clinic of Dr Verghese Verghese (Kottayam's leading Paediatrician and Feeler-up of Mothers). Rahel was with Ammu and Estha (who had insisted that he go along). Lenin was with his mother, Kalyani. Both Rahel and Lenin had the same complaint – Foreign Objects Lodged up their Noses. It seemed an extraordinary coincidence now, but somehow hadn't then. It was curious how politics lurked even in what children chose to stuff up their noses. She, the granddaughter of an Imperial Entomologist, he the son of a grass-roots Marxist Party worker. So, she a glass bead, and he a green gram.

The waiting room was full.

From behind the doctor's curtain, sinister voices murmured, interrupted by howls from savaged children. There was a clink of glass on metal, and the whisper and bubble of boiling water. A boy played with the wooden *Doctor is IN Doctor is OUT* sign on the wall, sliding the brass panel up and down. A feverish baby hiccupped on its mother's breast. The slow ceiling fan sliced the thick, frightened air into an unending spiral that spun slowly to the floor like the peeled skin of an endless potato.

No one read the magazines.

From below the scanty curtain that was stretched across the doorway that led directly onto the street came the relentless slip-slap of disembodied feet in slippers. The noisy, carefree world of Those with Nothing Up Their Noses.

Ammu and Kalyani exchanged children. Noses were pushed up, heads bent back, and turned towards the light to see if one mother could see what the other had missed. When that didn't work, Lenin, dressed like a taxi – yellow shirt, black stretchlon shorts – regained his mother's nylon lap (*and* his packet of chiclets). He sat on sari flowers and from that unassailable position of strength surveyed the scene impassively. He inserted his left forefinger deep into his unoccupied nostril and breathed noisily through his mouth. He had a neat side-parting. His hair was slicked down with Ayurvedic oil. The chiclets were his to *hold* before the doctor saw him, and to consume after. All was well with the world. Perhaps he was a little too young to know that Atmosphere in Waiting Room, plus Screams from Behind Curtain, ought logically to add up to a Healthy Fear of Dr V. V.

A rat with bristly shoulders made several busy journeys between the doctor's room and the bottom of the cupboard in the waiting room.

A nurse appeared and disappeared through the tattered-curtained doctor's door. She wielded strange weapons. A tiny vial. A rectangle of glass with blood smeared on it. A test tube of sparkling, back-lit urine. A stainless-steel tray of boiled needles. The hairs on her leg were pressed like coiled wires against her translucent white stockings. The box heels of her scuffed white sandals were worn away on the insides, and caused her feet to slope in, towards each other. Shiny black hairpins, like straightened snakes, clamped her starched nurse's cap to her oily head.

She appeared to have rat-filters on her glasses. She didn't seem to notice the bristly shouldered rat even when it scuttled right past her feet. She called out names in a deep voice, like a man's: 'A. Ninan . . . S. Kusumalatha . . . B. V. Roshini . . . N. Ambady.' She ignored the alarmed, spiralling air.

Estha's eyes were frightened saucers. He was mesmerized by the *Doctor is IN Doctor is OUT* sign.

A tide of panic rose in Rahel.

'Ammu, once again let's try.'

Ammu held the back of Rahel's head with one hand. With her thumb in her handkerchief she blocked the beadless nostril. All eyes in the waiting room were on Rahel. It was to be the performance of her life. Estha's expression prepared to blow its nose. Furrows gathered on his forehead and he took a deep breath.

Rahel summoned all her strength. *Please God, please make it come out.* From the soles of her feet, from the bottom of her heart, she blew into her mother's handkerchief.

And in a rush of snot and relief, it emerged. A little mauve bead in a glistening bed of slime. As proud as a pearl in an oyster. Children gathered around to admire it. The boy that was playing with the sign was scornful.

'I could easily do that!' he announced.

'Try it and see what a slap you'll get,' his mother said.

'Miss Rahel!' the nurse shouted and looked around.

'It's out!' Ammu said to the nurse. 'It's come out.' She held up her crumpled handkerchief.

The nurse had no idea what she meant.

'It's all right. We're leaving,' Ammu said. 'The bead's out.'

'Next,' the nurse said, and closed her eyes behind her rat-filters. ('It takes all kinds,' she told herself.) 'S. V. S. Kurup!'

The scornful boy set up a howl as his mother pushed him into the doctor's room.

Rahel and Estha left the clinic triumphantly. Little Lenin remained behind to have his nostril probed by Dr Verghese Verghese's cold steel implements, and his mother probed by other, softer ones.

That was Lenin then.

Now he had a house and a Bajaj scooter. A wife and an *issue.*

Rahel handed Comrade Pillai back the sachet of photographs and tried to leave.

'One mint,' Comrade Pillai said. He was like a flasher in a hedge. Enticing people with his nipples and then forcing pictures of his son on them. He flipped through the pack of photographs (a pictorial guide to Lenin's Life-in-a-Minute) to the last one. '*Orkunnundo?*'

It was an old black and white picture. One that Chacko took with the Rolleiflex camera that Margaret Kochamma had brought him as a Christmas present. All four of them were in it. Lenin, Estha, Sophie Mol and herself, standing in the front verandah of the Ayemenem House. Behind them Baby Kochamma's Christmas trimmings hung in loops from the ceiling. A cardboard star was tied to a bulb. Lenin, Rahel and Estha looked like frightened animals that had been caught in the headlights of a car. Knees pressed together, smiles frozen on their faces, arms pinned to their sides, chests swivelled to face the photograph. As though standing sideways was a sin.

Only Sophie Mol, with First World panache, had prepared herself, for her biological father's photo, a face. She had turned her eyelids inside out so that her eyes looked like pink-veined flesh petals (grey in a black-and white photograph). She wore a set of protruding false teeth cut from the yellow rind of a sweetlime. Her tongue pushed through the trap of teeth and had Mammachi's silver thimble fitted on the end of it. (She had hijacked it the day she arrived, and vowed to spend her holidays drinking only from a thimble.) She held out a lit candle in each hand. One leg of her denim bellbottoms was rolled up to expose a white, bony knee on which a face had been drawn. Minutes before that picture was taken, she had finished explaining patiently to Estha and Rahel (arguing away any evidence to the contrary, photographs, memories) how there was a pretty good chance that they were bastards, and what bastard really meant. This had entailed an involved, though somewhat inaccurate description of sex. 'See what they do is . . .'

That was only days before she died.

Sophie Mol.

Thimble-drinker.

Coffin-cartwheeler.

She arrived on the Bombay–Cochin flight. Hatted, bell-bottomed and Loved from the Beginning.

6

Cochin Kangaroos

At Cochin Airport, Rahel's new knickers were polka-dotted and still crisp. The rehearsals had been rehearsed. It was the Day of the Play. The culmination of the *What Will Sophie Mol Think?* week.

In the morning at the Hotel Sea Queen, Ammu – who had dreamed at night of dolphins and a deep blue – helped Rahel to put on her frothy Airport Frock. It was one of those baffling aberrations in Ammu's taste, a cloud of stiff yellow lace with tiny silver sequins and a bow on each shoulder. The frilled skirt was underpinned with buckram to make it flare. Rahel worried that it didn't really match her sunglasses.

Ammu held out the crisp matching knickers for her. Rahel, with her hands on Ammu's shoulders, climbed into her new knickers (left leg, right leg) and gave Ammu a kiss on each dimple (left cheek, right cheek). The elastic snapped softly against her stomach.

'Thank you, Ammu,' Rahel said.

'Thank you?' Ammu said.

'For my new frock and knickers,' Rahel said.

Ammu smiled. 'You're welcome, my sweetheart,' she said, but sadly.

You're welcome, my sweetheart.

The moth on Rahel's heart lifted a downy leg. Then put it back. Its little leg was cold. *A little less her mother loved her.*

The Sea Queen room smelled of eggs and filter coffee.

On the way to the car, Estha carried the Eagle vacuum flask with the tap water. Rahel carried the Eagle vacuum flask with the boiled water. Eagle vacuum flasks had Vacuum Eagles on them, with their wings spread, and a globe in their talons. Vacuum Eagles, the twins believed, watched the world all day and flew around their flasks all night. As silently as owls they flew, with the moon on their wings.

Estha was wearing a long-sleeved red shirt with a pointed collar and black drainpipe trousers. His puff looked crisp and surprised. Like well-whipped eggwhite.

Estha – with some basis, it must be admitted – said that Rahel looked stupid in her airport frock. Rahel slapped him, and he slapped her back.

They weren't speaking to each other at the airport.

Chacko, who usually wore a mundu, was wearing a funny tight suit and a shining smile. Ammu straightened his tie, which was odd and sideways. It had had its breakfast and was satisfied.

Ammu said, 'What's happened suddenly – to our Man of the Masses?'

But she said it with her dimples, because Chacko was so bursty. So very happy.

Chacko didn't slap her.

So she didn't slap him back.

From the Sea Queen florist Chacko had bought two red roses which he held carefully.

Fatly.

Fondly.

The airport shop, run by the Kerala Tourism Development Corporation, was crammed with Air India Maharajahs (small medium large), sandalwood elephants (small medium large) and papier-mâché masks of kathakali dancers (small medium large).

The smell of cloying sandalwood and terrycotton armpits (small medium large) hung in the air.

In the Arrivals Lounge, there were four life-sized cement kangaroos with cement pouches that said USE ME. In their pouches, instead of cement joeys, they had cigarette stubs, used matchsticks, bottle-caps, peanut shells, crumpled paper cups and cockroaches.

Red betel spit stains spattered their kangaroo stomachs like fresh wounds.

Red-mouthed smiles the Airport Kangaroos had.

And pink-edged ears.

They looked as though if you pressed them they might say 'Ma-ma' in empty battery voices.

When Sophie Mol's plane appeared in the skyblue Bombay–Cochin sky, the crowd pushed against the iron railing to see more of everything.

The Arrivals Lounge was a press of love and eagerness, because the Bombay–Cochin flight was the flight that all the Foreign Returnees came home on.

Their families had come to meet them. From all over Kerala. On long bus journeys. From Ranni, from Kumili, from Vizhinjam, from Uzhavoor. Some of them had camped at the airport overnight, and had brought their food with them. And tapioca chips and chakka velaichathu for the way back.

They were all there – the deaf ammoomas, the cantankerous, arthritic appoopans, the pining wives, scheming uncles, children with the runs. The fiancées to be reassessed. The teacher's husband still waiting for his Saudi visa. The teacher's husband's sisters waiting for their dowries. The wire-bender's pregnant wife.

'Mostly sweeper class,' Baby Kochamma said grimly, and looked away while a mother, not wanting to give up her Good Place near the railing, aimed her distracted baby's penis into an empty bottle while he smiled and waved at the people around him.

'Sssss . . .' his mother hissed. First persuasively, then savagely. But her baby thought he was the Pope. He smiled and waved and smiled and waved. With his penis in a bottle.

'Don't forget that you are Ambassadors of India,' Baby Kochamma told Rahel and Estha. 'You're going to form their First Impression of your country.'

Two-egg Twin Ambassadors. Their Excellencies Ambassador E(lvis). Pelvis, and Ambassador S(tick). Insect.

In her stiff lace dress and her fountain in a Love-in-Tokyo, Rahel looked like an Airport Fairy with appalling taste. She was hemmed in by humid hips (as she would be once again, at a funeral in a yellow church) and grim eagerness. She had her grandfather's moth on her heart. She turned away from the screaming steel bird in the skyblue sky that had her cousin in it, and what she saw was this: red-mouthed roos with ruby smiles moved cemently across the airport floor.

Heel and Toe
Heel and Toe

Long flatfeet.

Airport garbage in their baby bins.

The smallest one stretched its neck like people in English films who loosen their ties after office. The middle one rummaged in her pouch for a long cigarette stub to smoke. She found an old cashew nut in a dim plastic bag. She gnawed it with her front teeth like a rodent. The large one wobbled the standing up sign that said *Kerala Tourism Development Corporation Welcomes You* with a kathakali dancer doing a namasté. Another sign, unwobbled by a kangaroo, said: *emocleW ot eht ecipS tsaoC fo aidnI.*

Urgently, Ambassador Rahel burrowed through the press of people to her brother and co-Ambassador.

Estha look! Look Estha look!

Ambassador Estha wouldn't. Didn't want to. He watched the bumpy landing with his tap-water Eagle flask slung around him, and a bottomless-bottomful feeling: the Orangedrink Lemon-drink Man knew where to find him. In the factory in Ayemenem. On the banks of the Meenachal.

Ammu watched with her handbag.

Chacko with his roses.

Baby Kochamma with her sticking out neckmole.

Then the Bombay–Cochin people came out. From the cool air into the hot air. Crumpled people uncrumpled on their way to the Arrivals Lounge.

And there they were, the Foreign Returnees, in wash'n'wear suits and rainbow sunglasses. With an end to grinding poverty in their Aristocrat suitcases. With cement roofs for their thatched houses, and geysers for their parents' bathrooms. With sewage systems and septic tanks. Maxis and high heels. Puff sleeves and lipstick. Mixy-grinders and automatic flashes for their cameras. With keys to count, and cupboards to lock. With a hunger for kappa and meen vevichathu that they hadn't eaten for so long. With love and a lick of shame that their families who had come to meet them were so . . . so . . . gawkish. *Look at the way they dressed! Surely they had more suitable airport wear! Why did Malayalees have such awful teeth?*

And the airport itself! More like the local bus depot! The birdshit on the building! Oh the spitstains on the kangeroos!

Oho! Going to the dogs India is.

When long bus journeys, and overnight stays at the airport, were met by love and a lick of shame, small cracks appeared, which would grow and grow, and before they knew it, the

Foreign Returnees would be trapped outside the History House, and have their dreams redreamed.

Then, there, among the wash'n'wear suits and shiny suitcases, Sophie Mol.

Thimble-drinker.

Coffin-cartwheeler.

She walked down the runway, the smell of London in her hair. Yellow bottoms of bells flapped backwards around her ankles. Long hair floated out from under her straw hat. One hand in her mother's. The other swinging like a soldier's (lef, lef, lefrightlef).

There was
A girl
Tall and
Thin and
Fair
Her hair
Her hair
Was the delicate colourov
Gin–nnn–ger (leftleft, right)
There was
A girl –

Margaret Kochamma told her to Stoppit.

So she Stoppited.

Ammu said, 'Can you see her, Rahel?'

She turned around to find her crisp-knickered daughter communing with cement marsupials. She went and fetched her, scoldingly. Chacko said he couldn't take Rahel on his shoulders because he was already carrying something. Two roses red.

Fatly.

Fondly.

When Sophie Mol walked into the Arrivals Lounge, Rahel, overcome by excitement and resentment, pinched Estha hard. His skin between her nails. Estha gave her a Chinese Bangle, twisting the skin on her wrist different ways with each of his hands. Her skin became a welt and hurt. When she licked it, it tasted of salt. The spit on her wrist was cool and comfortable.

Ammu never noticed.

Across the tall iron railing that separated Meeters from the Met, and Greeters from the Gret, Chacko, beaming, bursting through his suit and sideways tie, bowed to his new daughter and ex-wife.

In his mind, Estha said, 'Bow.'

'Hello, ladies,' Chacko said in his Reading Aloud voice (last night's voice in which he said, *Love. Madness. Hope. Infinnate Joy*). 'And how was your journey?'

And the Air was full of Thoughts and Things to Say. But at times like these, only the Small Things are ever said. The Big Things lurk unsaid inside.

'Say Hello and How d'you do?' Margaret Kochamma said to Sophie Mol.

'Hello and How d'you do?' Sophie Mol said through the iron railing, to everyone in particular.

'One for you and one for you,' Chacko said with his roses.

'And Thank you?' Margaret Kochamma said to Sophie Mol.

'And Thank you?' Sophie Mol said to Chacko, mimicking her mother's question mark.

Margaret Kochamma shook her a little for her impertinence.

'You're welcome,' Chacko said. 'Now let me introduce everybody.' Then, more for the benefit of onlookers and eavesdroppers, because Margaret Kochamma needed no introduction really, 'My wife, Margaret.'

Margaret Kochamma smiled and wagged her rose at him. *Ex-wife, Chacko!* Her lips formed the words, though her voice never spoke them.

Anybody could see that Chacko was a proud and happy man to have had a wife like Margaret. White. In a flowered, printed frock with legs underneath. And brown back-freckles on her back. And arm-freckles on her arms.

But around her, the air was sad, somehow. And behind the smile in her eyes, the Grief was a fresh, shining blue. Because of a calamitous car crash. Because of a Joe-shaped hole in the Universe.

'Hello, all,' she said. 'I feel I've known you for years.'

Hello wall.

'My daughter, Sophie,' Chacko said, and laughed a small, nervous laugh that was worried, in case Margaret Kochamma said, 'Ex-daughter.' But she didn't. It was an easy-to-understand laugh. Not like the Orangedrink Lemondrink Man's laugh that Estha hadn't understood.

''llo,' Sophie Mol said.

She was taller than Estha. And bigger. Her eyes were bluegreyblue. Her pale skin was the colour of beach sand. But her hatted hair was beautiful, deep red-brown. And yes (oh yes!) she had Pappachi's nose waiting inside hers. An Imperial Entomologist's nose-within-a-nose. A moth-lover's nose. She carried her Made-in-England go-go bag that she loved.

'Ammu, my sister,' Chacko said.

Ammu said a grown-up's Hello to Margaret Kochamma and a children's Hell-oh to Sophie Mol. Rahel watched hawk-eyed to try and gauge how much Ammu loved Sophie Mol, but couldn't.

Laughter rambled through the Arrivals Lounge like a sudden breeze. Adoor Basi, the most popular, best-loved comedian in Malayalam cinema, had just arrived (Bombay–Cochin). Burdened with a number of small unmanageable packages and unabashed public adulation, he felt obliged to perform. He kept dropping his packages and saying, '*Ende Deivomay! Eee sadhanangal!*'

Estha laughed a high, delighted laugh.

'Ammu look! Adoor Basi's dropping his things!' Estha said. 'He can't even carry his things!'

'He's doing it deliberately,' Baby Kochamma said in a strange new British accent. 'Just *ignore* him.'

'He's a filmactor,' she explained to Margaret Kochamma and Sophie Mol, making Adoor Basi sound like a Mactor who did occasionally Fil. 'Just trying to attract attention,' Baby Kochamma said, and resolutely refused to have her attention attracted.

But Baby Kochamma was wrong. Adoor Basi *wasn't* trying to attract attention. He was only trying to deserve the attention that he had already attracted.

'My aunt, Baby,' Chacko said.

Sophie Mol was puzzled. She regarded Baby Kochamma with a beady-eyed interest. She knew of cow babies and dog babies. Bear babies – yes. (She would soon point out to Rahel a bat baby.) But *aunt* babies confounded her.

Baby Kochamma said, 'Hello, Margaret,' and 'Hello, Sophie Mol.' She said Sophie Mol was so beautiful that she reminded her of a wood-sprite. Of Ariel.

'D'you know who Ariel was?' Baby Kochamma asked Sophie Mol. 'Ariel in *The Tempest*?'

Sophie Mol said she didn't.

'"Where the bee sucks there suck I?"' Baby Kochamma said.

Sophie Mol said she didn't.

'"In a cowslip's bell I lie"?'

Sophie Mol said she didn't.

'Shakespeare's *The Tempest*?' Baby Kochamma persisted.

All this was of course primarily to announce her credentials to Margaret Kochamma. To set herself apart from the Sweeper Class.

'She's trying to boast,' Ambassador E. Pelvis whispered in Ambassador S. Insect's ear. Ambassador Rahel's giggle escaped in a blue-green bubble (the colour of a jackfruit fly) and burst in the hot airport air. Pffft! was the sound it made.

Baby Kochamma saw it, and knew that it was Estha who had started it.

'And now for the VIPs,' Chacko said (still using his Reading Aloud voice).

'My nephew, Esthappen.'

'Elvis Presley,' Baby Kochamma said for revenge. 'I'm afraid we're a little behind the times here.' Everyone looked at Estha and laughed.

From the soles of Ambassador Estha's beige and pointy shoes an angry feeling rose and stopped around his heart.

'How d'you do, Esthappen?' Margaret Kochamma said.

'Finethankyou.' Estha's voice was sullen.

'Estha,' Ammu said affectionately, 'when someone says How d'you do? You're supposed to say How d'you do? back. Not "Fine, thank you." Come on, say How do YOU do?'

Ambassador Estha looked at Ammu.

'Go on,' Ammu said to Estha. 'How do YOU do?'

Estha's sleepy eyes were stubborn.

In Malayalam Ammu said, 'Did you hear what I said?'

Ambassador Estha felt bluegreyblue eyes on him, and an Imperial Entomologist's nose. He didn't have a How do YOU do? in him.

'Esthappen!' Ammu said. And an angry feeling rose in her and stopped around her heart. A Far More Angry Than Necessary feeling. She felt somehow humiliated by this public revolt in her area of jurisdiction. She had wanted a smooth performance. A prize for her children in the Indo-British Behaviour Competition.

Chacko said to Ammu in Malayalam, 'Please. Later. Not now.'

And Ammu's angry eyes on Estha said, *All right. Later.*

And Later became a horrible, menacing, goose-bumpy word.

Lay.Ter.

Like a deep-sounding bell in a mossy well. Shivery, and furred. Like moth's feet.

The Play had gone bad. Like pickle in the monsoon.

'And my niece,' Chacko said. 'Where's Rahel?' He looked around and couldn't find her. Ambassador Rahel, unable to cope with see-sawing changes in her life, had ravelled herself like a sausage into the dirty airport curtain, and wouldn't unravel. A sausage with Bata sandals.

'Just ignore her,' Ammu said. 'She's just trying to attract attention.'

Ammu too was wrong. Rahel was only trying to not attract the attention that she deserved.

'Hello, Rahel,' Margaret Kochamma said to the dirty airport curtain.

'How do YOU do?' the dirty curtain replied in a mumble.

'Aren't you going to come out and say Hello?' Margaret Kochamma said in a kind-schoolteacher voice. (Like Miss Mitten's before she saw Satan in their eyes.)

Ambassador Rahel wouldn't come out of the curtain because she couldn't. She couldn't because she couldn't. Because Everything was wrong. And soon there would be a Lay Ter for both her and Estha.

Full of furred moths and icy butterflies. And deep-sounding bells. And moss.

And a Nowl.

The dirty airport curtain was a great comfort and a darkness and a shield.

'Just ignore her,' Ammu said, and smiled tightly.

Rahel's mind was full of millstones with bluegreyblue eyes.

Ammu loved her even less now. And it had come down to Brass Tacks with Chacko.

'Here comes the baggage!' Chacko said brightly. Glad to get away.

'Come, Sophiekins, let's get your bags.'

Sophiekins.

Estha watched as they walked along the railing, pushing through the crowds that moved aside, intimidated by Chacko's suit and sideways tie and his generally bursty demeanour. Because of the size of his stomach, Chacko carried himself in a way that made him appear to be walking uphill all the time. Negotiating optimistically the steep, slippery slopes of life. He walked on this side of the railing, Margaret Kochamma and Sophie Mol on that.

Sophiekins.

The Sitting Man with the cap and epaulettes, also intimidated by Chacko's suit and sideways tie, allowed him in to the baggage claim section.

When there was no railing left between them, Chacko kissed Margaret Kochamma, and then picked Sophie Mol up.

'The last time I did this I got a wet shirt for my pains,' Chacko said and laughed. He hugged her and hugged her and hugged her. He kissed her bluegreyblue eyes, her entomologist's nose, her hatted redbrown hair.

Then Sophie Mol said to Chacko, 'Ummm . . . excuse me? D'you think you could put me down now? I'm ummm . . . not really used to being carried.'

So Chacko put her down.

Ambassador Estha saw (with stubborn eyes) that Chacko's suit was suddenly looser, less bursty.

And while Chacko got the bags, at the dirty-curtained window Lay Ter became Now.

Estha saw how Baby Kochamma's neckmole licked its chops and throbbed with delicious anticipation. *Der-dhoom, der-dhoom.* It changed colour like a chameleon, Der-green, der-blueblack, der-mustardyellow.

Twins for tea
It would bea

'All right,' Ammu said. 'That's enough. Both of you. Come *out* of there, Rahel!'

Inside the curtain, Rahel closed her eyes and thought of the green river, of the quiet deep-swimming fish, and the gossamer wings of the dragonflies (that could see behind them) in the sun. She thought of her luckiest fishing rod that Velutha had made for her. Yellow bamboo with a float that dipped every time a foolish fish enquired. She thought of Velutha and wished she was with him.

Then Estha unravelled her. The cement kangaroos were watching.

Ammu looked at them. The Air was quiet except for the sound of Baby Kochamma's throbbing neckmole.

'So,' Ammu said.

And it was really a question. So?

And it hadn't an answer.

Ambassador Estha looked down, and saw that his shoes (from where the angry feelings rose) were beige and pointy. Ambassador Rahel looked down and saw that in her Bata sandals her toes were trying to disconnect themselves. Twitching to join someone else's feet. And that she couldn't stop them. Soon she'd be without toes and have a bandage like the leper at the level crossing.

'If you ever,' Ammu said, 'and I *mean* this, EVER, ever again disobey me in Public, I will see to it that you are sent away to somewhere where you will jolly well learn to behave. Is that clear?'

When Ammu was really angry, she said Jolly Well. Jolly Well was a deeply well with larfing dead people in it.

'Is. That. Clear?' Ammu said again.

Frightened eyes and a fountain looked back at Ammu.

Sleepy eyes and a surprised puff looked back at Ammu.

Two heads nodded three times.

Yes. It's. Clear.

But Baby Kochamma was dissatisfied with the fizzling out of a situation that had been so full of potential. She tossed her head.

'As if!' she said.

As if!

Ammu turned to her, and the turn of her head was a question.

'It's useless,' Baby Kochamma said. 'They're sly. They're uncouth. Deceitful. They're growing wild. You can't manage them.'

Ammu turned back to Estha and Rahel and her eyes were blurred jewels.

'Everybody says that children need a Baba. And I say no. Not *my* children. D'you know why?'

Two heads nodded.

'Why. Tell me,' Ammu said.

And not together, but almost, Esthappen and Rahel said: 'Because you're our Ammu and our Baba and you love us Double.'

'More than Double,' Ammu said. 'So remember what I told you. People's feelings are precious. And when you disobey me in Public, *every*body gets the wrong impression.'

'What Ambassadors and a half you've been!' Baby Kochamma said.

Ambassador E. Pelvis and Ambassador S. Insect hung their heads.

'And the other thing, Rahel,' Ammu said, 'I think it's high time that you learned the difference between CLEAN and DIRTY. Especially in this country.'

Ambassador Rahel looked down.

'Your dress is – was – CLEAN,' Ammu said. 'That curtain is DIRTY. Those kangaroos are DIRTY. Your hands are DIRTY.'

Rahel was frightened by the way Ammu said CLEAN and DIRTY so loudly. As though she was talking to a deaf person.

'Now, I want you to go and say Hello *properly*,' Ammu said. 'Are you going to do that or not?'

Two heads nodded twice.

Ambassador Estha and Ambassador Rahel walked towards Sophie Mol.

'Where d'you think people are sent to Jolly Well Behave?' Estha asked Rahel in a whisper.

'To the Government,' Rahel whispered back, because she knew.

'How do you do?' Estha said to Sophie Mol loud enough for Ammu to hear.

'Just like a laddoo one pice two,' Sophie Mol whispered to Estha. She had learned this in school from a Pakistani classmate.

Estha looked at Ammu.

Ammu's look said, *Never Mind Her As Long As You've Done The Right Thing.*

On their way across the airport car park, Hotweather crept into their clothes and dampened crisp knickers. The children lagged behind, weaving through parked cars and taxis.

'Does Yours hit you?' Sophie Mol asked.

Rahel and Estha, unsure of the politics of this, said nothing.

'Mine does,' Sophie Mol said invitingly. 'Mine even Slaps.'

'Ours doesn't,' Estha said loyally.

'Lucky,' Sophie Mol said.

Lucky rich boy with porketmunny. And a grandmother's factory to inherit. No worries.

They walked past the Class III Airport Workers' Union token one-day hunger strike. And past the people watching the Class III Airport Workers' Union token one-day hunger strike.

And past the people watching the people watching the people.

A small tin sign on a big banyan tree said *For VD Sex Complaints contact Dr O. K. Joy.*

'Who d'you love Most in the World?' Rahel asked Sophie Mol.

'Joe,' Sophie Mol said without hesitation. 'My dad. He died two months ago. We've come here to Recover from the Shock.'

'But Chacko's your dad,' Estha said.

'He's just my *real* dad,' Sophie Mol said. 'Joe's my dad. He never hits. Hardly ever.'

'How can he hit if he's dead?' Estha asked reasonably.

'Where's *your* dad?' Sophie Mol wanted to know.

'He's . . .' and Rahel looked at Estha for help.

'. . . not here.' Estha said.

'Shall I tell you my list?' Rahel asked Sophie Mol.

'If you like,' Sophie Mol said.

Rahel's 'list' was an attempt to order chaos. She revised it constantly, torn forever between love and duty. It was by no means a true gauge of her feelings.

'First Ammu and Chacko,' Rahel said. 'Then Mammachi –'

'Our grandmother,' Estha clarified.

'*More* than your brother?' Sophie Mol asked.

'We don't count,' Rahel said. 'And anyway he might change. Ammu says.'

'How d'you mean? Change into what?' Sophie Mol asked.

'Into a Male Chauvinist Pig,' Rahel said.

'Very unlikely,' Estha said.

'Anyway, after Mammachi, Velutha, and then –'

'Who's Velutha?' Sophie Mol wanted to know.

'A man we love,' Rahel said. 'And after Velutha, you,' Rahel said.

'Me? What d'you love me for?' Sophie Mol said.

'Because we're firstcousins. So I have to,' Rahel said piously.

'But you don't even know me,' Sophie Mol said. 'And anyway, I don't love you.'

'But you will, when you come to know me,' Rahel said confidently.

'I doubt it,' Estha said.

'Why not?' Sophie Mol said.

'Because,' Estha said. 'And anyway she's most probably going to be a dwarf.'

As though loving a dwarf was completely out of the question.

'I'm not,' Rahel said.

'You are,' Estha said.

'I'm not.'

'You are.'

'I'm not.'

'You are. We're twins,' Estha explained to Sophie Mol, 'and just see how much shorter she is.'

Rahel obligingly took a deep breath, threw her chest out and stood back to back with Estha in the airport car park, for Sophie Mol to see just how much shorter she was.

'Maybe you'll be a midget,' Sophie Mol suggested. 'That's taller than a dwarf and shorter than a . . . Human Being.'

The silence was unsure of this compromise.

In the doorway of the Arrivals Lounge, a shadowy, red-mouthed roo-shaped silhouette waved a cemently paw only at Rahel. Cement kisses whirred through the air like small helicopters.

'D'you know how to sashay?' Sophie Mol wanted to know.

'No. We don't sashay in India,' Ambassador Estha said.

'Well in England we do,' Sophie Mol said. 'All the models do. On television. Look – it's easy.'

And the three of them, led by Sophie Mol, sashayed across the airport car park, swaying like fashion models, Eagle flasks and Made-in-England go-go bags bumping around their hips. Damp dwarves walking tall.

Shadows followed them. Silver jets in a blue church sky, like moths in a beam of light.

The skyblue Plymouth with tailfins had a smile for Sophie Mol. A chromebumpered sharksmile.

A Paradise Pickles carsmile.

When she saw the carrier with the painted pickle bottles and the list of Paradise products, Margaret Kochamma said, 'Oh dear! I feel as though I'm in an advertisement!' She said Oh dear! a lot.

Oh dear! Oh dearohdear!

'I didn't know you did pineapple slices!' she said. 'Sophie loves pineapple, don't you, Soph?'

'Sometimes,' Soph said. 'And sometimes not.'

Margaret Kochamma climbed into the advertisement with her brown back-freckles and her arm-freckles and her flowered dress with legs underneath.

Sophie Mol sat in front between Chacko and Margaret Kochamma, just her hat peeping over the car seat. Because she was their daughter.

Rahel and Estha sat at the back.

The luggage was in the boot.

Boot was a lovely word. *Sturdy* was a terrible word.

Near Ettumanoor they passed a dead temple elephant, electrocuted by a high tension wire that had fallen on the road. An engineer from the Ettumanoor municipality was supervising the disposal of the carcass. They had to be careful because the decision would serve as precedent for all future Government Pachyderm Carcass Disposals. Not a matter to be treated lightly. There was a fire engine and some confused firemen. The municipal officer had a file and was shouting a lot. There was a Joy Ice Cream cart and a man selling peanuts in narrow cones of paper cleverly designed to hold not more than eight or nine nuts.

Sophie Mol said, 'Look, a dead elephant.'

Chacko stopped to ask whether it was by any chance Kochu Thomban (Little Tusker), the Ayemenem temple elephant who came to the Ayemenem House once a month for a coconut. They said it wasn't.

Relieved that it was a stranger, and not an elephant they knew, they drove on.

'Thang God,' Estha said.

'Than*k* God, Estha,' Baby Kochamma corrected him.

On the way, Sophie Mol learned to recognize the first whiff of the approaching stench of unprocessed rubber and to clamp her nostrils shut until long after the truck carrying it had driven past.

Baby Kochamma suggested a car song.

Estha and Rahel had to sing in English in obedient voices. Breezily. As though they hadn't been made to rehearse it all week long. Ambassador E. Pelvis and Ambassador S. Insect.

RejOice in the Lo-Ord Or-Orlways
And again I say re-jOice.

Their Prer NUN sea ayshun was perfect.

The Plymouth rushed through the green midday heat, promoting pickles on its roof, and the skyblue sky in its tailfins.

Just outside Ayemenem they drove into a cabbage-green butterfly (or perhaps it drove into them).

7

Wisdom Exercise Notebooks

In Pappachi's study, mounted butterflies and moths had disintegrated into small heaps of iridescent dust that powdered the bottom of their glass display cases, leaving the pins that had impaled them naked. Cruel. The room was rank with fungus and disuse. An old neon-green hula hoop hung from a wooden peg on the wall, a huge saint's discarded halo. A column of shining black ants walked across a windowsill, their bottoms tilted upwards, like a line of mincing chorus girls in a Busby Berkeley musical. Silhouetted against the sun. Buffed and beautiful.

Rahel (on a stool, on top of a table) rummaged in a book cupboard with dull, dirty glass panes. Her bare footprints were clear in the dust on the floor. They led from the door to the table (dragged to the bookshelf), to the stool (dragged to the table and lifted onto it). She was looking for something. Her life had a size and a shape now. She had half-moons under her eyes and a team of trolls on her horizon.

On the top shelf, the leather binding on Pappachi's set of *The Insect Wealth of India* had lifted off each book and buckled like corrugated asbestos. Silverfish tunnelled through the pages, burrowing arbitrarily from species to species, turning organized information into yellow lace.

Rahel groped behind the row of books and brought out hidden things.

A smooth seashell and a spiky one.

A plastic case for contact lenses. An orange pipette.

A silver crucifix on a string of beads. Baby Kochamma's rosary.

She held it up against the light. Each greedy bead grabbed its share of sun.

A shadow fell across the sunlit rectangle on the study floor. Rahel turned towards the door with her string of light.

'Imagine. It's still here. I stole it. After you were Returned.'

That word slipped out easily. *Returned.* As though that was what twins were meant for. To be borrowed and returned. Like library books.

Estha wouldn't look up. His mind was full of trains. He blocked the light from the door. An Estha-shaped hole in the Universe.

Behind the books, Rahel's puzzled fingers encountered something else. Another magpie had had the same idea. She brought it out and wiped the dust off with the sleeve of her shirt. It was a flat packet wrapped in clear plastic and stuck with Sellotape. A scrap of white paper inside it said *Esthappen and Rahel.* In Ammu's writing.

There were four tattered notebooks in it. On their covers they said *Wisdom Exercise Notebooks* with a place for *Name, School/College, Class, Subject.* Two had her name on them, and two Estha's.

Inside the back cover of one, something had been written in a child's handwriting. The laboured form of each letter and the irregular space between words was full of the struggle for control over the errant, self-willed pencil. The sentiment, in contrast, was lucid: *I Hate Miss Mitten and I Think Her gnickers are TORN.*

On the front of the book, Estha had rubbed out his surname with spit, and taken half the paper with it. Over the whole mess, he had written in pencil *Un-known.* Esthappen Un-known. (His surname postponed for the Time Being, while Ammu chose between her husband's name and her father's.) Next to *Class* it said: *6 years.* Next to *Subject* it said: *Story-writing.*

Rahel sat cross-legged (on the stool on the table).

'Esthappen Un-known,' she said. She opened the book and read aloud.

'When Ulyesses came home his son came and said father I thought you would not come back. many princes came and each wanted to marry Pen Lope, but Pen Lope said that the man who can stoot through the twelve rings can mary me. and everyone failed. and ulyesses came to the palace dressed liked a beggar and asked if he could try. the men all laughed at him and said if we cant do it you cant. ulyesses son stopped them and said let himtry and he took the bow and shot right through the twelve rings.'

Below this there were corrections from a previous lesson.

Ferus	Learned	Neither	Carriages	Bridge	Bearer	Fastened
Ferus	*Learned*	*Niether*	*Carriages*	*Bridge*	*Bearer*	*Fastened*
Ferus	*Learned*	*niether*				
Ferus	*Learned*	*Nieter*				

Laughter curled around the edges of Rahel's voice. '"Safety First,"' she announced. Ammu had drawn a wavy line down the length of the page with a red pen and written, *Margin? And joint handwriting in future, please!*

'When we walk on the road in the town,' cautious Estha's story went, *'we should always walk on the pavement. If you go on the pavement there is no traffic to cause accidnts, but on the main road there is so much dangerouse traffic that they can easily knock you down and make you senseless or a criple. If you break your head or back-bone you will be very unfortunate. policemen can direct the traffic so that there won't be too many invalids to go to hospitil. When we get out of the bus we should do so only after asking the conductor or we will be injured and make the doctors have*

a busy time. The job of a driver is very fatle His famly should be very angshios because the driver could easily be dead.'

'Morbid kid,' Rahel said to Estha. As she turned the page something reached into her throat, plucked her voice out, shook it down, and returned it without its laughing edges. Estha's next story was called *Little Ammu.*

In joint handwriting. The tails of the Ys and Gs were curled and looped. The shadow in the doorway stood very still.

'On Saturday we went to a bookshop in Kottayam to buy Ammu a present because her birthday is in 17th of novembre. We bote her a diary. We hid it in the coberd and then it began to be night. Then we said do you want to see your present she said yes I would like to see it. and we wrote on the paper For a Little Ammu with Love from Estha and Rahel and we gave it to Ammu and she said what a lovely present its just what I whanted and then we talked for a little while and we talked about the diary then we gave her a kiss and went to bed.

We talked with each other and went of to sleep. We had a little dream.

After some time I got up and I was very thirsty and I went to Ammu's room and said I am thirsty. Ammu gave me water and I was just going to my bed when Ammu called me and said come and sleep with me. and I lay at the back of Ammu and talked to Ammu and went of to sleep. After a little while I got up and we talked again and after that we had a mid-night feest. we had orange coffee bananana. afterwards Rahel came and we ate two more bananas and we gave a kiss to Ammu because it was her birthday afterwards we sang happy birthday. Then in the morning we had new cloths from Ammu as a back-present Rahel was a maharani and I was Little Nehru.'

Ammu had corrected the spelling mistakes, and below the essay had written: *If I am Talking to somebody, you may interrupt me only if it is very urgent. When you do, please say 'Excuse me'. I will punish you very severely if you disobey these instructions. Please complete your corrections.*

Little Ammu.

Who never completed *her* corrections.

Who had to pack her bags and leave. Because she had no Locusts Stand I. Because Chacko said she had destroyed enough already.

Who came back to Ayemenem with asthma and a rattle in her chest that sounded like a faraway man shouting.

Estha never saw her like that.

Wild. Sick. Sad.

The last time Ammu came back to Ayemenem, Rahel had just been expelled from Nazareth Convent (for decorating dung and slamming into seniors). Ammu had lost the latest of her succession of jobs – as a receptionist in a cheap hotel – because she had been ill and had missed too many days of work. The hotel couldn't afford that, they told her. They needed a healthier receptionist.

On that last visit, Ammu spent the morning with Rahel in her room. With the last of her meagre salary she had bought her daughter small presents wrapped in brown paper with coloured paper hearts pasted on. A packet of cigarette sweets, a tin Phantom pencil box and *Paul Bunyan* – a Junior Classics Illustrated comic. They were presents for a seven-year-old; Rahel was nearly eleven. It was as though Ammu believed that if she refused to acknowledge the passage of time, if she willed it to stand still in the lives of her twins, it would. As though sheer willpower was enough to suspend her children's childhoods until she could afford to have them living with her. Then they could take up from where they left off. Start again from seven. Ammu told Rahel that she had bought Estha a comic too, but that she'd kept it away for him until she got another job and could earn enough to rent a room for the three of them to stay together in. Then she'd go to Calcutta and fetch Estha, and he could have his comic. That day was not far off, Ammu said. It could happen *any* day. Soon rent would be no problem. She said she had applied for a UN job and they would all live in The Hague with a Dutch ayah to look after them. Or on the other hand, Ammu said, she might stay on in India and do what she had been planning to do all along – start a school. Choosing between a career in Education and a UN job wasn't easy, she said – but the thing to remember was that the very fact that she had a choice was a great privilege.

But for the Time Being, she said, until she made her decision, she was keeping Estha's presents away for him.

That whole morning Ammu talked incessantly. She asked Rahel questions, but never let her answer them. If Rahel tried to say something, Ammu would interrupt with a new thought or query. She seemed terrified of what adult thing her daughter might say and thaw Frozen Time. Fear made her garrulous. She kept it at bay with her babble.

She was swollen with cortisone, moonfaced, not the slender mother Rahel knew. Her skin was stretched over her puffy cheeks like shiny scar tissue that covers old vaccination marks. When she smiled, her dimples looked as though they hurt. Her curly hair had lost its sheen and hung around her swollen face like a dull curtain. She carried her breath in a glass inhaler in her tattered handbag. Brown Brovon fumes. Each breath she took was like a war won against the steely fist that was trying to squeeze the air from her lungs. Rahel watched her mother breathe. Each time she inhaled, the hollows near her collarbones grew steep and filled with shadows.

Ammu coughed up a wad of phlegm into her handkerchief and showed it to Rahel.

'You must always check it,' she whispered hoarsely, as though phlegm was an Arithmetic answer sheet that had to be revised before it was handed in. 'When it's white, it means it isn't ripe. When it's yellow and has a rotten smell, it's ripe and ready to be coughed out. Phlegm is like fruit. Ripe or raw. You have to be able to tell.'

Over lunch she belched like a truck-driver and said, 'Excuse me,' in a deep, unnatural voice. Rahel noticed that she had new, thick hairs in her eyebrows, long – like palps. Ammu smiled at the silence around the table as she picked fried emperor fish off the bone. She said that she felt like a road sign with birds shitting on her. She had an odd, feverish glitter in her eyes.

Mammachi asked her if she'd been drinking and suggested that she visit Rahel as seldom as possible.

Ammu got up from the table and left without saying a word. Not even goodbye. 'Go and see her off,' Chacko said to Rahel.

Rahel pretended she hadn't heard him. She went on with her fish. She thought of the phlegm and nearly retched. She hated her mother then. *Hated* her.

She never saw her again.

Ammu died in a grimy room in the Bharat Lodge in Alleppey, where she had gone for a job interview as someone's secretary. She died alone. With a noisy ceiling fan for company and no Estha to lie at the back of her and talk to her. She was thirty-one. Not old, not young, but a viable, die-able age.

She had woken up at night to escape from a familiar, recurrent dream in which policemen approached her with snicking scissors, wanting to hack off her hair. They did that in Kottayam to prostitutes whom they'd caught in the bazaar – branded them so that everybody would know them for what they were. *Veshyas.* So that new policemen on the beat would have no trouble identifying whom to harass. Ammu always noticed them in the market, the women with vacant eyes and forcibly shaved heads in the land where long, oiled hair was only for the morally upright.

That night in the lodge, Ammu sat up in the strange bed in the strange room in the strange town. She didn't know where she was, she recognized nothing around her. Only her fear was familiar. The faraway man inside her began to shout. This time the steely fist never loosened its grip. Shadows gathered like bats in the steep hollows near her collarbone.

The sweeper found her in the morning. He switched off the fan.

She had a deep blue sac under one eye that was bloated like a bubble. As though her eye had tried to do what her lungs couldn't. Some time close to midnight, the faraway man who lived in her chest had stopped shouting. A platoon of ants carried a dead cockroach sedately through the door, demonstrating what should be done with corpses.

The church refused to bury Ammu. On several counts. So Chacko hired a van to transport the body to the electric crematorium. He had her wrapped in a dirty bedsheet and laid out on a stretcher. Rahel thought she looked like a Roman Senator. *Et tu, Ammu!* she thought and smiled, remembering Estha.

It was odd driving through bright, busy streets with a dead Roman senator on the floor of the van. It made the blue sky bluer. Outside the van windows, people, like cut-out paper puppets, went on with their paper-puppet lives. Real life was inside the van. Where real death was. Over the jarring bumps and potholes in the road, Ammu's body jiggled and slid off the stretcher. Her head hit an iron bolt on the floor. She didn't wince or wake up. There was a hum in Rahel's head, and for the rest of the day Chacko had to shout at her if he wanted to be heard.

The crematorium had the same rotten, run-down air of a railway station, except that it was deserted. No trains, no crowds. Nobody except beggars, derelicts and the police-custody dead were cremated there. People who died with nobody to lie at the back of them and talk to them. When Ammu's turn came, Chacko held Rahel's hand tightly. She didn't want her hand held. She used the slickness of crematorium sweat to slither out of his grip. No one else from the family was there.

The steel door of the incinerator went up and the muted hum of the eternal fire became a red roaring. The heat lunged out at them like a famished beast. Then Rahel's Ammu was fed to it. Her hair, her skin, her smile. Her voice. The way she used Kipling to love her children before putting them to bed: *We be of one blood, ye and I.* Her good night kiss. The way she held their faces steady with one hand (squashed-cheeked, fish-mouthed) while she parted and combed their hair with the other. The way she held knickers out for Rahel to climb into. *Left leg, right leg.* All this was fed to the beast, and it was satisfied.

She was their Ammu *and* their Baba and she had loved them Double.

The door of the furnace clanged shut. There were no tears.

The crematorium 'In-charge' had gone down the road for a cup of tea and didn't come back for twenty minutes. That's how long Chacko and Rahel had to wait for the pink receipt that would entitle them to collect Ammu's remains. Her ashes. The grit from her bones. The teeth from her smile. The whole of her crammed into a little clay pot. Receipt No. Q498673.

Rahel asked Chacko how the crematorium management knew which ashes were whose. Chacko said they must have a system.

Had Estha been with them, he would have kept the receipt. He was the Keeper of Records. The natural custodian of bus tickets, bank receipts, cash memos, cheque book stubs. Little Man. He lived in a Cara-van. Dum dum.

But Estha wasn't with them. Everybody decided it was better this way. They wrote to him instead. Mammachi said Rahel should write too. Write what? *My dear Estha, How are you? I am well. Ammu died yesterday.*

Rahel never wrote to him. There are things that you can't

do – like writing letters to a part of yourself. To your feet or hair. Or heart.

In Pappachi's study, Rahel (not old, not young), with floor-dust on her feet, looked up from the Wisdom Exercise Notebook and saw that Esthappen Un-known was gone.

She climbed down (off the stool, off the table) and walked out to the verandah.

She saw Estha's back disappearing through the gate.

It was midmorning and about to rain again. The green – in the last moments of that strange, glowing, preshower light – was fierce.

A cock crowed in the distance and its voice separated into two. Like a sole peeling off an old shoe.

Rahel stood there with her tattered Wisdom notebooks. In the front verandah of an old house, below a button-eyed bison head, where years ago, on the day that Sophie Mol came, *Welcome Home, Our Sophie Mol* was performed.

Things can change in a day.

8

Welcome Home, Our Sophie Mol

It was a grand old house, the Ayemenem House, but aloof-looking. As though it had little to do with the people that lived in it. Like an old man with rheumy eyes watching children play, seeing only transience in their shrill elation and their whole-hearted commitment to life.

The steep, tiled roof had grown dark and mossy with age and rain. The triangular wooden frames fitted into the gables were intricately carved, the light that slanted through them and fell in patterns on the floor was full of secrets. Wolves. Flowers. Iguanas. Changing shape as the sun moved through the sky. Dying punctually, at dusk.

The doors had not two, but four shutters of panelled teak so that in the old days, ladies could keep the bottom half closed, lean their elbows on the ledge and bargain with visiting vendors without betraying themselves below the waist. Technically, they could buy carpets, or bangles, with their breasts covered and their bottoms bare. Technically.

Nine steep steps led from the driveway up to the front verandah. The elevation gave it the dignity of a stage and everything that happened there took on the aura and significance of performance. It overlooked Baby Kochamma's ornamental garden, the gravel driveway looped around it, sloping down towards the bottom of the slight hill that the house stood on.

It was a deep verandah, cool even at midday, when the sun was at its scorching best.

When the red cement floor was laid, the egg white from nearly nine hundred eggs went into it. It took a high polish.

Below the stuffed, button-eyed bison head, with the portraits of her father-in-law and mother-in-law on either side, Mammachi sat in a low wicker chair at a wicker table on which stood a green glass vase with a single stem of purple orchids curving from it.

The afternoon was still and hot. The Air was waiting.

Mammachi held a gleaming violin under her chin. Her opaque fifties sunglasses were black and slanty-eyed, with rhinestones on the corners of the frames. Her sari was starched and perfumed. Off-white and gold. Her diamond earrings shone in her ears like tiny chandeliers. Her ruby rings were loose. Her pale, fine skin was creased like cream on cooling milk and dusted with tiny red moles. She was beautiful. Old, unusual, regal.

Blind Mother Widow with a violin.

In her younger years with prescience, and good management, Mammachi had collected all her falling hair in a small, embroidered purse that she kept on her dressing table. When there was enough of it, she made it into a netted bun which she kept hidden in a locker with her jewellery. A few years earlier, when her hair began to thin and silver, to give it body, she wore her jet-black bun pinned to her small, silver head. In her book this was perfectly acceptable, since all the hair was hers. At night, when she took off her bun, she allowed her grandchildren to plait her remaining hair into a tight, oiled, grey rat's tail with a rubber band at the end. One plaited her hair, while the other counted her uncountable moles. They took turns.

On her scalp, carefully hidden by her scanty hair, Mammachi had raised, crescent-shaped ridges. Scars of old beatings from an old marriage. Her brass vase scars.

She played *Lentement* – a movement from the Suite 1 in D/G of

Handel's *Water Music*. Behind her slanted sunglasses, her useless eyes were closed, but she could see the music as it left her violin and lifted into the afternoon like smoke.

Inside her head, it was like a room with dark drapes drawn across a bright day.

As she played, her mind wandered back over the years to her first batch of professional pickles. How beautiful they had looked! Bottled and sealed, standing on a table near the head of her bed, so they'd be the first thing she would touch in the morning when she woke up. She had gone to bed early that night, but woke a little after midnight. She groped for them, and her anxious fingers came away with a film of oil. The pickle bottles stood in a pool of oil. There was oil everywhere. In a ring under her vacuum flask. Under her Bible. All over her bedside table. The pickled mangoes had absorbed oil and expanded, making the bottles leak.

Mammachi consulted the book that Chacko bought her, *Homescale Preservations*, but it offered no solutions. Then she dictated a letter to Annamma Chandy's brother-in-law, who was the Regional Manager of Padma Pickles in Bombay. He suggested that she increase the proportion of preservative that she used. And the salt. That had helped, but didn't solve the problem entirely. Even now, after all those years, Paradise Pickles' bottles still leaked a little. It was imperceptible, but they did still leak, and on long journeys their labels became oily and transparent. The pickles themselves continued to be a little on the salty side.

Mammachi wondered whether she would ever master the art of perfect preservation, and whether Sophie Mol would like some iced grape crush. Some cold purple juice in a glass.

Then she thought of Margaret Kochamma and the languid, liquid notes of Handel's music grew shrill and angry.

Mammachi had never met Margaret Kochamma. But she despised her anyway. *Shopkeeper's daughter* – was how Margaret

Kochamma was filed away in Mammachi's mind. Mammachi's world was arranged that way. If she was invited to a wedding in Kottayam, she would spend the whole time whispering to whoever she went with, 'The bride's maternal grandfather was my father's carpenter. Kunjukutty Eapen? His great-grandmother's sister was just a midwife in Trivandrum. My husband's family used to own this whole hill.'

Of course Mammachi would have despised Margaret Kochamma even if she had been heir to the throne of England. It wasn't just her working-class background Mammachi resented. She hated Margaret Kochamma for being Chacko's wife. She hated her for leaving him. But would have hated her even more had she stayed.

The day that Chacko prevented Pappachi from beating her (and Pappachi had murdered his chair instead), Mammachi packed her wifely luggage and committed it to Chacko's care. From then onwards he became the repository of all her womanly feelings. Her Man. Her only Love.

She was aware of his libertine relationships with the women in the factory, but had ceased to be hurt by them. When Baby Kochamma brought up the subject, Mammachi became tense and tight-lipped.

'He can't help having a Man's Needs,' she said primly.

Surprisingly, Baby Kochamma accepted this explanation, and the enigmatic, secretly thrilling notion of Men's Needs gained implicit sanction in the Ayemenem House. Neither Mammachi nor Baby Kochamma saw any contradiction between Chacko's Marxist mind and feudal libido. They only worried about the Naxalites, who had been known to force men from Good Families to marry servant girls whom they had made pregnant. Of course they did not even remotely suspect that the missile, when it *was* fired, the one that would annihilate the family's Good Name for ever, would come from a completely unexpected quarter.

Mammachi had a separate entrance built for Chacko's room, which was at the eastern end of the house, so that the objects of his 'Needs' wouldn't have to go traipsing *through* the house. She secretly slipped them money to keep them happy. They took it because they needed it. They had young children and old parents. Or husbands who spent all their earnings in toddy bars. The arrangement suited Mammachi, because in her mind, a fee *clarified* things. Disjuncted sex from love. Needs from Feelings.

Margaret Kochamma, however, was a different kettle of fish altogether. Since she had no means of finding out (though she did once try to get Kochu Maria to examine the bedsheets for stains), Mammachi could only hope that Margaret Kochamma was not intending to resume her sexual relationship with Chacko. While Margaret Kochamma was in Ayemenem Mammachi managed her otherwise unmanageable feelings by slipping money into the pockets of the dresses that Margaret Kochamma left in the laundry bin. Margaret Kochamma never returned the money simply because she never found it. Her pockets were emptied as a matter of routine by Aniyan the dhobi. Mammachi knew this, but preferred to construe Margaret Kochamma's silence as a tacit acceptance of payment for the favours Mammachi imagined she bestowed on her son.

So Mammachi had the satisfaction of regarding Margaret Kochamma as just another whore, Aniyan the dhobi was happy with his daily gratuity, and of course Margaret Kochamma remained blissfully unaware of the whole arrangement.

From its perch on the well, an untidy coucal called *Hwoop Hwoop* and shuffled its rust-red wings.

A crow stole some soap that bubbled in its beak.

In the dark, smoky kitchen, short Kochu Maria stood on her toes and iced the tall, double-deckered WELCOME HOME OUR SOPHIE MOL cake. Though even in those days most Syrian

Christian women had started wearing saris, Kochu Maria still wore her spotless half-sleeved white chatta with a V-neck and her white mundu, which folded into a crisp cloth fan on her behind. Kochu Maria's fan was more or less hidden by the blue and white checked, frilled, absurdly incongruous housemaid's apron that Mammachi insisted she wear inside the house.

She had short, thick forearms, fingers like cocktail sausages, and a broad fleshy nose with flared nostrils. Deep folds of skin connected her nose to either side of her chin, and separated that section of her face from the rest of it, like a snout. Her head was too large for her body. She looked like a bottled foetus that had escaped from its jar of formaldehyde in a Biology lab and unshrivelled and thickened with age.

She kept damp cash in her bodice which she tied tightly around her chest to flatten her unchristian breasts. Her kunukku earrings were thick and gold. Her earlobes had been distended into weighted loops that swung around her neck, her earrings sitting in them like gleeful children in a merry-go-(not all the way)round. Her right lobe had split open once and was sewn together again by Dr Verghese Verghese. Kochu Maria couldn't stop wearing her kunukku because if she did, how would people know that despite her lowly cook's job (seventy-five rupees a month) she was a Syrian Christian, Mar Thomite? Not a Pelaya, or a Pulaya, or a Paravan. But a Touchable, upper-caste Christian (into whom Christianity had seeped like tea from a teabag). Split lobes stitched back were a better option by far.

Kochu Maria hadn't yet made her acquaintance with the television addict waiting inside her. The Hulk Hogan addict. She hadn't yet seen a television set. She wouldn't have believed television existed. Had someone suggested that it did, Kochu Maria would have assumed that he or she was insulting her intelligence. Kochu Maria was wary of other people's versions of the outside world. More often than not, she took them to be a deliberate affront to her lack of education and (earlier) gullibility. In a determined reversal of her inherent nature, Kochu Maria now, as a policy, hardly ever believed anything that anybody said. A few months ago, in July, when Rahel told her that an American astronaut called Neil Armstrong had walked on the moon, she laughed sarcastically and said that a Malayali acrobat called O. Muthachen had done handsprings on the sun. With pencils up his nose. She was prepared to concede that Americans *existed* though she'd never seen one. She was even prepared to believe that Neil Armstrong might conceivably even be some absurd kind of name. But the walking on the moon bit? No sir. Nor did she trust the vague grey pictures that had appeared in the *Malayala Manorama* that she couldn't read.

She remained certain that Estha, when he said, '*Et tu, Kochu Maria!*' was insulting her in English. She thought it meant something like *Kochu Maria, you ugly black dwarf*. She bided her time, waiting for a suitable opportunity to complain about him.

She finished icing the tall cake. Then she tipped her head back and squeezed the leftover icing on to her tongue. Endless coils of chocolate toothpaste on a pink Kochu Maria tongue. When Mammachi called from the verandah ('Kochu Mariye! I hear the car!') her mouth was full of icing and she couldn't answer. When she finished, she ran her tongue over her teeth and then made a series of short smacking sounds with her tongue against her palate as though she'd just eaten something sour.

Distant skyblue carsounds (past the bus stop, past the school, past the yellow church and up the bumpy red road through the rubber trees) sent a murmur through the dim, sooty premises of Paradise Pickles.

The pickling (and the squashing, the slicing, boiling and stirring, the grating, salting, drying, the weighing and bottle sealing) stopped.

'*Chacko Saar vannu*,' the travelling whisper went. Chopping knives were put down. Vegetables were abandoned, half cut, on huge steel platters. Desolate bitter gourds, incomplete pineapples. Coloured rubber finger-guards (bright, like cheerful, thick condoms) were taken off. Pickled hands were washed and wiped on cobalt-blue aprons. Escaped wisps of hair were recaptured and returned to white headscarves. Mundus tucked up under aprons were let down. The gauze doors of the factory had sprung hinges, and closed noisily on their own.

And on one side of the driveway, beside the old well, in the shade of the kodam puli tree, a silent blue-aproned army gathered in the greenheat to watch.

Blue-aproned, white-capped, like a clot of smart blue and white flags.

Achoo, Jose, Yako, Anian, Elayan, Kuttan, Vijayan, Vawa, Joy, Sumathi, Ammal, Annamma, Kanakamma, Latha, Sushila, Vijayamma, Jollykutty, Mollykuty, Lucykutty, Beena Mol (girls with bus names). The early rumblings of discontent, concealed under a thick layer of loyalty.

The skyblue Plymouth turned in at the gate and crunched over the gravel driveway crushing small shells and shattering little red and yellow pebbles. Children tumbled out.

Collapsed fountains.

Flattened puffs.

Crumpled yellow bellbottoms and a go-go bag that was loved. Jet-lagged and barely awake. Then the swollen-ankled adults. Slow from too much sitting.

'Have you arrived?' Mammachi asked, turning her slanty dark glasses towards the new sounds: car doors slamming, getting-outedness. She lowered her violin.

'Mammachi!' Rahel said to her beautiful blind grandmother. 'Estha vomited! In the middle of *The Sound of Music*! And . . .'

Ammu touched her daughter gently. On her shoulder. And her touch meant *Shhhh* . . . Rahel looked around her and saw that she was in a Play. But she had only a small part.

She was just the landscape. A flower perhaps. Or a tree.

A face in the crowd. A townspeople.

Nobody said Hello to Rahel. Not even the Blue Army in the greenheat.

'Where is she?' Mammachi asked the car sounds. 'Where is my Sophie Mol? Come here and let me see you.'

As she spoke, the Waiting Melody that hung over her like a shimmering temple elephant's umbrella crumbled and gently fell about like dust.

Chacko, in his *What Happened to Our Man of the Masses?* suit and well-fed tie, led Margaret Kochamma and Sophie Mol triumphantly up the nine red steps like a pair of tennis trophies that he had recently won.

And once again, only the Small Things were said. The Big Things lurked unsaid inside. 'Hello, Mammachi,' Margaret Kochamma said in her kind-schoolteacher (that sometimes slapped) voice. 'Thank you for having us. We needed so much to get away.'

Mammachi caught a whiff of inexpensive perfume soured at the edges by airline sweat. (She herself had a bottle of Dior in its soft green leather pouch locked away in her safe.)

Margaret Kochamma took Mammachi's hand. The fingers were soft, the ruby rings were hard.

'Hello, Margaret,' Mammachi said (not rude, not polite), her dark glasses still on. 'Welcome to Ayemenem. I'm sorry I can't see you. As you must know, I am almost blind.' She spoke in a slow deliberate manner.

'Oh that's all right,' Margaret Kochamma said. 'I'm sure I look terrible anyway.' She laughed uncertainly, not sure if it was the right response.

'Wrong,' Chacko said. He turned to Mammachi, smiling a proud smile that his mother couldn't see. 'She's as lovely as ever.'

'I was very sorry to hear about . . . Joe,' Mammachi said. She sounded only a little sorry. Not very sorry.

There was a short, Sad-About-Joe silence.

'Where's my Sophie Mol?' Mammachi said. 'Come here and let your grandmother look at you.'

Sophie Mol was led to Mammachi. Mammachi pushed her dark sunglasses up into her hair. They looked up like slanting cat's eyes at the mouldy bison head. The mouldy bison said, '*No. Absolutely Not.*' In Mouldy Bisonese.

Even after her cornea transplant, Mammachi could only see light and shadow. If somebody was standing in the doorway, she could tell that someone was standing in the doorway. But not who it was. She could read a cheque, or a receipt, or a bank note only if it was close enough for her eyelashes to touch it. She would then hold it steady, and move her eye along it. Wheeling it from word to word.

The Townspeople (in her fairy frock) saw Mammachi draw Sophie Mol close to her eyes to look at her. To read her like a cheque. To check her like a bank note. Mammachi (with her better eye) saw redbrown hair (N . . . Nalmost blond), the curve of two fatfreckled cheeks (Nnnn . . . almost rosy), bluegreyblue eyes.

'Pappachi's nose,' Mammachi said. 'Tell me, are you a pretty girl?' she asked Sophie Mol.

'Yes,' Sophie Mol said.

'And tall?'

'Tall for my age,' Sophie Mol said.

'Very tall,' Baby Kochamma said. 'Much taller than Estha.'

'She's older,' Ammu said.

'Still . . .' Baby Kochamma said.

A little way away, Velutha walked up the shortcut through the rubber trees. Barebodied. A coil of insulated electrical wire was looped over one shoulder. He wore his printed dark blue and black mundu loosely folded up above his knees. On his back, his lucky leaf from the birthmark tree (that made the monsoons come on time). His autumn leaf at night.

Before he emerged through the trees and stepped into the driveway, Rahel saw him and slipped out of the Play and went to him.

Ammu saw her go.

Off stage, she watched them perform their elaborate Official Greeting. Velutha curtsied as he had been taught to, his mundu spread like a skirt, like the English dairymaid in *The King's Breafkast.* Rahel bowed (and said 'Bow'). Then they hooked little fingers and shook hands gravely with the mien of bankers at a convention.

In the dappled sunlight filtering through the dark green trees, Ammu watched Velutha lift her daughter effortlessly as though she was an inflatable child, made of air. As he tossed her up and she landed in his arms, Ammu saw on Rahel's face the high delight of the airborne young.

She saw the ridges of muscle on Velutha's stomach grow taught and rise under his skin like the divisions on a slab of chocolate. She wondered at how his body had changed – so quietly, from a flatmuscled boy's body into a man's body. Contoured and hard. A swimmer's body. A swimmer-carpenter's body. Polished with a high-wax body polish.

He had high cheekbones and a white, sudden smile.

It was his smile that reminded Ammu of Velutha as a little boy. Helping Vellya Paapen to count coconuts. Holding out little gifts he had made for her, flat on the palm of his hand so that she could take them without touching him. Boats, boxes, small windmills. Calling her Ammukutty. Little Ammu. Though she was so much less little than he was. When she looked at him now, she couldn't help thinking that the man he had become bore so little resemblance to the boy he had been. His smile was the only piece of baggage he had carried with him from boyhood into manhood.

Suddenly Ammu hoped that it *had* been him that Rahel saw in the march. She hoped it had been him that had raised his flag and knotted arm in anger. She hoped that under his careful cloak of cheerfulness, he housed a living, breathing anger against the smug, ordered world that she so raged against.

She hoped it had been him.

She was surprised at the extent of her daughter's physical ease with him. Surprised that her child seemed to have a sub-world that excluded *her* entirely. A tactile world of smiles and laughter that she, her mother, had no part in. Ammu recognized vaguely that her thoughts were shot with a delicate, purple tinge of envy. She didn't allow herself to consider whom it was that she envied. The man or her own child. Or just their world of hooked fingers and sudden smiles.

The man standing in the shade of the rubber trees with coins of sunshine dancing on his body, holding her daughter in his arms, glanced up and caught Ammu's gaze. Centuries telescoped into one evanescent moment. History was wrong-footed, caught off guard. Sloughed off like an old snakeskin. Its marks, its scars, its wounds from old wars and the walking backwards days all fell away. In its absence it left an aura, a palpable shimmering that was as plain to see as the water in a river or the sun in the sky. As plain to feel as the heat on a hot day, or the tug of a fish on a taut line. So obvious that no one noticed.

In that brief moment, Velutha looked up and saw things that he hadn't seen before. Things that had been out of bounds so far, obscured by history's blinkers.

Simple things.

For instance, he saw that Rahel's mother was a woman.

That she had deep dimples when she smiled and that they stayed on long after her smile left her eyes. He saw that her brown arms were round and firm and perfect. That her shoulders shone, but her eyes were somewhere else. He saw that when he gave her gifts they no longer needed to be offered flat on the palms of his hands so that she wouldn't have to touch him. His boats and boxes. His little windmills. He saw too that he was not necessarily the only giver of gifts. That *she* had gifts to give him too.

This knowing slid into him cleanly, like the sharp edge of a knife. Cold and hot at once. It only took a moment.

Ammu saw that he saw. She looked away. He did too. History's fiends returned to claim them. To rewrap them in its old, scarred pelt and drag them back to where they really lived. Where the Love Laws lay down who should be loved. And how. And how much.

Ammu walked up to the verandah, back into the Play. Shaking.

Velutha looked down at Ambassador S. Insect in his arms. He put her down. Shaking too.

'And look at you!' he said, looking at her ridiculous frothy frock. 'So beautiful! Getting married?'

Rahel lunged at his armpits and tickled him mercilessly. *Ickilee ickilee ickilee!*

'I *saw* you yesterday,' she said.

'Where?' Velutha made his voice high and surprised.

'Liar,' Rahel said. 'Liar and pretender. I did see you. You were a communist and had a shirt and a flag. *And* you ignored me.'

'*Aiyyo kashtam*,' Velutha said. 'Would I do that? *You* tell me, would Velutha *ever* do that? It must've been my Long-lost Twin brother.'

'Which Long-lost Twin brother?'

'Urumban silly . . . The one who lives in Kochi.'

'Who Urumban?' Then she saw the twinkle. 'Liar! You haven't got a twin brother! It wasn't Urumban! It was *you*!'

Velutha laughed. He had a lovely laugh that he really meant.

'Wasn't me,' he said. 'I was sick in bed.'

'See, you're smiling!' Rahel said. 'That means it was you. Smiling means, "It was you."'

'That's only in English!' Velutha said. 'In Malayalam my teacher always said, "Smiling means it wasn't me."'

It took Rahel a moment to sort that one out. She lunged at him once again. *Ickilee ickilee ickilee!*

Still laughing, Velutha looked into the Play for Sophie. 'Where's our Sophie Mol? Let's take a look at her. Did you remember to bring her, or did you leave her behind?'

'Don't look there,' Rahel said urgently.

She stood up on the cement parapet that separated the rubber trees from the driveway, and clapped her hands over Velutha's eyes.

'Why?' Velutha said.

'Because,' Rahel said, 'I don't want you to.'

'Where's Estha Mon?' Velutha said, with an Ambassador (disguised as a Stick Insect disguised as an Airport Fairy) hanging down his back with her legs wrapped around his waist, blindfolding him with her sticky little hands. 'I haven't seen him.'

'Oh we sold him in Cochin,' Rahel said airily. 'For a bag of rice. And a torch.'

The froth of her stiff frock pressed rough lace flowers into Velutha's back. Lace flowers and a lucky leaf bloomed on a black back.

But when Rahel searched the Play for Estha, she saw that he wasn't there.

Back inside the Play, Kochu Maria arrived, short, behind her tall cake.

'Cake's come,' she said, a little loudly, to Mammachi.

Kochu Maria always spoke a little loudly to Mammachi because she assumed that poor eyesight automatically affected the other senses.

'*Kando*, Kochu Mariye?' Mammachi said. 'Can you see our Sophie Mol?'

'*Kandoo*, Kochamma,' Kochu Maria said extra loud. 'I can see her.'

She smiled at Sophie, extra wide. She was exactly Sophie's height. More short than Syrian Christian, despite her best efforts.

'She has her mother's colour,' Kochu Maria said.

'Pappachi's nose,' Mammachi insisted.

'I don't know about that, but she's very beautiful,' Kochu Maria shouted. '*Sundarikutty*. She's a little angel.'

Littleangels were beach-coloured and wore bellbottoms.

Littledemons were mudbrown in Airport Fairy frocks with forehead bumps that might turn into horns. With Fountains in Love-in-Tokyos. And backward-reading habits.

And if you cared to look, you could see Satan in their eyes.

Kochu Maria took both Sophie's hands in hers, palms upward, raised them to her face and inhaled deeply.

'What's she doing?' Sophie wanted to know, tender London hands clasped in calloused Ayemenem ones. 'Who's she and why's she smelling my hands?'

'She's the cook,' Chacko said. 'That's her way of kissing you.'

'Kissing?' Sophie Mol was unconvinced, but interested.

'How marvellous!' Margaret Kochamma said. 'It's a sort of sniffing! Do the men and women do it to each other too?'

She hadn't meant it to sound quite like that, and she blushed. An embarrassed schoolteacher-shaped hole in the Universe.

'Oh, all the time!' Ammu said, and it came out a little louder than the sarcastic mumble that she had intended. 'That's how we make babies.'

Chacko didn't slap her.

So she didn't slap him back.

But the Waiting Air grew Angry.

'I think you owe my wife an apology, Ammu,' Chacko said, with a protective, proprietorial air, (hoping that Margaret Kochamma wouldn't say, '*Ex-wife, Chacko*!' and wag a rose at him).

'Oh no!' Margaret Kochamma said. 'It was my fault! I never meant it to sound quite like that . . . what I meant was – I mean it is fascinating to think that –'

'It was a perfectly legitimate question,' Chacko said. 'And I think Ammu ought to apologize.'

'Must we behave like some damn godforsaken tribe that's just been discovered?' Ammu asked.

'Oh dear!' Margaret Kochamma said.

In the angry quietness of the Play (the Blue Army in the greenheat still watching), Ammu walked back to the Plymouth, took out her suitcase, slammed the door, and walked away to her room, her shoulders shining. Leaving everybody to wonder where she had learned her effrontery from.

And truth be told, it was no small wondering matter.

Because Ammu had not had the kind of education, nor read the sorts of books, nor met the sorts of people, that might have influenced her to think the way she did.

She was just that sort of animal.

As a child, she had learned very quickly to disregard the Father Bear Mother Bear stories she was given to read. In her version, Father Bear beat Mother Bear with brass vases. Mother Bear suffered those beatings with mute resignation.

In her growing years, Ammu had watched her father weave his hideous web. He was charming and urbane with visitors, and stopped just short of fawning on them if they happened to be white. He donated money to orphanages and leprosy clinics. He worked hard on his public profile as a sophisticated, generous, moral man. But alone with his wife and children he turned into a monstrous, suspicious bully, with a streak of vicious cunning. They were beaten, humiliated and then made to suffer the envy of friends and relations for having such a wonderful husband and father.

Ammu had endured cold winter nights in Delhi hiding in the

mehndi hedge around their house (in case people from Good Families saw them) because Pappachi had come back from work out of sorts, and beaten her and Mammachi and driven them out of their home.

On one such night, Ammu, aged nine, hiding with her mother in the hedge, watched Pappachi's natty silhouette in the lit windows as he flitted from room to room. Not content with having beaten his wife and daughter (Chacko was away at school), he tore down curtains, kicked furniture and smashed a table lamp. An hour after the lights went out, disdaining Mammachi's frightened pleading, little Ammu crept back into the house through a ventilator to rescue her new gumboots that she loved more than anything else. She put them in a paper bag and crept back into the drawing room when the lights were suddenly switched on.

Pappachi had been sitting in his mahogany rocking chair all along, rocking himself silently in the dark. When he caught her, he didn't say a word. He flogged her with his ivory-handled riding crop (the one that he had held across his lap in his studio photograph). Ammu didn't cry. When he finished beating her he made her bring him Mammachi's pinking shears from her sewing cupboard. While Ammu watched, the Imperial Entomologist shred her new gumboots with her mother's pinking shears. The strips of black rubber fell to the floor. The scissors made snicking scissor-sounds. Ammu ignored her mother's drawn, frightened face that appeared at the window. It took ten minutes for her beloved gumboots to be completely shredded. When the last strip of rubber had rippled to the floor, her father looked at her with cold, flat eyes, and rocked and rocked and rocked. Surrounded by a sea of twisting, rubber snakes.

As she grew older, Ammu learned to live with this cold, calculating cruelty. She developed a lofty sense of injustice and the mulish, reckless streak that develops in Someone Small who has been bullied all their lives by Someone Big. She did exactly nothing to avoid quarrels and confrontations. In fact, it could be argued that she sought them out, perhaps even enjoyed them.

'Has she gone?' Mammachi asked the silence around her.

'She's gone,' Kochu Maria said loudly.

'Are you allowed to say "damn" in India?' Sophie Mol asked.

'Who said "damn"?' Chacko asked.

'She did,' Sophie Mol said. 'Aunty Ammu. She said, "some damn godforsaken tribe".'

'Cut the cake and give everybody a piece,' Mammachi said.

'Because in England, we're not,' Sophie Mol said to Chacko.

'Not what?' Chacko said.

'Allowed to say Dee Ay Em En,' Sophie Mol said.

Mammachi looked sightlessly out into the shining afternoon. 'Is everyone here?' she asked.

'*Oower*, Kochamma,' the Blue Army in the greenheat said. 'We're all here.'

Outside the Play, Rahel said to Velutha: '*We're* not here, are we? We're not even Playing.'

'That is Exactly Right,' Velutha said. 'We're not even Playing. But what I would like to know is, where is our Esthappappychachen Kuttappen Peter Mon?'

And that became a delighted, breathless, Rumplestiltskin-like dance among the rubber trees.

Oh Esthapappychachen Kuttappen Peter Mon,
Where, oh where have you gon?

And from Rumplestiltskin it graduated to the Scarlet Pimpernel.

We seek him here, we seek him there,
Those Frenchies seek him everywhere.

Is he in heaven? Is he in hell?
That demmedel-usive Estha – Pen?

Kochu Maria cut a sample piece of cake for Mammachi's approval.

'One piece each,' Mammachi confirmed to Kochu Maria, touching the piece lightly with rubyringed fingers to see if it was small enough.

Kochu Maria sawed up the rest of the cake messily, laboriously, breathing through her mouth, as though she was carving a hunk of roast lamb. She put the pieces on a large silver tray. Mammachi played a *Welcome Home, Our Sophie Mol* melody on her violin. A cloying, chocolate melody. Stickysweet, and meltybrown. Chocolate waves on a chocolate shore.

In the middle of the melody, Chacko raised his voice over the chocolate sound. 'Mamma!' he said (in his Reading Aloud voice). 'Mamma! That's enough! Enough violin!'

Mammachi stopped playing and looked in Chacko's direction, the bow poised in midair.

'Enough? D'you think that's enough, Chacko?'

'More than enough,' Chacko said.

'Enough's enough,' Mammachi murmured to herself. 'I think I'll stop now.' As though the idea had suddenly occurred to her.

She put her violin away into its black, violin-shaped box. It closed like a suitcase. And the music closed with it.

Click. And click.

Mammachi put her dark glasses on again. And drew the drapes across the hot day.

Ammu emerged from the house and called to Rahel.

'Rahel! I want you to have your afternoon nap! Come in after you've had your cake!'

Rahel's heart sank. Afternoon Gnap. She hated those.

Ammu went back indoors.

Velutha put Rahel down, and she stood forlornly at the edge of the driveway, on the periphery of the Play, a Gnap looming large and nasty on her horizon.

'And please stop being so over-familiar with that man!' Baby Kochamma said to Rahel.

'Over-familiar?' Mammachi said. 'Who is it, Chacko? Who's being over-familiar?'

'Rahel,' Baby Kochamma said.

'Over-familiar with *who*?'

'With whom,' Chacko corrected his mother.

'All right, with *whom* is she being over-familiar?' Mammachi asked.

'Your Beloved Velutha – whom else?' Baby Kochamma said, and to Chacko – 'Ask him where he was yesterday. Let's bell the cat once and for all.'

'Not now,' Chacko said.

'What's over-familiar?' Sophie Mol asked Margaret Kochamma, who didn't answer.

'Velutha? Is Velutha here? Are you here?' Mammachi asked the Afternoon.

'*Oower*, Kochamma.' He stepped through the trees into the Play.

'Did you find out what it was?' Mammachi asked.

'The washer in the foot-valve,' Velutha said. 'I've changed it. It's working now.'

'Then switch it on,' Mammachi said. 'The tank is empty.'

'That man will be our Nemesis,' Baby Kochamma said. Not because she was clairvoyant and had had a sudden flash of prophetic vision. Just to get him into trouble. Nobody paid her any attention.

'Mark my words,' she said bitterly.

'See her?' Kochu Maria said when she got to Rahel with her tray of cake. She meant Sophie Mol. 'When she grows up, she'll be our Kochamma, and she'll raise our salaries, and give us nylon saris for Onam.' Kochu Maria collected saris, though she hadn't ever worn one, and probably never would.

'So what?' Rahel said. 'By then I'll be living in Africa.'

'Africa?' Kochu Maria sniggered. 'Africa's full of ugly black people and mosquitoes.'

'You're the only one who's ugly,' Rahel said, and added (in English) 'Stupid dwarf!'

'What did you say?' Kochu Maria said threateningly. 'Don't tell me. I know. I heard. I'll tell Mammachi. Just wait!'

Rahel walked across to the old well where there were usually some ants to kill. Red ants that had a sour farty smell when they were squashed. Kochu Maria followed her with the tray of cake.

Rahel said she didn't want any of the stupid cake.

'*Kushumbi*,' Kochu Maria said. 'Jealous people go straight to hell.'

'Who's jealous?'

'I don't know. You tell me,' Kochu Maria said, with a frilly apron and a vinegar heart.

Rahel put on her sunglasses and looked back into the Play. Everything was Angry-coloured. Sophie Mol, standing between Margaret Kochamma and Chacko, looked as though she ought to be slapped. Rahel found a whole column of juicy ants. They were on their way to church. All dressed in red. They had to be killed before they got there. Squished and squashed with a stone. You can't have smelly ants in church.

The ants made a faint crunchy sound as life left them. Like an elf eating toast, or a crisp biscuit.

The Antly Church would be empty and the Antly Bishop would wait in his funny Antly Bishop clothes, swinging Frankincense in a silver pot. And nobody would arrive.

After he had waited for a reasonably Antly amount of time, he would get a funny Antly Bishop frown on his forehead, and shake his head sadly.

He would look at the glowing Antly stained-glass windows and when he finished looking at them, he would lock the church with an enormous key and make it dark. Then he'd go home to his wife, and (if she wasn't dead) they'd have an Antly Afternoon Gnap.

Sophie Mol, hatted, bellbottomed and Loved from the Beginning, walked out of the Play to see what Rahel was doing behind the well. But the Play went with her. Walked when she walked, stopped when she stopped. Fond smiles followed her. Kochu Maria moved the caketray out of the way of her adoring downwards smile as Sophie squatted down in the well-squelch (yellow bottoms of bells muddy wet now).

Sophie Mol inspected the smelly mayhem with clinical detachment. The stone was coated with crushed red carcasses and a few feebly waving legs.

Kochu Maria watched with her cake-crumbs.

The Fond Smiles watched Fondly.

Little Girls Playing.

Sweet.

One beach-coloured.

One brown.

One Loved.

One Loved a Little Less.

'Let's leave one alive so that it can be lonely,' Sophie Mol suggested.

Rahel ignored her and killed them all. Then in her frothy Airport Frock with matching knickers (no longer crisp) and unmatching sunglasses, she ran away. Disappeared into the green heat.

The Fond Smiles stayed on Sophie Mol, like a spotlight, thinking perhaps, that the sweet cousins were playing hide-and-seek, like sweet cousins often do.

9

Mrs Pillai, Mrs Eapen, Mrs Rajagopalan

The green-for-the-day had seeped from the trees. Dark palm leaves were splayed like drooping combs against the monsoon sky. The orange sun slid through their bent, grasping teeth.

A squadron of fruit bats sped across the gloom.

In the abandoned ornamental garden, Rahel, watched by lolling dwarves and a forsaken cherub, squatted by the stagnant pond and watched toads hop from stone to scummy stone. Beautiful Ugly Toads.

Slimy. Warty. Croaking.

Yearning, unkissed princes trapped inside them. Food for snakes that lurked in the long June grass. Rustle. Lunge. No more toad to hop from stone to scummy stone. No more prince to kiss.

It was the first night since she'd come that it hadn't rained.

Around now, Rahel thought, *if this were Washington, I would be on my way to work. The bus ride. The streetlights. The gas fumes. The shapes of people's breath on the bulletproof glass of my cabin. The clatter of coins pushed towards me in the metal tray. The smell of money on my fingers. The punctual drunk with sober eyes who arrives exactly at 10 p.m.: 'Hey, you! Black bitch! Suck my dick!'*

She owned seven hundred dollars. And a gold bangle with snakeheads. But Baby Kochamma had already asked her how much longer she planned to stay. And what she planned to do about Estha.

She had no plans.

No plans.

No Locusts Stand I.

She looked back at the looming, gabled, house-shaped hole in the Universe and imagined living in the silver bowl that Baby Kochamma had installed on the roof. It *looked* large enough for people to live in. Certainly it was bigger than a lot of people's homes. Bigger, for instance, than Kochu Maria's cramped quarters.

If they slept there, she and Estha, curled together like foetuses in a shallow steel womb, what would Hulk Hogan and Bam Bam Bigelow do? If the dish were occupied, where would *they* go? Would they slip through the chimney into Baby Kochamma's life and TV? Would they land on the old stove with a *Heeaagh!*, in their muscles and spangled clothes? Would the Thin People – the famine victims and refugees – slip through the cracks in the doors? Would Genocide slide between the tiles?

The sky was thick with TV. If you wore special glasses you could see them spinning through the sky among the bats and homing birds – blondes, wars, famines, football, food shows, coups d'état, hairstyles stiff with hairspray. Designer pectorals. Gliding towards Ayemenem like skydivers. Making patterns in the sky. Wheels. Windmills. Flowers blooming and unblooming.

Heeaagh!

Rahel returned to contemplating toads.

Fat. Yellow. From stone to scummy stone. She touched one gently. It moved its eyelids upwards. Funnily self-assured.

Nictitating membrane, she remembered she and Estha once spent a whole day saying. She and Estha and Sophie Mol.

Nictitating
ictitating
titating
itating
tating
ating
ting
ing

They were, all three of them, wearing saris (old ones, torn in half) that day, Estha was the draping expert. He pleated Sophie Mol's pleats. Organized Rahel's pallu and settled his own. They had red bindis on their foreheads. In the process of trying to wash out Ammu's forbidden kohl, they had smudged it all over their eyes, and on the whole looked like three raccoons trying to pass off as Hindu ladies. It was about a week after Sophie Mol arrived. A week before she died. By then she had performed unfalteringly under the twins' perspicacious scrutiny and had confounded all their expectations.

She had:

(a) Informed Chacko that even though he was her Real Father, she loved him less than Joe – (which left him available – even if not inclined – to be the surrogate father of certain two-egg persons greedy for his affection).

(b) Turned down Mammachi's offer that she replace Estha and Rahel as the privileged plaiter of Mammachi's nightly rat's tail and counter of moles.

(c) (& Most Important) – Astutely gauged the prevailing temper, and not just rejected, but rejected outright and extremely rudely, all of Baby Kochamma's advances and small seductions.

As if this were not enough, she also revealed herself to be human. One day the twins returned from a clandestine trip to the river (which had excluded Sophie Mol), and found her in the garden in tears, perched on the highest point of Baby

Kochamma's Herb Curl, 'Being Lonely,' as she put it. The next day Estha and Rahel took her with them to visit Velutha.

They visited him in saris, clumping gracelessly through red mud and long grass (*Nictitating ictitating tating ating ting ing*) and introduced themselves as Mrs Pillai, Mrs Eapen and Mrs Rajagopalan. Velutha introduced himself and his paralysed brother, Kuttappen (although he was fast asleep). He greeted them with the utmost courtesy. He addressed them all as Kochamma and gave them fresh coconut water to drink. He chatted to them about the weather. The river. The fact that in his opinion coconut trees were getting shorter by the year. As were the ladies in Ayemenem. He introduced them to his surly hen. He showed them his carpentry tools, and whittled them each a little wooden spoon.

It is only now, these years later, that Rahel with adult hindsight, recognized the sweetness of that gesture. A grown man entertaining three raccoons, treating them like real ladies. Instinctively colluding in the conspiracy of their fiction, taking care not to decimate it with adult carelessness. Or affection.

It is after all so easy to shatter a story. To break a chain of thought. To ruin a fragment of a dream being carried around carefully like a piece of porcelain.

To let it be, to travel with it, as Velutha did, is much the harder thing to do.

Three days before the Terror, he had let them paint his nails with red Cutex that Ammu had discarded. That's the way he was the day History visited them in the back verandah. A carpenter with gaudy nails. The posse of Touchable Policemen had looked at them and laughed.

'What's this?' one had said. 'AC-DC?'

Another lifted his boot with a millipede curled into the ridges of its sole. Deep rust brown. A million legs.

The last strap of light slipped from the cherub's shoulder. Gloom swallowed the garden. Whole. Like a python. Lights came on in the house.

Rahel could see Estha in his room, sitting on his neat bed. He was looking out through the barred window at the darkness. He couldn't see her, sitting outside in the darkness, looking in at the light.

A pair of actors trapped in a recondite play with no hint of plot or narrative. Stumbling through their parts, nursing someone else's sorrow. Grieving someone else's grief.

Unable, somehow, to change plays. Or purchase, for a fee, some cheap brand of exorcism from a counsellor with a fancy degree, who would sit them down and say, in one of many ways: 'You're not the Sinners. You're the Sinned Against. You were only children. You had no control. You are the *victims*, not the perpetrators.'

It would have helped if they could have made that crossing. If only they could have worn, even temporarily, the tragic hood of victimhood. Then they would have been able to put a face on it, and conjure up fury at what had happened. Or seek redress. And eventually, perhaps, exorcize the memories that haunted them.

But anger wasn't available to them and there was no face to put on this Other Thing that they held in their sticky Other Hands, like an imaginary orange. There was nowhere to lay it down. It wasn't theirs to give away. It would have to be held. Carefully and for ever.

Esthappen and Rahel both knew that there were several perpetrators (besides themselves) that day. But only one victim. And he had blood-red nails and a brown leaf on his back that made the monsoons come on time.

He left behind a hole in the Universe through which darkness poured like liquid tar. Through which their mother followed without even turning to wave goodbye. She left them behind, spinning in the dark, with no moorings, in a place with no foundation.

Hours later, the moon rose and made the gloomy python surrender what it had swallowed. The garden reappeared. Regurgitated whole. With Rahel sitting in it.

The direction of the breeze changed and brought her the sound of drums. A gift. The promise of a story. *Once upon a time,* they said, *there lived a*

Rahel lifted her head and listened.

On clear nights the sound of the chenda travelled up to a kilometre from the Ayemenem temple, announcing a kathakali performance.

Rahel went. Drawn by the memory of steep roofs and white walls. Of brass lamps lit and dark, oiled wood. She went in the hope of meeting an old elephant who wasn't electrocuted on the Kottayam–Cochin highway. She stopped by the kitchen for a coconut.

On her way out, she noticed that one of the gauze doors of the factory had come off its hinges and was propped against the doorway. She moved it aside and stepped in. The air was heavy with moisture, wet enough for fish to swim in.

The floor under her shoes was slick with monsoon scum. A small, anxious bat flitted between the roof beams.

The low cement pickle vats silhouetted in the gloom made the factory floor look like an indoor cemetery for the cylindrical dead.

The earthly remains of Paradise Pickles & Preserves.

Where long ago, on the day that Sophie Mol came, Ambassador E. Pelvis stirred a pot of scarlet jam and thought Two Thoughts. Where a red, tender-mango-shaped secret was pickled, sealed and put away.

It's true. Things can change in a day.

10

The River in the Boat

While the *Welcome Home, Our Sophie Mol* Play was being performed in the front verandah and Kochu Maria distributed cake to a Blue Army in the green heat, Ambassador E. Pelvis/S. Pimpernel (with a puff) of the beige and pointy shoes, pushed open the gauze doors to the dank and pickle-smelling premises of Paradise Pickles. He walked among the giant cement pickle vats to find a place to Think in. Ousa, the Bar Nowl, who lived on a blackened beam near the skylight (and contributed occasionally to the flavour of certain Paradise products), watched him walk.

Past floating yellow limes in brine that needed prodding from time to time (or else islands of black fungus formed like frilled mushrooms in a clear soup).

Past green mangoes, cut and stuffed with turmeric and chilli powder and tied together with twine. (They needed no attention for a while.)

Past glass casks of vinegar with corks.

Past shelves of pectin and preservatives.

Past trays of bitter gourd, with knives and coloured finger-guards.

Past gunny bags bulging with garlic and small onions.

Past mounds of fresh green peppercorns.

Past a heap of banana peels on the floor (preserved for the pigs' dinner).

Past the label cupboard full of labels.

Past the glue.

Past the glue-brush.

Past an iron tub of empty bottles floating in soapbubbled water.

Past the lemon squash.

The grape-crush.

And back.

It was dark inside, lit only by the light that filtered through the clotted gauze doors, and a beam of dusty sunlight (that Ousa didn't use) from the skylight. The smell of vinegar and asafoetida stung his nostrils, but Estha was used to it, loved it. The place that he found to Think in was between the wall and the black iron cauldron in which a batch of freshly boiled (illegal) banana jam was slowly cooling.

The jam was still hot and on its sticky scarlet surface, thick pink froth was dying slowly. Little banana bubbles drowning deep in jam and nobody to help them.

The Orangedrink Lemondrink Man could walk in any minute. Catch a Cochin–Kottayam bus and be there. And Ammu would offer him a cup of tea. Or pineapple squash perhaps. With ice. Yellow in a glass.

With the long iron stirrer. Estha stirred the thick, fresh jam.

The dying froth made dying frothly shapes.

A crow with a crushed wing.

A clenched chicken's claw.

A Nowl (not Ousa) mired in sickly jam.

A sadly swirl.

And nobody to help.

As Estha stirred the thick jam he thought Two Thoughts, and the Two Thoughts he thought, were these:

(a) *Anything can happen to Anyone.*

And

(b) *It's best to be prepared.*

Having thought these thoughts, Estha Alone was happy with his bit of wisdom.

As the hot magenta jam went round, Estha became a Stirring Wizard with a spoiled puff and uneven teeth, and then the Witches of Macbeth.

Fire burn, banana bubble.

Ammu had allowed Estha to copy Mammachi's recipe for banana jam into her new recipe book, black with a white spine.

Acutely aware of the honour that Ammu had bestowed on him, Estha had used both his best handwritings.

Banana Jam (in his *old* best writing)

Crush ripe banana. Add water to cover and cook on a very
hot fire till fruit is soft.
Sqweeze out juice by straining through course muslin.
Weigh equal quantity of sugar and keep by.
Cook fruit juice till it turns scarlet and about half the quantity
evapourates.

Prepare the gelatin (pectin) thus:
Proportion 1:5
ie: 4 teaspoons Pectin: 20 teaspoons sugar.

Estha always thought of Pectin as the youngest of three brothers with hammers, Pectin, Hectin and Abednego. He imagined them building a wooden ship in failing light and a drizzle. Like Noah's sons. He could see them clearly in his mind. Racing against time. The sound of their hammering echoing dully under the brooding, storm-coming sky. And nearby in the jungle, in the eerie, storm-coming light, animals queued up in pairs:

Girlboy.
Girlboy.
Girlboy.

Girlboy.

Twins were not allowed.

The rest of the recipe was in Estha's new best handwriting. Angular, spiky. It leaned backwards as though the letters were reluctant to form words, and the words reluctant to be in sentences:

Add the Pectin to concenterated juice. Cook for a few (5) minutes.
Use a strong fire, burning heavily all around.
Add the sugar. Cook until sheeting consistency is obtained.
Cool slowly.
Hope you will enjoy this recipe.

Apart from the spelling mistakes, the last line – *Hope you will enjoy this recipe* – was Estha's only augmentation of the original text.

Gradually, as Estha stirred, the banana jam thickened and cooled, and Thought Number Three rose unbidden from his beige and pointy shoes.

Thought Number Three was:

(c) *A boat.*

A boat to row across the river. Akkara. The Other Side. A boat to carry Provisions. Matches. Clothes. Pots and pans. Things they would need and couldn't swim with.

Estha's arm hairs stood on end. The jam-stirring became a boat-rowing. The round and round became a back and forth. Across a sticky scarlet river. A song from the Onam boatrace filled the factory. *'Thaiy thaiy thaka thaiy thaiy thome!'*

Enda da korangacha, chandi ithra thenjadu?
(Hey Mr Monkey man, why's your bum so red?)
Pandyill thooran poyappol nerakkamuthiri nerangi njan.
(I went for a shit to Madras, and scraped it till it bled.)

Over the somewhat discourteous questions and answers of the boatsong, Rahel's voice floated into the factory.

'Estha! Estha! Estha!'

Estha didn't answer. The chorus of the boatsong was whispered into the thick jam.

Theeyome
Thithome
Tharaka
Thithome
Theem

A gauze door creaked, and an Airport Fairy with hornbumps and yellow-rimmed red plastic sunglasses looked in with the sun behind her. The factory was Angry-coloured. The salted limes were red. The tender mangoes were red. The label cupboard was red. The dusty sunbeam (that Ousa never used) was red.

The gauze door closed.

Rahel stood in the empty factory with her Fountain in a Love-in-Tokyo. She heard a nun's voice singing the boatsong. A clear soprano wafting over vinegar fumes and pickle vats.

She turned to Estha bent over the scarlet broth in the black cauldron.

'What d'you want?' Estha asked without looking up.

'Nothing,' Rahel said.

'Then why have you come here?'

Rahel didn't reply. There was a brief, hostile silence.

'Why're you rowing the jam?' Rahel asked.

'India's a Free Country,' Estha said.

No one could argue with that.

India was a Free Country.

You could make salt. Row jam, if you wanted to.

The Orangedrink Lemondrink Man could just walk in through the gauze doors.

If he wanted to.

And Ammu would offer him pineapple juice. With ice.

Rahel sat on the edge of a cement vat (frothy ends of buckram and lace, delicately dipped in tender mango pickle) and tried on the rubber finger-guards. Three bluebottles fiercely fought the gauze doors, wanting to be let in. And Ousa the Bar Nowl watched the pickle-smelling silence that lay between the twins like a bruise.

Rahel's fingers were Yellow Green Blue Red Yellow.

Estha's jam was stirred.

Rahel got up to go. For her Afternoon Gnap.

'Where're you going?'

'Somewhere.'

Rahel took off her new fingers, and had her old finger-coloured fingers back. Not yellow, not green, not blue, not red. Not yellow.

'I'm going Akkara,' Estha said. Not looking up. 'To the History House.'

Rahel stopped and turned around, and on her heart a drab moth with unusually dense dorsal tufts unfurled its predatory wings.

Slow out.

Slow in.

'Why?' Rahel said.

'Because Anything can Happen to Anyone,' Estha said. 'It's Best to be Prepared.'

You couldn't argue with that.

Nobody went to Kari Saipu's house any more. Vellya Paapen claimed to be the last human being to have set eyes on it. He said that it was haunted. He had told the twins the story of his encounter with Kari Saipu's ghost. It happened two years ago, he said. He had gone across the river, hunting for a nutmeg tree to make a paste of nutmeg and fresh garlic for Chella, his wife, as she lay dying of tuberculosis. Suddenly he smelled cigar smoke (which he recognized at once, because Pappachi used to smoke the same brand). Vellya Paapen whirled around and hurled his sickle at the smell. He pinned the ghost to the trunk of a rubber tree, where, according to Vellya Paapen, it still remained. A sickled smell, that bled clear, amber blood, and begged for cigars.

Vellya Paapen never found the nutmeg tree, and had to buy himself a new sickle. But he had the satisfaction of knowing that his lightning-quick reflexes (despite his mortgaged eye) and his presence of mind had put an end to the bloodthirsty wanderings of a paedophile ghost.

As long as no one succumbed to its artifice and unsickled it with a cigar.

What Vellya Paapen (who knew most things) *didn't* know was that Kari Saipu's house was the History House (whose doors were locked and windows open). And that inside, map-breath'd ancestors with tough toe-nails whispered to the lizards on the wall. That History used the back verandah to negotiate its terms and collect its dues. That default led to dire consequences. That on the day History picked to square its books, Estha would keep the receipt for the dues that Velutha paid.

Vellya Paapen had no idea that Kari Saipu it was who captured dreams and redreamed them. That he plucked them from the minds of passers-by the way children pick currants from a cake. That the ones he craved most of all, the dreams he loved redreaming, were the tender dreams of two-egg twins.

Poor old Vellya Paapen, had he known then that History would choose him for its deputy, that it would be *his* tears that set the Terror rolling, perhaps he would not have strutted like a young cockerel in the Ayemenem bazaar, bragging of how he swam the river with his sickle in his mouth (sour, the taste of iron on his tongue). How he put it down for just one moment while he kneeled to wash the river-grit out of his mortgaged eye (there was grit in the river sometimes, particularly in the rainy months) when he caught the first whiff of cigar smoke. How he picked up his sickle, whirled around and sickled the smell that fixed the ghost for ever. All in a single, fluid, athletic motion.

By the time he understood his part in History's Plans, it was too late to retrace his steps. He had swept his footprints away himself. Crawling backwards with a broom.

In the factory the silence swooped down once more and tightened around the twins. But this time it was a different kind of silence. An old river silence. The silence of Fisher People and waxy mermaids.

'But communists don't believe in ghosts,' Estha said, as though they were continuing a discourse investigating solutions to the ghost problem. Their conversations surfaced and dipped like mountain streams. Sometimes audible to other people. Sometimes not.

'Are we going to become a communist?' Rahel asked.

'Might have to.'

Estha-the-Practical.

Distant cake-crumbled voices and approaching Blue Army footsteps caused the comrades to seal the secret.

It was pickled, sealed and put away. A red, tender mango-shaped secret in a vat. Presided over by a Nowl.

The Red Agenda was worked out and agreed upon:

Comrade Rahel would go for her Afternoon Gnap, then lie awake until Ammu fell asleep.

Comrade Estha would find the flag (that Baby Kochamma had been forced to wave), and wait for her by the river, and there they would:

(b) *Prepare to prepare to be prepared.*

A child's abandoned fairy frock (semi-pickled) stood stiffly on its own in the middle of Ammu's darkened bedroom floor.

Outside, the Air was Alert and Bright and Hot. Rahel lay next to Ammu, wide awake in her matching airport knickers. She could see the pattern of the cross-stitch flowers from the blue cross-stitch counterpane on Ammu's cheek. She could hear the blue cross-stitch afternoon.

The slow ceiling fan. The sun behind the curtains.

The yellow wasp wasping against the windowpane in a dangerous dzzzz.

A disbelieving lizard's blink.

High-stepping chickens in the yard.

The sound of the sun crinkling the washing. Crisping white bedsheets. Stiffening starched saris. Off-white and gold.

Red ants on yellow stones.

A hot cow feeling hot. *Amhoo.* In the distance.

And the smell of a cunning Englishman ghost, sickled to a rubber tree, asking courteously for a cigar.

'Umm . . . excuse me? You wouldn't happen to have an umm . . . cigar, would you?'

In a kind-schoolteacherly voice.

Oh *dear.*

And Estha waiting for her. By the river. Under the mangosteen tree that Reverend E. John Ipe had brought home from his visit to Mandalay.

What was Estha sitting on?

On what they always sat on under the mangosteen tree. Something grey and grizzled. Covered in moss and lichen, smothered in ferns. Something that the earth had claimed. Not a log. Not a rock . . .

Before she completed the thought, Rahel was up and running.

Through the kitchen, past Kochu Maria fast asleep. Thick-wrinkled like a sudden rhinoceros in a frilly apron.

Past the factory.

Tumbling barefoot through the greenheat, followed by a yellow wasp.

Comrade Estha was there. Under the mangosteen tree. With the red flag planted in the earth beside him. A Mobile Republic. A Twin Revolution with a Puff.

And what was he sitting on?

Something covered with moss, hidden by ferns.

Knock on it and it made a hollow knocked-on sound.

The silence dipped and soared and swooped and looped in figures of eight.

Jewelled dragonflies hovered like shrill children's voices in the sun.

Finger-coloured fingers fought the ferns, moved the stones, cleared the way. There was a sweaty grappling for an edge to hold on to. And a One Two and.

Things can change in a day.

It *was* a boat. A tiny wooden vallom.

The boat that Estha sat on and Rahel found.

The boat that Ammu would use to cross the river. To love by night the man her children loved by day.

So old a boat that it had taken root. Almost.

A grey old boatplant with boatflowers and boatfruit. And underneath, a boat-shaped patch of withered grass. A scurrying, hurrying boatworld.

Dark and dry and cool. Unroofed now. And blind.

White termites on their way to work.

White ladybirds on their way home.

White beetles burrowing away from the light.

White grasshoppers with whitewood violins.

Sad white music.

A white wasp. Dead.

A brittlewhite snakeskin, preserved in darkness, crumbled in the sun.

But would it do, that little vallom? Was it perhaps too old? Too dead? Was Akkara too far away for it?

Two-egg twins looked out across their river.

The Meenachal.

Greygreen. With fish in it. The sky and trees in it. And at night, the broken yellow moon in it.

When Pappachi was a boy, an old tamarind tree fell into it in a storm. It was still there. A smooth barkless tree, blackened by a surfeit of green water. Driftless driftwood.

The first third of the river was their friend. Before the Really Deep began. They knew the slippery stone steps (thirteen) before the slimy mud began. They knew the afternoon weed that flowed inwards from the backwaters of Komarakom. They knew the smaller fish. The flat, foolish pallathi, the silver paral, the wily, whiskered koori, the sometimes karimeen.

Here Chacko had taught them to swim (splashing around his ample uncle stomach without help). Here they had discovered for themselves the disconnected delights of underwater farting.

Here they had learned to fish. To thread coiling purple earthworms onto hooks on the fishing rods that Velutha made from slender culms of yellow bamboo.

Here they studied Silence (like the children of the Fisher Peoples), and learned the bright language of dragonflies.

Here they learned to Wait. To Watch. To think thoughts and not voice them. To move like lightning when the bendy yellow bamboo arced downwards.

So this first third of the river they knew well. The next two-thirds less so.

The second third was where the Really Deep began. Where the current was swift and certain (downstream when the tide was out, upstream, pushing up from the backwaters when the tide was in).

The third third was shallow again. The water brown and murky. Full of weeds and darting eels and slow mud that oozed through toes like toothpaste.

The twins could swim like seals and, supervised by Chacko, had crossed the river several times, returning panting and cross-eyed from the effort, with a stone, a twig or a leaf from the Other Side as testimony to their feat. But the middle of a respectable river, or the Other Side, was no place for children to Linger, Loll or Learn Things. Estha and Rahel accorded the second third and the third third of the Meenachal the deference it deserved. Still, swimming across was not the problem. Taking the boat with Things in it (so that they could *(b) Prepare to prepare to be prepared*) was.

They looked across the river with Old Boat eyes. From where they stood they couldn't see the History House. It was just a darkness beyond the swamp, at the heart of the abandoned rubber estate, from which the sound of crickets swelled.

Estha and Rahel lifted the little boat and carried it to the water. It looked surprised, like a grizzled fish that had surfaced from the deep. In dire need of sunlight. It needed scraping, and cleaning, perhaps, but nothing more.

Two happy hearts soared like coloured kites in a skyblue sky. But then, in a slow green whisper, the river (with fish in it, with the sky and trees in it), bubbled in.

Slowly the old boat sank, and settled on the sixth step.

And a pair of two-egg twin hearts sank and settled on the step above the sixth.

The deep-swimming fish covered their mouths with their fins and laughed sideways at the spectacle.

A white boat-spider floated up with the river in the boat, struggled briefly and drowned. Her white egg sac ruptured prematurely, and a hundred baby spiders (too light to drown, too small to swim), stippled the smooth surface of the green water, before being swept out to sea. To Madagascar, to start a new phylum of Malayali Swimming Spiders.

In a while, as though they'd discussed it (though they hadn't), the twins began to wash the boat in the river. The cobwebs, the mud, the moss and lichen floated away. When it was clean, they turned it upside down and hoisted it onto their heads. Like a combined hat that dripped. Estha uprooted the red flag.

A small procession (a flag, a wasp and a boat-on-legs) wended its knowledgeable way down the little path through the undergrowth. It avoided the clumps of nettles, and side-stepped known ditches and anthills. It skirted the precipice of the deep pit from which laterite had been quarried, and was now a still lake with steep orange banks, the thick, viscous water covered with a luminous film of green scum. A verdant, treacherous lawn, in which mosquitoes bred and the fish were fat but inaccessible.

The path, which ran parallel to the river, led to a little grassy clearing that was hemmed in by huddled trees: coconut, cashew, mango, bilimbi. On the edge of the clearing, with its back to the river, a low hut with walls of orange laterite plastered with mud and a thatched roof nestled close to the ground, as though it was listening to a whispered subterranean secret. The low walls of the hut were the same colour as the earth they stood on, and seemed to have germinated from a house-seed planted in the ground, from which right-angled ribs of earth had risen and enclosed space. Three untidy banana trees grew in the little front yard that had been fenced off with panels of woven palm leaves.

The boat-on-legs approached the hut. An unlit oil lamp hung on the wall beside the door, the patch of wall behind it was singed soot black. The door was ajar. It was dark inside. A black hen appeared in the doorway. She returned indoors, entirely indifferent to boat visits.

Velutha wasn't home. Nor Vellya Paapen. But someone was.

A man's voice floated out from inside and echoed around the clearing, making him sound lonely.

The voice shouted the same thing, over and over again, and

each time it climbed into a higher, more hysterical register. It was an appeal to an over-ripe guava threatening to fall from its tree and make a mess on the ground.

Pa pera-pera-pera-perakka
(Mr gugga-gug-gug-guava,)
Ende parambil thooralley.
(Don't shit here in my compound.)
Chetende parambil thoorikko,
(You can shit next door in my brother's compound,)
Pa pera-pera-pera-perakka.
(Mr gugga-gug-gug-guava.)

The shouter was Kuttappen, Velutha's older brother. He was paralysed from his chest downwards. Day after day, month after month, while his brother was away and his father went to work, Kuttappen lay flat on his back and watched his youth saunter past without stopping to say hello. All day he lay there listening to the silence of huddled trees with only a domineering black hen for company. He missed his mother, Chella, who had died in the same corner of the room that he lay in now. She had died a coughing, spitting, aching, phlegmy death. Kuttappen remembered noticing how her feet died long before she had. How the skin on them grew grey and lifeless. How fearfully he watched death creep over her from the bottom up. Kuttappen kept vigil on his own numb feet with mounting terror. Occasionally he poked at them hopefully with a stick that he kept propped up in the corner to defend himself against visiting snakes. He had no sensation in his feet at all, and only visual evidence assured him that they were still connected to his body, and were indeed his own.

After Chella died, he was moved into her corner, the corner that Kuttappen imagined was the corner of his home that Death had reserved to administer her deathly affairs. One corner for cooking, one for clothes, one for bedding rolls, one for dying in.

He wondered how long his would take, and what people who had more than four corners in their houses did with the rest of their corners. Did it give them a choice of corners to die in?

He assumed, not without reason, that he would be the first in his family to follow in his mother's wake. He would learn otherwise. Soon. Too soon.

Sometimes (from habit, from missing her), Kuttappen coughed like his mother used to, and his upper body bucked like a just-caught fish. His lower body lay like lead, as though it belonged to someone else. Someone dead whose spirit was trapped and couldn't get away.

Unlike Velutha, Kuttappen was a good, safe Paravan. He could neither read nor write. As he lay there on his hard bed, bits of thatch and grit fell onto him from the ceiling and mingled with his sweat. Sometimes ants and other insects fell with it. On bad days the orange walls held hands and bent over him, inspecting him like malevolent doctors, slowly, deliberately, squeezing the breath out of him and making him scream. Sometimes they receded of their own accord, and the room he lay in grew impossibly large, terrorizing him with the spectre of his own insignificance. That too made him cry out.

Insanity hovered close at hand, like an eager waiter at an expensive restaurant (lighting cigarettes, refilling glasses). Kuttappen thought with envy of mad men who could walk. He had no doubts about the equity of the deal; his sanity, for serviceable legs.

The twins put the boat down, and the clatter was met with a sudden silence from inside.

Kuttappen wasn't expecting anyone.

Estha and Rahel pushed open the door and went in. Small as they were, they had to stoop a little to go in. The wasp waited outside on the lamp.

'It's us.'

The room was dark and clean. It smelled of fish curry and woodsmoke. Heat cleaved to things like a low fever. But the mud floor was cool under Rahel's bare feet. Velutha's and Vellya Paapen's bedding was rolled up and propped against the wall. Clothes hung on a string. There was a low wooden kitchen shelf on which covered terracotta pots, ladles made of coconut shells and three chipped enamel plates with dark blue rims were arranged. A grown man could stand up straight in the centre of the room, but not along its sides. Another low door led to a backyard where there were more banana trees, beyond which the river glimmered through the foliage. A carpenter's work station had been erected in the backyard.

There were no keys or cupboards to lock.

The black hen left through the back door, and scratched abstractedly in the yard where woodshavings blew about like blonde curls. Judging from her personality, she appeared to have been reared on a diet of hardware: hasps and clasps and nails and old screws.

'*Aiyyo, Mon! Mol!* What must you be thinking? That Kuttappen's a basket case!' an embarrassed, disembodied voice said.

It took the twins a while for their eyes to grow accustomed to the dark. Then the darkness dissolved and Kuttappen appeared on his bed, a glistening genie in the gloom. The whites of his eyes were dark yellow. The soles of his feet (soft from so much lying down) stuck out from under the cloth that covered his legs. They were still stained a pale orange from years of walking barefoot on red mud. He had grey callouses on his ankles from the chafing of the rope that Paravans tied around their feet when they climbed coconut trees.

On the wall behind him there was a benign, mouse-haired calendar-Jesus with lipstick and rouge, and a lurid, jewelled heart glowing through his clothes. The bottom quarter of the calendar (the part with the dates on it) frilled out like a skirt. Jesus in a mini. Twelve layers of petticoats for the twelve months of the year. None had been torn out.

There were other things from the Ayemenem House that had either been given to them or salvaged from the rubbish bin. Rich things in a poor house. A clock that didn't work, a flowered tin waste-paper basket. Pappachi's old riding boots (brown, with green mould) with the cobbler's trees still in them. Biscuit tins with sumptuous pictures of English castles and ladies with bustles and ringlets.

A small poster (Baby Kochamma's, given away because of a damp patch) hung next to Jesus. It was a picture of a blonde child writing a letter, with tears falling down her cheeks. Underneath it said: *I'm writing to say I Miss You.* She looked as though she'd had a haircut, and it was her cropped curls that were blowing around Velutha's backyard.

A transparent plastic tube led from under the worn cotton sheet that covered Kuttappen to a bottle of yellow liquid that caught the shaft of light that came in through the door, and quelled a question that had been rising inside Rahel. She fetched him water in a steel tumbler from the clay koojah. She seemed to know her way around. Kuttappen lifted his head and drank. Some water dribbled down his chin.

The twins squatted on their haunches, like professional adult gossips in the Ayemenem market.

They sat in silence for a while. Kuttappen mortified, the twins preoccupied with boat thoughts.

'Has Chacko Saar's Mol come?' Kuttappen asked.

'Must have,' Rahel said laconically.

'Where's she?'

'Who knows? Must be around somewhere. We don't know.'

'Will you bring her here for me to see?'

'Can't,' Rahel said.

'Why not?'

'She has to stay indoors. She's very delicate. If she gets dirty she'll die.'

'I see.'

'We're not allowed to bring her here . . . and anyway, there's nothing to *see*,' Rahel assured Kuttappen. 'She has hair, legs, teeth – you know – the usual . . . only she's a little tall.' And that was the only concession she would make.

'Is that all?' Kuttappen said, getting the point very quickly. 'Then where's the point in seeing her?'

'No point,' Rahel said.

'Kuttappa, if a vallom leaks, is it very hard to mend?' Estha asked.

'Shouldn't be,' Kuttappen said. 'Depends. Why, whose vallom is leaking?'

'Ours – that we found. D'you want to see it?'

They went out and returned with the grizzled boat for the paralysed man to examine. They held it over him like a roof. Water dripped on him.

'First we'll have to find the leaks,' Kuttappen said. 'Then we'll have to plug them.'

'Then sandpaper,' Estha said. 'Then polish.'

'Then oars,' Rahel said.

'Then oars,' Estha agreed.

'Then offity off,' Rahel said.

'Where to?' Kuttappen asked.

'Just here and there,' Estha said airily.

'You must be careful,' Kuttappen said. 'This river of ours – she isn't always what she pretends to be.'

'What does she pretend to be?' Rahel asked.

'Oh . . . a little old church-going ammooma, quiet and clean . . . idi appams for breakfast, kanji and meen for lunch. Minding her own business. Not looking right or left.'

'And she's really a . . . ?'

'Really a wild thing . . . I can hear her at night – rushing past in the moonlight, always in a hurry. You must be careful of her.'

'And what does she really eat?'

'Really eat? Oh . . . Stoo . . . and . . .' He cast about for something English for the evil river to eat.

'Pineapple slices . . .' Rahel suggested.

'That's right! Pineapple slices and Stoo. And she drinks. Whisky.'

'And brandy.'

'And brandy. True.'

'And looks right *and* left.'

'True.'

'And minds *other* people's business . . .'

Esthappen steadied the little boat on the uneven earth floor with a few blocks of wood that he found in Velutha's workstation in the backyard. He gave Rahel a cooking ladle made of a wooden handle stuck through the polished half of a coconut shell.

The twins climbed into the vallom and rowed across vast, choppy waters.

With a *Thaiy thaiy thaka thaiy thaiy thome*. And a jewelled Jesus watching.

He walked on water. Perhaps. But could He have *swum* on land?

In matching knickers and dark glasses? With His Fountain in a Love-in-Tokyo? In pointy shoes and a puff? Would He have had the imagination?

Velutha returned to see if Kuttappen needed anything. From a distance he heard the raucous singing. Young voices, underlining with delight the scatology.

Hey Mr Monkey Man
Why's your BUM so RED?

I went for a SHIT to Madras
And scraped it till it BLED!

Temporarily, for a few happy moments, the Orangedrink Lemondrink Man shut his yellow smile and went away. Fear sank and settled at the bottom of the deep water. Sleeping a dog's sleep. Ready to rise and murk things at a moment's notice.

Velutha smiled when he saw the Marxist flag blooming like a tree outside his doorway. He had to bend low in order to enter his home. A tropical Eskimo. When he saw the children, something clenched inside him. And he couldn't understand it. He saw them every day. He loved them without knowing it. But it was different suddenly. Now. After History had slipped up so badly. No fist had clenched inside him before.

Her children, an insane whisper whispered to him.

Her eyes, *her* mouth. *Her* teeth.

Her soft, lambent skin.

He drove the thought away angrily. It returned and sat outside his skull. Like a dog.

'Ha!' he said to his young guests. 'And who, may I ask, are these Fisher Peoples?'

'Esthapappychachen Kuttappen Peter Mon. Mr and Mrs Pleasetomeetyou.' Rahel held out her ladle to be shaken in greeting.

It was shaken in greeting. Hers, then Estha's.

'And where, may I ask, are they off to by boat?'

'Off to Africa!' Rahel shouted.

'Stop *shouting*,' Estha said.

Velutha walked around the boat. They told him where they had found it.

'So it doesn't belong to anybody,' Rahel said a little doubtfully, because it suddenly occurred to her that it might. 'Ought we to report it to the police?'

'Don't be stupid,' Estha said.

Velutha knocked on the wood and then scraped a little patch clean with his nail.

'Good wood,' he said.

'It sinks,' Estha said. 'It leaks.'

'Can you mend it for us, Veluthapappychachen Peter Mon?' Rahel asked.

'We'll see about that,' Velutha said. 'I don't want you playing any silly games on this river.'

'We won't. We promise. We'll use it only when you're with us.'

'First we'll have to find the leaks . . .' Velutha said.

'Then we'll have to plug them!' the twins shouted, as though it was the second line of a well-known poem.

'How long will it take?' Estha asked.

'A day,' Velutha said.

'A *day*! I thought you'd say a month!'

Estha, delirious with joy, jumped on Velutha, wrapped his legs around his waist and kissed him.

The sandpaper was divided into exactly equal halves, and the twins fell to work with an eerie concentration that excluded everything else.

Boat-dust flew around the room and settled on hair and eyebrows. On Kuttappen like a cloud, on Jesus like an offering. Velutha had to prise the sandpaper out of their fingers.

'Not here,' he said firmly. 'Outside.'

He picked the boat up and carried it out. The twins followed, eyes fixed on their boat with unwavering concentration, starving puppies expecting to be fed.

Velutha set the boat up for them. The boat that Estha sat on, and Rahel found. He showed them how to follow the grain of the wood. He started them off on the sandpapering. When he returned indoors, the black hen followed him, determined to be wherever the boat wasn't.

Velutha dipped a thin cotton towel in an earthen pot of water. He squeezed the water out of it (savagely, as though it was an unwanted thought) and handed it to Kuttappen to wipe the grit off his face and neck.

'Did they say anything?' Kuttappen asked. 'About seeing you in the march?'

'No,' Velutha said. 'Not yet. They will though. They know.'

'For sure?'

Velutha shrugged and took the towel away to wash. And rinse. And beat. And wring. As though it was his ridiculous, disobedient brain.

He tried to hate her.

She's one of them, he told himself. *Just another one of them.*

He couldn't.

She had deep dimples when she smiled. Her eyes were always somewhere else.

Madness slunk in through a chink in History. It only took a moment.

An hour into the sandpapering, Rahel remembered her Afternoon Gnap. And she was up and running. Tumbling through the green afternoon heat. Followed by her brother and a yellow wasp.

Hoping, praying, that Ammu hadn't woken up and found her gone.

11

The God of Small Things

That afternoon, Ammu travelled upwards through a dream in which a cheerful man with one arm held her close by the light of an oil lamp. He had no other arm with which to fight the shadows that flickered around him on the floor.

Shadows that only he could see.

Ridges of muscle on his stomach rose under his skin like divisions on a slab of chocolate.

He held her close, by the light of an oil lamp, and he shone as though he had been polished with a high-wax body polish.

He could do only one thing at a time.

If he held her, he couldn't kiss her. If he kissed her, he couldn't see her. If he saw her, he couldn't feel her.

She could have touched his body lightly with her fingers, and felt his smooth skin turn to gooseflesh. She could have let her fingers stray to the base of his flat stomach. Carelessly, over those burnished chocolate ridges. And left patterned trails of bumpy gooseflesh on his body, like flat chalk on a blackboard, like a swathe of breeze in a paddyfield, like jet streaks in a blue church-sky. She could so easily have done that, but she didn't. He could have touched her too. But he didn't, because in the gloom beyond the oil lamp, in the shadows, there were metal folding chairs arranged in a ring and on the chairs there were people, with slanting rhinestone sunglasses, watching. They all held polished violins under their chins, the bows poised at identical angles. They all had their legs crossed, left over right, and all their left legs were shivering.

Some of them had newspapers. Some didn't. Some of them blew spit-bubbles. Some didn't. But they all had the flickering reflection of an oil lamp on each lens.

Beyond the circle of folding chairs was a beach littered with broken blue glass bottles. The silent waves brought new blue bottles to be broken, and dragged the old ones away in the undertow. There were jagged sounds of glass on glass. On a rock, out at sea, in a shaft of purple light, there was a mahogany and wicker rocking chair. Smashed.

The sea was black, the spume vomit green.

Fish fed on shattered glass.

Night's elbows rested on the water, and falling stars glanced off its brittle shards.

Moths lit up the sky. There wasn't a moon.

He could swim, with his one arm. She with her two.

His skin was salty. Hers too.

He left no footprints in sand, no ripples in water, no image in mirrors.

She could have touched him with her fingers, but she didn't. They just stood together.

Still.

Skin to skin.

A powdery, coloured breeze lifted her hair and blew it like a rippled shawl around his armless shoulder, that ended abruptly, like a cliff.

A thin red cow with a protruding pelvic bone appeared and swam straight out to sea without wetting her horns, without looking back.

Ammu flew through her dream on heavy, shuddering wings, and stopped to rest, just under the skin of it.

She had pressed roses from the blue cross-stitch counterpane on her cheek.

She sensed her children's faces hanging over her dream, like two dark, worried moons, waiting to be let in.

'D'you think she's dying?' she heard Rahel whisper to Estha.

'It's an afternoon-mare,' Estha-the-Accurate replied. 'She dreams a lot.'

If he touched her, he couldn't talk to her, if he loved her he couldn't leave, if he spoke he couldn't listen, if he fought he couldn't win.

Who was he, the one-armed man? Who *could* he have been? The God of Loss? The God of Small Things? The God of Goose Bumps and Sudden Smiles? Of Sourmetal Smells – like steel bus-rails and the smell of the bus conductor's hands from holding them?

'Should we wake her up?' Estha said.

Chinks of late afternoon light stole into the room through the curtains and fell on Ammu's tangerine-shaped transistor radio that she always took with her to the river. (Tangerine-shaped too, was the Thing that Estha carried into *The Sound of Music* in his sticky Other Hand.)

Bright bars of sunlight brightened Ammu's tangled hair. She waited, under the skin of her dream, not wanting to let her children in.

'She says you should never wake dreaming people suddenly,' Rahel said. 'She says they could easily have a Heart Attack.'

Between them they decided that it would be best to *disturb* her discreetly, rather than wake her suddenly. So they opened drawers, they cleared their throats, they whispered loudly, they hummed a little tune. They moved shoes. And found a cupboard door that creaked.

Ammu, resting under the skin of her dream, observed them and ached with her love for them.

The one-armed man blew out his lamp and walked across the jagged beach, away into the shadows that only he could see.

He left no footprints on the shore.

The folding chairs were folded. The black sea smoothed. The creased waves ironed. The spume rebottled. The bottle corked.

The night postponed till further notice.

Ammu opened her eyes.

It was a long journey that she made, from the embrace of the one-armed man to her unidentical two-egg twins.

'You were having an afternoon-mare,' her daughter informed her.

'It wasn't a mare,' Ammu said. 'It was a dream.'

'Estha thought you were dying.'

'You looked so sad,' Estha said.

'I was happy,' Ammu said, and realized that she had been.

'If you're happy in a dream, Ammu, does that count?' Estha asked.

'Does what count?'

'The happiness – does it count?'

She knew exactly what he meant, her son with his spoiled puff.

Because the truth is, that only what *counts* counts.

The simple, unswerving wisdom of children.

If you eat fish in a dream, does it count? Does it mean you've eaten fish?

The cheerful man without footprints – did *he* count?

Ammu groped for her tangerine transistor, and switched it on. It played a song from a film called *Chemmeen.*

It was the story of a poor girl who is forced to marry a fisherman from a neighbouring beach, though she loves someone else. When the fisherman finds out about his new wife's old lover, he sets out to sea in his little boat though he knows that a storm is brewing. It's dark, and the wind rises. A whirlpool spins up from the ocean bed. There is storm music, and the fisherman drowns, sucked to the bottom of the sea in the vortex of the whirlpool.

The lovers make a suicide pact, and are found the next morning, washed up on the beach with their arms around each other. So everybody dies. The fisherman, his wife, her lover, and a shark that has no part in the story, but dies anyway. The sea claims them all.

In the blue cross-stitch darkness laced with edges of light, with cross-stitch roses on her sleepy cheek, Ammu and her twins (one on either side of her), sang softly with the tangerine radio. The song that fisherwomen sang to the sad young bride as they braided her hair and prepared her for her wedding to a man she didn't love.

Pandoru mukkuvan muthinu poyi,
(Once a fisherman went to sea,)
Padinjaran kattathu mungi poyi,
(The West Wind blew and swallowed his boat,)

An Airport Fairy frock stood on the floor, supported by its own froth and stiffness. Outside in the mittam, crisp saris lay in rows and crispened in the sun. Off-white and gold. Small pebbles nestled in their starched creases and had to be shaken out before the saris were folded and taken in to be ironed.

Arayathi pennu pizhachu poyi,
(His wife on the shore went astray,)

The electrocuted elephant (not Kochu Thomban) in Ettumanoor was cremated. A giant burning ghat was erected on the highway. The engineers of the concerned municipality sawed off the tusks and shared them unofficially. Unequally. Eighty tins of pure ghee were poured over the elephant to feed the fire. The smoke rose in dense fumes and arranged itself in complex patterns against the sky. People crowded around at a safe distance, read meanings into them.

There were lots of flies.

Avaney kadalamma kondu poyi.
(So Mother Ocean rose and took him away.)

Pariah kites dropped into nearby trees, to supervise the supervision of the last rites of the dead elephant. They hoped, not without reason, for pickings of giant innards. An enormous gall bladder, perhaps. Or a charred, gigantic spleen.

They weren't disappointed. Nor wholly satisfied.

Ammu noticed that both her children were covered in a fine dust. Like two pieces of lightly sugar-dusted, unidentical cake. Rahel had a blonde curl lodged among her black ones. A curl from Velutha's backyard. Ammu picked it out.

'I've told you before,' she said. 'I don't want you going to his house. It will only cause trouble.'

What trouble, she didn't say. She didn't know.

Somehow, by not mentioning his name, she knew that she had drawn him into the tousled intimacy of that blue cross-stitch afternoon and the song from the tangerine transistor. By not mentioning his name, she sensed that a pact had been forged between her Dream and the World. And that the midwives of that pact, were, or would be, her sawdust coated two-egg twins.

She knew who he was – the God of Loss, the God of Small Things. Of *course* she did.

She switched off the tangerine radio. In the afternoon silence (laced with edges of light), her children curled into the warmth of her. The smell of her. They covered their heads with her hair. They sensed somehow that in her sleep she had travelled away from them. They summoned her back now with the palms of their small hands laid flat against the bare skin of her midriff. Between her petticoat and her blouse. They loved the fact that the brown of the backs of their hands was the exact brown of their mother's stomach skin.

'Estha, look,' Rahel said, plucking at the line of soft down that led southwards from Ammu's bellybutton.

'Here's where we kicked you.' Estha traced a wandering silver stretchmark with his finger.

'Was it in the bus, Ammu?'

'On the winding estate road?'

'When Baba had to hold your tummy?'

'Did you have to buy tickets?'

'Did we hurt you?'

And then, keeping her voice casual, Rahel's question: 'D'you think he may have lost our address?'

Just the hint of a pause in the rhythm of Ammu's breathing made Estha touch Rahel's middle finger with his. And middle finger to middle finger, on their beautiful mother's midriff, they abandoned that line of questioning.

'That's Estha's kick, and that's mine,' Rahel said. '. . . And that's Estha's and that's mine.'

Between them they apportioned their mother's seven silver stretchmarks. Then Rahel put her mouth on Ammu's stomach and sucked at it, pulling the soft flesh into her mouth and drawing her head back to admire the shining oval of spit and the faint red imprint of her teeth on her mother's skin.

Ammu wondered at the transparence of that kiss. It was a clear-as-glass kiss. Unclouded by passion or desire – that pair of dogs that sleeps so soundly inside children, waiting for them to grow up. It was a kiss that demanded no kiss-back.

Not a cloudy kiss full of questions that wanted answers. Like the kisses of cheerful one-armed men in dreams.

Ammu grew tired of their proprietary handling of her. She wanted her body back. It was hers. She shrugged her children off the way a bitch shrugs off her pups when she's had enough of them. She sat up and twisted her hair into a knot at the nape of her neck. Then she swung her legs off the bed, walked to the window and drew back the curtains.

Slanting afternoon light flooded the room and brightened two children on the bed.

The twins heard the lock turning in Ammu's bathroom door.

Click.

Ammu looked at herself in the long mirror on the bathroom door and the spectre of her future appeared in it to mock her. Pickled. Grey. Rheumy-eyed. Cross-stitch roses on a slack, sunken cheek. Withered breasts that hung like weighted socks. Dry as a bone between her legs, the hair feather white. Spare. As brittle as a pressed fern.

Skin that flaked and shed like snow.

Ammu shivered.

With that cold feeling on a hot afternoon that Life had been Lived. That her cup was full of dust. That the air, the sky, the trees, the sun, the rain, the light and darkness were all slowly turning to sand. That sand would fill her nostrils, her lungs, her mouth. Would pull her down, leaving on the surface a spinning swirl like crabs leave when they burrow downwards on a beach.

Ammu undressed and put a red toothbrush under a breast to see if it would stay. It didn't. Where she touched herself her flesh was taut and smooth. Under her hands her nipples wrinkled and hardened like dark nuts, pulling at the soft skin on her breasts. The thin line of down from her belly button led over the gentle curve of the base of her belly, to her dark triangle. Like an arrow directing a lost traveller. An inexperienced lover.

She undid her hair and turned around to see how long it had grown. It fell, in waves and curls and disobedient frizzy wisps – soft on the inside, coarser on the outside – to just below where her small, strong waist began its curve out towards her hips. The bathroom was hot. Small beads of sweat studded her skin like diamonds. Then they broke and trickled down. Sweat ran down the recessed line of her spine. She looked a little critically at her round, heavy behind. Not big in itself. Not big *per se* (as Chacko-of-Oxford would no doubt have put it). Big only because the rest of her was so slender. It belonged on another more voluptuous body.

She had to admit that they would happily support a toothbrush apiece. Perhaps two. She laughed out loud at the idea of walking naked down Ayemenem with an array of coloured toothbrushes sticking out from either cheek of her bottom. She silenced herself quickly. She saw a wisp of madness escape from its bottle and caper triumphantly around the bathroom.

Ammu worried about madness.

Mammachi said it ran in their family. That it came on people suddenly and caught them unawares. There was Pathil Ammai, who at the age of sixty-five began to take her clothes off and run naked along the river, singing to the fish. There was Thampi Chachen, who searched his shit every morning with a knitting needle for a gold tooth he had swallowed years ago. And Dr Muthachen, who had to be removed from his own wedding in a sack. Would future generations say, 'There was Ammu – Ammu Ipe. Married a Bengali. Went quite mad. Died young. In a cheap lodge somewhere.'

Chacko said that the high incidence of insanity among Syrian Christians was the price they paid for Inbreeding. Mammachi said it wasn't.

Ammu gathered up her heavy hair, wrapped it around her face, and peered down the road to Age and Death through its parted strands. Like a medieval executioner peering through the tilted eye-slits of his peaked black hood at the executionee. A slender, naked executioner with dark nipples and deep dimples when she smiled. With seven silver stretchmarks from her two-egg twins, born to her by candlelight amidst news of a lost war.

It wasn't what lay at the end of her road that frightened Ammu as much as the nature of the road itself. No milestones marked its progress. No trees grew along it. No dappled shadows shaded it. No mists rolled over it. No birds circled it. No twists, no turns or hairpin bends obscured even momentarily, her clear view of the end. This filled Ammu with an awful dread, because she was not the kind of woman who wanted her future told. She dreaded it too much. So if she were granted one small wish perhaps it would only have been Not to Know. Not to know what each day held in store for her. Not to know where she might be, next month, next year. Ten years on. Not to know which way her road might turn and what lay beyond the bend. And Ammu knew. Or *thought* she knew, which was really just as bad (because if in a dream you've eaten fish, it means you've eaten fish). And what Ammu knew (or thought she knew), smelled of the vapid, vinegary fumes that rose from the cement vats of Paradise Pickles. Fumes that wrinkled youth and pickled futures.

Hooded in her own hair, Ammu leaned against herself in the bathroom mirror and tried to weep.

For herself.

For the God of Small Things.

For the sugar-dusted twin midwives of her dream.

That afternoon – while in the bathroom the fates conspired to alter horribly the course of their mysterious mother's road, while in Velutha's backyard an old boat waited for them, while in a yellow church a young bat waited to be born – in their mother's bedroom, Estha stood on his head on Rahel's bum.

The bedroom with blue curtains and yellow wasps that worried the windowpanes. The bedroom whose walls would soon learn their harrowing secrets.

The bedroom into which Ammu would first be locked and then lock herself. Whose door, Chacko, crazed by grief, four days after Sophie Mol's funeral, would batter down.

'Get out of my house before I break every bone in your body!'

My house, *my* pineapples, *my* pickle.

After that for years Rahel would dream this dream: a fat man, faceless, kneeling beside a woman's corpse. Hacking its hair off. Breaking every bone in its body. Snapping even the little ones. The fingers. The ear bones cracked like twigs. *Snapsnap* the softsound of breaking bones. A pianist killing the piano keys. Even the black ones. And Rahel (though years later, in the Electric Crematorium, she would use the slipperiness of sweat to slither out of Chacko's grasp), loved them both. The player and the piano.

The killer and the corpse.

As the door was slowly battered down, to control the trembling of her hands, Ammu would hem the ends of Rahel's ribbons that didn't need hemming.

'Promise me you'll always love each other,' she'd say, as she drew her children to her.

'Promise,' Estha and Rahel would say. Not finding words with which to tell her that for them there *was* no Each, no Other.

Twin millstones and their mother. Numb millstones. What they had done would return to empty them. But that would be Later.

Lay Ter. A deep-sounding bell in a mossy well. Shivery and furred like moth's feet.

At the time, there would only be incoherence. As though meaning had slunk out of things and left them fragmented. Disconnected. The glint of Ammu's needle. The colour of a ribbon. The weave of the cross-stitch counterpane. A door slowly breaking. Isolated things that didn't *mean* anything. As though the intelligence that decodes life's hidden patterns – that connects reflections to images, glints to light, weaves to fabrics, needles to thread, walls to rooms, love to fear to anger to remorse – was suddenly lost.

'Pack your things and go,' Chacko would say, stepping over the debris. Looming over them. A chrome door handle in his hand. Suddenly strangely calm. Surprised at his own strength. His bigness. His bullying power. The enormity of his own terrible grief.

Red the colour of splintered doorwood.

Ammu, quiet outside, shaking inside, wouldn't look up from her unnecessary hemming. The tin of coloured ribbons would lie open on her lap, in the room where she had lost her Locusts Stand I.

The same room in which (after the Twin Expert from Hyderabad had replied), Ammu would pack Estha's little trunk and khaki holdall: 12 sleeveless cotton vests, 12 half-sleeved cotton vests. *Estha, here's your name on them in ink.* His socks. His drainpipe trousers. His pointy collared shirts. His beige and pointy shoes (from where the Angry Feelings came). His Elvis records. His calcium tablets and Vydalin syrup. His Free Giraffe (that came with the Vydalin). His Books of Knowledge Vols. 1–4. *No, sweetheart, there won't be a river there to fish in.* His white leather zip-up Bible with an Imperial Entomologist's amethyst cuff-link on the zip. His mug. His soap. His Advance Birthday Present that he *mustn't* open. Forty green inland letter forms. *Look, Estha, I've written our address on it. All you have to do is fold it. See if you can fold it yourself.* And Estha would fold the green inland letter neatly along the dotted lines that said *Fold here* and look up at Ammu with a smile that broke her heart.

Promise me you'll write? Even when you don't have any news?

Promise, Estha would say. Not wholly cognizant of his situation. The sharp edge of his apprehensions blunted by this sudden wealth of worldly possessions. They were His. And had his name on them in ink. They were to be packed into the trunk (with his name on it) that lay open on the bedroom floor.

The room to which, years later, Rahel would return and watch a silent stranger bathe. And wash his clothes with crumbling bright blue soap.

Flatmuscled, and honey coloured. Sea-secrets in his eyes. A silver raindrop on his ear.

Esthapappychachen Kuttappen Peter Mon.

12

Kochu Thomban

The sound of the chenda mushroomed over the temple, accentuating the silence of the encompassing night. The lonely, wet road. The watching trees. Rahel, breathless, holding a coconut, stepped into the temple compound through the wooden doorway in the high white boundary wall.

Inside, everything was white-walled, moss-tiled and moonlit. Everything smelled of recent rain. The thin priest was asleep on a mat in the raised stone verandah. A brass platter of coins lay near his pillow like a comic strip illustration of his dreams. The compound was littered with moons, one in each mud puddle. Kochu Thomban had finished his ceremonial rounds, and lay tethered to a wooden stake next to a steaming mound of his own dung. He was asleep, his duty done, his bowels empty, one tusk resting on the earth, the other pointed to the stars. Rahel approached quietly. She saw that his skin was looser than she remembered. He wasn't *Kochu* Thomban any more. His tusks had grown. He was *Vellya* Thomban now. The Big Tusker. She put the coconut on the ground next to him. A leathery wrinkle parted to reveal a liquid glint of elephant eye. Then it closed and long, sweeping lashes resummoned sleep. A tusk towards the stars.

June is low season for kathakali. But there are some temples that a troupe will not pass by without performing in. The Ayemenem temple wasn't one of them, but these days, thanks to its geography, things had changed.

In Ayemenem they danced to jettison their humiliation in the Heart of Darkness. Their truncated swimming pool performances. Their turning to tourism to stave off starvation.

On their way back from the Heart of Darkness, they stopped at the temple to ask pardon of their gods. To apologize for corrupting their stories. For encashing their identities. Misappropriating their lives.

On these occasions, a human audience was welcome, but entirely incidental.

In the broad, covered corridor – the colonnaded kuthambalam abutting the heart of the temple where the Blue God lived with his flute, the drummers drummed and the dancers danced, their colours turning slowly in the night. Rahel sat down cross-legged, resting her back against the roundness of a white pillar. A tall cannister of coconut oil gleamed in the flickering light of the brass lamp. The oil replenished the light. The light lit the tin.

It didn't matter that the story had begun, because kathakali discovered long ago that the secret of the Great Stories is that they *have* no secrets. The Great Stories are the ones you have heard and want to hear again. The ones you can enter anywhere and inhabit comfortably. They don't deceive you with thrills and trick endings. They don't surprise you with the unforeseen. They are as familiar as the house you live in. Or the smell of your lover's skin. You know how they end, yet you listen as though you don't. In the way that although you know that one day you will die, you live as though you won't. In the Great Stories you know who lives, who dies, who finds love, who doesn't. And yet you want to know again.

That is their mystery and their magic.

To the Kathakali Man these stories are his children and his childhood. He has grown up within them. They are the house he was raised in, the meadows he played in. They are his windows and his way of seeing. So when he tells a story, he handles it as he would a child of his own. He teases it. He punishes it. He sends it up like a bubble. He wrestles it to the ground and lets it go again. He laughs at it because he loves it. He can fly you across whole worlds in minutes, he can stop for hours to examine a wilting leaf. Or play with a sleeping monkey's tail. He can turn effortlessly from the carnage of war into the felicity of a woman washing her hair in a mountain stream. From the crafty ebullience of a rakshasa with a new idea into a gossipy Malayali with a scandal to spread. From the sensuousness of a woman with a baby at her breast into the seductive mischief of Krishna's smile. He can reveal the nugget of sorrow that happiness contains. The hidden fish of shame in a sea of glory.

He tells stories of the gods, but his yarn is spun from the ungodly, human heart.

The Kathakali Man is the most beautiful of men. Because his body *is* his soul. His only instrument. From the age of three it has been planed and polished, pared down, harnessed wholly to the task of story-telling. He has magic in him, this man within the painted mask and swirling skirts.

But these days he has become unviable. Unfeasible. Condemned goods. His children deride him. They long to be everything that he is not. He has watched them grow up to become clerks and bus conductors. Class IV non-gazetted officers. With unions of their own.

But he himself, left dangling somewhere between heaven and earth, cannot do what they do. He cannot slide down the aisles of buses, counting change and selling tickets. He cannot answer bells that summon him. He cannot stoop behind trays of tea and Marie biscuits.

In despair he turns to tourism. He enters the market. He hawks the only thing he owns. The stories that his body can tell.

He becomes a Regional Flavour.

In the Heart of Darkness they mock him with their lolling nakedness and their imported attention spans. He checks his rage and dances for them. He collects his fee. He gets drunk. Or smokes a joint. Good Kerala grass. It makes him laugh. Then he stops by the Ayemenem Temple, he and the others with him, and they dance to ask pardon of the gods.

Rahel (no Plans, no Locusts stand I), her back against a pillar, watched Karna praying on the banks of the Ganga. Karna, sheathed in his armour of light. Karna, melancholy son of Surya, God of Day. Karna the Generous. Karna the abandoned child. Karna the most revered warrior of them all.

That night Karna was stoned. His tattered skirt was darned. There were hollows in his crown where jewels used to be. His velvet blouse had grown bald with use. His heels were cracked. Tough. He stubbed his joints out on them.

But if he had had a fleet of make-up men waiting in the wings, an agent, a contract, a percentage of the profits – what then would he be? An impostor. A rich pretender. An actor playing a part. Could he be Karna? Or would he be too *safe* inside his pod of wealth? Would his money grow like a rind between himself and his story? Would he be able to touch its heart, its hidden secrets, in the way that he can now?

Perhaps not.

This man tonight is dangerous. His despair complete. This story is the safety net above which he swoops and dives like a brilliant clown in a bankrupt circus. It's all he has to keep him from crashing through the world like a falling stone. It is his colour and his light. It is the vessel into which he pours himself. It gives him shape. Structure. It harnesses him. It contains him. His Love. His Madness. His Hope. His Infinnate Joy. Ironically, his struggle is the reverse of an actor's struggle – he strives not to *enter* a part but to escape it. But this is what he cannot do. In his abject defeat lies his supreme triumph. He *is* Karna, whom the world has abandoned. Karna Alone. Condemned goods. A prince raised in poverty. Born to die unfairly, unarmed and alone at the hands of his brother. Majestic in his complete despair. Praying on the banks of the Ganga. Stoned out of his skull.

Then Kunti appeared. She too was a man, but a man grown soft and womanly, a man with breasts, from doing female parts for years. Her movements were fluid. Full of woman. Kunti, too, was stoned. High on the same shared joints. She had come to tell Karna a story.

Karna inclined his beautiful head and listened.

Red-eyed, Kunti danced for him. She told him of a young woman who had been granted a boon. A secret mantra that she could use to choose a lover from among the gods. Of how, with the imprudence of youth, the woman decided to test it to see if it really worked. How she stood alone in an empty field, turned her face to the heavens and recited the mantra. The words had scarcely left her foolish lips, Kunti said, when Surya, the God of Day, appeared before her. The young woman, bewitched by the beauty of the shimmering young god, gave herself to him. Nine months later she bore him a son. The baby was born sheathed in light, with gold earrings in his ears and a gold breastplate on his chest, engraved with the emblem of the sun.

The young mother loved her first-born son deeply, Kunti said, but she was unmarried and couldn't keep him. She put him in a reed basket and cast him away in a river. The child was found downriver by Adhirata, a charioteer. And named Karna.

Karna looked up at Kunti. *Who was she? Who was my mother? Tell me where she is. Take me to her.*

Kunti bowed her head. *She's here,* she said. *Standing before you.*

Karna's elation and anger at the revelation. His dance of confusion and despair. *Where were you,* he asked her, *when I needed you most? Did you ever hold me in your arms? Did you feed me? Did you ever look for me? Did you wonder where I might be?*

In reply Kunti took the regal face in her hands, green the face, red the eyes, and kissed him on his brow. Karna shuddered in delight. A warrior reduced to infancy. The ecstasy of that kiss. He dispatched it to the ends of his body. To his toes. His fingertips. His lovely mother's kiss. *Did you know how much I missed you?* Rahel could see it coursing through his veins, as clearly as an egg travelling down an ostrich's neck.

A travelling kiss whose journey was cut short by dismay when Karna realized that his mother had revealed herself to him only to secure the safety of her five other, more beloved sons – the Pandavas – poised on the brink of their epic battle with their one hundred cousins. It is *them* that Kunti sought to protect by announcing to Karna that she was his mother. She had a promise to extract.

She invoked the Love Laws.

They are your brothers. Your own flesh and blood. Promise me that you will not go to war against them. Promise me that.

Karna the Warrior could not make that promise, for if he did, he would have to revoke another one. Tomorrow he would go to war, and his enemies would be the Pandavas. They were the ones, Arjuna in particular, who had publicly reviled him for being a lowly charioteer's son. And it was Duryodhana, the eldest of the one hundred Kaurava brothers, that came to his rescue by gifting him a kingdom of his own. Karna, in return, had pledged Duryodhana eternal fealty.

But Karna the Generous could not refuse his mother what she asked of him. So he modified the promise. Equivocated. Made a small adjustment, took a somewhat altered oath.

I promise you this, Karna said to Kunti. *You will always have five sons. Yudhishtira I will not harm. Bhima will not die by my hand. The twins – Nakula and Sahadeva – will go untouched by me. But Arjuna –*

him I will make no promises about. I will kill him, or he will kill me. One of us will die.

Something altered in the air. And Rahel knew that Estha had come.

She didn't turn her head, but a glow spread inside her. *He's come*, she thought. *He's here. With me.*

Estha settled against a distant pillar and they sat through the performance like this, separated by the breadth of the kuthambalam, but joined by a story. And the memory of another mother.

The air grew warmer. Less damp.

Perhaps that evening had been a particularly bad one in the Heart of Darkness. In Ayemenem the men danced as though they couldn't stop. Like children in a warm house sheltering from a storm. Refusing to emerge and acknowledge the weather. The wind and thunder. The rats racing across the ruined landscape with dollar signs in their eyes. The world crashing around them.

They emerged from one story only to delve deep into another. From *Karna Shabadam* – Karna's Oath – to *Duryodhana Vadham* – the death of Duryodhana and his brother Dushasana.

It was almost four in the morning when Bhima hunted down vile Dushasana. The man who had tried publicly to undress the Pandavas' wife, Draupadi, after the Kauravas had won her in a game of dice. Draupadi (strangely angry only with the men that won her, not the ones that staked her), has sworn that she will never tie up her hair until it is washed in Dushasana's blood. Bhima has vowed to avenge her honour.

Bhima cornered Dushasana in a battlefield already strewn with corpses. For an hour they fenced with each other. Traded insults. Listed all the wrongs that each had done the other. When the light from the brass lamp began to flicker and die, they called a truce. Bhima poured the oil, Dushasana cleaned the charred wick. Then they went back to war. Their breathless battle spilled out of the kuthambalam and spun around the temple. They chased each other across the compound, twirling their papier-mâché maces. Two men in ballooning skirts and balding velvet blouses, vaulting over littered moons and mounds of dung, circling around the hulk of a sleeping elephant. Dushasana full of bravado one minute. Cringing the next. Bhima toying with him. Both stoned.

The sky was a rose bowl. The grey, elephant-shaped hole in the Universe agitated in his sleep, then slept again. Dawn was just breaking when the brute in Bhima stirred. The drums beat louder, but the air grew quiet and full of menace.

In the early morning light, Esthappen and Rahel watched Bhima fulfil his vow to Draupadi. He clubbed Dushasana to the floor. He pursued every feeble tremor in the dying body with his mace, hammering at it until it was stilled. An ironsmith flattening a sheet of recalcitrant metal. Systematically smoothing every pit and bulge. He continued to kill him long after he was dead. Then, with his bare hands he tore the body open. He ripped its innards out and stooped to lap blood straight from the bowl of the torn carcass, his crazed eyes peeping over the rim, glittering with rage and hate and mad fulfilment. Gurgling blood-bubbles pale pink between his teeth. Dribbling down his painted face, his neck and chin. When he had drunk enough, he stood up, bloody intestines draped around his neck like a scarf and went to find Draupadi and bathe her hair in fresh blood. He still had about him the aura of rage that even murder cannot quell.

There was madness there that morning. Under the rose bowl. It was no performance. Esthappen and Rahel recognized it. They had seen its work before. Another morning. Another stage. Another kind of frenzy (with millipedes on the soles of its shoes). The brutal extravagance of this matched by the savage economy of that.

They sat there, Quietness and Emptiness, frozen two-egg fossils, with hornbumps that hadn't grown into horns. Separated by the breadth of a kuthambalam. Trapped in the bog of a story that was and wasn't theirs. That had set out with the semblance of structure and order, then bolted like a frightened horse into anarchy.

Kochu Thomban woke and delicately cracked open his morning coconut.

The Kathakali Men took off their make-up and went home to beat their wives. Even Kunti, the soft one with breasts.

Outside and around, the little town masquerading as a village stirred and came to life. An old man woke and staggered to the stove to warm his peppered coconut oil.

Comrade Pillai. Ayemenem's egg-breaker and professional omletteer.

Oddly enough, it was he who had introduced the twins to kathakali. Against Baby Kochamma's better judgement, it was he who took them, along with Lenin, for all-night performances at the temple, and sat up with them till dawn, explaining the language and gesture of kathakali. Aged six, they had sat with him through this very story. It was he who had introduced them to Raudra Bhima – crazed, bloodthirsty Bhima in search of death and vengeance. 'He is searching for the beast that lives in him,' Comrade Pillai had told them – frightened, wide-eyed children – when the ordinarily good-natured Bhima began to bay and snarl.

Which beast in particular, Comrade Pillai didn't say. Searching for the *man* who lives in him was perhaps what he really meant, because certainly no beast has essayed the boundless, infinitely inventive art of human hatred. No beast can match its range and power.

The rose bowl dulled and sent down a warm grey drizzle. As Estha and Rahel stepped through the temple gateway, Comrade

K. N. M. Pillai stepped in, slick from his oil bath. He had sandalwood paste on his forehead. Raindrops stood out on his oiled skin like studs. In his cupped palms he carried a small heap of fresh jasmine.

'Oho!' he said in his piping voice 'You are here! So still you are interested in your Indian culture? Goodgood. Very good.'

The twins, not rude, not polite, said nothing. They walked home together. He and She. We and Us.

13

The Pessimist and the Optimist

Chacko had moved out of his room and would sleep in Pappachi's study so that Sophie Mol and Margaret Kochamma could have his room. It was a small room, with a window that overlooked the dwindling, somewhat neglected rubber plantation that Reverend E. John Ipe had bought from a neighbour. One door connected it to the main house and another (the separate entrance that Mammachi had installed for Chacko to pursue his 'Men's Needs' discreetly) led directly out into the side mittam.

Sophie Mol lay asleep on a little camp cot that had been made up for her next to the big bed. The drone of the slow ceiling fan filled her head. Bluegreyblue eyes snapped open.

A Wake

A Live

A Lert

Sleep was summarily dismissed.

For the first time since Joe had died, he was not the first thing that she thought about when she woke up.

She looked around the room. Not moving, just swivelling her eyeballs. A captured spy in enemy territory, plotting her spectacular escape.

A vase of awkwardly arranged hibiscus, already drooping, stood on Chacko's table. The walls were lined with books. A glass-paned cupboard was crammed with damaged balsa airplanes. Broken butterflies with imploring eyes. A wicked king's wooden wives languishing under an evil wooden spell.

Trapped.

Only one, her mother, Margaret, had escaped to England.

The room went round in the calm, chrome centre of the silver ceiling fan. A beige gecko, the colour of an undercooked biscuit, regarded her with interested eyes. She thought of Joe. Something shook inside her. She closed her eyes.

The calm, chrome centre of the silver ceiling fan went round inside her head.

Joe could walk on his hands. And when he cycled downhill, he could put the wind inside his shirt.

On the next bed, Margaret Kochamma was still asleep. She lay on her back with her hands clasped together just below her ribcage. Her fingers were swollen and her wedding band looked uncomfortably tight. The flesh of her cheeks fell away on either side of her face, making her cheekbones look high and prominent, and pulling her mouth downwards into a mirthless smile that contained just a glimmer of teeth. She had tweezed her once bushy eyebrows into the currently fashionable, pencil-thin arcs which gave her a slightly surprised expression even in her sleep. The rest of her expressions were growing back in a nascent stubble. Her face was flushed. Her forehead glistened. Underneath the flush, there was a paleness. A staved-off sadness.

The thin material of her dark blue and white flowered cotton-polyester dress had wilted and clung limply to the contours of her body, rising over her breasts, dipping along the line between her long, strong legs – as though it too was unaccustomed to the heat and needed a nap.

On the bedside table there was a silver-framed black-and-white wedding picture of Chacko and Margaret Kochamma taken outside the church in Oxford. It was snowing a little. The first flakes of fresh snow lay on the street and sidewalk. Chacko was dressed like Nehru. He wore a white churidar and a black shervani. His shoulders were dusted with snow. There was a rose in his buttonhole, and the tip of his handkerchief, folded into a triangle, peeped out of his breast pocket. On his feet he wore polished black Oxfords. He looked as though he was laughing at himself and the way he was dressed. Like someone at a fancy-dress party.

Margaret Kochamma wore a long, foaming gown and a cheap tiara on her cropped, curly hair. Her veil was lifted off her face. She was as tall as he was. They looked happy. Thin and young, scowling from the sun in their eyes. Her thick, dark eyebrows were knitted together and somehow made a lovely contrast to the frothy, bridal white. A scowling cloud with eyebrows. Behind them stood a large matronly woman with thick ankles and all the buttons done up on her long overcoat. Margaret Kochamma's mother. She had her two little granddaughters on either side of her, in pleated tartan skirts, stockings and identical fringes. They were both giggling with their hands over their mouths. Margaret Kochamma's mother was looking away, out of the photograph, as though she would rather not have been there.

Margaret Kochamma's father had refused to attend the wedding. He disliked Indians, he thought of them as sly, dishonest people. He couldn't believe that his daughter was marrying one.

In the right-hand corner of the photograph, a man wheeling his bicycle along the kerb had turned to stare at the couple.

Margaret Kochamma was working as a waitress at a café in Oxford when she first met Chacko. Her family lived in London. Her father owned a bakery. Her mother was a milliner's assistant. Margaret Kochamma had moved out of her parents' home a year ago, for no greater reason than a youthful assertion of independence. She intended to work and save enough money to put herself through a teacher training course, and then look for a job at a school. In Oxford she shared a small flat with a friend. Another waitress in another café.

Having made the move, Margaret Kochamma found herself becoming exactly the kind of girl her parents wanted her to be. Faced with the Real World, she clung nervously to old remembered rules, and had no one but herself to rebel against. So even up at Oxford, other than playing her gramophone a little louder than she was permitted at home, she continued to lead the same small, tight life that she imagined she had escaped.

Until Chacko walked into the café one morning.

It was the summer of his final year at Oxford. He was alone. His rumpled shirt was buttoned up wrong. His shoelaces were untied. His hair, carefully brushed and slicked down in front, stood up in a stiff halo of quills at the back. He looked like an untidy, beatified porcupine. He was tall, and underneath the mess of clothes (inappropriate tie, shabby coat), Margaret Kochamma could see that he was well-built. He had an amused air about him, and a way of narrowing his eyes as though he was trying to read a faraway sign and had forgotten to bring his glasses. His ears stuck out on either side of his head like teapot handles. There was something contradictory about his athletic build and his dishevelled appearance. The only sign that a fat man lurked inside him was his shining, happy cheeks.

He had none of the vagueness or the apologetic awkwardness that one usually associates with untidy, absent-minded men. He looked cheerful, as though he was with an imaginary friend whose company he enjoyed. He took a seat by the window and sat down with an elbow on the table and his face cupped in the palm of his hand, smiling around the empty café as though he was considering striking up a conversation with the furniture. He ordered coffee with that same friendly smile, but without really appearing to notice the tall, bushy eyebrowed waitress who took his order.

She winced when he put two heaped spoons of sugar into his extremely milky coffee.

Then he asked for fried eggs on toast. More coffee, and strawberry jam.

When she returned with his order, he said, as though he was continuing an old conversation, 'Have you heard about the man who had twin sons?'

'No,' she said, setting down his breakfast. For some reason (natural prudence perhaps, and an instinctive reticence with foreigners) she did not evince the keen interest that he seemed to expect from her about the Man with Twin Sons. Chacko didn't seem to mind.

'A man had twin sons,' he told Margaret Kochamma. 'Pete and Stuart. Pete was an Optimist and Stuart was a Pessimist.'

He picked the strawberries out of the jam and put them on one side of his plate. The rest of the jam he spread in a thick layer on his buttered toast.

'On their thirteenth birthday their father gave Stuart – the Pessimist – an expensive watch, a carpentry set and a bicycle.'

Chacko looked up at Margaret Kochamma to see if she was listening.

'And Pete's – the Optimist's – room, he filled with horse dung.'

Chacko lifted the fried eggs onto the toast, broke the brilliant, wobbling yokes and spread them over the strawberry jam with the back of his teaspoon.

'When Stuart opened his presents he grumbled all morning. He hadn't wanted a carpentry set, he didn't like the watch and the bicycle had the wrong kind of tyres.'

Margaret Kochamma had stopped listening because she was riveted by the curious ritual unfolding on his plate. The toast with jam and fried egg was cut into neat little squares. The dejammed strawberries were summoned one by one, and sliced into delicate pieces.

'When the father went to Pete's – the Optimist's – room, he couldn't see Pete, but he could hear the sound of frantic shovelling and heavy breathing. Horse dung was flying all over the room.'

Chacko had begun to shake with silent laughter in anticipation of the end of his joke. With laughing hands, he placed a sliver of strawberry on each bright yellow and red square of toast – making the whole thing look like a lurid snack that an old woman might serve at a bridge party.

'"What in heaven's name are you doing?" the father shouted to Pete.'

Salt and pepper was sprinkled on the squares of toast. Chacko paused before the punch line, laughing up at Margaret Kochamma, who was smiling at his plate.

'A voice came from deep inside the dung. "Well, Father," Pete said, "if there's so much shit around, there has to be a pony somewhere!"'

Chacko, holding a fork and a knife in each hand, leaned back in his chair in the empty café, and laughed his high, hiccupping, infectious, fat man's laugh till the tears poured down his cheeks. Margaret Kochamma, who had missed most of the joke, smiled. Then she began to laugh at his laugh. Their laughs fed each other and climbed to a hysterical pitch. When the owner of the café appeared, he saw a customer (not a particularly desirable one), and a waitress (an only averagely desirable one), locked in a spiral of hooting, helpless laughter.

Meanwhile, another customer (a regular), had arrived unnoticed, and waited to be served.

The owner cleaned some already-clean glasses clinking them together noisily, and clattered crockery on the counter to convey his displeasure to Margaret Kochamma. She tried to compose herself before she went to take the new order. But she had tears in her eyes, and had to stifle a fresh batch of giggles, which made the hungry man whose order she was taking look up from his menu card, his thin lips pursed in silent disapproval.

She stole a glance at Chacko, who looked at her and smiled. It was an insanely friendly smile.

He finished his breakfast, paid, and left.

Margaret Kochamma was reproached by her employer and given a lecture on Café Ethics. She apologized to him. She was truly sorry for the way she had behaved.

That evening, after work, she thought about what had happened and was uncomfortable with herself. She was not usually frivolous, and didn't think it right to have shared such uncontrolled laughter with a complete stranger. It seemed such an over-familiar, intimate thing to have done. She wondered what had made her laugh so much. She knew it wasn't the joke.

She thought of Chacko's laugh, and a smile stayed in her eyes for a long time.

Chacko began to visit the café quite often.

He always came with his invisible companion and his friendly smile. Even when it wasn't Margaret Kochamma who served him, he sought her out with his eyes, and they exchanged secret smiles that invoked the joint memory of their Laugh.

Margaret Kochamma found herself looking forward to the Rumpled Porcupine's visits. Without anxiety, but with a sort of creeping affection. She learned that he was a Rhodes Scholar from India. That he read Classics. And rowed for Balliol.

Until the day she married him she never believed that she would ever consent to be his wife.

A few months after they began to go out together, he began to smuggle her into his rooms, where he lived like a helpless, exiled prince. Despite the best efforts of his scout and cleaning lady, his room was always filthy. Books, empty wine bottles, dirty underwear and cigarette butts littered the floor. Cupboards were dangerous to open because clothes and books and shoes would cascade down and some of his books were heavy enough to inflict real damage. Margaret Kochamma's tiny, ordered life relinquished itself to this truly baroque bedlam with the quiet gasp of a warm body entering a chilly sea.

She discovered that underneath the aspect of the Rumpled Porcupine, a tortured Marxist was at war with an impossible, incurable Romantic – who forgot the candles, who broke the wine glasses, who lost the ring. Who made love to her with a passion that took her breath away. She had always thought of herself as a somewhat uninteresting, thick-waisted, thick-ankled girl. Not bad-looking. Not special. But when she was with Chacko, old limits were pushed back. Horizons expanded.

She had never before met a man who spoke of the world – of what it was, and how it came to be, or what he thought would become of it – in the way in which other men she knew discussed their jobs, their friends or their weekends at the beach.

Being with Chacko made Margaret Kochamma feel as though her soul had escaped from the narrow confines of her island country into the vast, extravagant spaces of his. He made her feel as though the world belonged to them – as though it lay before them like an opened frog on a dissecting table, begging to be examined.

In the year she knew him, before they were married, she discovered a little magic in herself, and for a while felt like a blithe genie released from her lamp. She was perhaps too young to realize that what she assumed was her love for Chacko was actually a tentative, timorous acceptance of herself.

As for Chacko, Margaret Kochamma was the first female friend he had ever had. Not just the first woman that he had slept with, but his first real companion. What Chacko loved most about her was her self-sufficiency. Perhaps it wasn't remarkable in the average English woman, but it was remarkable to Chacko.

He loved the fact that Margaret Kochamma didn't cling to him. That she was uncertain about her feelings for him. That he never knew till the last day whether or not she would marry him. He loved the way she would sit up naked in his bed, her long white back swivelled away from him, look at her watch and say in her practical way – 'Oops, I must be off.' He loved the way she wobbled to work every morning on her bicycle. He encouraged their differences in opinion, and inwardly rejoiced at her occasional outbursts of exasperation at his decadence.

He was grateful to her for not wanting to look after him. For not offering to tidy his room. For not being his cloying mother. He grew to depend on Margaret Kochamma for not depending on him. He adored her for not adoring him.

Of his family Margaret Kochamma knew very little. He seldom spoke of them.

The truth is that in his years at Oxford, Chacko rarely thought of them. Too much was happening in his life and Ayemenem seemed so far away. The river too small. The fish too few.

He had no pressing reasons to stay in touch with his parents. The Rhodes Scholarship was generous. He needed no money. He was deeply in love with his love for Margaret Kochamma and had no room in his heart for anyone else.

Mammachi wrote to him regularly, with detailed descriptions of her sordid squabbles with her husband and her worries about Ammu's future. He hardly ever read a whole letter. Sometimes he never bothered to open them at all. He never wrote back.

Even the one time he did return (when he stopped Pappachi from hitting Mammachi with the brass vase, and a rocking chair was murdered in the moonlight), he was hardly aware of how stung his father had been, or his mother's redoubled adoration of him, or his young sister's sudden beauty. He came and went in a trance, yearning from the moment he arrived to return to the long-backed white girl who waited for him.

The winter after he came down from Balliol (he did badly in his exams), Margaret Kochamma and Chacko were married. Without her family's consent. Without his family's knowledge.

They decided that he should move into Margaret Kochamma's flat (displacing the Other waitress in the Other café) until he found himself a job.

The timing of the wedding couldn't have been worse.

Along with the pressures of living together came penury. There was no longer any scholarship money, and there was the full rent of the flat to be paid.

With the end to his rowing came a sudden, premature, middle-aged spread. Chacko became a Fat Man, with a body to match his laugh.

A year into the marriage, and the charm of Chacko's studently sloth wore off for Margaret Kochamma. It no longer amused her that while she went to work, the flat remained in the same filthy mess that she had left it in. That it was impossible for him even to consider making the bed, or washing clothes or dishes. That he didn't apologize for the cigarette burns in the new sofa. That he seemed incapable of buttoning up his shirt, knotting his tie *and* tying his shoe laces before presenting himself for a job interview. Within a year she was prepared to exchange the frog on the dissecting table for some small, practical concessions. Such as a job for her husband and a clean home.

Eventually Chacko got a brief, badly paid assignment with the Overseas Sales Department of the India Tea Board. Hoping that this would lead to other things, Chacko and Margaret moved to London. To even smaller, more dismal rooms. Margaret Kochamma's parents refused to see her.

She had just discovered that she was pregnant when she met Joe. He was an old school friend of her brother's. When they met, Margaret Kochamma was physically at her most attractive. Pregnancy had put colour in her cheeks and brought a shine to her thick, dark hair. Despite her marital troubles, she had that air of secret elation, that affection for her own body that pregnant women often have.

Joe was a biologist. He was updating the third edition of a

dictionary of Biology for a small publishing house. Joe was everything that Chacko wasn't.

Steady. Solvent. Thin.

Margaret Kochamma found herself drawn towards him like a plant in a dark room towards a wedge of light.

When Chacko finished his assignment and couldn't find another job, he wrote to Mammachi, telling her of his marriage and asking for money. Mammachi was devastated, but secretly pawned her jewellery and arranged for money to be sent to him in England. It wasn't enough. It was never enough.

By the time Sophie Mol was born, Margaret Kochamma realized that for herself and her daughter's sake, she *had* to leave Chacko. She asked him for a divorce.

Chacko returned to India, where he found a job easily. For a few years he taught at the Madras Christian College, and after Pappachi died, he returned to Ayemenem with his Bharat bottle-sealing machine, his Balliol oar and his broken heart.

Mammachi joyfully welcomed him back into her life. She fed him, she sewed for him, she saw to it that there were fresh flowers in his room every day. Chacko needed his mother's adoration. Indeed, he *demanded* it, yet he despised her for it and punished her in secret ways. He began to cultivate his corpulence and general physical dilapidation. He wore cheap, printed Terylene bush shirts over his white mundus and the ugliest plastic sandals that were available in the market. If Mammachi had guests, relatives, or perhaps an old friend visiting from Delhi, Chacko would appear at her tastefully laid dining table – adorned with her exquisite orchid arrangements and best china – and worry an old scab, or scratch the large, black oblong calluses he had cultivated on his elbows.

His special targets were Baby Kochamma's guests – Catholic bishops or visiting clergy – who often dropped by for a snack.

In their presence Chacko would take off his sandals and air a revolting, pus-filled diabetic boil on his foot.

'Lord have mercy upon this poor leper,' he would say, while Baby Kochamma tried desperately to distract them from the spectacle by picking out the biscuit crumbs and bits of banana chips that littered their beards.

But of all the secret punishments that Chacko tormented Mammachi with, the worst and most mortifying of all, was when he reminisced about Margaret Kochamma. He spoke of her often and with a peculiar pride. As though he admired her for having divorced him.

'She traded me in for a better man,' he would say to Mammachi, and she would flinch as though he had denigrated her instead of himself.

Margaret Kochamma wrote regularly, giving Chacko news of Sophie Mol. She assured him that Joe made a wonderful, caring father and that Sophie Mol loved him dearly – facts that gladdened and saddened Chacko in equal measure.

Margaret Kochamma was happy with Joe. Happier perhaps than she would have been had she not had those wild, precarious years with Chacko. She thought of Chacko fondly, but without regret. It simply did not occur to her that she had hurt him as deeply as she had, because she still thought of herself as an ordinary woman, and him as an extraordinary man. And because Chacko had not then, or since, exhibited any of the usual symptoms of grief and heartbreak, Margaret Kochamma just assumed that he felt it had been as much of a mistake for him as it had been for her. When she told him about Joe he had left sadly, but quietly. With his invisible companion and his friendly smile.

They wrote to each other frequently, and over the years their relationship matured. For Margaret Kochamma it became a comfortable, committed friendship. For Chacko it was a way, the *only* way, of remaining in touch with the mother of his child and the only woman he had ever loved.

When Sophie Mol was old enough to go to school, Margaret Kochamma enrolled herself in a teacher training course, and then got a job as a junior school teacher in Clapham. She was in the staff room when she was told about Joe's accident. The news was delivered by a young policeman who wore a grave expression and carried his helmet in his hands. He had looked strangely comical, like a bad actor auditioning for a solemn part in a play. Margaret Kochamma remembered that her first instinct when she saw him had been to smile.

For Sophie Mol's sake, if not her own, Margaret Kochamma did her best to face the tragedy with equanimity. To *pretend* to face the tragedy with equanimity. She didn't take time off from her job. She saw to it that Sophie Mol's school routine remained unchanged – *Finish your homework. Eat your egg. No, we can't not go to school.*

She concealed her anguish under the brisk, practical mask of a schoolteacher. The stern, schoolteacher-shaped hole in the Universe (who sometimes slapped).

But when Chacko wrote inviting her to Ayemenem, something inside her sighed and sat down. Despite everything that had happened between her and Chacko, there was nobody in the world she would rather spend Christmas with. The more she considered it, the more tempted she was. She persuaded herself that a trip to India would be just the thing for Sophie Mol.

So eventually, though she knew that her friends and colleagues at the school would think it odd – her running back to her first husband just as soon as her second one had died – Margaret Kochamma broke her term deposit and bought two airline tickets. London–Bombay–Cochin.

She was haunted by that decision for as long as she lived.

She took with her to her grave the picture of her little daughter's body laid out on the chaise longue in the drawing room of the Ayemenem House. Even from a distance, it was obvious that she was dead. Not ill or asleep. It was something to do with the way she lay. The angle of her limbs. Something to do with Death's authority. Its terrible stillness.

Green weed and river grime were woven into her beautiful redbrown hair. Her sunken eyelids were raw, nibbled at by fish. (O yes they do, the deepswimming fish. They sample everything.) Her mauve corduroy pinafore said *Holiday!* in a tilting, happy font. She was as wrinkled as a dhobi's thumb from being in water for too long.

A spongy mermaid who had forgotten how to swim.

A silver thimble clenched, for luck, in her little fist.

Thimble-drinker.

Coffin-cartwheeler.

Margaret Kochamma never forgave herself for taking Sophie Mol to Ayemenem. For leaving her there alone over the weekend while she and Chacko went to Cochin to confirm their return tickets.

IT WAS ABOUT NINE in the morning when Mammachi and Baby Kochamma got news of a white child's body found floating downriver where the Meenachal broadens as it approaches the backwaters. Estha and Rahel were still missing.

Earlier that morning the children – all three of them – hadn't appeared for their morning glass of milk. Baby Kochamma and Mammachi thought that they might have gone down to the river for a swim, which was worrying because it had rained heavily the previous day and a good part of the night. They knew that the river could be dangerous. Baby Kochamma sent Kochu Maria to look for them but she returned without them. In the chaos that ensued after Vellya Paapen's visit, nobody could remember when they had actually last seen the children. They hadn't been uppermost on anybody's mind. They could have been missing all night.

Ammu was still locked into her bedroom. Baby Kochamma had the keys. She called through the door to ask Ammu whether she had any idea where the children might be. She tried to keep the panic out of her voice, make it sound like a casual enquiry. Something crashed against the door. Ammu was incoherent with rage and disbelief at what was happening to her – at being locked away like the family lunatic in a medieval household. It was only later, when the world collapsed around them, after Sophie Mol's body was brought to Ayemenem, and Baby Kochamma unlocked her, that Ammu sifted through her rage to try to make sense of what had happened. Fear and apprehension forced her to think clearly, and it was only then that she remembered what she had said to her twins when they came to her bedroom door and asked her why she had been locked up. The careless words she hadn't meant.

'Because of you!' Ammu had screamed. 'If it wasn't for you I wouldn't be here! None of this would have happened! I wouldn't be here! I would have been free! I should have dumped you in an orphanage the day you were born! *You're* the millstones round my neck!'

She couldn't see them crouched against the door. A Surprised Puff and a Fountain in a Love-in-Tokyo. Bewildered Twin Ambassadors of God-knows-what. Their Excellencies Ambassadors E. Pelvis and S. Insect.

'Just go away!' Ammu had said. 'Why can't you just go away and leave me alone?'

So they had.

But when the only answer Baby Kochamma got to her question about the children was something crashing against Ammu's bedroom door, she went away. A slow dread built up inside her as she began to make the obvious, logical and completely mistaken connections between the night's happenings and the missing children.

The rain had started early the previous afternoon. Suddenly the hot day darkened and the sky began to clap and grumble. Kochu Maria, in a bad mood for no particular reason, was in the kitchen standing on her low stool savagely cleaning a large fish, working up a smelly blizzard of fish scales. Her gold earrings swung fiercely. Silver fish scales flew around the kitchen, landing on kettles, walls, vegetable peelers, the fridge handle. She ignored Vellya Paapen when he arrived at the kitchen door, drenched and shaking. His real eye was bloodshot and he looked as though he had been drinking. He stood there for ten minutes waiting to be noticed. When Kochu Maria finished the fish and started on the onions, he cleared his throat and asked for Mammachi. Kochu Maria tried to shoo him away, but he wouldn't go. Each time he opened his mouth to speak, the smell of arrack on his breath hit Kochu Maria like a hammer. She had never seen him like this before, and was a little frightened. She had a pretty good idea of what it was all about, so she eventually decided that it would be best to call Mammachi. She shut the kitchen door, leaving Vellya Paapen outside in the back mittam, weaving drunkenly in the driving rain. Though it was December, it rained as though it was June. *Cyclonic disturbance,* the newspapers called it the next day. But by then nobody was in any condition to read the papers.

Perhaps it was the rain that drove Vellya Paapen to the kitchen door. To a superstitious man, the relentlessness of that unseasonal downpour could have seemed like an omen from an angry god. To a drunk superstitious man, it could have seemed like the beginning of the end of the world. Which, in a way, it was.

When Mammachi arrived in the kitchen, in her petticoat and pale pink dressing gown with rickrack edging, Vellya Paapen climbed up the kitchen steps and offered her his mortgaged eye. He held it out in the palm of his hand. He said he didn't deserve it and wanted her to have it back. His left eyelid drooped over his empty socket in an immutable, monstrous wink. As though everything that he was about to say was part of an elaborate prank.

'What is it?' Mammachi asked, stretching her hand out, thinking perhaps that for some reason Vellya Paapen was returning the kilo of red rice she had given him that morning.

'It's his eye,' Kochu Maria said loudly to Mammachi, her own eyes bright with onion tears. By then Mammachi had already touched the glass eye. She recoiled from its slippery hardness. Its slimy marbleness.

'Are you drunk?' Mammachi said angrily to the sound of the rain. 'How dare you come here in this condition?'

She groped her way to the sink, and soaped away the sodden Paravan's eye-juices. She smelled her hands when she'd finished. Kochu Maria gave Vellya Paapen an old kitchen cloth to wipe himself with, and said nothing when he stood on the topmost step, almost inside her Touchable kitchen, drying himself, sheltered from the rain by the sloping overhang of the roof.

When he was calmer, Vellya Paapen returned his eye to its rightful socket and began to speak. He started by recounting to Mammachi how much her family had done for his. Generation for generation. How, long before the communists thought of it, Reverend E. John Ipe had given his father, Kelan, title to the land on which their hut now stood. How Mammachi had paid for his eye. How she had organized for Velutha to be educated and given him a job . . .

Mammachi, though annoyed at his drunkenness, wasn't averse to listening to bardic stories about herself and her family's Christian munificence. Nothing prepared her for what she was about to hear.

Vellya Paapen began to cry. Half of him wept. Tears welled up in his real eye and shone on his black cheek. With his other eye he stared stonily ahead. An old Paravan, who had seen the Walking Backwards days, torn between Loyalty and Love.

Then the Terror took hold of him and shook the words out of him. He told Mammachi what he had seen. The story of the little boat that crossed the river night after night, and who was in it. The story of a man and woman, standing together in the moonlight. Skin to skin.

They went to Kari Saipu's House, Vellya Paapen said. The white man's demon had entered them. It was Kari Saipu's revenge for what he, Vellya Paapen, had done to him. The boat (that Estha sat on and Rahel found) was tethered to the tree stump next to the steep path that led through the marsh to the abandoned rubber estate. He had seen it there. Every night. Rocking on the water. Empty. Waiting for the lovers to return. For hours it waited. Sometimes they only emerged through the long grass at dawn. Vellya Paapen had seen them with his own eye. Others had seen them too. The whole village knew. It was only a matter of time before Mammachi found out. So Vellya Paapen had come to tell Mammachi himself. As a Paravan and a man with mortgaged body parts, he considered it his duty.

The lovers. Sprung from his loins and hers. His son and her daughter. They had made the unthinkable thinkable and the impossible really happen.

Vellya Paapen kept talking. Weeping. Retching. Moving his mouth. Mammachi couldn't hear what he was saying. The sound of the rain grew louder and exploded in her head. She didn't hear herself shouting.

Suddenly the blind old woman in her rickrack dressing gown and her thin grey hair plaited into a rat's tail stepped forward and pushed Vellya Paapen with all her strength. He stumbled backwards, down the kitchen steps and lay sprawled in the wet mud. He was taken completely by surprise. Part of the taboo of being an Untouchable was expecting not to be touched. At least not in these circumstances. Of being locked into a physically impregnable cocoon.

Baby Kochamma, walking past the kitchen, heard the commotion. She found Mammachi spitting into the rain, THOO! THOO! THOO! and Vellya Paapen lying in the slush, wet, weeping, grovelling. Offering to kill his son. To tear him limb from limb.

Mammachi was shouting, 'Drunken dog! Drunken Paravan liar!'

Over the din Kochu Maria shouted Vellya Paapen's story to Baby Kochamma. Baby Kochamma recognized at once the immense potential of the situation, but immediately anointed her thoughts with unctuous oils. She bloomed. She saw it as God's Way of punishing Ammu for her sins and simultaneously avenging her (Baby Kochamma's) humiliation at the hands of Velutha and the men in the march – the *Modalali Mariakutty* taunts, the forced flag-waving. She set sail at once. A ship of goodness ploughing through a sea of sin.

Baby Kochamma put her heavy arm around Mammachi.

'It must be true,' she said in a quiet voice. 'She's quite capable of it. And so is he. Vellya Paapen would not lie about something like this.'

She asked Kochu Maria to get Mammachi a glass of water and a chair to sit on. She made Vellya Paapen repeat his story, stopping him every now and then for details – Whose boat? How often? How long had it been going on?

When Vellya Paapen finished, Baby Kochamma turned to Mammachi. 'He must go,' she said. 'Tonight. Before it goes any further. Before we are completely ruined.'

Then she shuddered her schoolgirl shudder. That was when she said: *'How could she stand the smell? Haven't you noticed? They have a particular smell, these Paravans.'*

With that olfactory observation, that specific little detail, the Terror unspooled.

Mammachi's rage at the old one-eyed Paravan standing in the rain, drunk, dribbling and covered in mud was redirected into a cold contempt for her daughter and what she had done. She thought of her naked, coupling in the mud with a man who was nothing but a filthy *coolie*. She imagined it in vivid detail: a Paravan's coarse black hand on her daughter's breast. His mouth on hers. His black hips jerking between her parted legs. The sound of their breathing. His particular Paravan smell. *Like animals*, Mammachi thought and nearly vomited. *Like a dog with a bitch on heat.* Her tolerance of 'Men's Needs' as far as her son was concerned, became the fuel for her unmanageable fury at her daughter. She had defiled generations of breeding (The Little Blessed One, blessed personally by the Patriarch of Antioch, an Imperial Entomologist, a Rhodes Scholar from Oxford) and brought the family to its knees. For generations to come, *for ever* now, people would point at them at weddings and funerals. At baptisms and birthday parties. They'd nudge and whisper. It was all finished now.

Mammachi lost control.

They did what they had to do, the two old ladies. Mammachi provided the passion. Baby Kochamma the Plan. Kochu Maria was their midget lieutenant. They locked Ammu up (tricked her into her bedroom) before they sent for Velutha. They knew that they had to get him to leave Ayemenem before Chacko returned. They could neither trust nor predict what Chacko's attitude would be.

It wasn't entirely their fault, though, that the whole thing spun out of control like a deranged top. That it lashed out at those that crossed its path. That by the time Chacko and Margaret Kochamma returned from Cochin, it was too late.

The fisherman had already found Sophie Mol.

Picture him.

Out in his boat at dawn, at the mouth of the river he has known all his life. It is still quick and swollen from the previous night's rain. Something bobs past in the water and the colours catch his eye. Mauve. Red-brown. Beach sand. It moves with the current, swiftly towards the sea. He sends out his bamboo pole to stop it and draw it towards him. It's a wrinkled mermaid. A mer-child. A mere mer-child. With red-brown hair. With an Imperial Entomologist's nose, and a silver thimble clenched for luck in her fist. He pulls her out of the water into his boat. He puts his thin cotton towel under her, she lies at the bottom of his boat with his silver haul of small fish. He rows home – *Thaiy thaiy thakka thaiy thaiy thome* – thinking how wrong it is for a fisherman to believe that he knows his river well. *No one* knows the Meenachal. No one knows what it may snatch or suddenly yield. Or when. That is what makes fishermen pray.

At the Kottayam police station, a shaking Baby Kochamma was ushered into the Station House Officer's room. She told Inspector Thomas Mathew of the circumstances that had led to the sudden dismissal of a factory worker. A Paravan. A few days ago he had tried to, to . . . to force himself on her niece, she said. A divorcée with two children.

Baby Kochamma misrepresented the relationship between Ammu and Velutha, not for Ammu's sake, but to contain the scandal and salvage the family reputation in Inspector Thomas Mathew's eyes. It didn't occur to her that Ammu would later invite shame upon herself – that she would go to the police and try and set the record straight. As Baby Kochamma told her story, she began to believe it.

Why wasn't the matter reported to the police in the first place, the Inspector wanted to know.

'We are an old family,' Baby Kochamma said. 'These are not things we want talked about . . .'

Inspector Thomas Mathew, receding behind his bustling Air India moustache, understood perfectly. He had a Touchable wife, two Touchable daughters – whole Touchable generations waiting in their Touchable wombs . . .

'Where is the molestee now?'

'At home. She doesn't know I've come here. She wouldn't have let me come. Naturally – she's frantic with worry about the children. Hysterical.'

Later, when the real story reached Inspector Thomas Mathew, the fact that what the Paravan had taken from the

Touchable Kingdom had not been snatched but *given*, concerned him deeply. So after Sophie Mol's funeral, when Ammu went to him with the twins to tell him that a mistake had been made and he tapped her breasts with his baton, it was not a policeman's spontaneous brutishness on his part. He knew exactly what he was doing. It was a premeditated gesture, calculated to humiliate and terrorize her. An attempt to instil order into a world gone wrong.

Still later, when the dust had settled and he had had the paperwork organized, Inspector Thomas Mathew congratulated himself for the way it had all turned out.

But now, he listened carefully and courteously as Baby Kochamma constructed her story.

'Last night it was getting dark – about seven in the evening – when he came to the house to threaten us. It was raining very heavily. The lights had gone out and we were lighting the lamps when he came,' she told him. 'He knew that the man of the house, my nephew, Chacko Ipe, was – is – away in Cochin. We were three women alone in the house.' She paused to let the Inspector imagine the horrors that could be visited by a sex-crazed Paravan on three women alone in a house.

'We told him that if he did not leave Ayemenem quietly we would call the police. He started off by saying that my niece had *consented*, can you imagine? He asked us what proof we had of what we were accusing him of. He said that according to the Labour Laws we had no grounds on which to dismiss him. He was very calm. "The days are gone," he told us, "when you can kick us around like dogs . . ."' By now Baby Kochamma sounded utterly convincing. Injured. Incredulous.

Then her imagination took over completely. She didn't describe how Mammachi had lost control. How she had gone up to Velutha and spat right into his face. The things she had said to him. The names she had called him.

Instead she described to Inspector Thomas Mathew how it

was not just *what* Velutha had said that had made her come to the police, but the *way* he said it. His complete lack of remorse, which was what had shocked her most. As though he was actually *proud* of what he had done. Without realizing it herself, she grafted the manner of the man who had humiliated her during the march onto Velutha. She described the sneering fury in his face. The brassy, insolence in his voice that had so frightened her. That made her sure that his dismissal and the children's disappearance were not, could not possibly be, unconnected.

She had known the Paravan since he was a child, Baby Kochamma said. He had been educated by her family, in the Untouchables' school started by her father, Punnyan Kunju (Mr Thomas Mathew must know who he was? Yes, of course) . . . He was trained to be a carpenter by her family, the house he lived in was given to his grandfather by her family. He owed everything to her family.

'You people,' Inspector Thomas Mathew said, 'first you spoil these people, carry them about on your head like trophies, then when they misbehave you come running to us for help.'

Baby Kochamma lowered her eyes like a chastised child. Then she continued her story. She told Inspector Thomas Mathew how in the last few weeks she had noticed some presaging signs, some insolence, some rudeness. She mentioned seeing him in the march on the way to Cochin and the rumours that he was or had been a Naxalite. She didn't notice the faint furrow of worry that this piece of information produced on the Inspector's brow.

She had warned her nephew about him, Baby Kochamma said, but never in her wildest dreams had she thought that it would ever come to this. A beautiful child was dead. Two children were missing.

Baby Kochamma broke down.

Inspector Thomas Mathew gave her a cup of police tea. When she was feeling a little better, he helped her to set down all she had told him in her FIR. He assured Baby Kochamma of the Full Co-operation of the Kottayam Police. The rascal would be caught before the day was out, he said. A Paravan with a pair of two-egg twins, hounded by history – he knew there weren't many places for him to hide.

Inspector Thomas Mathew was a prudent man. He took one precaution. He sent a Jeep to fetch Comrade K. N. M. Pillai to the police station. It was crucial for him to know whether the Paravan had any political support or whether he was operating alone. Though he himself was a Congress man, he did not intend to risk any run-ins with the Marxist Government. When Comrade Pillai arrived, he was ushered into the seat that Baby Kochamma had only recently vacated. Inspector Thomas Mathew showed him Baby Kochamma's FIR. The two men had a conversation. Brief, cryptic, to the point. As though they had exchanged numbers and not words. No explanations seemed necessary. They were not friends, Comrade Pillai and Inspector Thomas Mathew, and they didn't trust each other. But they understood each other perfectly. They were both men whom childhood had abandoned without a trace. Men without curiosity. Without doubt. Both in their own way truly, terrifyingly adult. They looked out at the world and never wondered how it worked, because they knew. *They* worked it. They were mechanics who serviced different parts of the same machine.

Comrade Pillai told Inspector Thomas Mathew that he was acquainted with Velutha, but omitted to mention that Velutha was a member of the Communist Party, or that Velutha had knocked on his door late the previous night, which made Comrade Pillai the last person to have seen Velutha before he disappeared. Nor, though he knew it to be untrue, did Comrade Pillai refute the allegation of attempted rape in Baby Kochamma's FIR. He merely assured Inspector Thomas Mathew that as far as he was concerned Velutha did not have the patronage or the protection of the Communist Party. That he was on his own.

After Comrade Pillai left, Inspector Thomas Mathew went over their conversation in his mind, teasing it, testing its logic, looking for loopholes. When he was satisfied, he instructed his men.

Meanwhile, Baby Kochamma returned to Ayemenem. The Plymouth was parked in the driveway. Margaret Kochamma and Chacko were back from Cochin.

Sophie Mol was laid out on the chaise longue.

When Margaret Kochamma saw her little daughter's body, shock swelled in her like phantom applause in an empty auditorium. It overflowed in a wave of vomit and left her mute and empty-eyed. She mourned two deaths, not one. With the loss of Sophie, Joe died again. And this time there was no homework to finish or egg to eat. She had come to Ayemenem to heal her wounded world, and had lost all of it instead. She shattered like glass.

Her memory of the days that followed was fuzzy. Long, dim hours of thick, furry-tongued serenity (medically administered by Dr Verghese Verghese), lacerated by sharp, steely slashes of hysteria, as keen and cutting as the edge of a new razor blade.

She was vaguely conscious of Chacko – concerned and gentle-voiced when he was by her side – otherwise incensed, blowing like an enraged wind through the Ayemenem House. So different from the amused Rumpled Porcupine she had met that longago Oxford morning at the café.

She remembered faintly the funeral in the yellow church. The sad singing. A bat that had bothered someone. She remembered the sounds of doors being battered down, and frightened women's voices. And how at night the bush crickets had sounded like creaking stairs and amplified the fear and gloom that hung over the Ayemenem House.

She never forgot her irrational rage at the other two younger children who had for some reason been spared. Her fevered mind fastened like a limpet onto the notion that Estha was somehow responsible for Sophie Mol's death. Odd, considering that Margaret Kochamma didn't know that it was Estha – Stirring Wizard with a Puff who had rowed jam and thought Two Thoughts – Estha who had broken rules and rowed Sophie Mol and Rahel across the river in the afternoons in a little boat, Estha who had abrogated a sickled smell by waving a Marxist flag at it. Estha who had made the back verandah of the History House their home away from home, furnished with a grass mat and most of their toys – a catapult, an inflatable goose, a Qantas koala with loosened button eyes. And finally, on that dreadful night, Estha who had decided that though it was dark and raining, the Time Had Come for them to run away, because Ammu didn't want them any more.

Despite not knowing any of this, why did Margaret Kochamma blame Estha for what had happened to Sophie? Perhaps she had a mother's instinct.

Three or four times, swimming up through thick layers of drug-induced sleep, she had actually sought Estha out and slapped him until someone calmed her down and led her away. Later, she wrote to Ammu to apologize. By the time the letter arrived, Estha had been Returned and Ammu had had to pack her bags and leave. Only Rahel remained in Ayemenem to accept, on Estha's behalf, Margaret Kochamma's apology. *I can't imagine what came over me*, she wrote. *I can only put it down to the effect of the tranquillizers. I had no right to behave the way I did, and want you to know that I am ashamed and terribly, terribly sorry.*

Strangely, the person that Margaret Kochamma never thought about was Velutha. Of him she had no memory at all. Not even what he looked like.

Perhaps this was because she never really knew him, nor ever heard what happened to him.

The God of Loss.

The God of Small Things.

He left no footprints in sand, no ripples in water, no image in mirrors.

After all, Margaret Kochamma wasn't with the platoon of Touchable policemen when they crossed the swollen river. Their wide khaki shorts rigid with starch.

The metallic clink of handcuffs in someone's heavy pocket.

It is unreasonable to expect a person to remember what she didn't know had happened.

SORROW, HOWEVER, was still two weeks away on that blue cross-stitch afternoon, as Margaret Kochamma lay jet-lagged and still asleep. Chacko, on his way to see Comrade K. N. M. Pillai, drifted past the bedroom window like an anxious, stealthy whale intending to peep in to see whether his wife (*Ex-wife, Chacko!*) and daughter were awake and needed anything. At the last minute his courage failed him and he floated fatly by without looking in. Sophie Mol (A wake, A live, A lert) saw him go.

She sat up on her bed and looked out at the rubber trees. The sun had moved across the sky and cast a deep house-shadow across the plantation, darkening the already dark-leafed trees. Beyond the shadow, the light was flat and gentle. There was a diagonal slash across the mottled bark of each tree through which milky rubber seeped like white blood from a wound, and dripped into the waiting half of a coconut shell that had been tied to the tree.

Sophie Mol got out of bed and rummaged through her sleeping mother's purse. She found what she was looking for – the keys to the large, locked suitcase on the floor, with its airline stickers and baggage tags. She opened it and rooted through the contents with all the delicacy of a dog digging up a flowerbed. She upset stacks of lingerie, ironed skirts and blouses, shampoos, creams, chocolate, Sellotape, umbrellas, soap (and other bottled London smells), quinine, aspirin, broad spectrum antibiotics. 'Take everything,' her colleagues had advised Margaret Kochamma in concerned voices. 'You never know.' Which was their way of saying to a colleague travelling to the Heart of Darkness that:

(a) Anything Can Happen To Anyone.

So

(b) It's Best to be Prepared.

Sophie Mol eventually found what she had been looking for.

Presents for her cousins. Triangular towers of Toblerone chocolate (soft and slanting in the heat). Socks with separate multi-coloured toes. And two ballpoint pens – the top halves filled with water in which a cut-out collage of a London streetscape was suspended. Buckingham Palace and Big Ben. Shops and people. A red double-decker bus propelled by an air-bubble floated up and down the silent street. There was something sinister about the absence of noise on the busy ballpoint street.

Sophie Mol put the presents into her go-go bag, and went forth into the world. To drive a hard bargain. To negotiate a friendship.

A friendship that, unfortunately, would be left dangling. Incomplete. Flailing in the air with no foothold. A friendship that never circled around into a story, which is why, far more quickly than ever should have happened, Sophie Mol became a Memory, while The Loss of Sophie Mol grew robust and alive. Like a fruit in season. Every season.

14

Work is Struggle

Chacko took the shortcut through the tilting rubber trees so that he would have to walk only a very short stretch down the main road to Comrade K. N. M. Pillai's house. He looked faintly absurd, stepping over the carpet of dry leaves in his tight airport suit, his tie blown over his shoulder.

Comrade Pillai wasn't in when Chacko arrived. His wife, Kalyani, with fresh sandalwood paste on her forehead, made him sit down on a steel folding chair in their small front room and disappeared through the bright pink, nylon, lace-curtained doorway into a dark adjoining room where the small flame from a large brass oil lamp flickered. The cloying smell of incense drifted through the doorway, over which a small wooden placard said, *Work is Struggle. Struggle is Work.*

Chacko was too big for the room. The blue walls crowded him. He glanced around, tense and a little uneasy. A towel dried on the bars of the small green window. The dining table was covered with a bright flowered plastic tablecloth. Midges whirred around a bunch of small bananas on a blue-rimmed white enamel plate. In one corner of the room there was a pile of green unhusked coconuts. A child's rubber slippers lay pigeon-toed in the bright parallelogram of barred sunlight on the floor. A glass-paned cupboard stood next to the table. It had printed curtains hanging on the inside, hiding its contents.

Comrade Pillai's mother, a minute old lady in a brown blouse and off-white mundu, sat on the edge of the high wooden bed that was pushed against the wall, her feet dangling high above the floor. She wore a thin white towel arranged diagonally over her chest and slung over one shoulder. A funnel of mosquitoes, like an inverted dunce cap, whined over her head. She sat with her cheek resting in the palm of her hand, bunching together all the wrinkles on that side of her face. Every inch of her, even her wrists and ankles, were wrinkled. Only the skin on her throat was taut and smooth, stretched over an enormous goitre. Her fountain of youth. She stared vacantly at the wall opposite her, rocking herself gently, grunting regular, rhythmic little grunts, like a bored passenger on a long bus journey.

Comrade Pillai's SSLC, BA and MA certificates were framed and hung on the wall behind her head.

On another wall was a framed photograph of Comrade Pillai garlanding Comrade E. M. S. Namboodiripad. There was a microphone on a stand, shining in the foreground with a sign that said *Ajantha.*

The rotating table fan by the bed measured out its mechanical breeze in exemplary, democratic turns – first lifting what was left of Old Mrs Pillai's hair, then Chacko's. The mosquitoes dispersed and reassembled tirelessly.

Through the window Chacko could see the tops of buses, luggage in their luggage racks, as they thundered by. A Jeep with a loudspeaker drove past, blaring a Marxist Party song whose theme was Unemployment. The chorus was in English, the rest of it in Malayalam.

> No vacancy! No vacancy!
> *Wherever in the world a poor man goes,*
> No no no no no vacancy!

'No' pronounced to rhyme with door.

Kalyani returned with a stainless-steel glass of filter coffee and a stainless-steel plate of banana chips (bright yellow with little black seeds in the centre) for Chacko.

'He has gone to Olassa. He'll be back any time now,' she said. She referred to her husband as *addeham* which was the respectful form of 'he', whereas 'he' called her 'edi' which was, approximately, 'Hey, you!'

She was a lush, beautiful woman with golden brown skin and huge eyes. Her long frizzy hair was damp and hung loose down her back, plaited only at the very end. It had wet the back of her tight, deep red blouse and stained it a tighter, deeper red. From where the sleeves ended, her soft arm-flesh swelled and dropped over her dimpled elbows in a sumptuous bulge. Her white mundu and kavani were crisp and ironed. She smelled of sandalwood and the crushed green gram that she used instead of soap. For the first time in years, Chacko watched her without the faintest stirring of sexual desire. He had a wife (*Ex-wife, Chacko!*) at home. With arm freckles and back freckles. With a blue dress and legs underneath.

Young Lenin appeared at the door in red stretchlon shorts. He stood on one thin leg like a stork and twisted the pink lace curtain into a pole, staring at Chacko with his mother's eyes. He was six now, long past the age of pushing things up his nose.

'Mon, go and call Latha,' Mrs Pillai said to him.

Lenin remained where he was, and still staring at Chacko, screeched effortlessly, in the way only children can.

'Latha! Latha! You're wanted!'

'Our niece from Kottayam. His elder brother's daughter,' Mrs Pillai explained. 'She won the First Prize for Elocution at the Youth Festival in Trivandrum last week.'

A combative-looking young girl of about twelve or thirteen appeared through the lace curtain. She wore a long, printed skirt that reached all the way down to her ankles and a short, waist-length white blouse with darts that made room for future breasts. Her oiled hair was parted into two halves. Each of her tight, shining plaits was looped over and tied with ribbons so that they hung down on either side of her face like the outlines of large, drooping ears that hadn't been coloured in yet.

'D'you know who this is?' Mrs Pillai asked Latha.

Latha shook her head.

'Chacko saar. Our factory Modalali.'

Latha stared at him with a composure and a lack of curiosity unusual in a thirteen-year-old.

'He studied in London Oxford,' Mrs Pillai said. 'Will you do your recitation for him?'

Latha complied without hesitation. She planted her feet slightly apart.

'Respected Chairman,' she bowed to Chacko, 'mydearjudges and . . .' she looked around at the imaginary audience crowded into the small, hot room, 'beloved friends.' She paused theatrically.

'Today I would like to recite to you a poem by Sir Walter Scott entitled "Lochinvar".' She clasped her hands behind her back. A film fell over her eyes. Her gaze was fixed unseeingly just above Chacko's head. She swayed slightly as she spoke. At first Chacko thought it was a Malayalam translation of 'Lochinvar'. The words ran into each other. The last syllable of one word attached itself to the first syllable of the next. It was rendered at remarkable speed.

'O, young Lochin varhas scum out of the vest,
Through wall the vide Border his teed was the bes;
Tand savissgood broadsod heweapon sadnun,
Nhe rod all unarmed, and he rod all lalone.'

The poem was interspersed with grunts from the old lady on the bed, which no one except Chacko seemed to notice.

'Nhe swam the Eske river where ford there was none;
Buttair he alighted at Netherby Gate,
The bridehad cunsended, the gallantcame late.'

Comrade Pillai arrived mid-poem, a sheen of sweat glazed his skin, his mundu was folded up over his knees, dark sweatstains spread under his Terylene armpits. In his late thirties, he was an unathletic, sallow little man. His legs were already spindly and his taut, distended belly, like his tiny mother's goitre, was completely at odds with the rest of his thin, narrow body and alert face. As though something in their family genes had bestowed on them compulsory bumps that appeared randomly in different parts of their bodies.

His neat pencil moustache divided his upper lip horizontally into half and ended exactly in line with the ends of his mouth. His hairline had begun to recede and he made no attempt to hide it. His hair was oiled and combed back off his forehead. Clearly youth was not what he was after. He had the easy authority of the Man of the House. He smiled and nodded a greeting to Chacko, but did not acknowledge the presence of his wife or his mother.

Latha's eyes flicked towards him for permission to continue with the poem. It was granted. Comrade Pillai took off his shirt, rolled it into a ball and wiped his armpits with it. When he finished, Kalyani took it from him and held it as though it was a gift. A bouquet of flowers. Comrade Pillai, in his sleeveless vest, sat on a folding chair and pulled his left foot up onto his right thigh. Through the rest of his niece's recitation, he sat staring meditatively down at the floor, his chin cupped in the palm of his hand, tapping his right foot in time with the metre and cadence of the poem. With his other hand he massaged the exquisitely arched instep of his left foot.

When Latha finished, Chacko applauded with genuine kindness. She did not acknowledge his applause with even a flicker of a smile. She was like an East German swimmer at a local competition. Her eyes were firmly fixed on Olympic Gold. Any lesser achievement she took as her due. She looked at her uncle for permission to leave the room.

Comrade Pillai beckoned to her and whispered in her ear, 'Go and tell Pothachen and Mathukutty that if they want to see me, they should come immediately.'

'No, comrade, really . . . I won't have anything more,' Chacko said, assuming that Comrade Pillai was sending Latha off for more snacks. Comrade Pillai, grateful for the misunderstanding, perpetuated it.

'No no no. Hah! What is this? . . . Edi Kalyani, bring a plate of those avalose oondas.'

As an aspiring politician, it was essential for Comrade Pillai to be seen in his chosen constituency as a man of influence. He wanted to use Chacko's visit to impress local supplicants and Party Workers. Pothachen and Mathukutty, the men he had sent for, were villagers who had asked him to use his connections at the Kottayam hospital to secure nursing jobs for their daughters. Comrade Pillai was keen that they be *seen* waiting outside his house for their appointment with him. The more people that were seen waiting to meet him, the busier he would appear, the better the impression he would make. And if the waiting people saw that the factory Modalali himself had come to see him, on *his* turf, he knew it would give off all sorts of useful signals.

'So! Comrade!' Comrade Pillai said, after Latha had been dispatched and the avalose oondas had arrived. 'What is the news? How is your daughter adjusting?' He insisted on speaking to Chacko in English.

'Oh fine. She's fast asleep right now.'

'Oho. Jet lag, I suppose,' Comrade Pillai said, pleased with himself for knowing a thing or two about international travel.

'What's happening in Olassa? A Party meeting?' Chacko asked.

'Oh, nothing like that. My sister Sudha met with fracture sometime back,' Comrade Pillai said, as though Fracture were a visiting dignitary. 'So I took her to Olassa Moos for some medications. Some oils and all that. Her husband is in Patna, so she is alone at in-laws' place.'

Lenin gave up his post at the doorway, placed himself between his father's knees and picked his nose.

'What about a poem from you, young man?' Chacko said to him. 'Doesn't your father teach you any?'

Lenin stared at Chacko, giving no indication that he had either heard or understood what Chacko said.

'He knows everything,' Comrade Pillai said. 'He is genius. In front of visitors only he's quiet.'

Comrade Pillai jiggled Lenin with his knees.

'Lenin Mon, tell Comrade Uncle the one Pappa taught you. *Friends Romans countrymen . . .*'

Lenin continued his nasal treasure hunt.

'Come on, Mon, it's only our Comrade Uncle –'

Comrade Pillai tried to kick-start Shakespeare. '*Friends, Romans, countrymen, lend me your* – ?'

Lenin's unblinking gaze remained on Chacko. Comrade Pillai tried again.

'. . . *lend me your* – ?'

Lenin grabbed a handful of banana chips and bolted out of the front door. He began to race up and down the strip of front yard between the house and road, braying with an excitement that he couldn't understand. When he had worked some of it off his run turned into a breathless, high-kneed gallop.

'*lend me yawYERS*;'

Lenin shouted from the yard, over the sound of a passing bus.

'I cometoberry Caeser, not to praise him.
Theevil that mendoo lives after them,
The goodisoft interred with their bones;'

He shouted it fluently, without faltering once. Remarkable, considering he was only six and didn't understand a word of what he was saying. Sitting inside, looking out at the little dust-devil whirling in his yard (future service contractor with a baby and Bajaj scooter), Comrade Pillai smiled proudly.

'He's standing first in class. This year he will be getting double-promotion.'

There was a lot of ambition packed into that little hot room.

Whatever Comrade Pillai stored in his curtained cupboard, it wasn't broken balsa airplanes.

Chacko, on the other hand, from the moment he had entered the house, or perhaps from the moment Comrade Pillai had arrived, had undergone a curious process of invalidation. Like a general who had been stripped of his stars, he limited his smile. Contained his expansiveness. Anybody meeting him there for the first time might have thought him reticent. Almost timid.

With a street-fighter's unerring instincts, Comrade Pillai knew that his straitened circumstances (his small, hot house, his grunting mother, his obvious proximity to the toiling masses) gave him a power over Chacko that in those revolutionary times no amount of Oxford education could match.

He held his poverty like a gun to Chacko's head.

Chacko brought out a crumpled piece of paper on which he had tried to sketch the rough layout for a new label that he wanted Comrade K. N. M. Pillai to print. It was for a new product that Paradise Pickles & Preserves planned to launch in the spring. Synthetic Cooking Vinegar. Drawing was not one of Chacko's strengths, but Comrade Pillai got the general gist. He was familiar with the logo of the kathakali dancer, the slogan under his skirt that said *Emperors of the Realm of Taste* (his idea) and the typeface they had chosen for Paradise Pickles & Preserves.

'Design is same. Only difference is in text, I suppose,' Comrade Pillai said.

'And the colour of the border,' Chacko said. 'Mustard instead of red.'

Comrade Pillai pushed his spectacles up into his hair in order to read aloud the text. The lenses immediately grew fogged with hairoil.

'*Synthetic Cooking Vinegar*,' he said. 'This all is in caps, I suppose.'

'Prussian Blue,' Chacko said.

'*Prepared from Acetic Acid*?'

'Royal Blue,' Chacko said. 'Like the one we did for green pepper in brine.'

'*Net Contents. Batch No., Mfg date, Expiry Date, Max Rtl Pr. Rs* . . . same Royal Blue colour but c. and l.c.?'

Chacko nodded.

'*We hereby certify that the vinegar in this bottle is warranted to be of the nature and quality which it purports to be. Ingredients: Water and Acetic Acid.* This will be red colour, I suppose.'

Comrade Pillai used 'I suppose' to disguise questions as statements. He hated asking questions unless they were personal ones. Questions signified a vulgar display of ignorance.

By the time they finished discussing the label for the vinegar, Chacko and Comrade Pillai had each acquired personal mosquito funnels.

They agreed on a delivery date.

'So yesterday's march was a success?' Chacko said, finally broaching the real reason for his visit.

'Unless and until demands are met, comrade, we cannot say it is Success or Non-success.' A pamphleteering inflection crept into Comrade Pillai's voice. 'Until then, struggle must continue.'

'But Response was good,' Chacko prompted, trying to speak in the same idiom.

'That is of course there,' Comrade Pillai said. 'Comrades

have presented Memorandum to Party High Command. Now let us see. We have only to wait and watch.'

'We passed them on the road yesterday,' Chacko said. 'The procession.'

'On the way to Cochin, I suppose,' Comrade Pillai said. 'But according to Party sources Trivandrum Response was much more better.'

'There were thousands of comrades in Cochin too,' Chacko said. 'In fact my niece saw our young Velutha among them.'

'Oho. I see.' Comrade Pillai was caught off guard. Velutha was a topic he had planned to broach with Chacko. Some day. Eventually. But not this straightforwardly. His mind hummed like the table fan. He wondered whether to make use of the opening that was being offered to him, or to leave it for another day. He decided to use it now.

'Yes. He is good worker,' he said thoughtfully. 'Highly intelligent.'

'He is,' Chacko said. 'An excellent carpenter with an engineer's mind. If it wasn't for –'

'Not *that* worker, comrade,' Comrade Pillai said. '*Party* worker.'

Comrade Pillai's mother continued to rock and grunt. There was something reassuring about the rhythm of the grunts. Like the ticking of a clock. A sound you hardly noticed, but would miss if it stopped.

'Ah, I see. So he's a card-holder?'

'Oh yes,' Comrade Pillai said softly. 'Oh yes.'

Perspiration trickled through Chacko's hair. He felt as though a company of ants was touring his scalp. He scratched his head for a long time, with both his hands. Moving his whole scalp up and down.

'*Oru kaaryam parayattey?*' Comrade Pillai switched to Malayalam and a confiding, conspiratorial voice. 'I'm speaking as a friend, *keto*. Off the record.'

Before he continued, Comrade Pillai studied Chacko, trying to gauge his response. Chacko was examining the grey paste of sweat and dandruff lodged under his fingernails.

'That Paravan is going to cause trouble for you,' he said. 'Take it from me . . . get him a job somewhere else. Send him off.'

Chacko was puzzled at the turn the conversation had taken. He had only intended to find out what was happening, where things stood. He had expected to encounter antagonism, even confrontation, and instead was being offered sly, misguided collusion.

'Send him away? But why? I have no objections to him being a card-holder. I was just curious, that's all . . . I thought perhaps you had been speaking to him,' Chacko said. 'But I'm sure he's just experimenting, testing his wings, he's a sensible fellow, Comrade. I trust him . . .'

'Not like that,' Comrade Pillai said. 'He may be very well okay as a person. But other workers are not happy with him. Already they are coming to me with complaints . . . You see, Comrade, from local standpoint, these caste issues are very deep-rooted.'

Kalyani put a steel tumbler of steaming coffee on the table for her husband.

'See her, for example. Mistress of this house. Even she will never allow Paravans and all that into her house. Never. Even *I* cannot persuade her. My own wife. Of course inside the house she is Boss.' He turned to her with an affectionate, naughty smile. '*Allay edi*, Kalyani?'

Kalyani looked down and smiled, coyly acknowledging her bigotry.

'You see?' Comrade Pillai said triumphantly. 'She understands English very well. Only doesn't speak.'

Chacko smiled half-heartedly.

'You say my workers are coming to you with complaints . . .'

'Oh yes, correct,' Comrade Pillai said.

'Anything specific?'

'Nothing specifically as such,' Comrade K. N. M. Pillai said. 'But see, Comrade, any benefits that you give him, naturally others are resenting it. They see it as a partiality. After all, whatever job he does, carpenter or electrician or whateveritis, for them he is just a Paravan. It is a conditioning they have from birth. This I myself have told them is wrong. But frankly speaking, Comrade, Change is one thing. Acceptance is another. You should be cautious. Better for him you send him off . . .'

'My dear fellow,' Chacko said. 'That's impossible. He's invaluable. He practically runs the factory . . . and we can't solve the problem by sending all the Paravans away. Surely we have to learn to deal with this nonsense.'

Comrade Pillai disliked being addressed as My Dear Fellow. It sounded to him like an insult couched in good English, which, of course, made it a double-insult – the insult itself, and the fact that Chacko thought he wouldn't understand it. It spoiled his mood completely.

'That may be,' he said caustically. 'But Rome was not built in a day. Keep it in mind, Comrade, that this is not your Oxford college. For you what is a nonsense, for Masses it is something different.'

Lenin, with his father's thinness and his mother's eyes, appeared at the door, out of breath. He had finished shouting the whole of Mark Antony's speech and most of 'Lochinvar' before he realized that he had lost his audience. He repositioned himself between Comrade Pillai's parted knees.

He clapped his hands over his father's head, creating mayhem in the mosquito funnel. He counted the squashed carcasses on his palms. Some of them bloated with fresh blood. He showed them to his father, who handed him over to his mother to be cleaned up.

Once again the silence between them was appropriated by

old Mrs Pillai's grunts. Latha arrived with Pothachen and Mathukutty. The men were made to wait outside. The door was left ajar. When Comrade Pillai spoke next, he spoke in Malayalam and made sure it was loud enough for his audience outside.

'Of course the proper forum to air workers' grievances is through the Union. And in this case, when Modalali himself is a Comrade, it is a shameful matter for them not to be unionized and join the Party Struggle.'

'I've thought of that,' Chacko said. 'I am going to formally organize them into a union. They will elect their own representatives.'

'But Comrade, you cannot stage their revolution for them. You can only create awareness. Educate them. They must launch their *own* struggle. *They* must overcome their fears.'

'Of whom?' Chacko smiled. 'Me?'

'No, not you, my dear Comrade. Of centuries of oppression.'

Then Comrade Pillai, in a hectoring voice, quoted Chairman Mao. In Malayalam. His expression curiously like his niece's.

'Revolution is not a dinner party. Revolution is an insurrection, an act of violence in which one class overthrows another.'

And so, having bagged the contract for the Synthetic Cooking Vinegar labels, he deftly banished Chacko from the fighting ranks of the Overthrowers to the treacherous ranks of the To Be Overthrown.

They sat beside each other on steel folding chairs, on the afternoon of the Day that Sophie Mol Came, sipping coffee and crunching banana chips. Dislodging with their tongues the sodden yellow mulch that stuck to the roofs of their mouths.

The Small Thin Man and the Big Fat Man. Comic book adversaries in a still-to-come war.

It turned out to be a war which, unfortunately for Comrade Pillai, would end almost before it began. Victory was gifted to him wrapped and be-ribboned, on a silver tray. Only then, when it was too late, and Paradise Pickles slumped softly to the floor without so much as a murmur or even the pretence of resistance – did Comrade Pillai realize that what he really needed was the process of war more than the outcome of victory. War could have been the stallion that he rode, part of, if not all, the way to the Legislative Assembly, whereas victory left him no better off than when he started out.

He broke the eggs but burned the omelette.

Nobody ever learned the precise nature of the role that Comrade Pillai played in the events that followed. Even Chacko – who knew that the fervent, high-pitched speeches about Rights of Untouchables ('Caste is Class, comrades') delivered by Comrade Pillai during the Marxist Party siege of Paradise Pickles, were pharisaic – never learned the whole story. Not that he cared to find out. By then, numbed by the loss of Sophie Mol, he looked out at everything with a vision smudged with grief. Like a child touched by tragedy, who grows up suddenly and abandons his playthings, Chacko dumped his toys. Pickle Baron dreams and the People's War joined the racks of broken airplanes in his glass-paned cupboard. After Paradise Pickles closed down, some rice-fields were sold (along with their mortgages) to pay off the bank loans. More were sold to keep the family in food and clothes. By the time Chacko emigrated to Canada, the family's only income came from the rubber estate that adjoined the Ayemenem House and the few coconut trees in the compound. This was what Baby Kochamma and Kochu Maria lived off after everybody else had died, left, or been Returned.

To be fair to Comrade Pillai, he did not plan the course of events that followed. He merely slipped his ready fingers into History's waiting glove.

It was not entirely his fault that he lived in a society where a man's death could be more profitable than his life had ever been.

Velutha's last visit to Comrade Pillai – after his confrontation with Mammachi and Baby Kochamma – and what had passed between them, remained a secret. The last betrayal that sent Velutha across the river, swimming against the current, in the dark and rain, well in time for his blind date with history.

VELUTHA CAUGHT the last bus back from Kottayam where he was having the canning machine mended. He ran into one of the other factory workers at the bus stop, who told him with a smirk that Mammachi wanted to see him. Velutha had no idea what had happened and was completely unaware of his father's drunken visit to the Ayemenem House. Nor did he know that Vellya Paapen had been sitting for hours at the door of their hut, still drunk, his glass eye and the edge of his axe glittering in the lamplight, waiting for Velutha to return. Nor that poor paralysed Kuttappen, numb with apprehension, had been talking to his father continuously for two hours, trying to calm him down, all the time straining his ears for the sound of a footstep or the rustle of undergrowth so that he could shout a warning to his unsuspecting brother.

Velutha didn't go home. He went straight to the Ayemenem House. Though, on the one hand, he was taken by surprise, on the other, he knew, had known, with an ancient instinct, that one day History's twisted chickens would come home to roost. Through the whole of Mammachi's outburst he remained restrained and strangely composed. It was a composure born of extreme provocation. It stemmed from a lucidity that lies beyond rage.

When Velutha arrived, Mammachi lost her bearings and spewed her blind venom, her crass, insufferable insults, at a panel in the sliding-folding door until Baby Kochamma tactfully swivelled her around and aimed her rage in the right direction, at Velutha standing very still in the gloom. Mammachi continued her tirade, her eyes empty, her face twisted and ugly, her anger propelling her towards Velutha until she was shouting right into his face and he could feel the spray of her spit and smell the stale tea on her breath. Baby Kochamma stayed close to Mammachi. She said nothing, but used her hands to modulate Mammachi's fury, to stoke it anew. An encouraging pat on the back. A reassuring arm around the shoulders. Mammachi was completely unaware of the manipulation.

Just *where* an old lady like her – who wore crisp ironed saris and played the *Nutcracker Suite* on the violin in the evenings – had learned the foul language that Mammachi used that day was a mystery to everybody (Baby Kochamma, Kochu Maria, Ammu in her locked room) who heard her.

'Out!' she had screamed, eventually. 'If I find you on my property tomorrow I'll have you castrated like the pariah dog that you are! I'll have you killed!'

'We'll see about that,' Velutha said quietly.

That was all he said. And that was what Baby Kochamma in Inspector Thomas Mathew's office, enhanced and embroidered into threats of murder and abduction.

Mammachi spat into Velutha's face. Thick spit. It spattered across his skin. His mouth and eyes.

He just stood there. Stunned. Then he turned and left.

As he walked away from the house, he felt his senses had been honed and heightened. As though everything around him had been flattened into a neat illustration. A machine drawing with an instruction manual that told him what to do. His mind, desperately craving some kind of mooring, clung to details. It labelled each thing it encountered.

Gate, he thought as he walked out of the gate. *Gate. Road. Stones. Sky. Rain.*

Gate.
Road.
Stones.
Sky.
Rain.

The rain on his skin was warm. The laterite rock under his feet jagged. He knew where he was going. He noticed everything. Each leaf. Each tree. Each cloud in the starless sky. Each step he took.

Koo-koo kookum theevandi
Kooki paadum theevandi
Rapakal odum theevandi
Thalannu nilkum theevandi

That was the first lesson he had learned in school. A poem about a train.

He began to count. Something. Anything. *One two three four five six seven eight nine ten eleven twelve thirteen fourteen fifteen sixteen seventeen eighteen nineteen twenty twenty-one twenty-two twenty-three twenty-four twenty-five twenty-six twenty-seven twenty-eight twenty-nine . . .*

The machine drawing began to blur. The clear lines to smudge. The instructions no longer made sense. The road rose to meet him and the darkness grew dense. Glutinous. Pushing through it became an effort. Like swimming underwater.

It's happening, a voice informed him. *It has begun.*

His mind, suddenly impossibly old, floated out of his body and hovered high above him in the air, from where it jabbered useless warnings.

It looked down and watched a young man's body walk through the darkness and the driving rain. More than anything else that body wanted to sleep. Sleep and wake up in another world. *With the smell of her skin in the air that he breathed. Her body on his. He might never see her again. Where was she? What had they done to her? Had they hurt her?*

He kept walking. His face was neither lifted towards the rain, nor bent away from it. He neither welcomed it, nor warded it off.

Though the rain washed Mammachi's spit off his face, it didn't stop the feeling that somebody had lifted off his head and vomited into his body. Lumpy vomit dribbling down his insides. Over his heart. His lungs. The slow thick drip into the pit of his stomach. All his organs awash in vomit. There was nothing that rain could do about that.

He knew what he had to do. The instruction manual directed him. He had to get to Comrade Pillai. He no longer knew why. His feet took him to Lucky Press, which was locked, and then across the tiny yard to Comrade Pillai's house.

Just the effort of lifting his arm to knock exhausted him.

Comrade Pillai had finished his avial and was squashing a ripe banana, extruding the sludge through his closed fist into his plate of curd, when Velutha knocked. He sent his wife to open the door. She returned looking sulky, and, Comrade Pillai thought, suddenly sexy. He wanted to touch her breast immediately. But he had curd on his fingers and there was someone at the door. Kalyani sat on the bed and absent-mindedly patted Lenin, who was asleep next to his tiny grandmother, sucking his thumb.

'Who is it?'

'That Paapen Paravan's son. He says it's urgent.'

Comrade Pillai finished his curd unhurriedly. He waggled his fingers over his plate. Kalyani brought water in a little stainless-steel container and poured it out for him. The leftover morsels of food in his plate (a dry red chilli, and stiff angular brushes of sucked and spat-out drumsticks) rose and floated. She brought him a hand-towel. He wiped his hands, belched his appreciation, and went to the door.

'*Enda?* At this time of the night?'

As he replied, Velutha heard his own voice beat back at him as though it had hit a wall. He tried to explain what had happened, but he could hear himself slipping into incoherence. The man he was talking to was small and far away, behind a wall of glass.

'This is a little village,' Comrade Pillai was saying. 'People talk. I listen to what they say. It's not as though I don't know what's been going on.'

Once again Velutha heard himself say something which made no difference to the man he spoke to. His own voice coiled around him like a snake.

'Maybe,' Comrade Pillai said. 'But Comrade, you should know that Party was not constituted to support workers' indiscipline in their private life.'

Velutha watched Comrade Pillai's body fade from the door. His disembodied, piping voice stayed on and sent out slogans. Pennants fluttering in an empty doorway.

It is not in the Party's interests to take up such matters.

Individuals' interest is subordinate to the organization's interest.

Violating Party Discipline means violating Party Unity.

The voice went on. Sentences disaggregated into phrases. Words.

Progress of the Revolution.

Annihilation of the Class Enemy.

Comprador capitalist.

Spring-thunder.

And there it was again. Another religion turned against itself. Another edifice constructed by the human mind, decimated by human nature.

Comrade Pillai shut the door and returned to his wife and dinner. He decided to eat another banana.

'What did he want?' his wife asked, handing him one.

'They've found out. Someone must have told them. They've sacked him.'

'Is that all? He's lucky they haven't had him strung up from the nearest tree.'

'I noticed something strange . . .' Comrade Pillai said as he peeled his banana. 'The fellow had red varnish on his nails . . .'

Standing outside in the rain, in the cold, wet light from the single streetlight, Velutha was suddenly overcome by sleep. He had to force his eyelids to stay open.

Tomorrow, he told himself. *Tomorrow when the rain stops.*

His feet walked him to the river. As though they were the leash and he were the dog.

History walking the dog.

15

The Crossing

It was past midnight. The river had risen, its waters quick and black, snaking towards the sea, carrying with it cloudy night skies, a whole palm frond, part of a thatched fence, and other gifts the wind had given it.

In a while the rain slowed to a drizzle and then stopped. The breeze shook water from the trees and for a while it rained only under trees, where shelter had once been.

A weak, watery moon filtered through the clouds and revealed a young man sitting on the topmost of thirteen stone steps that led into the water. He was very still, very wet. Very young. In a while he stood up, took off the white mundu he was wearing, squeezed the water from it and twisted it around his head like a turban. Naked now, he walked down the thirteen stone steps into the water and further, until the river was chest high. Then he began to swim with easy, powerful strokes, striking out towards where the current was swift and certain, where the Really Deep began. The moonlit river fell from his swimming arms like sleeves of silver. It took him only a few minutes to make the crossing. When he reached the other side he emerged gleaming and pulled himself ashore, black as the night that surrounded him, black as the water he had crossed.

He stepped onto the path that led through the swamp to the History House.

He left no ripples in the water.

No footprints on the shore.

He held his mundu spread above his head to dry. The wind lifted it like a sail. He was suddenly happy. *Things will get worse*, he thought to himself. *Then better*. He was walking swiftly now, towards the Heart of Darkness. As lonely as a wolf.

The God of Loss.

The God of Small Things.

Naked but for his nail varnish.

16

A Few Hours Later

Three children on the river bank. A pair of twins and another, whose mauve corduroy pinafore said *Holiday!* in a tilting, happy font.

Wet leaves in the trees shimmered like beaten metal. Dense clumps of yellow bamboo drooped into the river as though grieving in advance for what they knew was going to happen. The river itself was dark and quiet. An absence rather than a presence, betraying no sign of how high and strong it really was.

Estha and Rahel dragged the boat out of the bushes where they usually hid it. The paddles that Velutha had made were hidden in a hollow tree. They set it down in the water and held it steady for Sophie Mol to climb in. They seemed to trust the darkness and moved up and down the glistening stone steps as surefooted as young goats.

Sophie Mol was more tentative. A little frightened of what lurked in the shadows around her. She had a cloth bag with food purloined from the fridge slung across her chest. Bread, cake, biscuits. The twins, weighed down by their mother's words

If it weren't for you I would be free. I should have dumped you in an orphanage the day you were born. You're the millstones round my neck –

carried nothing. Thanks to what the Orangedrink Lemondrink Man did to Estha, their Home away from Home was already equipped. In the two weeks since Estha rowed scarlet jam and

Thought Two Thoughts, they had squirrelled away Essential Provisions: matches, potatoes, a battered saucepan, an inflatable goose, socks with multicoloured toes, ballpoint pens with London buses and the Qantas koala with loosened button eyes.

'What if Ammu finds us and *begs* us to come back?'

'Then we will. But only if she begs.'

Estha-the-Compassionate.

Sophie Mol had convinced the twins that it was *essential* that she go along too. That the absence of children, *all* children, would heighten the adults' remorse. It would make them truly sorry, like the grown-ups in Hamelin after the Pied Piper took away all their children. They would search everywhere and just when they were sure that all three of them were dead, they would return home in triumph. Valued, loved, and needed more than ever. Her clinching argument was that if she were left behind she might be tortured and forced to reveal their hiding place.

Estha waited until Rahel got in, then took his place, sitting astride the little boat as though it were a seesaw. He used his legs to push the boat away from the shore. As they lurched into the deeper water they began to row diagonally upstream, against the current, the way Velutha had taught them to. ('If you want to end up there, you must aim *there*.')

In the dark they couldn't see that they were in the wrong lane on a silent highway full of muffled traffic. That branches, logs, parts of trees, were motoring towards them at some speed.

They were past the Really Deep, only yards from the Other Side, when they collided with a floating log and the little boat tipped over. It had happened to them often enough on previous expeditions across the river, and they would swim after the boat and, using it as a float, dog-paddle to the shore. This time, they couldn't see their boat in the dark. It was swept away in the current. They headed for the shore, surprised at how much effort it took them to cover that short distance.

Estha managed to grab a low branch that arched down into the water. He peered downriver through the darkness to see if he could see the boat at all.

'I can't see anything. It's gone.'

Rahel, covered in slush, clambered ashore and held a hand out to help Estha pull himself out of the water. It took them a few minutes to catch their breath and register the loss of the boat. To mourn its passing.

'And all our food is spoiled,' Rahel said to Sophie Mol and was met with silence. A rushing, rolling, fishswimming silence.

'Sophie Mol?' she whispered to the rushing river. 'We're here! Here! Near the Illimba tree!'

Nothing.

On Rahel's heart Pappachi's moth snapped open its sombre wings.

Out.

In.

And lifted its legs.

Up.

Down.

They ran along the bank calling out to her. But she was gone. Carried away on the muffled highway. Greygreen. With fish in it. With the sky and trees in it. And at night the broken yellow moon in it.

There was no storm-music. No whirlpool spun up from the inky depths of the Meenachal. No shark supervised the tragedy.

Just a quiet handing over ceremony. A boat spilling its cargo. A river accepting the offering. One small life. A brief sunbeam. With a silver thimble clenched for luck in its little fist.

It was four in the morning, still dark, when the twins, exhausted, distraught and covered in mud, made their way through the swamp and approached the History House. Hansel and Gretel in a ghastly fairy tale in which their dreams would be captured and redreamed. They lay down in the back verandah on a grass mat with an inflatable goose and a Qantas koala bear. A pair of damp dwarves, numb with fear, waiting for the world to end.

'D'you think she's dead by now?'

Estha didn't answer.

'What's going to happen?'

'We'll go to jail.'

He Jolly Well knew. Little Man. He lived in a cara-van. Dum dum.

They didn't see someone else lying asleep in the shadows. As lonely as a wolf. A brown leaf on his black back. That made the monsoons come on time.

17

Cochin Harbour Terminus

In his clean room in the dirty Ayemenem House, Estha (not old, not young) sat on his bed in the dark. He sat very straight. Shoulders squared. Hands in his lap. As though he was next in line for some sort of inspection. Or waiting to be arrested.

The ironing was done. It sat in a neat pile on the ironing board. He had done Rahel's clothes as well.

It was raining steadily. Night rain. That lonely drummer practising his roll long after the rest of the band has gone to bed.

In the side mittam, by the separate 'Men's Needs' entrance, the chrome tailfins of the old Plymouth gleamed momentarily in the lightning. For years after Chacko left for Canada, Baby Kochamma had had it washed regularly. Twice a week for a small fee, Kochu Maria's brother-in-law who drove the yellow municipal garbage truck in Kottayam would drive into Ayemenem (heralded by the stench of Kottayam's refuse, which lingered long after he had gone) to divest his sister-in law of her salary and drive the Plymouth around to keep its battery charged. When she took up television, Baby Kochamma dropped the car and the garden simultaneously. Tutti-frutti.

With every monsoon, the old car settled more firmly into the ground. Like an angular, arthritic hen settling stiffly on her clutch of eggs. With no intention of ever getting up. Grass grew around its flat tyres. The Paradise Pickles & Preserves signboard rotted and fell inwards like a collapsed crown.

A creeper stole a look at itself in the remaining mottled half of the cracked driver's mirror.

A sparrow lay dead on the back seat. She had found her way in through a hole in the windscreen, tempted by some seat-sponge for her nest. She never found her way out. No one noticed her panicked car-window appeals. She died on the back seat, with her legs in the air. Like a joke.

Kochu Maria was asleep on the drawing-room floor, curled into a comma in the flickering light of the television that was still on. American policemen were stuffing a hand-cuffed teenaged boy into a police car. There was blood spattered on the pavement. The police car lights flashed and a siren wailed a warning. A wasted woman, the boy's mother perhaps, watched fearfully from the shadows. The boy struggled. They had used a mosaic blur on the upper part of his face so that he couldn't sue them. He had caked blood all over his mouth and down the front of his T-shirt like a red bib. His baby-pink lips were lifted off his teeth in a snarl. He looked like a werewolf. He screamed through the car window at the camera.

'I'm fifteen years old and I wish I were a better person than I am. But I'm not. Do you want to hear my pathetic story?'

He spat at the camera and a missile of spit splattered over the lens and dribbled down.

Baby Kochamma was in her room, sitting up in bed, filling in a Listerine discount coupon that offered a two-rupee rebate on their new 500ml bottle and two-thousand-rupee gift vouchers to the Lucky Winners of their lottery.

Giant shadows of small insects swooped along the walls and ceiling. To get rid of them Baby Kochamma had put out the lights and lit a large candle in a tub of water. The water was already thick with singed carcasses. The candlelight accentuated her rouged cheeks and painted mouth. Her mascara was smudged. Her jewellery gleamed.

She tilted the coupon towards the candle.

Which brand of mouthwash do you usually use?

Listerine, Baby Kochamma wrote in a hand grown spidery with age.

State the reasons for your preference:

She didn't hesitate. *Tangy Taste. Fresh Breath.* She had learned the smart, snappy language of television commercials.

She filled in her name and lied about her age.

Under *Occupation:* she wrote, *Ornamental Gardening (Dip) Roch. USA.*

She put the coupon into an envelope marked *RELIABLE MEDICOS, KOTTAYAM.* It would go with Kochu Maria in the morning, when she went into town on her Bestbakery cream-bun expedition.

Baby Kochamma picked up her maroon diary which came with its own pen. She turned to 19 June and made a fresh entry. Her manner was routine. She wrote: *I love you I love you.*

Every page in the diary had an identical entry. She had a case full of diaries with identical entries. Some said more than just that. Some had the day's accounts, To-do lists, snatches of favourite dialogue from favourite soaps, But even these entries all began with the same words: *I love you I love you.*

Father Mulligan had died four years ago of viral hepatitis, in an ashram north of Rishikesh. His years of contemplation of Hindu scriptures had led initially to theological curiosity, but eventually to a change of faith. Fifteen years ago, Father Mulligan became a Vaishnava. A devotee of Lord Vishnu. He stayed in touch with Baby Kochamma even after he joined the ashram. He wrote to her every Diwali and sent her a greeting card every New Year. A few years ago he sent her a photograph of himself addressing a gathering of middle-class Punjabi widows at a spiritual camp. The women were all in white with their sari palloos drawn over their heads. Father Mulligan was in saffron. A yolk addressing a sea of boiled eggs. His white beard and hair were long, but combed and groomed. A saffron Santa with votive ash on his forehead. Baby Kochamma couldn't believe it. It was the only thing he ever sent her that she hadn't kept. She was offended by the fact that he had actually, eventually, renounced his vows, but not for her. For other vows. It was like welcoming someone with open arms, only to have him walk straight past into someone else's.

Father Mulligan's death did not alter the text of the entries in Baby Kochamma's diary, simply because as far as she was concerned, it did not alter his availability. If anything, she possessed him in death in a way that she never had while he was alive. At least her memory of him was *hers.* Wholly hers. Savagely, fiercely, hers. Not to be shared with Faith, far less with competing co-nuns, and co-sadhus or whatever it was they called themselves. Co-swamis.

His rejection of her in life (gentle and compassionate though it was) was neutralized by death. In her memory of him, he embraced her. Just her. In the way a man embraces a woman. Once he was dead, Baby Kochamma stripped Father Mulligan of his ridiculous saffron robes and reclothed him in the Coca-Cola cassock she so loved. (Her senses feasted, between changes, on that lean, concave, Christ-like body.) She snatched away his begging bowl, pedicured his horny Hindu soles and gave him back his comfortable sandals. She reconverted him into the high-stepping camel that came to lunch on Thursdays.

And every night, night after night, year after year, in diary after diary after diary, she wrote: *I love you I love you.*

She put the pen back into the pen-loop and shut the diary. She took off her glasses, dislodged her dentures with her tongue, severing the strands of saliva that attached them to her gums like the sagging strings of a harp, and dropped them into a glass of Listerine. They sank to the bottom and sent up little bubbles, like prayers. Her nightcap. A clenched-smile soda. Tangy teeth in the morning.

Baby Kochamma settled back on her pillow and waited to hear Rahel come out of Estha's room. They had begun to make her uneasy, both of them. A few mornings ago she had opened her window (for a Breath of Fresh Air) and caught them red-handed in the act of Returning From Somewhere. Clearly they had spent the whole night out. Together. Where could they have been? What and how much did they remember? When would they leave? What were they doing, sitting together in the dark for so long? She fell asleep propped up against her pillows, thinking that perhaps, over the sound of the rain and the television, she hadn't heard Estha's door open. That Rahel had gone to bed long ago.

She hadn't.

Rahel was lying on Estha's bed. She looked thinner lying down. Younger. Smaller. Her face was turned towards the window beside the bed. Slanting rain hit the bars of the window-grill and shattered into a fine spray over her face and her smooth bare arm. Her soft, sleeveless T-shirt was a glowing yellow in the dark. The bottom half of her, in blue jeans, melted into the darkness.

It was a little cold. A little wet. A little quiet. The Air.

But what was there to say?

From where he sat, at the end of the bed, Estha, without turning his head, could see her. Faintly outlined. The sharp line of her jaw. Her collarbones like wings that spread from the base of her throat to the ends of her shoulders. A bird held down by skin.

She turned her head and looked at him. He sat very straight. Waiting for the inspection. He had finished the ironing.

She was lovely to him. Her hair. Her cheeks. Her small, clever-looking hands.

His sister.

A nagging sound started up in his head. The sound of passing trains. The light and shade and light and shade that falls on you if you have a window seat.

He sat even straighter. Still, he could see her. Grown into their mother's skin. The liquid glint of her eyes in the dark. Her small straight nose. Her mouth, full lipped. Something wounded-looking about it. As though it was flinching from something. As though long ago someone – a man with rings – had hit her across it. A beautiful, hurt mouth.

Their beautiful mother's mouth, Estha thought. Ammu's mouth.

That had kissed his hand through the barred train window. First class, on the Madras Mail to Madras.

'Bye, Estha. Godbless, Ammu's mouth had said. Ammu's trying-not-to-cry mouth.

The last time he had seen her.

She was standing on the platform of the Cochin Harbour Terminus, her face turned up to the train window. Her skin grey, wan, robbed of its luminous sheen by the neon station light. Daylight stopped by trains on either side. Long corks that kept the darkness bottled in. The Madras Mail. The Flying Rani.

Rahel held by Ammu's hand. A mosquito on a leash. A Refugee Stick Insect in Bata sandals. An Airport Fairy at a railway station. Stamping her feet on the platform, unsettling clouds of settled station-filth. Until Ammu shook her and told her to Stoppit and she Stoppited. Around them the hostling-jostling crowd.

Scurrying hurrying buying selling luggage trundling porter paying children shitting people spitting coming going begging bargaining reservation-checking.

Echoing stationsounds.

Hawkers selling coffee. Tea.

Gaunt children, blonde with malnutrition, selling smutty

magazines and food they couldn't afford to eat themselves.

Melted chocolates. Cigarette sweets.

Orangedrinks.

Lemondrinks.

CocaColaFantaicecreamrosemilk.

Pink-skinned dolls. Rattles. Love-in-Tokyos.

Hollow plastic parakeets full of sweets with heads you could unscrew.

Yellow-rimmed red sunglasses.

Toy watches with the time painted on them.

A cartful of defective toothbrushes.

The Cochin Harbour Terminus.

Grey in the stationlight. Hollow people. Homeless. Hungry. Still touched by last year's famine. Their revolution postponed for the Time Being by Comrade E. M. S. Namboodiripad (*Soviet Stooge, Running Dog*). The former apple of Peking's eye.

The air was thick with flies.

A blind man without eyelids and eyes as blue as faded jeans, his skin pitted with smallpox scars, chatted to a leper without fingers, taking dexterous drags from scavenged cigarette stubs that lay beside him in a heap.

'What about you? When did *you* move here?'

As though they had had a choice. As though they had *picked* this for their home from a vast array of posh housing estates listed in a glossy pamphlet.

A man sitting on a red weighing machine unstrapped his artificial leg (knee downwards) with a black boot and nice white sock painted on it. The hollow, knobbled calf was pink, like proper calves should be. (When you recreate the image of man, why repeat God's mistakes?) Inside it he stored his ticket. His towel. His stainless-steel tumbler. His smells. His secrets. His love. His madness. His hope. His infinnate joy. His real foot was bare.

He bought some tea for his tumbler.

An old lady vomited. A lumpy pool. And went on with her life.

The Stationworld. Society's circus. Where, with the rush of commerce, despair came home to roost and hardened slowly into resignation.

But this time, for Ammu and her two-egg twins, there was no Plymouth window to watch it through. No net to save them as they vaulted through the circus air.

Pack your things and leave, Chacko had said. Stepping over a broken door. A handle in his hand. And Ammu, though her hands were trembling, hadn't looked up from her unnecessary hemming. A tin of ribbons lay open on her lap.

But Rahel had. Looked up. And seen that Chacko had disappeared and left a monster in his place.

A thick-lipped man with rings, cool in white, bought Scissors cigarettes from a platform vendor. Three packs. To smoke in the train corridor.

For Men of Action
SatisfAction.

He was Estha's escort. A Family Friend who happened to be going to Madras. Mr Kurien Maathen.

Since there was going to be a grown-up with Estha anyway, Mammachi said there was no need to waste money on another ticket. Baba was buying Madras–Calcutta. Ammu was buying Time. She too had to pack her things and leave. To start a new life, in which she could afford to keep her children. Until then, it had been decided that one twin could stay in Ayemenem. Not both. Together they were trouble. *nataS ni rieht seye.* They had to be separated.

Maybe they're right, Ammu's whisper said as she packed his trunk and holdall. *Maybe a boy does need a Baba.*

The thick-lipped man was in the coupé next to Estha's. He said he'd try and change seats with someone once the train started.

For now he left the little family alone.

He knew that a hellish angel hovered over them. Went where they went. Stopped where they stopped. Dripping wax from a bent candle.

Everybody knew.

It had been in the papers. The news of Sophie Mol's death, of the police 'Encounter' with a Paravan charged with kidnapping and murder. Of the subsequent Communist Party siege of Paradise Pickles & Preserves, led by Ayemenem's own Crusader for Justice and Spokesman of the Oppressed. Comrade K. N. M. Pillai claimed that the Management had implicated the Paravan in a false police case because he was an active member of the Communist Party. That they wanted to eliminate him for indulging in 'Lawful Union Activities'.

All that had been in the papers. The Official Version.

Of course the thick-lipped man with rings had no idea about the other version.

The one in which a posse of Touchable Policemen crossed the Meenachal river, sluggish and swollen with recent rain, and picked their way through the wet undergrowth, clumping into the Heart of Darkness.

18

The History House

A posse of Touchable Policemen crossed the Meenachal river, sluggish and swollen with recent rain, and picked their way through the wet undergrowth, the clink of handcuffs in someone's heavy pocket.

Their wide khaki shorts were rigid with starch, and bobbed over the tall grass like a row of stiff skirts, quite independent of the limbs that moved inside them.

There were six of them. Servants of the State.

P oliteness
O bedience
L oyalty
I ntelligence
C ourtesy
E fficiency.

The Kottayam Police. A cartoonplatoon. New-Age princes in funny pointed helmets. Cardboard lined with cotton. Hairoil stained. Their shabby khaki crowns.

Dark of Heart.

Deadlypurposed.

They lifted their thin legs high, clumping through tall grass. Ground creepers snagged in their dewdamp leghair. Burrs and grass flowers enhanced their dull socks. Brown millipedes slept in the soles of their steel-tipped, Touchable boots. Rough grass left their legskin raw, crisscrossed with cuts. Wet mud farted under their feet as they squelched through the swamp.

They trudged past darter birds on the tops of trees, drying their sodden wings spread out like laundry against the sky. Past egrets. Cormorants. Adjutant storks. Sarus cranes looking for space to dance. Purple herons with pitiless eyes. Deafening, their *wraark wraark wraark*. Motherbirds and their eggs.

The early morning heat was full of the promise of worse to come.

Beyond the swamp that smelled of still water, they walked past ancient trees cloaked in vines. Gigantic mani plants. Wild pepper. Cascading purple acuminus.

Past a deepblue beetle balanced on an unbending blade of grass.

Past giant spider webs that had withstood the rain and spread like whispered gossip from tree to tree.

A banana flower sheathed in claret bracts hung from a scruffy, torn-leafed tree. A gem held out by a grubby schoolboy. A jewel in the velvet jungle.

Crimson dragonflies mated in the air. Doubledeckered. Deft. One admiring policeman watched and wondered briefly about the dynamics of dragonfly sex, and what went into what. Then his mind clicked to attention and Police Thoughts returned.

Onwards.

Past tall anthills congealed in the rain. Slumped like drugged sentries asleep at the gates of Paradise.

Past butterflies drifting through the air like happy messages. Huge ferns.

A chameleon.

A startling shoeflower.

The scurry of grey jungle fowl running for cover.

The nutmeg tree that Vellya Paapen hadn't found.

A forked canal. Still. Choked with duckweed. Like a dead

green snake. A tree trunk fallen over it. The Touchable policemen minced across. Twirling polished bamboo batons.

Hairy fairies with lethal wands.

Then the sunlight was fractured by thin trunks of tilting trees. Dark of Heartness tiptoed into the Heart of Darkness. The sound of stridulating crickets swelled.

Grey squirrels streaked down mottled trunks of rubber trees that slanted towards the sun. Old scars slashed across their bark. Sealed. Healed. Untapped.

Acres of this, and then, a grassy clearing. A house.

The History House.

Whose doors were locked and windows open.

With cold stone floors and billowing, ship-shaped shadows on the walls.

Where waxy ancestors with tough toe-nails and breath that smelled of yellow maps whispered papery whispers.

Where translucent lizards lived behind old paintings.

Where dreams were captured and re-dreamed.

Where an old Englishman ghost, sickled to a tree, was abrogated by a pair of two-egg twins – a Mobile Republic with a Puff who had planted a Marxist flag in the earth beside him. As the platoon of policemen minced past they didn't hear him beg. In his kind-missionary voice. *Excuse me, would you, umm . . . you wouldn't happen to umm . . . I don't suppose you'd have a cigar on you? No? . . . No, I didn't think so.*

The History House.

Where, in the years that followed, the Terror (still-to-come) would be buried in a shallow grave. Hidden under the happy humming of hotel cooks. The humbling of old communists. The slow death of dancers. The toy histories that rich tourists came to play with.

It was a beautiful house.

White-walled once. Red-roofed. But painted in weather-colours now. With brushes dipped in nature's palette. Moss-green. Earthbrown. Crumbleblack. Making it look older than it really was. Like sunken treasure dredged up from the ocean bed. Whale-kissed and barnacled. Swaddled in silence. Breathing bubbles through its broken windows.

A deep verandah ran all around. The rooms themselves were recessed, buried in shadow. The tiled roof swept down like the sides of an immense, upside-down boat. Rotting beams supported on once-white pillars had buckled at the centre, leaving a yawning, gaping hole. A History hole. A History-shaped hole in the Universe through which, at twilight, dense clouds of silent bats billowed like factory smoke and drifted into the night.

They returned at dawn with news of the world. A grey haze in the rosy distance that suddenly coalesced and blackened over the house before it plummeted through the History hole like smoke in a film running backwards.

All day they slept, the bats. Lining the roof like fur. Spattering the floors with shit.

The policemen stopped and fanned out. They didn't really need to, but they liked these Touchable games.

They positioned themselves strategically. Crouching by the broken, low stone boundary wall.

Quick Piss.

Hotfoam on warmstone. Police-piss.

Drowned ants in yellow bubbly.

Deep breaths.

Then together, on their knees and elbows, they crept towards the house. Like Film-policemen. Softly, softly through the grass. Batons in their hands. Machine-guns in their minds. Responsibility for the Touchable future on their thin but able shoulders.

They found their quarry in the back verandah. A Spoiled Puff. A Fountain in a Love-in-Tokyo. And in another corner (as lonely as a wolf) – a carpenter with blood-red nails.

Asleep. Making nonsense of all that Touchable cunning.

The Surpriseswoop.

The Headlines in their heads.

DESPERADO CAUGHT IN POLICE DRAGNET.

For this insolence, this spoiling-the-fun, their quarry paid. Oh yes.

They woke Velutha with their boots.

Esthappen and Rahel woke to the shout of sleep surprised by shattered kneecaps.

Screams died in them and floated belly up, like dead fish. Cowering on the floor, rocking between dread and disbelief, they realized that the man being beaten was Velutha. Where had he come from? What had he done? Why had the policemen brought him here?

They heard the thud of wood on flesh. Boot on bone. On teeth. The muffled grunt when a stomach is kicked in. The muted crunch of skull on cement. The gurgle of blood on a man's breath when his lung is torn by the jagged end of a broken rib.

Blue-lipped and dinner-plate-eyed, they watched, mesmerized by something that they sensed but didn't understand: the absence of caprice in what the policemen did. The abyss where anger should have been. The sober, steady brutality, the economy of it all.

They were opening a bottle.

Or shutting a tap.

Cracking an egg to make an omelette.

The twins were too young to know that these were only history's henchmen. Sent to square the books and collect the dues from those who broke its laws. Impelled by feelings that were primal yet paradoxically wholly impersonal. Feelings of contempt born of inchoate, unacknowledged fear – civilization's fear of nature, men's fear of women, power's fear of powerlessness.

Man's subliminal urge to destroy what he could neither subdue nor deify.

Men's Needs.

What Esthappen and Rahel witnessed that morning, though they didn't know it then, was a clinical demonstration in controlled conditions (this was not war after all, or genocide) of human nature's pursuit of ascendancy. Structure. Order. Complete monopoly. It was human history, masquerading as God's Purpose, revealing herself to an under-age audience.

There was nothing accidental about what happened that morning. Nothing *incidental.* It was no stray mugging or personal settling of scores. This was an era imprinting itself on those who lived in it.

History in live performance.

If they hurt Velutha more than they intended to, it was only because any kinship, any connection between themselves and him, any implication that if nothing else, at least biologically he was a fellow creature – had been severed long ago. They were not arresting a man, they were exorcizing fear. They had no instrument to calibrate how much punishment he could take. No means of gauging how much or how permanently they had damaged him.

Unlike the custom of rampaging religious mobs or conquering armies running riot, that morning in the Heart of Darkness the posse of Touchable Policemen acted with economy, not frenzy. Efficiency, not anarchy. Responsibility, not hysteria. They didn't tear out his hair or burn him alive. They didn't hack off his genitals and stuff them in his mouth. They didn't rape him. Or behead him.

After all, they were not battling an epidemic. They were merely inoculating a community against an outbreak.

In the back verandah of the History House, as the man they loved was smashed and broken, Mrs Eapen and Mrs Rajagopalan, Twin Ambassadors of God-knows-what, learned two new lessons.

Lesson Number One:
Blood barely shows on a Black Man. (Dum dum)
And
Lesson Number Two:
It smells, though.
Sicksweet.
Like old roses on a breeze. (Dum dum)

'*Madiyo?*' one of History's Agents asked.

'*Madi aayirikkum,*' another replied.

Enough?

Enough.

They stepped away from him. Craftsmen assessing their work. Seeking aesthetic distance.

Their Work, abandoned by God and History, by Marx, by Man, by Woman and (in the hours to come) by Children, lay folded on the floor. He was semi-conscious, but wasn't moving.

His skull was fractured in three places. His nose and both his cheekbones were smashed, leaving his face pulpy, undefined. The blow to his mouth had split open his upper lip and broken six teeth, three of which were embedded in his lower lip, hideously inverting his beautiful smile. Four of his ribs were splintered, one had pierced his left lung, which was what made him bleed from his mouth. The blood on his breath bright red. Fresh. Frothy. His lower intestine was ruptured and haemorrhaged, the blood collected in his abdominal cavity. His spine was damaged in two places, the concussion had paralysed his right arm and resulted in a loss of control over his bladder and rectum. Both his knee caps were shattered.

Still they brought out the handcuffs.

Cold.

With the sourmetal smell. Like steel bus-rails and the bus conductor's hands from holding them. That was when they noticed his painted nails. One of them held them up and waved the fingers coquettishly at the others. They laughed. 'What's this?' in a high falsetto. 'AC-DC?'

One of them flicked at his penis with his stick. 'Come on, show us your special secret. Show us how big it gets when you blow it up.' Then he lifted his boot (with millipedes curled into its sole) and brought it down with a soft thud.

They locked his arms across his back.

Click.

And click.

Below a Lucky Leaf. An autumn leaf at night. That made the monsoons come on time.

He had goosebumps where the handcuffs touched his skin.

'It isn't him,' Rahel whispered to Estha. 'I can tell. It's his twin brother. Urumban. From Kochi.'

Unwilling to seek refuge in fiction, Estha said nothing.

Someone was speaking to them. A kind Touchable policeman. Kind to his kind.

'Mon, Mol, are you all right? Did he hurt you?'

And not together, but almost, the twins replied in a whisper. 'Yes. No.'

'Don't worry. You're safe with us now.'

Then the policemen looked around and saw the grass mat.

The pots and pans.

The inflatable goose.

The Qantas koala with loosened button eyes.

The ballpoint pens with London's streets in them.

Socks with separate coloured toes.

Yellow-rimmed red plastic sunglasses.

A watch with the time painted on it.

'Whose are these? Where did they come from? Who brought them?' An edge of worry in the voice.

Estha and Rahel, full of fish, stared back at him.

The policemen looked at one another. They knew what they had to do.

The Qantas koala they took for their children.

And the pens and socks. Police children with multi-coloured toes.

They burst the goose with a cigarette. *Bang.* And buried the rubber scraps.

Yooseless goose. Too recognizable.

The glasses one of them wore. The others laughed so he kept them on for a while. The watch they all forgot. It stayed behind in the History House. In the back verandah. A faulty record of the time. Ten to two.

They left.

Six princes, their pockets stuffed with toys.

A pair of two-egg twins.

And the God of Loss.

He couldn't walk. So they dragged him.

Nobody saw them.

Bats, of course, are blind.

19

Saving Ammu

At the police station, Inspector Thomas Mathew sent for two Coca-Colas. With straws. A servile constable brought them on a plastic tray and offered them to the two muddy children sitting across the table from the Inspector, their heads only a little higher than the mess of files and papers on it.

So once again, in the space of two weeks, bottled Fear for Estha. Chilled. Fizzed. Sometimes Things went worse with Coca-Cola.

The fizz went up his nose. He burped. Rahel giggled. She blew through her straw till the drink bubbled over onto her dress. All over the floor. Estha read aloud from the board on the wall.

'ssenetilo**P**,' he said. 'ssenetilo**P**, ecneideb**O**,'

'ytlayo**L**, ecnegilletn**I**,' Rahel said.

'ysetruo**C**.'

'ycneiciff**E**.'

To his credit, Inspector Thomas Mathew remained calm. He sensed the growing incoherence in the children. He noted the dilated pupils. He had seen it all before . . . the human mind's escape valve. Its way of managing trauma. He made allowances for that, and couched his questions cleverly. Innocuously. Between 'When is your birthday, Mon?' and 'What's your favourite colour, Mol?'

Gradually, in a fractured, disjointed fashion, things began to fall into place. His men had briefed him about the pots and pans. The grass mat. The impossible-to-forget toys. They began to make sense now. Inspector Thomas Mathew was not amused. He sent a Jeep for Baby Kochamma. He made sure that the children were not in the room when she arrived. He didn't greet her.

'Have a seat,' he said.

Baby Kochamma sensed that something was terribly wrong.

'Have you found them? Is everything all right?'

'Nothing is all right,' the Inspector assured her.

From the look in his eyes and the tone of his voice, Baby Kochamma realized that she was dealing with a different person this time. Not the accommodating police officer of their previous meeting. She lowered herself into a chair. Inspector Thomas Mathew didn't mince his words.

The Kottayam police had acted on the basis of an FIR filed by *her*. The Paravan had been caught. Unfortunately he had been badly injured in the encounter and in all likelihood would not live through the night. But now the children said that they had gone of their own volition. Their boat had capsized and the English child had drowned by accident. Which left the police saddled with the Death in Custody of a technically innocent man. True, he was a Paravan. True, he had misbehaved. But these were troubled times and technically, as per the law, he was an innocent man. There was no *case*.

'Attempted rape?' Baby Kochamma suggested weakly.

'*Where* is the rape-victim's complaint? Has it been filed? Has she made a statement? Have you brought it with you?' The Inspector's tone was belligerent. Almost hostile.

Baby Kochamma looked as though she had shrunk. Pouches of flesh hung from her eyes and jowls. Fear fermented in her and the spit in her mouth turned sour. The Inspector pushed a glass of water towards her.

'The matter is very simple. Either the rape-victim must file a complaint. Or the children must identify the Paravan as their abductor in the presence of a police witness. Or.' He waited for Baby Kochamma to look at him. 'Or I must charge you with lodging a false FIR. Criminal offence.'

Sweat stained Baby Kochamma's light blue blouse dark blue. Inspector Thomas Mathew didn't hustle her. He knew that given the political climate, he himself could be in very serious trouble. He was aware that Comrade K. N. M. Pillai would not pass up this opportunity. He kicked himself for acting so impulsively. He used his printed hand-towel to reach inside his shirt and wipe his chest and armpits. It was quiet in his office. The sounds of police-station activity, the clumping of boots, the occasional howl of pain from somebody being interrogated, seemed distant, as though they were coming from somewhere else.

'The children will do as they're told,' Baby Kochamma said. 'If I could have a few moments alone with them?'

'As you wish.' The Inspector rose to leave the office.

'Please give me five minutes before you send them in.'

Inspector Thomas Mathew nodded his assent and left.

Baby Kochamma wiped her shining, sweaty face. She stretched her neck, looking up at the ceiling in order to wipe the sweat from crevices between her rolls of neckfat with the end of her pallu. She kissed her crucifix.

Hail Mary, full of grace . . .

The words of the prayer deserted her.

The door opened. Estha and Rahel were ushered in. Caked with mud. Drenched in Coca-Cola.

The sight of Baby Kochamma made them suddenly sober. The moth with unusually dense dorsal tufts spread its wings over both their hearts. *Why had she come? Where was Ammu? Was she still locked up?*

Baby Kochamma looked at them sternly. She said nothing for a long time. When she spoke her voice was hoarse and unfamiliar.

'Whose boat was it? Where did you get it from?'

'Ours. That we found. Velutha mended it for us,' Rahel whispered.

'How long have you had it?'

'We found it the day Sophie Mol came.'

'And you stole things from the house and took them across the river in it?'

'We were only playing . . .'

'*Playing?* Is that what you call it?'

Baby Kochamma looked at them for a long time before she spoke again.

'Your lovely little cousin's body is lying in the drawing room. The fish have eaten out her eyes. Her mother can't stop crying. Is that what you call *playing*?'

A sudden breeze made the flowered window curtain billow. Outside Rahel could see Jeeps parked. And walking people. A man was trying to start his motorcycle. Each time he jumped on the kick-starter lever, his helmet slipped to one side.

Inside the Inspector's room, Pappachi's Moth was on the move.

'It's a terrible thing to take a person's life,' Baby Kochamma said. 'It's the worst thing that anyone can ever do. Even *God* doesn't forgive that. You know that, don't you?'

Two heads nodded twice.

'And yet –' she looked sadly at them, 'you did it.' She looked them in the eye. 'You are murderers.' She waited for this to sink in.

'You know that I know that it wasn't an accident. I know how jealous of her you were. And if the judge asks me in court I'll have to tell him, won't I? I can't tell a lie, can I?' She patted the chair next to her. 'Here, come and sit down –'

Four cheeks of two obedient bottoms squeezed into it.

'I'll have to tell them how it was strictly against the Rules for you to go alone to the river. How you forced her to go with you although you knew that she couldn't swim. How you pushed her out of the boat in the middle of the river. It wasn't an accident, was it?'

Four saucers stared back at her. Fascinated by the story she was telling them. *Then what happened?*

'So now you'll have to go to jail,' Baby Kochamma said kindly. 'And your mother will go to jail because of you. Would you like that?'

Frightened eyes and a fountain looked back at her.

'Three of you in three different jails. Do you know what jails in India are like?'

Two heads shook twice.

Baby Kochamma built up her case. She drew (from her imagination) vivid pictures of prison life. The cockroach-crisp food. The *chhi-chhi* piled in the toilets like soft brown mountains. The bedbugs. The beatings. She dwelled on the long years Ammu would be put away because of them. How she would be an old, sick woman with lice in her hair when she came out – if she didn't die in jail, that was. Systematically, in her kind, concerned voice she conjured up the macabre future in store for them. When she had stamped out every ray of hope, destroyed their lives completely, like a fairy godmother she presented them with a solution. God would never forgive them for what they had done, but here on Earth there was a way of undoing some of the damage. Of saving their mother from humiliation and suffering on their account. Provided they were prepared to be practical.

'Luckily,' Baby Kochamma said, 'luckily for you, the police have made a mistake. A *lucky* mistake.' She paused. 'You know what it is, don't you?'

There were people trapped in the glass paperweight on the policeman's desk. Estha could see them. A waltzing man and a waltzing woman. She wore a white dress with legs underneath.

'Don't you?'

There was paperweight waltz music. Mammachi was playing it on her violin.

Ra-ra-ra-ra-rum.

Parum-parum.

'The thing is,' Baby Kochamma's voice was saying, 'what's done is done. The Inspector says he's going to die anyway. So it won't really matter to him what the police think. What matters is whether you want to go to jail and make Ammu go to jail because of *you*. It's up to you to decide that.'

There were bubbles inside the paperweight which made the man and woman look as though they were waltzing underwater. They looked happy. Maybe they were getting married. She in her white dress. He in his black suit and bow-tie. They were looking deep into each other's eyes.

'If you want to save her, all you have to do, is to go with the Uncle with the big *meeshas*. He'll ask you a question. One question. All you have to do is to say "Yes". Then we can all go home. It's so easy. It's a small price to pay.'

Baby Kochamma followed Estha's gaze. It was all she could do to prevent herself from taking the paperweight and flinging it out of the window. Her heart was hammering.

'So!' she said, with a bright, brittle smile, the strain beginning to tell in her voice. 'What shall I tell the Inspector Uncle? What have we decided? D'you want to save Ammu or shall we send her to jail?'

As though she was offering them a choice of two treats. Fishing or Bathing the pigs? Bathing the pigs or fishing?

The twins looked up at her. Not together (but almost) two frightened voices whispered, 'Save Ammu.'

In the years to come they would replay this scene in their heads. As children. As teenagers. As adults. Had they been deceived into doing what they did? Had they been tricked into condemnation?

In a way, yes. But it wasn't as simple as that. They both knew that they had been given a choice. And how quick they had been in the choosing! They hadn't given it more than a second of thought before they looked up and said (not together, but almost) – 'Save Ammu.' Save us. Save our mother.

Baby Kochamma beamed. Relief worked like a laxative. She needed to go to the bathroom. Urgently. She opened the door and asked for the Inspector.

'They're good little children,' she told him when he came. 'They'll go with you.'

'No need for both. One will serve the purpose,' Inspector Thomas Matthew said. 'Any one. Mon. Mol. Who wants to come with me?'

'Estha.' Baby Kochamma chose. Knowing him to be the more practical of the two. The more tractable. The more far-sighted. The more responsible. 'You go. Goodboy.'

Little Man. He lived in a cara-van. Dum dum.

Estha went.

Ambassador E. Pelvis. With saucer-eyes and a spoiled puff. A short ambassador flanked by tall policemen, on a terrible mission deep into the bowels of the Kottayam police station. Their footsteps echoing on the flagstone floor.

Rahel remained behind in the Inspector's office and listened to the rude sounds of Baby Kochamma's relief dribbling down the sides of the Inspector's pot in his attached toilet. 'The flush doesn't work,' she said when she came out. 'It's so annoying.' Embarrassed that the Inspector would see the colour and consistency of her stool.

The lockup was pitch-dark. Estha could see nothing, but he could hear the sound of rasping, laboured breathing. The smell of shit made him retch. Someone switched on the light. Bright. Blinding. Velutha appeared on the scummy, slippery floor. A mangled genie invoked by a modern lamp. He was naked, his soiled mundu had come undone. Blood spilled from his skull like a secret. His face was swollen and his head look liked a pumpkin, too large and heavy for the slender stem it grew from. A pumpkin with a monstrous upside-down smile. Police boots stepped back from the rim of a pool of urine spreading from him, the bright, bare electric bulb reflected in it.

Dead fish floated up in Estha. One of the policemen prodded Velutha with his foot. There was no response. Inspector Thomas Mathew squatted on his haunches and raked his Jeep key across the sole of Velutha's foot. Swollen eyes opened. Wandered. Then focused through a film of blood on a beloved child. Estha imagined that something in him smiled. Not his mouth, but some other unhurt part of him. His elbow perhaps. Or shoulder.

The Inspector asked his question. Estha's mouth said Yes.

Childhood tiptoed out.

Silence slid in like a bolt.

Someone switched off the light and Velutha disappeared.

On their way back in the police Jeep, Baby Kochamma stopped at Reliable Medicos for some Calmpose. She gave them two each. By the time they reached Chungam Bridge their eyes were beginning to close. Estha whispered something into Rahel's ear.

'You were right. It wasn't him. It was Urumban.'

'Thang god,' Rahel whispered back.

'Where d'you think he is?'

'Escaped to Africa.'

They were handed over to their mother fast asleep, floating on this fiction.

Until the next morning, when Ammu shook it out of them. But by then it was too late.

Inspector Thomas Mathew, a man of experience in these matters, was right. Velutha didn't live through the night.

Half an hour past midnight, Death came for him.

And for the little family curled up and asleep on a blue cross-stitch counterpane? What came for them?

Not death. Just the end of living.

After Sophie Mol's funeral, when Ammu took them back to the police station and the Inspector chose his mangoes (*Tap, tap*), the body had already been removed. Dumped in the *themmady kuzhy* – the pauper's pit – where the police routinely dump their dead.

When Baby Kochamma heard about Ammu's visit to the police station, she was terrified. Everything that she, Baby Kochamma, had done, had been premised on one assumption. She had gambled on the fact that Ammu, whatever else she did, however angry she was, would never publicly admit to her relationship with Velutha. Because, according to Baby Kochamma, that would amount to destroying herself and her children. For ever. But Baby Kochamma hadn't taken into account the Unsafe Edge in Ammu. The Unmixable Mix – the infinite tenderness of motherhood, the reckless rage of a suicide bomber.

Ammu's reaction stunned her. The ground fell away from under her feet. She knew she had an ally in Inspector Thomas Mathew. But how long would that last? What if he were transferred and the case reopened? It was possible – considering the shouting, sloganeering crowd of Party workers that Comrade K. N. M. Pillai had managed to assemble outside the gate. That prevented the labourers from coming to work, and left vast quantities of mangoes, bananas, pineapple, garlic and ginger rotting slowly on the premises of Paradise Pickles.

Baby Kochamma knew she had to get Ammu out of Ayemenem as soon as possible.

She managed that by doing what she was best at. Irrigating her fields, nourishing her crops with other people's passions.

She gnawed like a rat into the godown of Chacko's grief.

Within its walls she planted an easy, accessible target for his insane anger. It wasn't hard for her to portray Ammu as the person actually responsible for Sophie Mol's death. Ammu and her two-egg twins.

Chacko breaking down doors was only the sad bull thrashing at the end of Baby Kochamma's leash. It was *her* idea that Ammu be made to pack her bags and leave. That Estha be Returned.

20

The Madras Mail

And so, at the Cochin Harbour Terminus, Estha Alone at the barred train window. Ambassador E. Pelvis. A millstone with a puff. And a green-wavy, thick-watery, lumpy, seaweedy, floaty, bottomless-bottomful feeling. His trunk with his name on it was under his seat. His tiffin box with tomato sandwiches and his Eagle flask with an eagle was on the little folding table in front of him.

Next to him an eating lady in a green and purple Kanjeevaram sari and diamonds clustered like shining bees on each nostril offered him yellow laddoos in a box. Estha shook his head. She smiled and coaxed, her kind eyes disappeared into slits behind her glasses. She made kissing sounds with her mouth.

'Try one. Verrrry sweet,' she said in Tamil. *Rombo maduram.*

'Sweet,' her oldest daughter, who was about Estha's age, said in English

Estha shook his head again. The lady ruffled his hair and spoiled his puff. Her family (husband and three children) was already eating. Big round yellow laddoo crumbs on the seat. Trainrumbles under their feet. The blue nightlight not yet on.

The eating lady's small son switched it on. The eating lady switched it off. She explained to the child that it was a sleeping light. Not an awake light.

Every First Class train thing was green. The seats green. The berths green. The floor green. The chains green. Darkgreen Lightgreen.

TO STOP TRAIN PULL CHAIN, it said in green.

OT POTS NIART LLUP NIAHC, Estha thought in green.

Through the window bars, Ammu held his hand.

'Keep your ticket carefully,' Ammu's mouth said. Ammu's trying-not-to-cry mouth. 'They'll come and check.'

Estha nodded down at Ammu's face tilted up to the train window. At Rahel, small and smudged with station dirt. All three of them bonded by the certain, separate knowledge that they had loved a man to death.

That wasn't in the papers.

It took the twins years to understand Ammu's part in what had happened. At Sophie Mol's funeral and in the days before Estha was Returned, they saw her swollen eyes, and with the self-centredness of children, held themselves wholly culpable for her grief.

'Eat the sandwiches before they get soggy,' Ammu said. 'And don't forget to write.'

She scanned the fingernails of the little hand she held, and slid a black sickle of dirt from under the thumb-nail.

'And look after my sweetheart for me. Until I come and get him.'

'When, Ammu? When will you come for him?'

'Soon.'

'But when? When eggzackly?'

'Soon, sweetheart. As soon as I can.'

'Month-after-next? Ammu?' Deliberately making it a long time away so that Ammu would say, *Before that, Estha. Be practical. What about your studies?*

'As soon as I get a job. As soon as I can go away from here and get a job,' Ammu said.

'But that will be never!' A wave of panic. A bottomless-bottomful feeling.

The eating lady eavesdropped indulgently.

'See how nicely he speaks English,' she said to her children in Tamil.

'But that will be never,' her oldest daughter said combatively. 'En ee vee ee aar. Never.'

By 'never' Estha had only meant that it would be too far away. That it wouldn't be *now*, wouldn't be *soon*.

By 'never' he hadn't meant Not Ever.

But that's how the words came out.

But that will be never!

For Never they just took the O and T out of Not Ever.

They?

The Government.

Where people were sent to Jolly Well Behave.

And that's how it had all turned out.

Never. Not Ever.

It was *his* fault that the faraway man in Ammu's chest stopped shouting. *His* fault that she died alone in the lodge with no one to lie at the back of her and talk to her.

Because he was the one that had *said* it. *But Ammu that will be never!*

'Don't be silly, Estha. It'll be soon,' Ammu's mouth said. 'I'll be a teacher. I'll start a school. And you and Rahel will be in it.'

'And we'll be able to afford it because it will be ours!' Estha said with his enduring pragmatism. His eye on the main chance. Free bus rides. Free funerals. Free education. Little Man. He lived in a cara-van. Dum dum.

'We'll have our own house,' Ammu said.

'A little house,' Rahel said.

'And in our school we'll have classrooms and blackboards,' Estha said.

'And chalk.'

'And Real Teachers teaching.'

'And proper punishments,' Rahel said.

This was the stuff their dreams were made of. On the day that Estha was Returned. Chalk. Blackboards. Proper punishments.

They didn't ask to be let off lightly. They only asked for punishments that fitted their crimes. Not ones that came like cupboards with built-in bedrooms. Not ones you spent your whole life in, wandering through its maze of shelves.

Without warning the train began to move. Very slowly.

Estha's pupils dilated. His nails dug into Ammu's hand as she walked along the platform. Her walk turning into a run as the Madras Mail picked up speed.

Godbless, my baby. My sweetheart. I'll come for you soon!

'Ammu!' Estha said as she disengaged her hand. Prising loose small finger after finger. 'Ammu! Feeling vomity!' Estha's voice lifted into a wail.

Little Elvis the Pelvis with a spoiled, special-outing puff. And beige and pointy shoes. He left his voice behind.

On the station platform Rahel doubled over and screamed and screamed.

The train pulled out. The light pulled in.

TWENTY-THREE YEARS LATER, Rahel, dark woman in a yellow T-shirt, turns to Estha in the dark.

'Esthapappychachen Kuttappen Peter Mon,' she says.

She whispers.

She moves her mouth.

Their beautiful mother's mouth.

Estha, sitting very straight, waiting to be arrested, takes his fingers to it. To touch the words it makes. To keep the whisper. His fingers follow the shape of it. The touch of teeth. His hand is held and kissed.

Pressed against the coldness of a cheek, wet with shattered rain.

Then she sat up and put her arms around him. Drew him down beside her.

They lay like that for a long time. Awake in the dark. Quietness and Emptiness.

Not old. Not young.

But a viable die-able age.

They were strangers who had met in a chance encounter.

They had known each other before Life began.

There is very little that anyone could say to clarify what happened next. Nothing that (in Mammachi's book) would separate Sex from Love. Or Needs from Feelings.

Except perhaps that no Watcher watched through Rahel's eyes. No one stared out of a window at the sea. Or a boat in the river. Or a passer-by in the mist in a hat.

Except perhaps that it was a little cold. A little wet. But very quiet. The Air.

But what was there to say?

Only that there were tears. Only that Quietness and Emptiness fitted together like stacked spoons. Only that there was a snuffling in the hollows at the base of a lovely throat. Only that a hard honey-coloured shoulder had a semi-circle of teethmarks on it. Only that they held each other close, long after it was over. Only that what they shared that night was not happiness, but hideous grief.

Only that once again they broke the Love Laws. That lay down who should be loved. And how. And how much.

On the roof of the abandoned factory, the lonely drummer drummed. A gauze door slammed. A mouse rushed across the factory floor. Cobwebs sealed old pickle vats. Empty, all but one – in which a small heap of congealed white dust lay. Bone dust from a Bar Nowl. Long dead. Pickledowl.

In answer to Sophie Mol's question: *Chacko, where do old birds go to die? Why don't dead ones fall like stones from the sky?*

Asked on the evening of the day she arrived. She was standing on the edge of Baby Kochamma's ornamental pond looking up at the kites wheeling in the sky.

Sophie Mol. Hatted, bellbottomed and Loved from the Beginning.

Margaret Kochamma (because she knew that when you travel to the Heart of Darkness (b) *Anything can Happen to Anyone*) called her in to have her regimen of pills. Filaria. Malaria. Diarrhoea.

She had no prophylaxis, unfortunately, for Death by Drowning.

Then it was time for dinner.

'Supper, silly,' Sophie Mol said when Estha was sent to call her.

At *supper silly*, the children sat at a separate smaller table. Sophie Mol, with her back to the grown ups, made gruesome faces at the food. Every mouthful she ate was displayed to her admiring younger cousins, half-chewed, mulched, lying on her tongue like fresh vomit.

When Rahel did the same, Ammu saw her and took her to bed.

Ammu tucked her naughty daughter in and switched off the light. Her good-night kiss left no spit on Rahel's cheek and Rahel could tell that she wasn't really angry.

'You're not angry, Ammu.' In a happy whisper. *A little more her mother loved her.*

'No.' Ammu kissed her again. 'Good night, sweetheart. Godbless.'

'Good night, Ammu. Send Estha soon.'

And as Ammu walked away she heard her daughter whisper, 'Ammu!'

'What is it?'

'We be of one blood, ye and I.'

Ammu leaned against the bedroom door in the dark, reluctant to return to the dinner table where the conversation circled like a moth around the white child and her mother as though they were the only source of light. Ammu felt that she would die, wither and die, if she heard another word. If she had to endure another minute of Chacko's proud, tennis-trophy smile. Or the undercurrent of sexual jealousy that emanated from Mammachi. Or Baby Kochamma's conversation that was designed to exclude Ammu and her children, to inform them of their place in the scheme of things.

As she leaned against the door in the darkness, she felt her dream, her afternoon-mare move inside her like a rib of water rising from the ocean, gathering into a wave. The cheerful one-armed man with salty skin and a shoulder that ended abruptly like a cliff emerged from the shadows of the jagged beach and walked towards her.

Who was he?

Who could he have been?

The God of Loss.

The God of Small Things.

The God of Goose Bumps and Sudden Smiles.

He could do only one thing at a time.

If he touched her, he couldn't talk to her, if he loved her he couldn't leave, if he spoke he couldn't listen, if he fought he couldn't win.

Ammu longed for him. Ached for him with the whole of her biology.

She returned to the dinner table.

21

The Cost of Living

When the old house had closed its bleary eyes and settled into sleep, Ammu, wearing one of Chacko's old shirts over a long white petticoat, walked out onto the front verandah. She paced up and down for a while. Restless. Feral. Then she sat on the wicker chair below the mouldy, button-eyed bison head and the portraits of the Little Blessed One and Aleyooty Ammachi that hung on either side of it. Her twins were sleeping the way they did when they were exhausted – with their eyes half open, two small monsters. They got that from their father.

Ammu switched on her tangerine transistor. A man's voice crackled through it. An English song she hadn't heard before.

She sat there in the dark. A lonely, lambent woman looking out at her embittered aunt's ornamental garden, listening to a tangerine. To a voice from far away. Wafting through the night. Sailing over lakes and rivers. Over dense heads of trees. Past the yellow church. Past the school. Bumping up the dirt road. Up the steps of the verandah. To her.

Barely listening to the music, she watched the frenzy of insects flitting around the light, vying to kill themselves.

The words of the song exploded in her head.

There's no time to lose
I heard her say
Cash your dreams before

They slip away
Dying all the time
Lose your dreams and you
Will lose your mind.

Ammu drew her knees up and hugged them. She couldn't believe it. The cheap coincidence of those words. She stared fiercely out at the garden. Ousa the Bar Nowl flew past on a silent nocturnal patrol. The fleshy anthuriums gleamed like gunmetal.

She remained sitting for a while. Long after the song had ended. Then suddenly she rose from her chair and walked out of her world like a witch. To a better, happier place.

She moved quickly through the darkness, like an insect following a chemical trail. She knew the path to the river as well as her children did and could have found her way there blindfolded. She didn't know what it was that made her hurry through the undergrowth. That turned her walk into a run. That made her arrive on the banks of the Meenachal breathless. Sobbing. As though she was late for something. As though her life depended on getting there in time. As though she knew he would be there. Waiting. As though *he* knew she would come.

He did.

Know.

That knowledge had slid into him that afternoon. Cleanly. Like the sharp edge of a knife. When history had slipped up. While he had held her little daughter in his arms. When her eyes had told him he was not the only giver of gifts. That she had gifts to give him too, that in return for his boats, his boxes, his small windmills, she would trade her deep dimples when she smiled. Her smooth brown skin. Her shining shoulders. Her eyes that were always somewhere else.

He wasn't there.

Ammu sat on the stone steps that led to the water. She buried her head in her arms, feeling foolish for having been so sure. So *certain.*

Further downstream in the middle of the river, Velutha floated on his back, looking up at the stars. His paralysed brother and his one-eyed father had eaten the dinner he had cooked them and were asleep. So he was free to lie in the river and drift slowly with the current. A log. A serene crocodile. Coconut trees bent into the river and watched him float by. Yellow bamboo wept. Small fish took coquettish liberties with him. Pecked him.

He flipped over and began to swim. Upstream. Against the current. He turned towards the bank for one last look, treading water, feeling foolish for having been so sure. So *certain.*

When he saw her the detonation almost drowned him. It took all his strength to stay afloat. He trod water, standing in the middle of a dark river.

She didn't see the knob of his head bobbing over the dark river. He could have been anything. A floating coconut. In any case she wasn't looking. Her head was buried in her arms.

He watched her. He took his time.

Had he known that he was about to enter a tunnel whose only egress was his own annihilation, would he have turned away?

Perhaps.

Perhaps not.

Who can tell?

He began to swim towards her. Quietly. Cutting through the water with no fuss. He had almost reached the bank when she looked up and saw him. His feet touched the muddy riverbed. As he rose from the dark river and walked up the stone steps, she saw that the world they stood in was his. That he belonged to it. That it belonged to him. The water. The mud. The trees.

The fish. The stars. He moved so easily through it. As she watched him she understood the quality of his beauty. How his labour had shaped him. How the wood he fashioned had fashioned him. Each plank he planed, each nail he drove, each thing he made, had moulded him. Had left its stamp on him. Had given him his strength, his supple grace.

He wore a thin white cloth around his loins, looped between his dark legs. He shook the water from his hair. She could see his smile in the dark. His white, sudden smile that he had carried with him from boyhood into manhood. His only luggage.

They looked at each other. They weren't thinking any more. The time for that had come and gone. Smashed smiles lay ahead of them. But that would be later.

Lay Ter.

He stood before her with the river dripping from him. She stayed sitting on the steps, watching him. Her face pale in the moonlight. A sudden chill crept over him. His heart hammered. It was all a terrible mistake. He had misunderstood her. The whole thing was a figment of his imagination. This was a trap. There were people in the bushes. Watching. She was the delectable bait. How could it be otherwise? They had seen him in the march. He tried to make his voice casual. Normal. It came out in a croak.

'Ammukutty . . . what is it?'

She went to him and laid the length of her body against his. He just stood there. He didn't touch her. He was shivering. Partly with cold. Partly terror. Partly aching desire. Despite his fear his body was prepared to take the bait. It wanted her. Urgently. His wetness wet her. She put her arms around him.

He tried to be rational: *What's the worst thing that can happen? I could lose everything. My job. My family. My livelihood. Everything.*

She could hear the wild hammering of his heart.

She held him till it calmed down. Somewhat.

She unbuttoned her shirt. They stood there. Skin to skin.

Her brownness against his blackness. Her softness against his hardness. Her nut-brown breasts (that wouldn't support a toothbrush) against his smooth ebony chest. She smelled the river on him. His Particular Paravan smell that so disgusted Baby Kochamma. Ammu put out her tongue and tasted it, in the hollow of his throat. On the lobe of his ear. She pulled his head down towards her and kissed his mouth. A cloudy kiss. A kiss that demanded a kiss-back. He kissed her back. First cautiously. Then urgently. Slowly his arms came up behind her. He stroked her back. Very gently. She could feel the skin on his palms. Rough. Calloused. Sandpaper. He was careful not to hurt her. She could feel how soft she felt to him. She could feel herself through him. Her skin. The way her body existed only where he touched her. The rest of her was smoke. She felt him shudder against her. His hands were on her haunches (that could support a whole array of toothbrushes), pulling her hips against his, to let her know how much he wanted her.

Biology designed the dance. Terror timed it. Dictated the rhythm with which their bodies answered each other. As though they knew already that for each tremor of pleasure they would pay with an equal measure of pain. As though they knew that how far they went would be measured against how far they would be taken. So they held back. Tormented each other. Gave of each other slowly. But that only made it worse. It only raised the stakes. It only cost them more. Because it smoothed the wrinkles, the fumble and rush of unfamiliar love and roused them to fever pitch.

Behind them the river pulsed through the darkness, shimmering like wild silk. Yellow bamboo wept.

Night's elbows rested on the water and watched them.

They lay under the mangosteen tree, where only recently a grey old boatplant with boatflowers and boatfruit had been uprooted by a Mobile Republic. A wasp. A flag. A surprised puff. A Fountain in a Love-in-Tokyo.

The scurrying, hurrying, boatworld was already gone.
The White termites on their way to work.
The White ladybirds on their way home.
The White beetles burrowing away from the light.
The White grasshoppers with whitewood violins.
The sad white music.
All gone.

Leaving a boat-shaped patch of bare dry earth, cleared and ready for love. As though Esthappen and Rahel had prepared the ground for them. Willed this to happen. The twin midwives of Ammu's dream.

Ammu, naked now, crouched over Velutha, her mouth on his. He drew her hair around them like a tent. Like her children did when they wanted to exclude the outside world. She slid further down, introducing herself to the rest of him. His neck. His nipples. His chocolate stomach. She sipped the last of the river from the hollow of his navel. She pressed the heat of his erection against her eyelids. She tasted him, salty, in her mouth. He sat up and drew her back to him. She felt his belly tighten under her, hard as a board. She felt her wetness slipping on his skin. He took her nipple in his mouth and cradled her other breast in his calloused palm. Velvet gloved in sandpaper.

At the moment that she guided him into her, she caught a passing glimpse of his youth, his *youngness*, the wonder in his eyes at the secret he had unearthed and she smiled down at him as though he was her child.

Once he was inside her, fear was derailed and biology took over. The cost of living climbed to unaffordable heights; though later, Baby Kochamma would say it was a Small Price to Pay.

Was it?

Two lives. Two children's childhoods.

And a history lesson for future offenders.

Clouded eyes held clouded eyes in a steady gaze and a luminous woman opened herself to a luminous man. She was as wide and deep as a river in spate. He sailed on her waters. She could feel him moving deeper and deeper into her. Frantic. Frenzied. Asking to be let in further. Further. Stopped only by the shape of her. The shape of him. And when he was refused, when he had touched the deepest depths of her, with a sobbing, shuddering sigh, he drowned.

She lay against him. Their bodies slick with sweat. She felt his body drop away from her. His breath become more regular. She saw his eyes clear. He stroked her hair, sensing that the knot that had eased in him was still tight and quivering in her. Gently he turned her over on her back. He wiped the sweat and grit from her with his wet cloth. He lay over her, careful not to put his weight on her. Small stones pressed into the skin of his forearms. He kissed her eyes. Her ears. Her breasts. Her belly. Her seven silver stretchmarks from her twins. The line of down that led from her navel to her dark triangle, that told him where she wanted him to go. The inside of her legs, where her skin was softest. Then carpenter's hands lifted her hips and an untouchable tongue touched the innermost part of her. Drank long and deep from the bowl of her.

She danced for him. On that boat-shaped piece of earth. She lived.

He held her against him, resting his back against the mangosteen tree, while she cried and laughed at once. Then, for what seemed like an eternity, but was really no more than five minutes, she slept leaning against him, her back against his chest. Seven years of oblivion lifted off her and flew into the shadows on weighty, quaking wings. Like a dull, steel peahen. And on Ammu's Road (to Age and Death) a small, sunny meadow appeared. Copper grass spangled with blue butterflies. Beyond it, an abyss.

Slowly the terror seeped back into him. At what he had done. At what he knew he would do again. And again.

She woke to the sound of his heart knocking against his chest.

As though it was searching for a way out. For that movable rib. A secret sliding-folding panel. His arms were still around her, she could feel the muscles move while his hands played with a dry palm frond. Ammu smiled to herself in the dark, thinking how much she loved his arms – the shape and strength of them, how safe she felt resting in them when actually it was the most dangerous place she could be.

He folded his fear into a perfect rose. He held it out in the palm of his hand. She took it from him and put it in her hair.

She moved closer, wanting to be within him, to touch more of him. He gathered her into the cave of his body. A breeze lifted off the river and cooled their warm bodies.

It was a little cold. A little wet. A little quiet. The Air.

But what was there to say?

An hour later Ammu disengaged herself gently.

'I have to go.'

He said nothing, didn't move. He watched her dress.

Only one thing mattered now. They knew that it was all they could ask of each other. The only thing. Ever. They both knew that.

Even later, on the thirteen nights that followed this one, instinctively they stuck to the Small Things. The Big Things ever lurked inside. They knew that there was nowhere for them to go. They had nothing. No future. So they stuck to the small things.

They laughed at ant-bites on each other's bottoms. At clumsy caterpillars sliding off the ends of leaves, at overturned beetles that couldn't right themselves. At the pair of small fish that always sought Velutha out in the river and bit him. At a particularly devout praying mantis. At the minute spider who lived in a crack in the wall of the black verandah of the History House and camouflaged himself by covering his body with bits of rubbish – a sliver of wasp wing. Part of a cobweb. Dust. Leaf rot.

The empty thorax of a dead bee. *Chappu Thamburan*, Velutha called him. Lord Rubbish. One night they contributed to his wardrobe – a flake of garlic skin – and were deeply offended when he rejected it along with the rest of his armour from which he emerged – disgruntled, naked, snot-coloured. As though he deplored their taste in clothes. For a few days he remained in this suicidal state of disdainful undress. The rejected shell of garbage stayed standing, like an outmoded world-view. An antiquated philosophy. Then it crumbled. Gradually *Chappu Thamburan* acquired a new ensemble.

Without admitting it to each other or themselves, they linked their fates, their futures (their Love, their Madness, their Hope, their Infinnate Joy) to his. They checked on him every night (with growing panic as time went by) to see if he had survived the day. They fretted over his frailty. His smallness. The adequacy of his camouflage. His seemingly self-destructive pride. They grew to love his eclectic taste. His shambling dignity.

They chose him because they knew that they had to put their faith in fragility. Stick to Smallness. Each time they parted, they extracted only one small promise from each other.

'Tomorrow?'

'Tomorrow.'

They knew that things could change in a day. They were right about that.

They were wrong about *Chappu Thamburan*, though. He outlived Velutha. He fathered future generations.

He died of natural causes.

That first night, on the day that Sophie Mol came, Velutha watched his lover dress. When she was ready she squatted facing him. She touched him lightly with her fingers and left a trail of goosebumps on his skin. Like flat chalk on a blackboard. Like breeze in a paddyfield. Like jet-streaks in a blue church sky. He took her face in his hands and drew it towards his. He closed his eyes and smelled her skin. Ammu laughed.

Yes, Margaret, she thought. *We do it to each other too.*

She kissed his closed eyes and stood up. Velutha with his back against the mangosteen tree watched her walk away.

She had a dry rose in her hair.

She turned to say it once again: *'Naaley.'*

Tomorrow.